MAXIMAL
RESERVE

MAXIMAL RESERVE

A Novel

By Sam Batterman

Deep River
BOOKS

Sisters, Oregon

Maximal Reserve
© 2011 by Sam Batterman

Published by
Deep River Books
Sisters, Oregon
http://www.deepriverbooks.com

ISBN-10: 1-935265-52-0
ISBN-13: 9781935265528

Library of Congress Control Number: 2010942342

Printed in the USA

Cover design by Joe Bailen, Contajus Designs

For Susan—
My loving wife, my best friend, my partner through it all.

MAXIMAL RESERVE
Property of Axcess Energy Corporation

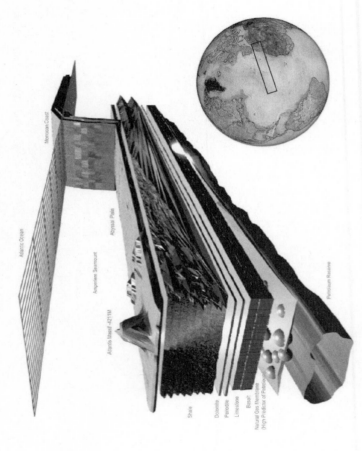

Atlantic Ocean

Moroccan Coast

Ampeniere Seamount

Abyssal Plain

Atlantis Massif -4211M

Shale

Dolomite

Peridotie

Limestone

Basalt

Natural Gas Membrane
(High Predictor of Petroleum)

Petroleum Reserve

Even by the God of thy father, who shall help thee; and by the Almighty, who shall bless thee with blessings of heaven above, blessings of the deep that lieth under, blessings of the breasts, and of the womb.

Genesis 49:25

And of Asher he said, Let Asher be blessed with children; let him be acceptable to his brethren, and let him dip his foot in oil.

Deuteronomy 33:24

And the word of the LORD came unto me, saying, Son of man, set thy face against Gog, the land of Magog, the chief prince of Meshech and Tubal, and prophesy against him, and say, Thus saith the Lord GOD; Behold, I am against thee, O Gog, the chief prince of Meshech and Tubal: and I will turn thee back, and put hooks into thy jaws, and I will bring thee forth, and all thine army, horses and horsemen, all of them clothed with all sorts of armour, even a great company with bucklers and shields, all of them handling swords.

Ezekiel 38:1–4

Prologue

TORONTO

Heavy metal music blasted across the small apartment as rain droplets gyrated on the smudged window glass. The small spheres of water multiplied a hundredfold the bright hues of neon light coming from across the street.

Jackson Sanders popped the tabbed lid of a high-energy drink and gulped down a third of the can without taking his eyes off the thirty-inch computer monitor dwarfing his desk. A strange image was spread across the display, a branching, root-like shape with tapered cylinders that sprouted from a single point. The shape's surface was wire-framed and broken into thousands of triangles. Depths measured in kilometers ran along a vertical axis.

Jack moved the mouse while holding down the right button, and the entire scene shifted slowly in three dimensions as if his head were at the center of the display. The lights on the front of his computer flickered at high speed, trying to keep up with the eyes and actions of its user.

The powerful computer was losing the battle.

Clicking on a few of the colorful triangles, Jack measured the distance between two points on the display. He knew this strange digital domain better than his messy apartment.

"There it is," he mumbled, pulling out a notepad with a University of Waterloo at Toronto crest on the cover. He wrote quickly, the scrawl indecipherable to all but himself. Years of e-mail exchanges and multiple instant-messenger sessions open at any given time had long ago ruined any appreciation he'd had for good penmanship.

A new track began to play, but its volume and vigor were the same. Jack's head bobbed with the syncopated rhythm. He continued writing in the tattered notepad at a mad pace when a small icon began flashing on his virtual desktop.

Jack frowned and clicked on the icon. A window sprang up, showing a grid of video feeds covering the hallway outside his apartment, the stairwell leading to the second floor, and the back alley below his rain-covered window.

Jack had written the program for surveillance purposes. The small fortune tied up in his workstations, servers, and networking could fetch quite a reward at a local pawn shop or fund a junkie's habit for the next few months, so this gave him a way to keep an eye on the area. The program was simple: it allowed him to view the grainy black-and-white images coming from the cameras and look for big changes between frames—arriving or departing parties in the apartment complex.

Jack squinted at the low-quality images. Three men in black coats and jeans, with crew cuts and the physique of soldiers, were coming up the stairwell.

Jack didn't recognize them. He glanced at his watch: 10:30 p.m.

The bars don't close for another three hours; they're not students, Jack thought.

One of the video feeds went to static. The stairwell feed was out. Jack's already caffeinated body amped up with adrenaline.

He'd known this day was coming.

Jack watched the men approach the surveillance cameras. It seemed they knew where the cameras were. The remaining feeds blurred rapidly and then succumbed to static.

Jack pulled the hard drive connected to his nine-thousand-dollar workstation, and the monitor went blank. He ran to the kitchenette and opened the microwave door, shoving the hard drive into the small oven and cramming in a dozen CDs and DVDs from a shoebox on a bookshelf. He slammed the microwave door shut and pushed the "Popcorn" button. The appliance hummed as it destroyed the magnetic characteristics of the storage media.

Jack bounded from the kitchenette across his rumpled bed, the mattress groaning from a dozen broken springs. He grabbed his backpack and shoved the university notepads containing his indecipherable scrawl into it.

A polite knock came at the door as Jack opened the raindrop-covered window as quietly as possible. He took one last look around his apartment and glanced at the lightning forking behind the tinted glass of the microwave door as the hard drive was destroyed.

Jack stepped out onto the small balcony and fire escape. Inside the apartment, polite knocking had turned into pounding. The balcony was crowded: a mountain bike, a hibachi for warmer weather, and a dead plant left little room for anything or anyone else.

Jack picked up the light, titanium-framed mountain bike and threw it over the ledge of the balcony. It bounced off a pile of trash bags and landed on the street ten feet below. There was no time to carry it down to the street carefully like he normally did.

As he stepped to the rusting ladder of the fire escape, he heard the apartment door splinter and crack as the men broke through. Jack flicked the latch for the ladder, and the rusty steel rungs flew down to the street.

Jack bailed over the side of the balcony and made his way down the slippery ladder to the alley below. As his sneakers hit the asphalt, he heard the men rummaging through all the things in his apartment.

Jack smiled. They wouldn't find what they were looking for.

He mounted his bike and pedaled with all his might down the alley, avoiding a homeless man and a dumpster on the way to Front Street. As he left the alley he heard a gruff voice yell, "There he is!" The squelch of a two-way radio followed before the sounds of the city at night extinguished the shouting from the apartment raid.

Jack pedaled quickly, weaving between parking meters and parked cars as he headed toward Roger's Center and the downtown area. The rain stung his eyes, and he felt numb with the wind sweeping the street. As he reached the corner, he saw the CN Tower looming above him with spotlights shining on its three soaring concrete sides. Behind him the squealing tires of a speeding car announced a vehicle entering the street a hundred yards back.

A black Escalade SUV roared toward him. Jack could see neon lights reflecting in its polished grill. He stood up on the bike and pumped the pedals while careening down the smooth concrete, ducking the grid-like arrangement of trees growing out of sidewalk-level planters. He passed over the boulevard and into Roundhouse Park. A bus horn sounded, startling him, and a late-shift city bus roared past, nearly turning him into a splattered bug on its windshield.

Exhausted, his lungs burning, Jack looked behind him. No one was following. There were no main roads into the park.

He was safe, and he flashed a smile of relief.

Jack's smile disappeared as the high beams of the SUV glinted through the dark. The vehicle smashed over the median and into the courtyard of the park. Orange sparks flew from the car's transmission and undercarriage as automotive steel and concrete paving met.

Jack increased his speed, pedaling like a man possessed—too fast, much too fast.

Another car screeched into the far end of the park, cutting off the Lake Shore Drive ramp. Instinctively, Jack hit the brakes, and the mountain bike lost its traction on the park's wet cobblestones and crashed onto its side. The bike and its passenger slid for a dozen feet before running into a park bench. Spokes bent under the impact, and the chain broke and slithered across the sidewalk into the grass like a wounded snake.

Dazed, Jack pulled his bleeding leg from under the wrecked bike, grabbed his backpack from the pavement, and hobbled toward a crescent-shaped grove of pine trees.

A *bleep* sounded in the night air, and a tuft of grass flew up just to his left. Jack ambled to the right, and another pistol flashed, the bullet clipping his foot. He fell to the wet grass. Three long shadows stretched across the park lawn, blotting out the city lights behind them. They clustered together, and two of them looked over their shoulders in opposite directions, checking for unwanted observers.

"No!" said Jack, trembling and raising his right hand toward the man in the center of the group. "Please," he pleaded. "I won't tell anyone, I promise."

"You're right about that, Jack," said the man in the middle, twisting a silencer on the front of his pistol and pointing it at Jack's forehead.

The orange glow from the muzzle blast lit up Jack's terrified eyes for the last time.

"Get the backpack!" said the assassin.

"Got it!" said one of his accomplices, rummaging through the contents of the blood-spattered backpack. He held out a notebook with the university logo. The embossed crest gleamed in the town car's headlights. The other man knelt down and collected the empty shells from the wet lawn.

"Make sure you grab his wallet and phone, and let's get out of here," said the leader, flipping open his cell phone and snapping a photo of Jack's shattered body. He stored the picture and dialed a number. The three men walked back toward the still-idling Escalade, leaving Jack's lifeless form behind on the wet lawn.

"Yes, we took care of it; nothing's left. The secret's still safe. We'll be there in the morning. We're heading to the airport now."

Chapter One
The Interview

Philip Channing sat in the ripped-vinyl driver's seat of his car and examined his face and hair in the rearview mirror, adjusting his necktie one more time and giving an awkward smile. He closed his eyes and rehearsed his answers to the questions that would come at him in the next two hours. He gulped and cheered himself on as if he were in some sort of otherworldly race with himself as both player and spectator.

Okay, this is it. This is for all the marbles. Come on, Phil!

He lifted the door latch and stepped out into the bright Texas sunlight and humid air. As he closed the car door, something beneath the rusty hulk creaked. The college beater had served him well for six years, but now, parked next to Lexuses, BMWs, and SUVs, it seemed out of its element. *Kinda like me.* He scanned the parking lot, pictured the drivers of the cars, and grinned.

I'm not worthy!

Phil opened his leather-bound notepad and double-checked his arsenal of résumés and recommendation letters. He glanced at his watch and began the long walk to the security building over two hundred yards away. He had searched for a visitor parking spot upon arrival, but all the slots were filled. Instead of risking a parking ticket he couldn't afford—or worse, the towing of his decrepit but critically needed conveyance—he'd decided to join the rank and file in parking in the distant employee parking lot.

If all went well, his car would soon belong there.

As Phil walked behind the shiny cars, he wondered how he had ended up here at the Axcess Energy Company. Axcess was *the* enemy when he was in school. It was the eight-hundred-pound gorilla of the energy market that was poisoning the earth by belching its fossil fuels into the planet's precious and fragile atmosphere, practically stomping on the polar ice caps with its enormous carbon footprint.

He thought through a hundred lectures from guest speakers and liberal professors who had lambasted and accused Axcess of raping the natural resources of the planet for the purposes of greed and short-term stock value. As a freshman he had even participated in an on-campus protest against the corporate leviathan.

But that was a long time ago.

Phil looked up into the cloudless sky as he did a quick calculation of how much his education had cost him and his parents. Eighty thousand dollars in tuition funds, lab fees, and overall living debt was enough to bring sobriety to any environmental zealot drunk with dogma. Things were different now: more pragmatic, less idealistic. In short, he needed a job.

His parents, a proud blue-collar worker and a schoolteacher, had done what they could to help him—sacrificing their early retirements and driving used cars instead of new ones to help fund his education, first in an expensive prep school and then during his undergraduate years. Phil sometimes felt guilty about his parents' sacrifices, but now, alone in the world after their deaths—his mom in a tragic auto accident and his dad from a fast-moving cancer in Phil's sophomore year of college—he knew this interview was the door to making their investments in his life pay off.

Only a few weeks before, he had packed all his earthly belongings into his deathtrap and driven to Austin. It was a far warmer climate than Toronto's, where the typically Canadian winter was made even colder by freezing wind from Lake Ontario, plunging the temperature to zero and below in the winter months. The routine of graduate school was wearing off. He was responsible for himself now, and maybe soon—he hoped—for Lisa. His parents were gone, Lisa's parents still looked at him like he was a bum off the streets, he was in a boatload of debt, and he needed something to *do*. Something worthwhile and challenging, something that wasn't just school.

Yes, he needed this job—badly.

Three weeks earlier he had endured a technical interview with three of Axcess's most brilliant petroleum engineers: Scott Ward, Gorin Vladofsky, and Caleb Mosha. Phil had met Caleb in Toronto; his niece was dating Phil's best friend, Jack Sanders. It was Caleb who had made the interview with the energy company possible.

All three men worked for Dr. John Chambers—the legend, the iconoclast, the maverick. Chambers was the man to work for in the energy sector, more dynamic even than Glenn Martin, Axcess's CEO. Chambers was so important to the future of the energy company that the board gave him absolute flexibility in his research programs. Chambers's attitude was well-known: first, break all the rules; second, slay sacred cows. Chambers was highly regarded in academic communities and feared in the halls of business and government. His ideas and theories were always radical and challenged the status quo at every turn. Just like Phil.

The guardhouse was still a hundred yards away when Phil's cell phone rang. He fumbled with his notepad and dug through every pocket of his suit searching for the phone. He looked at the display: *Lisa Baton*. Phil smiled at the name and the photo that accompanied the call. He pressed "Take Call" with his nail-bitten thumb and heard the most beautiful voice in the world.

"Hi, Phil, I know you're getting ready to get all nervous and everything, but remember: regardless of what happens, I still love you and I still think you are the best geophysicist/computer science guy on the planet."

"Lisa, I think I'm the *only* geophysicist/computer science guy on the planet—at least the only one out of work," Phil replied.

Her response came quickly, as if Lisa had known he would say that. "True, but even if there were hordes of your kind, you'd still be the most handsome."

Even though the two had been dating for four years, she could still make him blush. "Thanks . . . I think," said Phil, stepping through the guardhouse door and getting in line with a dozen other people jockeying for position to register their visits.

Lisa's tone changed as she sensed Phil's attention being pulled away from the conversation. "Seriously, just do your best and let things happen. I'll be praying for you. I love you!"

"I love you too," said Phil a little too loudly as a lady in front of him turned around, smiled, and winked at him. Red-faced, Phil shoved his phone back into his suit pocket and wished there was another line he could get into.

A few uncomfortable minutes later, the security officer waved and said, "Next please," breaking the unspoken tension with the woman whose body language still showed she thought Phil was flirting with her.

After the woman went through the security turnstile, Phil stepped to the counter and smiled. The bored security guard stared at him with the biggest bags under his eyes that Phil had ever seen.

"I'm here for an interview with Dr. John Chambers," said Phil cheerfully.

"Good for you," said the security officer. "Do you have ID?"

Phil worked his way through all the pockets in his suit, producing his cell phone, car keys, a pen, and finally his wallet. The droopy-eyed security guard watched the stack of personal items grow on the counter in front of him.

"Here you go," Phil said, handing his driver's license over the counter. "Sorry, I rarely wear a suit."

"I wouldn't have guessed," said the security guard. A few moments later a black-and-white label rolled out of a printer. The guard peeled the wax-paper backing off the label and stuck it onto a temporary badge that said ESCORT REQUIRED in big red letters.

"Walk up the sidewalk to the main lobby and wait for your escort."

"Thanks," said Phil, smiling at the guard as he stepped through the turnstile. The security guard was already processing the next visitor.

The walk was quick. A small cement sidewalk skirted a perfectly manicured lawn and freshly mulched flowerbeds. The glass-and-steel office complex soared a dozen stories above the lawn and gleamed in the morning sun. Phil could see people in their offices, gathering in conference rooms, and walking across glass-enclosed sky bridges between the buildings, all preparing for a busy and productive day.

The beauty of the place seemed lost on the employees who were scurrying past, drinking coffee, checking voice mail, and typing on their BlackBerrys while juggling briefcases and messenger bags. Phil decided to pop open his cell phone and join the fun.

The welcome screen appeared on his phone and displayed his communication status:

New Text Messages: 0

New E-mail Messages: 0

Well, so much for that.

Phil flipped the phone closed as he reached the glass doors of the visitor center lobby. The lobby was a huge atrium, and sunlight radiated through the skylights, illuminating the beautiful marble floor of the visitor center. Phil looked along the wood-paneled walls where supposedly artistic and valuable sculptures were positioned in regular intervals. The rare oil paintings on the walls and benches made of beautiful wood were carefully interspersed, reminding Phil of an art gallery, not of the lair of a corporate beast that wanted to melt the Arctic.

A pleasant voice pulled Phil from his admiration of the lobby and back into reality. "Mr. Channing?"

Phil spun around and found an attractive, thirty-something woman dressed in a conservative navy business suit. She extended her hand.

"Mr. Channing, I'm Sarah Rogers, Dr. Chambers's administrative assistant. I'll be taking you to the conference room where the interview will be occurring today."

"Hello," said Phil, trying not to look like a goon. "It's a pleasure to meet you."

Phil walked alongside Sarah toward an elevator at the end of the hall, passing through a gauntlet of security guards who were eyeballing badges and checking for escorts. As they walked, Phil tried to break the awkward silence.

"It sure is pretty outside. What a wonderful facility you have here." He cleared his throat. Exactly how stupid and obvious could he sound, anyway?

They both stepped into the elevator, and Sarah pressed the button for the fourth floor. "Axcess is a wonderful place to work, Philip; they have a heart for the environment and a mind for American prosperity." Her tone was even with no inflection, giving no indication that she knew her response was weird and sounded way too recorded.

Phil pretended to glance at the back of the elevator, but he was really looking at the back of Sarah Rogers for a pull string showing that she was, in fact, a robot.

The elevator dinged, and the door slid open, revealing a wide-open reception area surrounded by spacious conference rooms. The sprawling campus of the corporation could be seen beyond windows that wrapped around the entire floor.

"How many people work at this facility?" asked Phil, admiring the rectangles of perfectly mowed lawns and glass-and-concrete structures outside the window.

"Around five thousand. Austin is the headquarters and the largest of all Axcess's sites. Now then, Dr. Chambers will be here in a minute. May I get you some water or anything?" Sarah said.

"No, thank you. I'm fine."

Sarah smiled and left the conference room. Phil put his leather notepad on the enormous oval table and walked around it to gaze out over the campus. He smiled as he looked through the glass and indulged in a quick fantasy that he had worked here for ten years and this was his corner office.

"Nice view, isn't it?" came a booming voice. Phil jumped, bumping into the windowpane. He was thankful for the safety glass; otherwise, he would have been plummeting some four stories to his doom.

"Dr. Chambers!" Phil responded as he tried to cross the space between them with some class and dignity to shake the famous scientist's hand. The older man smiled kindly at the young, eager recruit. Chambers was tall and thin in an athletic way and slightly balding with a close-shorn salt-and-pepper beard. He was dressed all in black, with the enigmatic noir look popularized by Steve Jobs. The Apple CEO had given his most successful product launches dressed in all black, and now technologists the world over emulated his "Geek Chic" look.

"I've been following your academic career for a very long time, Phil. Your professors give you the highest praise," said Chambers, inviting Phil to sit in the plush chair and taking a seat across from him. "They say you are one of the brightest minds to come through the university in quite a while. In fact, they call you the hottest data visualization specialist on the planet."

Phil paused. He wasn't sure how to respond to this praise. Should he look confident, or would that come across as arrogant? He managed to flash a subtle smile. Chambers's magnetism was legendary, and here in the presence of the icon, Phil felt the man's charisma envelop him like an energy field. Chambers instantly made you want to work for him.

The man leaned forward and focused all his attention on Phil. "So why are you bailing out now?"

Phil wasn't exactly sure what he meant. "Excuse me?"

Chambers clarified his question without so much as a blink of an eyelash. "Why aren't you staying to get your doctorate? With the kind of work you did in graduate school, you could be done pretty quickly."

Time seemed to stop. Phil felt a bead of sweat roll down his face. The energy emanating from the man tangled around him. He knew the right answers, of course. Everything he should say to make him sound like a good candidate for the job. But under such pressure, he felt the strange urge to speak his mind—as if that's what Chambers wanted.

Phil took a deep breath. "I've been in college and grad school for six years. I have double majors in geology and computer science and a master's in petroleum exploration. And you're right, I could keep going, but I want to use my education now. I want to work on great projects with people who will challenge me and make me better. I already have a master's degree—some would say that means I've mastered the subject, but how can that be? I've never made a commercial contribution to a company, and I've only seen the data and situations that an academic institution can provide. Frankly, Dr. Chambers, I want more."

Chambers beamed. It was the right answer.

"I do plan on going back to get my doctorate, but only after I have the experience that would make it valuable." There. He had hedged his bet properly.

"One of the researchers on my team, Caleb Mosha, brought you to my attention four years ago. You went to school with his niece, didn't you?"

"Yes, Aliya is dating one of my best friends. We double-dated a lot in school," answered Phil. "Actually, we all did everything together."

"All?" asked Chambers, raising his eyebrow.

"Aliya and her boyfriend and Lisa—she's my girlfriend. She lives here in town and works for the state."

Chambers looked at his cell phone and set it to vibrate before staring directly at Phil, taking in his every facial expression. "If it's not completely obvious by this point, Phil, I want you to work for me, on a project that I'm certain will define both of our careers. Since you went through the technical wringer a few weeks ago with the staff, I just want to answer any questions you might have and try to help you with your decision."

Chambers paused for a full minute, his eyes drilling into Phil's, who responded in kind, like a corporate version of a first-one-who-blinks-is-a-rotten-egg contest. Silence boomed in Phil's ears. Suddenly his mouth was dry, and he wished he had taken the robot up on her water offer.

Here goes. Phil licked his lips. He only had one question. "Well, to be honest, Dr. Chambers, I want to know more about the project. I need to know more about the actual work I'd be doing here at Axcess."

Chambers seemed a bit surprised. "You mean they didn't tell you anything about our project during the technical interview?"

"No, sir, most of their questions revolved around the project I worked on a few years ago. That project involved using commodity-based computer grids to solve uncertainty around seismic data, but nothing about the actual job at Axcess was discussed."

"Leave it to the nerds and the lawyers to goof up a good thing," Chambers muttered.

"Excuse me?"

"Nothing." Chambers glanced beyond Phil for a moment, his attention lost in the sprawling campus of Axcess Energy. A smile crept across his face, and he snapped his fingers. "Do you have a passport?"

"Um, yes," said Phil. *Where is he going with this?*

"I want to show you what you'll be working on. Are you available for, say, thirty hours?" asked Chambers as he stood up and dialed his assistant. He looked back at the young recruit. "Or are you doing something more important?"

How can I argue with that? Phil asked himself.

"Sarah, please have a limousine come around front for me." Chambers snapped the phone shut.

"Thirty hours? You mean right now?" asked Phil, glancing at his business suit and wing-tip shoes. "What do I need to bring?"

"No time like the present," said Chambers. "We'll stop by your apartment before the airport so you can get your stuff. We're heading for a research rig, so dress like you're going camping. Oh, and one more thing. It's going to be windy."

Stop by my apartment? How does he know—wait a minute—did he just say airport?

Chambers strode quickly from the conference room with Phil running close behind to keep up. When the elevator reached the lobby, a black limousine pulled around to the front of the complex, and Phil and Chambers jumped in.

■ ■ ■ ■

Phil opened the door of his apartment and ducked inside. The place was a mess, and he was glad Chambers hadn't asked to come in. That would've been a job killer for sure.

He pulled back a curtain and looked at the limo idling in the parking lot. Chambers was on his cell phone, and he spotted Phil looking out the window. He smiled and tapped his watch.

Phil ran to the bedroom and grabbed a duffel bag from the closet. He grabbed a shaving bag from the bathroom, a toothbrush, and all the typical things for an overnight hotel stay. He threw a pair of jeans, a few T-shirts, and a sweatshirt into the duffel, cramming them down with his hands and forcing the zipper shut. He pulled his cell phone out of his pocket. It was dead.

There was no time to charge the battery.

He grabbed the power cord for charging his laptop and stuffed it and the computer into his backpack. Running to the kitchen, he picked up the landline and dialed Lisa's number. Phil glanced at the refrigerator and wondered how many science experiments were growing in there. Cleaning had not been his top priority over the past few weeks. Phil's OCD took over, and he moved the trash can in front of the refrigerator with his legs. While the phone connection was being made, he started throwing things away—eggs, milk, and a head of lettuce that was already turning brown. The trash can was filling up fast.

"Hello?"

Phil cocked his neck to hold the phone against his shoulder and continued purging the refrigerator of its perishables.

"Lisa! You won't believe the day I'm having."

"You're already back at home? Why didn't you call me after you got out? How'd the interview go? Tell me everything!" The questions whizzed across Phil's mind like arrows.

"Listen, hon, I'm not done with the interview. I'm at the apartment packing for an, um, a business trip."

"A business trip? Phil, what are you talking about?" Phil could tell from Lisa's tone that she was confused and quickly heading toward annoyed.

"Well, let's just say they want to show me something to help me make up my mind. I think they really want me on board. It's weird and mysterious, but I can't say no."

There was silence on the other end of the line before Lisa spoke up. "Okay, well, where are you going? Will you be back for dinner? We were going to celebrate your interview tonight."

He slammed the fridge door shut. *Dinner? Blast! I forgot!*

"I think we're going to have to postpone dinner, sweetheart. They told me thirty hours, and to pack jeans like I was going camping. No suits or ties."

There was a pause on the other end.

Lisa's disappointment was obvious, but she came through as she always did. "Okay, Phil, we'll celebrate when you get back. I don't like this mysterious trip—it's not very corporate—but I trust *you* . . ."

"Thanks, honey. I love you!"

"I love you too. Be safe and call me when you can. Bye."

Phil hung up the phone, grateful for an understanding girlfriend. They had dated all through college, and she really was his best friend. She trusted him and he trusted her.

Phil tied a knot at the top of the heavy trash bag and swung it over his shoulder like a homeless man's version of Santa Claus. He grabbed the duffel and his backpack with his other hand and scanned the room quickly for anything that needed to be unplugged, turned off, or worried about while he was away. Nothing.

He ran out the front door and lobbed the overstuffed trash bag into the dumpster as he ran to the waiting limousine and a business trip that he was sure would be unusual.

Chapter Two

Deep Pathfinder

The Sikorsky SH-3 Sea King helicopter flew low over the Atlantic. The sky was overcast, and the ride was bumpy and noisy. The helicopter had a peculiar smell: a strange mixture of grease and old canvas. Phil's head vibrated as he held onto the canvas-webbed seat with white knuckles. The heater vent for the cabin was located behind his head, and the heat was firing directly down his neck. Phil's neck and shoulders ached. He had been in the helicopter too long as it had hopscotched across the Atlantic from oil platform to oil platform, refueling along the way.

Phil's headset came alive with Dr. Chambers's voice. The charismatic engineer was sitting in front of him, facing the cockpit. "So, Phil, how's it feel to be in a helicopter that's older than everyone else in here?"

"Um, not so good," said Phil. He looked out the window at the white caps on the waves and the horizon of the ocean blending with the sky in a gray haze. He felt as green around the gills as he was sure he looked.

Gorin Vladofsky, one of the three men who had done Phil's technical interview, sat in front of him. He was a Russian with a chip on his shoulder. His interviewing style was jarring and belittling: a mixture of arcane questions about Russian trivia, mathematics, and seismology that only a person with Gorin's exact experience and credentials would know, all fired at the interviewee in barrages.

Most of Phil's answers to Gorin's questions had been the same: "I don't know." Given a choice of going through that interview again or having his kidneys harvested by the black market, Phil figured he would pick the organ harvest every time. He shuddered.

"There it is!" yelled Gorin, breaking suddenly from his statuesque pose. The headache-inducing drone of the chopper's turbine engine competed handily with the man's voice, and Phil put his hand to his ear—the universal symbol for "I'm sorry, I'm deaf." Gorin frowned and pointed toward the left side of the helicopter.

Phil craned his neck to look out the Plexiglas windows and saw a large research ship with smaller support ships orbiting it. Even from this distance, the sheer size of the operation was impressive. The research vessel had at least five decks and was painted white with a thick orange stripe running along its hull. The orange and white paint reflected like a mirror in the ocean waves lapping up to the steel hull. Hundreds of rectangular portholes lined the hull, and two huge black anchors stared out from the bow like the eyes of some strange, weeping sea monster. Faint waterfalls of rust ran from the anchor sockets down the hull and into the gray-blue water of the Atlantic.

The pilot's voice came over the headset. "Okay, we're going in. You can expect a bit of chop." Phil gave an extra tug on his lap belt as the helicopter banked steeply and reduced its altitude.

The Sea King approached the ship's stern, where a small helipad rose from the deck and sat on a maze of steel girders welded to the hull. Beyond the helipad, various cranes and platforms were visible before the large cabin and control area, which sprouted high into the air and bristled with a bird's nest of antennas, microwave disks, and rotating radars.

The helicopter touched down and Phil gave a sigh of relief, grabbing his duffel bag and slinging his backpack over one shoulder. Support crew came to the door and rolled it open, patting their heads and pointing to the whirling helicopter blades above them.

The sign language was pretty clear. *Duck or lose your melon.*

As happy as Phil was to get off the helicopter of death, the ship's stability seemed even worse, if that was even possible. The deck pitched and yawed beneath his feet, and he gripped the handrail tightly as he made it off the helipad and walked down a ramp to the main deck six feet below.

The turbines of the helicopter changed pitch as the pilot gave it increased power. Rotor wash stung Phil's face with miniature rain pellets, and the white helicopter lifted up from the pad, rotated on its axis, and sped away into the overcast sky.

As the thumping of the helicopter blades decreased in the distance, the sounds of the research ship took over. Phil heard men talking over the loudspeaker and the outboard motor of a small dinghy bringing people to the larger research ship from the smaller boats that circled the research vessel like parasites.

Dr. Chambers slapped Phil on the back. "Welcome to the *Deep Pathfinder.* You're gonna love it!"

Gorin walked past Phil and slammed him in the back, harder than Chambers had—noticeably harder. His voice was heavy with a Russian accent. "Compared to Siberia or the Ukraine, this is like haven."

Don't you mean heaven? Phil let it slide and followed the team to the control deck.

Scott Ward was waiting at the railing for them. He was middle-aged, six feet tall with a shock of jet black hair. He was wearing old, faded jeans and a light windbreaker with an Axcess Energy logo.

"You've met Dr. Ward before," said Chambers.

"Yes, it's good to see you again, Phil," said Ward.

Gorin, Ward, Phil, and Dr. Chambers stepped through a hatch, and after a short trip down the hallway turned left into a berthing compartment. Six bunk beds with barely enough room to get between them were positioned three per side. One of the beds was already taken, and the men ahead of Phil quickly threw their luggage and duffels on the lowest of the available beds.

Phil looked at the vacant top bunk, about eleven inches from the ceiling, where the marine gray paint was beginning to peel. Phil frowned and grudgingly placed his bags on the top bunk, hoping they wouldn't sleep much.

"Sorry, Phil. You're not sleeping here. Bring your bags," said Chambers.

Gorin mocked him again. "Stinks to be the new guy, eh, comrade?"

14   Sam Batterman

Comrade? Give me a break. The Soviet Union is long gone, buddy. We won. You lost. Next!

Phil re-slung his bags over his shoulder.

Chambers checked his watch. "We'd better hurry; they're launching in five minutes." Packed into the berthing compartment like sardines, each man took a turn to rotate in the opposite direction and head down the hallway to a set of stairs lined with handrails that led to the control deck.

The control center was a bewildering array of glowing panels with buttons, flat LCD panels with weather and status reports from various parts of the ship, and hand controls for steering the massive boat through the bucking waves of the ocean. An overweight man wearing all denim and a long red beard stood in the center of the floor eating a huge sandwich.

Dr. Chambers cut in front of the others and shook the man's hand. "Phil Channing, I'd like to introduce you to Captain Roger Shubert," said Dr. Chambers, placing his hand on Phil's shoulder. Shubert stopped chewing for a second and said, with his mouth full of half-eaten sandwich, "New employee?"

He stuck out his hand and engulfed Phil's in what could have been mistaken for a bear paw, squeezing until Phil's knuckles cracked.

"Not yet, but by tonight I think we'll have our answer," grinned Chambers.

A voice came over the loudspeaker. "Captain, preparations for launching THEO are complete."

Phil mouthed the word silently at Dr. Chambers. "THEO?"

The captain grasped the transmitter, which disappeared instantly in his humongous hands, and clicked off a reply. "Very well, let's get this thing underway—port side, stand by."

Dr. Chambers led Phil to a window overlooking the port-side support deck. A large deep-sea submersible stood perched on an orange gantry. It was about the size of a smart car, with no portholes or people-sized hatches.

"It's remote?" asked Phil.

"Absolutely. We are going over four thousand meters down today. A bit risky for people, but robots, they don't care about the long descent, and they are expendable."

Scott Ward spoke up. "Expendable? That's a weird thing to say about something we spent over ten million dollars on."

"Ten million dollars is nothing," said Chambers, waving his hand dismissively. "If we find what I expect to find, ten million bucks will seem like the best investment any company in the history of the world has ever made."

Phil cocked his head. "What are you expecting to find with this thing? Atlantis?"

Dr. Chambers laughed. "It's funny you should say that. Come with me."

Chapter Three
Phil Meets THEO

P hil followed Dr. Chambers and the other men back down the steel railing and made his way past a stack of cargo boxes and spools of coiled cabling. As he came around the corner, he was startled by the submersible dangling perilously from a steel hook at the end of a robotic crane arm. The vehicle looked like a cross between a devilish sea creature and a high-tech crab, without the smooth hull of a submarine. Thick steel plating girded its frame in an angular arrangement.

Chambers looked at Scott Ward. "Since you designed this wonderful device, care to do the honors?"

Ward smiled and leaned an arm on the side of the strange crablike vehicle. "THEO, meet Philip. Philip . . . THEO."

Phil raised his hand in an awkward greeting. "Um, hi," said Phil. Gorin guffawed.

"THEO is our eyes, ears, arms, and brain when we descend to the hydrothermal field 3.2 miles beneath our feet." Ward walked around the side of the submersible and pointed out its attributes. "THEO doesn't move fast; it's not designed for speed. It's made for exploring and loitering. It's a lot like Gorin in that regard."

Phil gave a courtesy laugh and stopped when he saw he was the only one laughing. Gorin looked confused, as if American humor was beneath him. He sniffed at Ward.

"It uses these six thrusters to make it very maneuverable in the water," said Ward, patting one of the small vent-covered propellers. "These robotic arms allow us to perform retrieval and movement tasks in pressure that would instantly kill human beings."

Two black arms about six feet long rested under a glass dome filled with cameras and thermal imaging devices. "The arms have roughly the same degree of freedom that we do." Ward nodded at an engineer standing on a platform above the men, who was holding what looked like a remote-control transmitter for a model airplane. Suddenly THEO's arms twitched, moving independently and reaching out with smooth, precise motion.

It was the motion that got Phil's attention. It was human, not jerky or convulsing like most robots.

Ward continued. "There's a steel basket underneath that can carry two hundred and fifty pounds of samples or whatever we want to bring back to the surface."

"Cool," said Phil, still watching the claw-like arms move about. "How'd you get the motion so smooth?"

"Instead of the arms simply being on or off, we transition between the two states, almost like an animator might draw in-between frames that blur the difference between key poses," said Ward.

"Are you using fuzzy math or harmonic motion to do that?" asked Phil.

Ward raised his eyebrows, impressed with the young man's guess. "Harmonic motion."

"Bah, that was an easy one!" bellowed Gorin. Phil just smiled at the Russian.

Phil stepped up to the craft for a closer inspection, touching its cold metal skin. "How long can it stay under?"

"THEO is battery powered, but it can stay down around twelve hours. Considering that it takes two hours to get down and another two to return to the surface, we need every second."

Phil moved to the front of the vehicle where he had seen the thick plastic dome. "The eyes of the beast, huh?"

"That's right. THEO carries four video cameras and has sonar, an altimeter, and other sensors for measuring ambient temperature, water salinity and acidity . . . the works."

Phil squatted down to look at the belly of the crab. He noticed a latticework of hollow cylinders that looked like dozens and dozens of tube mailers welded together.

"What's this?"

Gorin pushed to the front, elbowing Ward and Chambers out of the way.

"That is my creation," he said, puffing out his chest before kneeling on the deck next to Phil. "These are extremely sophisticated sonar acoustic transponders, more sophisticated than anything else on the craft."

"You mean they're hydrophones?" asked Phil.

"No, no, no. They are much, much more complicated than just hydrophones."

Scott Ward chuckled a bit before interjecting, "Actually Phil, they really are *just* hydrophones. We drop them along the ocean floor and use them to map the hydrothermal field acoustically instead of dragging them on the surface or just below the surface as is conventionally done."

Gorin looked at Ward with disgust. "You have no respect for the work I do. When I was in Russia, they trusted me with ballistic missiles—"

Scott Ward cut him off. "Yes, I know. You remind us every day of the millions of lives that were in the balance and that your superior engineering prowess staved off a nuclear winter."

Phil laughed for the first time in what seemed like twenty-four hours, and Gorin scowled. "You see, you have turned our guest against me in no time flat."

"What's the source of the sound wave these instruments measure when they're on the ocean floor?" asked Phil, trying to show Gorin he was still interested and even a little impressed.

Gorin's pride visibly swelled, and his voice crooned like he was talking about a grandchild. "We have an air gun that we place a short distance away from the hydrophones, and the hydrophones pick up the reflected sound waves from the rock structures below the ocean floor. That's how we get superior readings."

Phil squatted down near the instrument pack and began asking the arrogant Russian question after question, trying to show interest in the invention Gorin was so proud of. Scott Ward and John Chambers glanced meaningfully at each other as they watched Phil purposefully drop his knowledge and bond with the Russian engineer.

"I think I'm starting to like this kid," said Ward.

Chambers nodded. "Me too—from the moment I met him." He yelled up to the captain. "Okay, lower away!"

The team of scientists stepped away from the submersible as the strong hydraulic arms lifted it from the deck and slowly began to lower the vehicle into the choppy water. Ward pointed to the snake-like umbilical attached to the top of the craft as a deckhand carefully gave it slack. "That cable has the topside feeds for camera, sensors, and sonar, and it also allows us to send commands."

Phil nodded his head, watching THEO slowly submerge beneath the waves. "This is really cool, but what does it have to do with oil and the Axcess Energy Company?" His voice betrayed a little of his doubt. *What can I do to help here? I'm not a mechanical engineer. I can't hold a candle to these guys. They're not just exploring; they're creating artificial creatures!*

"Come with me." Chambers waved to Phil to follow him as he moved up a stairway to a large steel platform where an object was covered in an all-weather tarp. Phil loped along behind him.

"THEO is only part of the strategy. We use it to place acoustic beacons around undersea vents and mountainous regions. But to get larger surveys of the structures under the ocean floor, we use the Manta Ray." Chambers unlatched a bungee cord and pulled the tarp back, revealing a strange, aircraft-like vehicle. "Dr. Ward, this is your baby," said Chambers.

Scott Ward rolled his eyes at the formality and jumped in. "Phil, this is what we call the Manta Ray. It's the result of my doctoral work at Cornell Theory Center: a high-speed submersible that can fly over the ocean floor and distribute a swarm of sonar probes. I built THEO as an early prototype, but the Manta Ray is what will give us the ability to do this seismic study with speed and hyper-accuracy."

Ward ran his hand across the smooth, dark finish of the vehicle. "It's milled from titanium and designed to survive depths of over six miles."

"So it delivers seismic probes like an aircraft dropping paratroopers?" asked Phil.

"Exactly like that. The Manta will fly a preprogrammed route, typically across a wide, flat area, and eject these things." Ward opened a panel that slowly opened like a bomb bay door, exposing the internals of the craft. "This is a rotary launcher that stores the probes. At certain programmed intervals it will drop a probe onto the ocean floor and continue flying to the next point."

Phil squatted down and studied the probes. They were all disc-shaped and black. They reminded Phil of the Roomba floor-cleaning robots he had seen in television commercials. "How many can you hold on the launcher?"

"About a hundred. Once the probes hit the ocean floor, they send sonic waves into the strata and then relay the telemetry—the results of the sonic reflections—back to the Manta, which consolidates all the data into one big set."

"How big is the data set?" asked Phil, his voice warming. Now he was getting somewhere. Seismic data—big data sets of seismic data—was what had brought him to Chambers's attention. There were only a handful of people on the planet who had even the first clue about how to make sense of that much information—and Phil was one of those few people who could do the task.

"Multiple terabytes—most likely in the range of ten terabytes," answered Ward. Chambers studied Phil and watched the recognition of the role he could play bloom on his new recruit's face.

"Ten trillion numbers is a lot of information," said Phil with a smile. "You need me to help make sense of it all."

Phil kept his excitement in check and returned his interest to the probes that the submersible would drop for deep-sea readings. "Is that it for the probe, or is it reusable?" asked Phil.

"Nope, the probes communicate with one another using, um . . . signals." Phil cocked his head at Ward's dramatic change of vocabulary: he'd gone from open to guarded.

"Are you using Extreme Low Frequency like a nuclear sub?" asked Phil.

"No, no way. ELF is way too slow. We are sucking up terabytes of data, so we use a proprietary mechanism to transmit. Otherwise, it would take thousands of years just to collect the signals."

Trade secret then, Phil thought. He let it drop.

Ward continued, "Then each probe will reposition itself for another reading, making sure not to overlap, but always covering the ground in an optimal fashion."

Phil stood. He could no longer hold back on his most important question.

"So the big question is, why would an oil company need both deep and broad seismic surveys of an area of the earth that can't be reached by contemporary drilling technologies?"

Ward smiled approvingly. Gorin grunted and rolled his eyes as if the question was obvious and should have been asked earlier in the conversation.

"That was the question we were all waiting for," said Chambers.

Chapter Four
The Mountain at the Bottom of the Atlantic

Phil descended stairs and moved through hatches and bulkheads until he found himself buried in the bowels of the *Deep Pathfinder*. Chambers and Ward walked in front of him, and Gorin followed along behind. They stopped at a formidable door made of reinforced steel with thick metal hinges and a security access pad.

"Are you sure you want to do this?" Ward asked Chambers, gesturing toward Phil.

"Oh, yes, I'm quite sure this will put young Mr. Channing over the top on his decision." Dr. Chambers paused for a moment as if second-guessing himself, and then turned and faced Phil.

"Now listen, young man. What you are about to see is top secret for our department. You've signed a nondisclosure agreement and our other confidentiality forms, so if a word of this comes out, a raft of lawsuits will land on your head. Understand?"

"I understand," said Phil. *Like there's any other answer to be given out here in the middle of the Atlantic.* Nervous excitement pumped through his body. Chambers wanted him badly—badly enough to take a big risk. This job was going to be more than he'd ever dreamed.

"Good!" Chambers slid his access card through the reader and entered a PIN. An indicator light glowed green, and the latches on the thick steel door released.

Phil walked through the bulkhead into a spherical room that reminded him of a planetarium, its walls sloping into a hemisphere of smooth panels. Gorin pulled the hatch closed behind them, and the lights dimmed. There was a stainless-steel circular table in the center of the room with a round bench that seemed to orbit it. It reminded Phil of an outdoor table at a fast-food joint. The walls glowed with a blue light until bubbles began to rise on the right side of the room. Dappled sunlight, refracted by the ocean, danced in the ceiling.

Phil couldn't control his excitement as he put the puzzle pieces together. This was the ocean—they were looking at the world underwater. "It's coming from the submersible, isn't it?"

"Yes, it is. Watch this." Chambers pressed a few buttons on a console on the sloped wall, and a heads-up display appeared on one of the panels. The depth was increasing as the submersible continued its dive.

100, 110, 120, 130, 140 . . .

Phil watched the counter grow, noting that the sunlight from the surface was becoming dimmer with every click. Similar digital gauges were recording salinity, acidity, temperature, and other measurements. Fish were flying through the dark blue space, dodging the submersible at the last second before zooming over the top or the side. Phil found himself ducking and bobbing, trying to avoid the incoming fish missiles. Gorin began to chuckle and imitate the young recruit's jerking motions.

Phil ignored the annoying Russian. "How long until we reach the bottom?"

"Two hours, but we have plenty to keep us occupied in the meantime," said Chambers with a smile. "Normally, we would let Caleb Mosha talk you through this next part—he's the real expert. Unfortunately, he's doing some work in Israel right now. He's looking for proof of our theory in the Lost City Vent Field."

"Lost City Vent Field? What theory?" asked Phil.

Chambers nodded at Ward and pressed another button on the wall console, and the submersible's environment temporarily disappeared.

"Let's start with why we're really here." Ward sat down at the table with Phil. "How were you taught that oil is formed?"

Suddenly Phil felt like he was back in the middle of an interview, and he didn't understand where this line of questioning was going. Why toss out such a simple, well-understood question?

He formed his words slowly. "Well, oil is a hydrocarbon. It's generally acknowledged that oil is a byproduct of ancient vegetation and other life forms that were sealed under the crust of the earth and put under enormous pressure."

"So you're a biogenic formation fan, are you?" asked Dr. Chambers.

Phil parsed the semantics in a moment: *Bio = life. Genic = generated by genes—life—ancient life.* "Yes, I guess I am."

Ward thrummed the steel table with his fingers. "Well, the good news is that you have a lot of company."

"Especially in America," Gorin piped up in his thick Russian accent, ending with a chortle.

Chambers crossed his arms over his chest and stared down at Phil. "But no one in this room agrees with you."

Phil cleared his throat. Were they setting him up? "Biogenic oil formation is the foundation of all modern petroleum exploration. It's how oil reserves are predicted, surveyed, and exploited. Even the commercials that Axcess Energy used to run on TV when I was a little kid showed a dinosaur turning into oil."

Phil felt his blood pressure rising as he stood his ground. "You know, you could say that Axcess Energy has done more to propagate biogenic formation than anyone else in the industry."

The silence in the room was deafening. Phil felt a little embarrassed and tried to lower his voice and bring the question back to the scientists in the room. He wondered if he'd just blown his chance to join this elite group of explorers. "If you don't believe in the biogenic formation theory, what theory do you accept?"

The other men exchanged glances before Chambers took the lead. "It's good to see you'll stand for something. That's an important trait—especially for this team."

"Up until last year about this time, we all agreed with you," said Ward.

"Except for me," said Gorin proudly. "I've known longer than anyone here that oil did not form in a biogenic fashion." Ward rolled his eyes at the boasting Russian.

Phil was confused. "What happened a year ago?"

"The discovery of Lost City," said Chambers.

Phil had never heard of it. "What Lost City? Wait . . . you don't mean Atlantis, do you?"

The men in the room laughed. "No, it's not Atlantis."

"It's bigger than Atlantis," said Ward. The laughter died down, and seriousness returned.

Chambers typed a few commands on a keyboard, and the spherical screen displayed a map of the ocean floor. Phil recognized it immediately. "That's the Mid-Atlantic Ridge."

"Very good. As you probably know, the Mid-Atlantic Ridge runs along the floor of the Atlantic like the seam of a baseball. The Pacific has a ridge too, but not quite as pronounced. Now, the U.S. Navy and other agencies have been mapping the ocean for decades. It was very important in the Cold War to know where these geologic features were on the ocean floor. It's important for national security reasons—submarines and electronic warfare—things like that."

Chambers moved the mouse, and the display zoomed into the Mid-Atlantic Ridge as if the scientists were flying in an airplane. It reminded Phil of flying over the Rocky Mountains en route to Denver. But unlike the mountains of the west, which were all of similar height, here a huge rock formation bulged from the ocean floor with an enormous domed cap. The other underwater mountains seemed to shrink away from the titan formation.

"This is Atlantis Massif," said Chambers.

"Wow. That thing sticks out like a sore thumb," said Phil. "Why is it so different from everything else?"

"That's why we're here," said Ward. "Nobody knows. There are some strange things about this area of the ridge that we think are profoundly different from anywhere else on earth. We call this area Lost City, and one of the big questions surrounding it is how this mountain formed."

Chambers adjusted his glasses. "Atlantis Massif is fourteen thousand feet tall and about ten miles across—about the same size as Mount Rainier in Washington State. Something is causing it to bulge up like that off the seafloor."

"Is it sitting on a volcano?" asked Phil.

"That's what we thought initially," Ward answered. "This whole ridge is very seismically active. So that's the first thing that comes to mind—but there is no volcano insofar as we can detect. It's something else entirely."

Phil studied the topology of the mountain. "These ripples on the surface of Atlantis Massif are really weird. I don't think I've ever seen anything like that on a mountain range."

Gorin grunted at the all-too-obvious comment by the rookie. Chambers beamed. "Good observation, young man."

Chambers moved the mouse pointer over the mountain looming on the display. "These marks, or corrugations as we like to call them, seem to be evidence that the entire mountain formed under the rift valley of the Mid-Atlantic Ridge a few miles away. But as the surface plates expanded and pulled away from one another, it was like pulling a rug out from under a piece of furniture."

Scott Ward stepped up to the map and pointed at a deep gash on the ocean floor that ran east to west near the strange mountain. "There's more. It looks like several thousands of years ago, the Mid-Atlantic Ridge near this Atlantis Fracture Zone may have been seismically active."

Ward waved his hand over the mountain and the image split away, showing a cross section of the inside of the mountain.

"Cool," said Phil. "But I'm still waiting on the connection to Axcess Energy."

An animation began to play, depicting the mountain slowly bulging and morphing into its giant form from a flat, featureless plane on the ocean floor. Ward narrated, ignoring Phil's question entirely. "During that time, the magma chambers may have become so over-pressurized from an influx of melted rock from the mantle that their roofs fractured. The basalt would have rushed upward from the chamber in a tight rift, called a dike. This force would breach the seafloor and create an eruption of basalt. The super-hot basalt would then cool extremely fast because of the near-freezing water. If you notice, this stuff cooled so quickly that a thin layer of glass formed on it like obsidian."

An image of jet-black glass coating a basaltic rock appeared on the screen near the cross section.

Phil stepped closer to the screen, and Chambers zoomed the display nearer to the giant mountain. Phil felt like he was mountain climbing in reverse as the digital terrain moved up the screen in front of him. Chambers released the mouse, and the movement stopped. Phil wobbled a bit on his legs, dizzy from the digital flight down the mountain. "Whoa."

Gorin chuckled and imitated the young recruit's instability by pretending he was drunk and wobbling around in the tight space.

A picture of the fractured ocean floor—ripped open in a huge gash—filled the display. "The rocks down here in the ridge are different from what you'd expect. It's mostly peridotite," said Ward.

Phil was shocked. "Peridotite? But that's usually found much deeper in the earth. How's it getting pushed up here?" He ran his hand along the screen as if he could explore the physical ridge from here.

"That's something we don't know yet. We were hoping that would be your area of research. The rocks in that mountain are not the usual black basalt that makes up most of the ocean floor. Instead, the mountain is made of this dense green rock, peridotite—which as you mentioned is found only in the mantle."

Chambers stepped back from the display. "Somehow, this rock from deep in the earth—at least a few miles down—has been brought to the surface and lifted up to form the Atlantis Massif."

"There's more, Phil," said Ward. "These ridges are venting like black smokers—except they aren't black smokers."

Phil thought back to sophomore geology class. Black smokers: hydrothermal vents on the ocean floor spewing superheated water into the ocean's cold depth from deep in the earth.

"On our last trip we collected some of this bubbling, petroleum-rich liquid from the vents using THEO. We were expecting to find carbon 12. That's what you'd expect to find in petroleum—*if* it was associated with biological origins."

"Right. So what did you find?" asked Phil.

"We found carbon 13," answered Ward, waiting for Phil to put the pieces together.

Phil's mind whirled and he spoke out loud as he reasoned it out. "Okay, so most geologists assume the carbon present in hydrocarbons—especially coal and oil—is organic carbon, which would make it carbon 12 . And carbon 12 is far more abundant than carbon 13—by a ratio of a 100:1. Nothing short of a nuclear reaction can change carbon 12 to carbon 13 and vice versa, so these are separate, naturally occurring elements."

"Go on," prodded Chambers.

"Photosynthesis, which is the key process of all biological plants, preferentially selects carbon 12 over carbon 13. And you're saying that carbon 13 appears to be formed from the mantle of the earth, rather than from biological material settled on the ocean floor. So petroleum, or at least this petroleum, is not biological—it's not life-based. It's, to use your word, abiogenic."

Chambers smiled. Phil was a quick study. That was one of a hundred reasons why he wanted him on the team. "That's what it looks like."

Phil couldn't contain himself. "Well, that's incredible news! That means that there might not really be an energy crisis. It could be evidence that oil is abundant and isn't nearly exhausted. In fact, it can't be exhausted. How did you find this out? Who else knows?" asked Phil, looking around the room for answers.

Ward and Gorin exchanged glances that almost showed pity for the naive but excited young man.

"People know about the *theory*, but the Atlantis Massif may be proof, and almost nobody outside of our team knows about it," said Chambers.

Gorin's voice boomed and echoed in the spherical chamber. "But in Russia we have known about this theory for years—since the late 1940s. It was the Russian Petroleum Industry that discovered this by drilling past the Crystalline Basement and discovering huge reserves."

"Wait . . . this has been known in Russia for decades?" asked Phil. "How come I've never heard of it? I'm a geophysicist with a concentration in hydrocarbon exploration, for pete's sake!"

"There are over seven hundred papers published. Many of them are available to anyone who asks," said Ward.

"How come nobody in North America acknowledges this yet?" asked Phil.

Scott Ward smiled at Phil's incredulity. "Some are starting to put the pieces together, Phil. Take me, for example. When I worked at Jet Propulsion Labs in Pasadena, we discovered that Titan, a moon around Saturn, seemed to have methane pockets. Now, methane is normally associated with life, and we know that Titan does not support life. So those discoveries led me to think that the production of methane does not require biologic origin. There is also evidence that hydrothermal vents may exist on Jupiter's moon Europa, and there might even be vents on Mars."

Phil was shaking his head, a smile starting to play on his face. But he'd grabbed onto another fact from Scott's story. "Wait, why would an oil-exploration geologist be working at JPL?"

Scott Ward smiled. "Because I'm not a geologist. I'm an astronomer." Scott nodded his head toward Gorin. "He's not a geologist either."

"I'm a mathematician," said Gorin.

Phil was confused. "Dr. Chambers?"

"I'm a chemist, Phil. You're the only geophysicist in the room."

Phil was taken aback. If he joined this team, it would be *his* reputation as a geophysicist that would be challenged—no one else was in the firing line. These other men were in different fields. Why hadn't he known that?

The phone on the wall rang, and Chambers picked it up. After a moment, he smiled. "THEO is coming up on the vents."

Chapter Five
White Smoker

P hil's head was spinning, and he sat down on the metal bench. This small multidisciplinary team had discovered something fantastic—unbelievable—amazing.

If it was really true, then there was no energy crisis. The earth wasn't running out of "fossil" fuels—it actually created petroleum naturally deep in its bowels. And the proof might be sitting right below their feet.

The display on the spherical surface became active again, reflecting the crushing, punishing environment enveloping the THEO submersible. The water was no longer blue. It was pitch black. No sunlight from the surface reached down here.

An odd, pale fish swam toward the submarine and turned at the last moment. Its eyes were dull gray and featureless. Light had never been seen by the creature.

Strange green flashes pulsed from a few fluorescing marine animals disturbed by THEO as it descended through the blackness.

"Turn on the auxiliary floods," said Ward. Gorin typed at a keyboard, and a moment later the deep black became a bit grayer. *Like high beams in thick fog,* Phil thought.

The sonar began to ping more frequently as the craft descended. A ghostly white spire appeared at the bottom of the screen. It revealed itself slowly before looming like a giant sequoia on the spherical screen, pure white against the stark dark contrast of ocean surrounding it. A bubbling vent of superheated water, rich in minerals, gurgled from a jagged, brittle-looking opening. The heated water blurred the edges of the cream-colored spire like summer heat on an asphalt highway.

The chimney belched its contents into the dark water, turning the blackness into a milky white, bubbling fountain. The difference between this vent and its more familiar black smoker cousins was not lost on Phil.

"Like I said, *not* like a black smoker," said Ward.

Phil was amazed at the size of the chimney as its thick mid-body came into view. "How big is this thing?"

"This is the small one. It's over thirty meters tall. The biggest we've found is over ten stories tall. It's made mostly of carbonate, which is typically very strong, but we had a chimney fall down last year that was the size of a three-story building."

Phil was mesmerized by the sand-castle-like structure. "Carbonate—you mean this is mostly just limestone secreted from the water?"

"Yep. It seems to share some properties with coral as well," said Chambers.

THEO reached the bottom of the chimney and slowly panned its camera toward the top of the spire. "They look clean," Phil said. "Not like the black smokers—you know how they are, all covered in particulates, microbial colonies, swarms of shrimp. There are no clams, mussels, or tube worms on the cooler areas of these vents."

Ward nodded. "Good observation. We don't know why that is—but we suspect the fluid being ejected is not supportive to life. The temperature of the venting fluid is about 170° F. If you consider that the ocean temperature here is 37° F, that's pretty amazing."

Phil agreed. "So this is the water you sampled and found carbon 13?"

"Yes. It's not totally petroleum, but there are trace amounts. We think there might be a gas pocket below Atlantis Massif . . ."

Phil finished Ward's sentence, ". . . and gas pockets are good predictors for oil reserves."

"That's right. Now you get it. So this might be both the evidence of abiogenic oil production inside the earth and also a huge, bountiful oil reserve—all in one."

Phil put his hands to his head, overwhelmed by the visuals and disclosures in the last hour. "It's so deep, though, the ability to find the reserve may be the easy part," he said. "Figuring out how to recover the oil at this depth may be nearly impossible."

"That's why we want you on the team," said Ward. "Your background and research in taking huge seismic data sets and understanding the underground features of possible oil reserves will be critical here."

"Hey, the batteries aren't getting any stronger while you persist in your emotional bear hug with the youngster," bellowed Gorin.

Phil cocked an eyebrow. *Youngster? Did he actually call me a youngster?*

Gorin typed on the keyboard, and an overlay of a green grid filled the screen, superimposing itself over the live camera feeds of the ocean floor. "Those hydrophones that you saw under the submersible will help us here," said Gorin between keystrokes.

The submersible began to run a preprogrammed course along the floor of the ocean, moving first to the bottom, leftmost corner of the grid and firing its thrusters to position itself perfectly within the digital square.

"What's it doing?" asked Phil.

Ward pointed to the grid points on the screen. "It will make its way across this grid and deposit those acoustic beacons on every fifth grid point. When we fire them off, they will survey the ocean bedrock with sonar, record the data, transmit it back to the submersible, and then transmit the entire reading up through the umbilical to the *Deep Pathfinder*."

"How powerful are they? I mean, how far down will the sound waves penetrate?"

"We should get returns up to seven miles down. That's deeper and better than almost anything else in this neighborhood."

Phil counted the rows and columns of the large grid and performed a few mental calculations based on the area of the return and the amount of data each beacon would generate.

"That's going to be one huge data set! Scott wasn't kidding when he said ten terabytes."

Chambers smiled. "Like I said, that's where you come in. There's no doubt that making sense of a sea of data is going to be a challenge. What's the largest set you've ever worked on?"

"Well, I won a national visualization award a few years back for visualizing two terabytes, but no one has ever done anything with ten—not even with five. Most academicians would say it's impossible for the human mind to comprehend that much information."

"Are you up for this?" Chambers asked point-blank.

Before Phil could respond, the captain's voice came over the intercom. "Dr. Chambers. The Sea King is here to take your visitor back."

Scott Ward motioned to Gorin, and they both shook Phil's hand and stepped out of the spherical projection room, leaving Phil and Dr. Chambers alone.

As the hatch closed, Dr. Chambers turned to Phil. "Well, son, it's time to make a decision. You've seen all of our cards. You've seen what's at stake, and I need you to help us make this breakthrough. I may have misled you a bit at the beginning, pretending we were all geophysicists, but you see where the energy industry has gone with only one discipline on board."

Phil felt his ego flair a bit, but he knew he had already made his decision the moment he heard about the Atlantis Massif and the deep-sea bubbling vents. He took a deep breath and jumped.

"Dr. Chambers, I want this job. It's a huge challenge—a challenge that will push me to the outer limits of what's possible. I can see that I can work well with your team, and I know this is the project for me."

Dr. Chambers raised an eyebrow, but he was clearly pleased. He was used to getting his recruits, but usually after a lot more platitudes and a lot more perks. "We haven't even talked about salary or benefits. Doesn't any of that play into your decision?"

"Sure it does, but money isn't everything. I need something to believe in passionately. I can make money anywhere—but here, working on this," Phil pointed at the white smoker looming on the screen like a ghostly sand castle, "I can make a real difference, and you know it."

Dr. Chambers smiled at the comment. Not cocky, but confident—full of conviction. "Great. Welcome aboard." He handed Phil a manila folder stuffed with documents. "You need to get these signed and back to Human Resources as quickly as possible. When can you start?"

Phil looked at his watch and calculated the return trip and number of time zone changes. "Thirty-six hours?"

Chambers smiled. "Perfect. The data acquisition should be done by then." The phone on the wall rang again; the captain was getting impatient waiting for the helicopter to leave. "Well, your chopper's waiting, Phil."

Phil grabbed his backpack and duffel and headed for the hatch. Chambers pulled a check from his pocket and held it out to Phil with a smile. "Oh, one more thing: here's your signing bonus. Now, if you decide not to take the job, you've got to give that back."

Phil decided to look at the check. He had no clue what his starting salary would be.

$20,000.00

Phil rubbed his eyes and tried to speak, but nothing came out. He cleared his throat and tried again.

"Th-th-ank you, Dr. Chambers."

"Happy to do it, Phil. Now get to the helicopter. You've got a lot of work ahead of you."

Phil shook Chambers's hand and headed for the helicopter pad.

After a quick wave, a crewman pulled the door closed, and the Sea King picked up into a hover before spinning around and heading back toward the shore of the United States a thousand miles away. Ward, Chambers, and Gorin watched the helicopter disappear into a cloud bank. Ward looked happy. "I'm glad we got him. He's the only chance we have of this thing seeing the light of day."

"The innocence of youth," said Chambers with a grim smile. He was suddenly filled with guilt, as if he were luring someone pure and innocent into a crime family.

"He has no idea what we're up against."

Chapter Six
High Society

Phil lay crashed on his bed in a deep sleep when his alarm clock woke him. He looked at the clock and blearily made out the time: 4:30 p.m. He was exhausted and jet-lagged, tired from multiple landings on deep-sea oil-drilling platforms that allowed the helicopter to refuel before finally landing in Jacksonville, Florida, and taking the red-eye to Austin.

His flight to Austin hadn't allowed any sleep either: a screaming baby next to him had thrown up on him not once, but three times. When the town car service finally dropped him off at his apartment, he barely had the strength to draw the shades and fall into bed at 7:00 a.m. Fortunately he'd remembered to set the alarm, knowing he would be in la-la land for the remainder of the day if nothing woke him.

He ran his hand over his face, wiping the sleep from his eyes. His beard had thirty-six hours of growth, and he smelled bad. He stumbled to the bathroom for a quick shower and shave. He only had forty minutes to be out of the apartment and on his way to his date with Lisa.

. . . .

An hour later, Phil pulled into the parking lot at The River's Edge, the fin-
est restaurant in Austin. As Phil waited in the valet line, he grew more and more
uncomfortable with the luxury cars lined up ahead of him. Phil looked in the
rearview mirror and adjusted his blue and gold striped tie as a jacketed valet
approached the beater. The valet couldn't have been more than seventeen.

"Would you like us to park your—um, car?" asked the adolescent, staring
at the never-waxed paint of the car.

"Sure," said Phil, hopping out with the rusted hinge making a strange
shrieking noise, "but remember, if it gets a scratch on it, I'm coming after you."
Phil handed the young man a wad of crumpled dollar bills. He tried to hold
a serious expression as the valet looked at the rusted hulk and measured the
words he had just been threatened with. Phil turned and walked toward the
lobby of the restaurant with a silly grin on his face.

Lisa was on her cell phone as he walked into the opulent lobby. She waved
and shot him a smile. She looked amazing. She had just come from work at the
governor's office where she was a media liaison with the commerce department of Austin, and she was dressed in a navy business jacket with charcoal
slacks. Her slender but athletic body made Phil's heart rate skyrocket.

She was wearing her brunette hair long and full, and it cascaded over her
shoulders until it reached midway down her back. Long hair in the business
world was a no-no, but she wore it like a badge of honor, almost daring a chau-
vinist to make an inappropriate comment. Though she was a knockout, Lisa
wasn't afraid to show her feminine side in the dog-eat-dog man's world she
found herself in.

Phil waved back to her and talked with the hostess, informing her that
the Channing party had arrived. He had been to this restaurant before with
Lisa. She liked this place. It was good for her career, and it was *the* place to be
seen in the city. The River's Edge was right in the downtown district, nestled
up against the river that meandered through the city of Austin. The decor
was amazing: inlaid wooden floors with rustic stone walls and a maze of deep
leather booths that obscured and concealed intimate conversations between
parties. The restaurant was a place for deal-making—wheeling and dealing—
just like in the movies.

Lisa had been born for this environment, but Phil felt out of place. As he watched the rich and famous enter the lobby, he thought about his preferred dinner plan: pizza and an action flick on his carpeted apartment floor.

Lisa ended the call and walked over to Phil. "Hi, honey, how was your business trip?" she asked, giving him a lingering kiss.

"Um, the trip was memorable," said Phil, mentally reliving the early morning flight. Fortunately the hostess chimed "Channing party" just as he began to relive the screaming, barfing baby incident of that morning's red-eye.

The hostess seated them in a booth that faced the main floor with a view of the Austin skyline. The water reflected the downtown skyscrapers, and the sun was painting the sky rust-orange with pink and purple feathered lines.

As the hostess disappeared, Lisa reached across the table and grabbed Phil's hand. "So did you get the job?"

"Yep, I signed all the papers on the way back last night. I'm going to take it."

Lisa beamed and squeezed his hand. "I'm so proud of you, Phil. It's not easy to get into Axcess. You know what else?"

"What?"

"Your dad would be proud too. I know he would."

A bittersweet, shallow grin appeared on Phil's face. "I think so too." He cleared his throat. "I'm starving. I haven't eaten all day." He glanced at the menu. Plated dishes with names he couldn't pronounce and prices he couldn't have afforded two days before ran down the page. The last time they'd eaten here he'd had to dig out of credit-card debt for a single dinner. This new job would change that.

Silence marched on for a moment as Lisa pretended to study the entrée list. She bit her lip, restraining the question she was dying to ask.

"One twenty," said Phil with a muffled voice from behind the menu.

"What!" she said in an urgent but whispered way. Lisa pulled the top of Phil's menu down and saw that he was smiling ear-to-ear like a Cheshire cat at the announcement of his salary.

"That's unheard of. They must want you pretty badly!"

"Oh, and they also gave me this," said Phil, sliding the signing bonus across the table.

Lisa was stunned as she looked at the amount on the check. "Twenty thousand dollars to sign on? They really pulled out all the stops, didn't they?" She felt the embossed company logo at the top of the check.

"I could buy a real hot car now." Phil buttered his roll, his tone purposely casual.

"It's not a bad idea," Lisa countered. Phil scrunched up his nose at her. He knew she didn't care.

"Where will you be working?" she asked, sliding the check back over.

"In Austin on the main campus, about fifteen minutes from here."

"When do you start?" she asked.

"Tomorrow, although the team won't be back from the site until next week," said Phil, grabbing more bread from the basket.

"Where exactly did they take you, Phil?"

"The middle of the Atlantic Ocean," he said. "It was amazing. I think they are onto something that will rip a hole in the oil industry. I've never seen anything like what I saw with them."

Lisa sat back and regarded him with an amazed smile. She knew that Phil was up to speed on the very latest in oil discovery methods and techniques. If this was new to him, it was something truly amazing. The salary, the signing bonus, the special recruitment technique—it was all starting to make some sense.

Lisa's eyes glanced up the center of the restaurant, and her demeanor abruptly changed. "Oh, my word," she said, pulling her cloth napkin up and dabbing her mouth.

Phil turned as he took a big bite of dinner roll, wondering what would engender such a self-conscious response from Lisa.

"My boss is here, and he's coming over here with the governor," she said.

The warning wasn't soon enough for Phil, who was chewing the roll just as the elected official arrived at the table.

"Hello, Lisa, how are you doing this evening?"

Lisa smiled and shook the governor's hand like he was the pope. Roger Wyngate was tall, in his early fifties with just a hint of a belly. He was dressed in an eastern executive-style suit—more Maryland than Texas. The suit alone was probably worth more than all Phil's earthly goods combined.

Phil struggled to swallow the dry bread without requiring a Heimlich maneuver that would doom his girlfriend's career prospects.

Lisa introduced him, trying to stall for time and hoping that Phil wouldn't spew dinner roll on her boss. "Governor Wyngate, I'd like to introduce you to my friend, Phil Channing."

"Aha . . . the friend," said the governor, shaking Phil's hand with a wink.

Phil stood as best he could in the booth, smiled, and gave a solid shake. "Governor," he said, dutifully nodding but avoiding a full bow.

"Don't let this one get away, she's a great gal," said the governor in a Texas drawl.

Phil grinned. "Oh, I don't intend to." He glanced back at Lisa, who was blushing.

"I hear you are interviewing at Axcess Energy, son," said Wyngate. Lisa looked a little embarrassed; obviously she had blabbed at work.

"Yes, sir, I just took a job there as an exploration scientist."

"Well, that's wonderful news, Phil. Axcess is a great company," said the governor, squeezing Phil's hand like a roughneck on an oil rig. "I'll actually be out there next week for an analyst briefing by the CEO, Glenn Martin. He's a friend of mine, you know."

Name-dropping, the main activity of the rich and famous, thought Phil as he watched the governor's attention shift to Lisa.

Governor Wyngate moved closer to Lisa's side of the table. "How's the planning coming for that meeting, Lisa?"

Lisa went into business mode. It was like watching a butterfly emerge from a cocoon. "We're all set, sir, just a few last-minute changes to the speech, but nothing major. We'll have some great attendees in the crowd. We even have the environmentalist lobby sending some heavy hitters."

Phil looked at the man standing next to the governor. He seemed uninterested in the conversation and was checking his voice mail.

The governor noticed Phil's attention on his colleague and put his right hand on the aloof man's shoulder. "This is David Rohm; he's my commerce secretary."

"And my boss," added Lisa.

Rohm was tall and thin—runner thin. He had salt-and-pepper short-cropped hair and a chiseled jaw. But it was his eyes that captured Phil's attention. Brown, almost black irises, and eyes that appeared sunken with deep bags beneath them. His conservative dark suit and starched white shirt amplified his severe look.

Phil made a snap judgment about the commerce secretary: he didn't like this man at all.

Rohm's thin lips curled into a smile that was more of a chore than a courtesy and continued listening to his messages as he shook Phil's hand. Phil and everyone else could see that he had no interest in Lisa's boyfriend.

"Very good; we'll talk later, Lisa. I've interrupted your dinner enough for one evening. You two enjoy yourselves," said the governor.

"Nice to meet you, sir," said Phil, returning a quick handshake.

The governor spotted another couple he knew and made his way over to their booth. David Rohm walked behind him, constantly checking his cell phone for messages.

"Nice guy," said Phil, taking another bite from his dinner roll and gesturing toward Rohm. "Very friendly—he should run for public office or something."

Lisa smirked. Phil kept going.

"Yes, that David Rohm is a lively guy. I'd just as soon get a tax audit from the IRS than go somewhere with him."

"Shhh," said Lisa, looking over her shoulder. "You want to get me fired or something? He's my boss."

The waiter came over to the table, and they ordered dinner. Phil, ever the meat eater, ordered The Cowboy, a twelve-ounce filet smothered in blue cheese. Lisa ordered the petit filet and a house salad.

With the order out of the way, Phil looked across the table and smiled at Lisa. She was beautiful, and he had always wondered why God had sent her his way and what in the world she found in him.

"I'm so glad you moved down here. I missed you," said Lisa, squeezing his hand.

"Me too. This is a cool town, and I sure won't miss the winters in Toronto." Phil looked up at the ceiling. "There's another reason I like this place—let me think—oh, yeah," said Phil, giving Lisa a squeeze back. "It just so happens that *you* are here too."

Phil had remained in Toronto to finish school while Lisa returned to Austin and landed her great job. They had e-mailed and instant messaged numerous times a day, keeping communication going and the spark alive. But regardless of technology, long-distance relationships were not easy.

Their dinner arrived, and the steaks bubbled and sizzled on their plates.

"I'll pray," said Phil. They both bowed their heads and continued holding hands.

"Father, thank you for all of your blessings to Lisa and me. Thank you for bringing us together, and thank you for this wonderful evening. Bless this food to our bodies and thank you for the wonderful jobs you have brought to both of us. Amen."

They looked up and noticed that a few of the patrons had been watching them. Phil didn't care. He really did have much to be thankful for. Just eating dinner without saying thank you to God seemed rude and insulting.

"Tell me about Dr. Chambers," said Lisa, cutting her steak.

"I think if you looked up charisma in the dictionary you'd find his picture. He has an aura around him—almost a magnetic field. He makes you want to work for him. He makes you want his thoughts and praise."

"That's the way he comes across in interviews," said Lisa. Chambers had been in numerous television talk shows and newspaper articles over the years, and he was one of the most famous people in Austin.

Lisa took a sip of water and blinked her eyes. "One of my contacts is bothering me. I'll be right back." She slid from the leather bench and headed for the ladies' room. Phil continued to watch the governor and his commerce secretary work the room.

Lisa's high heels clacked on the marble floor as she made her way to the sink. She looked at herself briefly in the mirror, checking her ensemble and hair and then carefully working the contact out of her eyeball.

As Lisa was cleaning her contact lens, another woman came into the restroom. She was blonde, wearing black slacks and a white silk blouse. She smiled at Lisa. "Those things can be a pain, huh?"

Lisa smiled and nodded as best she could as she refitted the lens on her eye. The other woman walked along the length of the bathroom, surveying the open stall doors and seemingly studying the room.

"You're Lisa Baton, aren't you?" asked the woman.

Lisa was a little startled. Yes, she worked for the governor, but she was hardly high-profile.

"Yes . . ."

"I'm Sheridan Preston, reporter for *The Austin Chronicle*," she said extending her hand.

Lisa timidly shook the woman's hand. She had a deep mistrust of reporters. Everyone in the office did. The people around the governor spent a lot of time fixing the mistakes of sloppy reporters. And suddenly Lisa realized why Sheridan had studied the room so carefully: she wanted to make sure they were alone.

"What do you know about a Russian Oil Company called LukZag Petroleum?"

"Only what I read in the paper," said Lisa. She was nervous, like everything she was saying was being recorded.

"That's funny, because your boss, David Rohm, meets with them frequently. Did you know they are building an oil pipeline across Turkey to supply the Middle East with natural gas?"

Lisa's surprised expression gave her away. "Why would my boss be meeting with an international oil company? His responsibilities are to the workers and economy of Texas. I'm sure you're mistaken."

"I'm not mistaken, Lisa. Rohm has interests way outside those of Texas. LukZag is also known to be controlled by the Russian Mafia. And I'm not talking about the good-looking guys you see in the *Godfather* movies either. These are the most ambitious and most dangerous of the criminal underworld in Russia."

The reporter pulled a stack of photos from a folder under her arm, placing them one by one on the countertop. The first showed Rohm at the airport, then Rohm at a dinner meeting with an overlook of Istanbul in the background window, Muslim prayer towers and domed structures against a sunset sky. Preston continued to produce photo after photo, and a damning collage materialized on the granite countertop before Lisa's eyes.

"I've followed Rohm to Turkey numerous times, Lisa. He's been there three times in the last month alone. Why is the governor's office involved with this Russian oil company?" Sheridan fished.

"I have no comment. I should get going," Lisa said, stuffing her saline bottle into her handbag.

"He's also making stops in Libya and Syria on these trips," said Preston.

Russia, Libya, Syria—not the best countries to be associated with as governor of the great state of Texas. Lisa felt like she was being told she had a terminal illness—as if the last few minutes of revelation from this reporter had altered her future in some immeasurable way.

Lisa stopped stuffing things into her handbag and exhaled, looking at the marble floor. "Why are you telling me these things?" Lisa's voice cracked a bit.

Preston handed her a business card. "Because I think that the governor, Rohm, and possibly a good chunk of the administration are involved with something they shouldn't be involved with."

Sheridan smiled at Lisa. "You seem like a good person to me, Lisa. Not every reporter is evil. I've been researching this for over a year, so consider everything in here as off the record. I won't reach out to you again, so if you need anything, contact me—but don't wait too long."

Sheridan Preston placed a business card in Lisa's hand, turned, and walked out of the ladies' room. Lisa leaned against the counter. She felt like she had been punched in the gut. She waited a few more minutes before returning to the booth where Phil had finished his dinner.

She sat down in the leather booth with less elegance than normal and looked down at her plate of food. She had lost her appetite.

Phil's face flashed with a combination of relief and concern. "Are you okay? I was beginning to get worried."

Lisa glanced around the restaurant. "Yeah, I'm fine," she said without emotion. She didn't see Sheridan Preston anywhere.

Phil knew better. "You don't look fine. You look . . . well, scared."

Their waiter approached the booth. "How was dinner?" he asked, glancing at the couple's plates. Phil's plate was immaculate, so clean it looked like food hadn't even been there. Lisa's was barely touched.

"It was amazing, thank you," said Phil. Lisa simply pushed the plate toward the center of the table as she looked over the divider and into the other side of the restaurant.

"Would you like to see the dessert menu?" asked the waiter. Phil glanced at Lisa, who continued to look around the restaurant. She was zoned out. Something was seriously wrong.

"Not tonight. Just the check, please," said Phil.

Chapter Seven
Drive Home

Phil waited with Lisa as the valet brought her car around to the entrance of the restaurant. Lisa was quiet, as if a switch had been thrown in the middle of dinner. She had been excited about the job offer, about his prospects for the future, about seeing the governor in the restaurant—and then silence. It was very unlike Lisa to downshift like this.

Finally, Phil got the courage to ask. "What's wrong?"

Lisa looked around her at the social elite leaving and arriving at the five-star restaurant. "Not here. I'll tell you in the car."

The valet with the scruffy hair finally pulled around, and they got into Lisa's car—a blue sedan with nice leather seats, a gift from her dad upon graduation from college. Phil gave the valet a nice tip and opened the driver's door for Lisa, then quickly ran to the passenger's side.

"What about your car?" asked Lisa.

"This is more important. We'll get mine later."

Lisa drove slowly down the road and pulled off to a parking lot that over-looked the river and the western side of the city. Phil leaned over and took her hand. "Okay, what's going on?"

Lisa tried to keep it together, but the emotion was too much. "A reporter came into the ladies' room. She was from *The Austin Chronicle*." Her voice cracked as she talked.

Phil's world did not include reporters, only nerds and geeks. He began to say something sarcastic, but Lisa's obvious distress stopped him. He remained silent as she continued.

"She said that David Rohm, my boss, is involved with a Russian oil company: LukZag Petroleum."

"LukZag?" echoed Phil. The company had been in the news frequently with their pipeline project that zigzagged through politically unstable countries. "Why would the secretary of commerce in Texas be involved with them?"

"That's what I asked," said Lisa, dabbing her eye with the corner of a crumpled tissue fished from her purse. "She said he's been meeting with them for over a year, secretly. She also said he's been making stops in Syria and Libya."

Phil's mind whirled with the scenario. "So . . . maybe he's trying to involve local petroleum projects or engineering firms in the building of the pipeline. It could be any number of things, Lisa. It doesn't have to be anything sinister."

Lisa wiped her eyes. "Maybe. But she said she's been following him for a year—a year, Phil! That means he's been hiding this from me the entire time."

"What are you going to do?" asked Phil.

Lisa's breathing was staggered, and she took a deep breath, trying to reset to a normal rhythm. "Nothing for now, but you can bet I'll be looking at everything Rohm does now with suspicion." Her emotion was heading toward anger as she thought more about it. "It's just that I should've known. I mean, I would know if he was up to—"

Lisa's cell phone rang, interrupting. She looked at the display. "It's Aliya," she said.

Before Phil could say to call her back, Lisa answered the call.

"Hello?"

The voice of her friend from college caused the tear to stop for a moment as her face showed enjoyment. But just moments into the conversation, the pleasure on Lisa's face disappeared. "Wait! *What?* Say that again."

She glanced at Phil, who mouthed, *What's going on?*

Lisa looked down, avoiding Phil's gaze as if the information she had just heard was shameful or unbearable. He took her hand. It was tense, her body wound tight like a spring.

Phil handed Lisa a handkerchief from his sport-coat pocket. He never used them, but his father had never gone anywhere without them, and carrying a handkerchief was a way to honor his memory. A tradition observed and handed down, but never adopted functionally.

Lisa dabbed her eyes as she listened. "I'm so sorry, Aliya. I don't know what to say, but we love you and we're praying for you."

A moment later she hung up.

Phil reached over and slowly turned her face to his, knowing the news was bad. "Hey, what's going on? Lisa?"

He had never seen her like this.

She sniffed and pulled her hands across her cheeks. She looked at Phil as if she was holding a secret that would change his life.

She was.

"Jack was killed two nights ago."

Phil's face became ashen. "Jack—Jack Sanders? What do you mean?"

"Jack was murdered in Toronto two nights ago."

Now it was Phil's turn to turn a blank stare toward the horizon.

"Do they know who did it?" Phil slumped in the passenger seat, overcome with strange emotions: sadness—rage—loss—denial. Jack—a free spirit to be sure and probably bordering on crazy, but a loyal friend. They had been in many of the same computer classes, and Jack and Aliya had double-dated often with Phil and Lisa. The emotions swirled and morphed in his mind like a swarm of mad hornets. "And why? It just seems so . . . meaningless."

"She didn't say—I don't think she knows. Poor Aliya. I feel so bad for her," said Lisa.

Neither of them knew what to say, and they sat silently watching the Texas sun weigh on the distant horizon.

Chapter Eight

First Day

P hil marched into the lobby of Axcess the next morning, ready to put a dent in the universe. The loss of Jack had awakened him to the brevity of life. He was ready to make his mark. After signing in at the security desk, he waited for the human-resources representative to arrive. A few minutes later a woman in her thirties, wearing a white blouse and a navy skirt, approached him. "Philip Channing?"

Phil smiled and greeted the woman.

"Mr. Channing, my name is Rose Stanton. I'm the director of human resources. Let's go to my office." Rose led Phil through the security checkpoint and down the hall through double-glass doors to her office. As she took her seat, she was all business. "Mr. Channing, have you signed all the papers?"

"Yes, ma'am," said Phil politely, opening a manila folder and laying the employee agreement and other official-looking papers in front of her.

"Very good. Now, you realize that your first paycheck will be deposited in your specified bank account three weeks from tomorrow, and then they

will follow in a bimonthly cycle on the fifteenth and the end of the month—
the twenty-eighth for February, the thirtieth for April, and the thirty-first for
months like July. Understand?"

Phil nodded.

Rose riffled through the papers and checked off a list. "It looks like everything is in order. Now, here's your badge. It will let you into the floors and
rooms that you are assigned to. You cannot go to floors that you are not assigned to with this badge. When you enter the elevator, you place the card in
the access slot and press the button of the floor you want. Okay?"

"Yes," said Phil, smiling as he looked at his gleaming badge. Even though
his employee photo looked like something from America's Most Wanted, this
was beginning to feel official.

"One last thing, and that's regarding Toilet Day," said Rose with a smirk.

Phil leaned forward, cocking his head a bit. "Did you say . . . Toilet Day?"

Rose laughed; the term always made new employees do a double take.
"It's the day all your paperwork gets processed. It takes place about two weeks
from tomorrow. Benefit cards are sent, you can charge food in the cafeteria to
your employee badge, and the 401k draw begins. In short, everything starts
working. We call it Toilet Day as if the toilets will start flushing for you. Fortunately, the actual toilets work from day one."

"Thank goodness," said Phil, relieved he wouldn't have to be outside using
the bushes in the landscaping of the corporate campus.

Rose stood and shook Phil's hand. "Welcome to Axcess Energy. Enjoy
your first day."

"Thank you." Even as his excitement grew, a wave of guilt washed over Phil
as he thought about his friend Jack and the strange way his life had ended. He
closed his eyes tightly, sighed, and marched through the double-glass doors to
the elevators with a new determination in his step. He was ready to work, to
apply his college and graduate knowledge, and to help Dr. Chambers and the
team he had joined. He was ready to set the world on fire. For his parents—for
Lisa—for Jack. And for himself. He looked at his paper as the elevator opened
for his floor assignment.

Department of Data Recovery and Exploration Development
(Floor B2)

Cool.

He was interrupted by half-a-dozen people who joined him in the glass-and-chrome elevator before it started upward. Phil glanced at the buttons for the floors: they were all lit up. The elevator shaft was all glass, and Phil looked out the back window at the sprawling campus.

The elevator dinged, and the floor readout appeared: L2. One person got off, the doors closed, and the elevator again headed upward.

Ding. L3. A few more people bailed out. Phil could feel his excitement growing. *The new guy gets the top-floor office!* He wondered if he would have an assistant; he was, after all, working on a new oil field—the lifeblood of the company.

The final floor dinged: L4. The last person got out, looking back at Phil as if he was on the wrong train. Phil opened his employee folder and reexamined his assignment. *Floor B2.* He studied the keypad from top to bottom: L4, L3 L2, Lobby, B1, B2. *Hmmm.*

Phil tried to act like he knew what he was doing, but he felt like an idiot. He pressed B2, the elevator doors closed on the top floor, and the elevator headed downward. The top floors disappeared quickly, and as the elevator passed the lobby, the beautiful back-window view of the corporate campus was replaced by steam pipes, electrical conduits, and a maze of plumbing. B1 went by, and the plumbing got thicker and more complex.

Finally the door dinged. The hallway outside the elevator was dusty, as if the cleaning crew had never been down here. Phil stepped out into the dimly lit hall. He half-expected to find a fossil down at this level, etched in the wall and surrounded by plumbing pipes and conduits from the Jurassic Period of business. Phil felt like he was buried in the deep geologic time when the company had first started. There was a trash chute and a service elevator at the leftmost edge of the hallway and a stairway to the upper levels.

Well, at least if there's a fire in the building, I have a fighting chance.

Phil walked to the only door on the right side of the elevator. The steel door had an older department's name on it, with black letters that were peeling off but still easily discernible:

DISCOVERY & DEVELOPMENT

Phil pulled his badge through the security lock, and the red light turned green. The click of the latch disengaging echoed for a moment down the empty hall. Phil pushed the door open, not sure what to expect.

The lights in the room were off. Only the dancing screen savers on three computer screens provided light. Phil groped the wall for the light switch and finally found it. The room was about forty feet long and thirty feet wide. Four cubicles were arranged two across from each other with a single aisle between the connected sets.

He easily found Scott Ward's desk. A large Cornell pennant was thumb-tacked to the wall, and all of Scott's coffee mugs had Cornell Theory Center logos. Phil had visited the CTC a number of times during graduate school, and many of his friends worked there. He thought about how fortunate he was to be working with such bright people.

The desk directly across from Ward's had to belong to Dr. Chambers. The chemistry books and MIT paraphernalia gave it away instantly. The third cubicle was Gorin's. It was a mess, stacked up with data tapes and adorned with half-empty soda cans accumulating dust.

The last cubicle was empty of personal or professional items, and Phil presumed it was his. Three boxes were stacked on the desk: a computer, a display monitor, and another box that Phil assumed were programs and peripherals to go with the other boxes.

Phil pulled his suit jacket off, laid it over a chair, and got to work hooking up the computer. As he plugged in the mouse and keyboard, he engaged in a fantasy.

"Mrs. Smith, please bring me some coffee and get me the Putman account," he said in a deep voice, trying his best to sound professional. He looked over his shoulder at the empty room and the dancing screen savers and laughed as loud as he wanted.

Chapter Nine
The Manta

The pulleys on the marine crane strained under the weight as the cables lowered the Manta Ray into the choppy Atlantic. The otherworldly craft looked as if it could change its mind at any moment about an underwater mission and fly off to explore Mars instead. Scott Ward watched from mid-ship, cradling a cup of coffee, and smiled as the craft entered the gray-blue water. All his years of research in self-organizing behavior were about to be put into something useful.

A group of divers clustered around the submersible, babying it as it lowered into the waves. Finally, one of the divers reached up and unlatched the steel hook from the anchor point on its dorsal side.

The Manta's systems came online and performed a diagnostic, transmitting the results of each test to the navigation chamber inside the *Deep Pathfinder*.

John Chambers and Gorin watched as the digital screen in front of them turned green across the board.

ELECTRICAL SYSTEMS POWERED UP: NO FAULTS
BALLAST & VENTING: ALL SYSTEMS NOMINAL
PROPULSION: ALL SYSTEMS NOMINAL
HYDRAULICS: ALL SYSTEMS NOMINAL
COMMUNICATIONS: ALL SYSTEMS NOMINAL
NAVIGATION: ALL SYSTEMS NOMINAL
INERTIAL GUIDANCE: ALL SYSTEMS NOMINAL

The list continued to build for a few more seconds, and Chambers spoke into the microphone boom. "All systems check out—green across the board. Manta Ray is now fully autonomous." Gorin crossed his fingers and pressed a button on the console between the two men. Chambers found it disturbing and amusing that the hardheaded mathematician would resort to superstition.

An announcement came over the loudspeaker. "Manta Ray is freed up. Good hunting, big fella."

Water vapor blew into the air as the Manta Ray began to slowly empty its ballast of air and consume the salty water of the Atlantic Ocean. The black, bat-like shape submerged beneath the chop and continued venting. Streams of bubbles emanated from multiple ports on its belly and dorsal surfaces.

The Manta's thrusters, propellers on the back and sides and below the vehicle, took turns firing short bursts into the water, adjusting the pitch, yaw, and roll of the vehicle as it began its long dive.

"Next stop, the abyssal plain," said Chambers gleefully.

The Manta slowly pitched downward, looking more like a killer whale than an advanced submersible, and its rear thrusters churned up bubbles, propelling it into the depths.

"How long?" asked Gorin, tapping nervously on the control panel. Chambers could see that the Russian was due his cigarette; he had lost track of how many coffin nails this man inhaled per day. His clothes reeked of tobacco.

"About forty-five minutes. Go ahead and go topside. I'll make an announcement when we start the run."

Gorin stepped out of the control center and ran up the stairwell, leaving Chambers alone with the instruments that were recording the Manta's every move.

■ ■ ■ ■

The Manta dove through the ocean water. At first, the shade of the water around the craft had been translucent blue—almost completely clear, full of light and the interplay of refracted colors from the support ships—but now, almost a thousand feet down, the water had become darker than any night on the surface. There were no stars to provide guidance, not even a twilight tint or a crescent moon to provide direction. There was no light here.

The Manta Ray didn't care. It was a machine, completely self-guided and simply carrying out the instructions it was programmed to perform. The internal guidance computer analyzed its position and orientation in space, the salinity of the water, and the pressure on the hull and responded with equal and opposite reactions if deemed necessary. The Manta was aware of but not concerned about the massive pressure of the ocean that was deftly looking—lurking—for any weakness in its titanium fabrication to crush it into an unrecognizable shape at the bottom of the Atlantic.

It was the perfect explorer, possessed of only the will to achieve its goal.

The Manta passed an angler fish that swerved away from it, barely missing becoming the deep-sea equivalent of a bug on a car's windshield.

The Manta's guidance computer sensed that the depth and position for its mission was quickly arriving. A diving plane on the back of the vehicle angled upward, and the craft moved into a cruising attitude and away from its deep-dive approach. The floor of the Atlantic was now approaching, looking like the surface of another planet. The rocky floor was mostly barren. Craggy hills and vents made occasional appearances, as did deep-sea coral fanning out from the bottom. Even here, in a mostly hostile environment, life still existed and even thrived, waiting for crumbs of decaying biological matter to fall through the deep blue night and land nearby.

Inside the Manta, the rotary launcher began to spin and adjust itself, preparing to jettison the sensor pods onto the ocean floor. The rotor spun fifteen degrees, and a set of springs pushed a pod into position on the launcher.

Ka-chung!

The pod fired out from the bottom of the Manta. It flipped over and over like a poker chip for a few moments in the current and turbulence behind the Manta before becoming autonomous itself. Small thrusters fired brief bursts, and the disc-shaped pod wobbled a few times before settling onto the floor of the abyssal plain. A sandy plume blossomed around the disc as it landed.

The small sensor blasted a sound wave deep into the earth and began to listen for the resulting reflections of sound from the underlying rock structure of the ocean floor. Once that area of the seafloor was examined, the sensor fired its thrusters and moved to another area, checking with its neighboring sensor pods for optimal positioning.

A hundred yards away, the Manta released another pod.

As the Manta continued its flight path along the ocean floor depositing its sensors, it began to work on its other job: streaming the data results of the survey back to the surface.

▪ ▪ ▪ ▪

Gorin stood at the rail looking out across the chop and took a final drag of his cigarette before tossing the butt into the ocean.

The loudspeaker squealed to life with the voice of John Chambers. "Hey, you guys, the results from the survey are starting to arrive!" The excitement in his voice was contagious, and Gorin and Scott Ward almost collided in the stairway as they made their way to the command center.

Chambers squinted as the airlock door swung open, and Gorin and Ward stepped through. The light from outside pierced through the darkness, dilating the operator's eyes. "Quick! Close the door. This is amazing!"

The large-format display on the wall was black, but small, colored shapes were beginning to appear. The colors and shapes seemed random at first, but after a few iterations, structure began to emerge. Data from the sensors began to fill in the holes and seams of empty space. Caverns, pockets, walls, and cavities took positions on the screen.

The detail of the massive structure was sketchy in the beginning, but as the pods continued to rain sonic waves into the area, the resolution of the massive underground structure became clearer and cleaner.

"How wide is it?" asked Gorin.

Chambers clicked on an icon on the screen and dragged a line across the features of the display as it continued to build.

"It's four hundred and eighty-six miles across right here."

Silence filled the room. Only the fans of the computer equipment could be heard.

"That's impossible!" growled the Russian. "The largest commercial oil field in the world is the Ghawar Field in Al-Ahsa, and it's only nineteen miles wide, maybe one hundred and seventy miles long. You're claiming—"

"I'm not claiming anything, you lunatic," said Chambers, clearly ticked off. "You asked me how wide this was, and I measured it. We don't even know anything about the volume or the contents yet, so just hold your horses."

Gorin plopped into a chair and crossed his arms like a rebellious teenager.

Chambers and Ward ignored the pouting Russian and continued watching the results of the data come in.

"Let me show you something," said Chambers as he typed some commands on his keyboard. The screen containing the sonic results faded from the display but continued blinking in the bottom, signifying it was running in the background. "Remember all those Cold War surveys we pulled from the naval research archives that contained anomalous readings around Atlantis Massif?"

Ward nodded.

"Well, I've simply pieced together where those anomalies were located, starting with Atlantis Massif, and connected the dots." Chambers continuously typed as he spoke.

The display filled with a globe which spun on its axis, positioning the observers over the Mid-Atlantic Ridge and directly over Atlantis Massif.

"Okay, so we know that there were strange readings south of the Marsala Seamount, here." Chambers clicked on the globe, and a small flashing marker appeared just east of the Atlantis Massif. "There's another one here, south of the Konstanitov Ridge." Another flashing marker took its place.

Chambers continued his march across the Atlantic, and a line of flashing markers followed him as he approached the Moroccan coastline and passed the Ampiere Seamount, heading under Tunisia, south of the Terrible Bank, and through the Mediterranean, veering north of the Irving Seamount, and stopping just off the coast of Palestine.

The final marker was on land: southeast of Jerusalem. Scott Ward recognized it immediately. "Etsba Elohim," he whispered.

The flashing markers, like a giant arrow, pointed across the Atlantic and directly at a spot south of the Dead Sea. The room was deadly silent for a moment as the men came to grips with the implications.

"If this is true, it will change the strategic balance of the world's markets and focus," said Ward. "It will make Israel the most important, most wealthy country on the planet."

Chambers put his hand on Ward's shoulder and stood from his chair. "We won't know until we stitch all these structures together and look at the volume of petroleum that the reserve contains. Let's get these tapes to Phil as soon as possible and get those sensor pods out of the water."

Chambers opened the hatch and stepped out of the control room, looking at the rusty orange sun on a collision course with the horizon. "We're almost out of daylight."

Chapter Ten

Red Tape

P hil sat dumbfounded, staring at the e-mail that was expanded to fill the whole of his display.

Mr. Channing:

We have received your request to load the dataset AM5612 and have scheduled it for approximately three months from now. The priority of your data load is not high enough to preempt other data loads that are ahead of your request in the queue.

As the date for the load draws nearer, we will be in contact with you.

Dr. Chaz Hiezwald

Data Systems/AXCESS ENERGY CORPORATION

He looked at the stack of high-capacity data tapes containing raw data from Gorin's sophisticated instrument packs. They stood three feet high on his desk, having arrived the day before wrapped in multicolored stickers.

URGENT!
FRAGILE!
OVERNIGHT DELIVERY

There was a handwritten note from Dr. Chambers included in the package.

Do WHATEVER it takes to get this analyzed!
—Chambers

A chime emanated from his computer's speaker, and an e-mail icon popped up on the system tray.

New mail! Phil clicked on the new message, neatly ordered at the top of the mail list.

Mr. Channing:
I have reviewed your requisition request for a new data server for $25,000.00. Unfortunately, it failed our Finance and Internal Expense audits and it will not be fulfilled. Please note that we show you have requested this item multiple times in the past week. It is unlikely that the audit profile for your work level will change in the near future.
Please contact us with any questions you have.
Lorraine Sophig
Corporate Requisitions/AXCESS ENERGY
CORPORATION

Phil kicked his trash can in frustration. Papers and a decaying apple core from breakfast the day before spilled on the floor. He looked around sheepishly, embarrassed for losing his cool in such an adolescent way. His gaze fell across the vacant desks of Gorin and Scott Ward.

He sighed in loud frustration. *They're still away on the survey trip to Atlantis Massif, and I'm stuck here trying to get terabytes of data loaded with bureaucratic overlords standing in my way.*

The office was quiet. The only sound was the HVAC equipment in the room next door. Beyond his cube was a twenty-square-foot void filled with old cardboard boxes and no overhead lights. Phil looked at the rotting apple core and listened to the white noise of the fans for a moment before an idea hit him.

A great idea—a fantastic idea—a crazy idea, and for sure, an expensive idea.

Well, expensive from his perspective anyway.

The cleaning people barely come down here. No one ever visits. This place could be a German discotheque, and no one would ever know.

Phil picked up the crumpled note from Dr. Chambers and muttered out loud. "Well, you said 'whatever,' so that's what I'm going to do."

He opened his wallet and counted out the money from his signing bonus. He laid out a stack of large-denomination bills before him. He'd never seen that much money before, and he could hear his father mentally chiding him for keeping that kind of cash in his wallet, where it could easily be stolen. *I haven't had time to open a savings account yet,* he explained to no one, and laughed at the absurd thought. He hadn't had any money to save until this week.

Phil took a quick look at equipment on the Internet, comparing prices, and then stuck half the cash in an envelope and put it in his front pocket. He took another two thousand dollars out, stuck it in another envelope, and wrote "Rent and Food" on the front. The rest he put back in his wallet.

He grabbed his backpack and headed for the elevator. As it dinged and reached the lobby, Phil squinted at the bright Texas sun bursting through the glass-plated, art-covered lobby. He felt like a troll, living in a cave and seeing the sun for the first time. He walked through the security turnstiles and headed for the parking lot.

■ ■ ■ ■

An hour later, Phil was driving down the freeway with a case of Ramen noodles and four boxes of Saltines in the back of his rusting car—his supply of food for the next few weeks before his first check as an employee of Axcess Energy arrived. Not the healthiest, but possibly the cheapest form of nutrition, with enough salt to give him hypertension after a month.

He looked in the rearview mirror and saw traffic splitting a hundred yards back to pass him on either side. He had his foot to the floor, but the speedometer said only fifty-five. Phil had a love-hate relationship with his car at the best of times, but today he was in a hurry. Today the relationship was definitely more on the hate side.

What a piece of junk!

Phil saw his exit and put the blinker on, pulling out of the suicidal traffic and into the parking lot of a massive electronics store. He lifted the door latch and stepped out. *I can't believe I'm going to do this.* He slammed the door of the eyesore and was thankful that it didn't fall off onto the pavement.

Phil thought about calling Lisa, but he knew that she'd tell him he was crazy. *I'm sure it would be in a loving tone, though,* he thought with a smile. Thinking about Lisa always made him smile.

Phil commandeered a shopping cart and wheeled it over to the computer section. He grabbed ten bundles of Ethernet CAT-5 cables and tossed them into the cart, mentally starting a tab for how much he was spending. Next he wheeled over to the routers and threw three boxes of broadband routers in. Moments later he grabbed a bunch of power strips and four home-theater projectors with mounting brackets. A dozen one-Terabyte hard drives seemingly jumped into his cart as he wheeled over toward the gaming section of the store.

Phil slowed down as he reached the gaming console row. He heard someone breathing behind him—big-time heavy breathing.

He turned around slowly, expecting to see a yak or some kind of woolly mammoth that had traveled through a time warp to punish him for using his signing bonus to buy computer junk.

Instead he found Eugene, the electronics specialist.

Eugene was about five hundred pounds, with thick glasses and a smear of mustard on his white work shirt. A pocket protector was jammed with every imaginable variety of pencil and pen. A forty-four-ounce soft drink was cradled in both his hands, and he had a strange look in his eyes as he gazed covetously at Phil's cart of nerd stuff, a cross between psycho-killer and puppy love.

Phil wasn't sure which part of the look made him more nervous.

A store manager two rows over scowled at Eugene's giant cup of pop. "No drinks on the store floor, Gene, for the tenth time." Eugene ignored the manager and took a sip from the Big Gulp. The manager stormed away in a huff.

Eugene looked back at Phil. "He'll get over it." The contents of Phil's shopping cart had his attention now. "Wow! Like, what are you building?" Eugene asked, fawning over the cart. "Like, the ultimate home theater?"

"Not quite," smiled Phil. "Hey, listen, Gene. Do you mind if I call you Gene?" Eugene shook his head as he slurped on the giant drink held in his stubby fingers.

Phil tried to be as persuasive as possible and strained to make eye contact with Eugene through his smudged, thick, plastic-rimmed glasses. "Great. Do you work on commission, Gene?"

"Yes, I do. They pay us diddly-squat here, so commission is everything."

Before Eugene could launch into a manifesto against his employer that would land him on the FBI's top ten list, Phil stepped in. "I'm going to make your day, my friend."

"You are?" More slurping came from the Big Gulp, but this time at a faster tempo, as if the slurps were a barometer to Eugene's excitement level.

"Yes, sir. You see, I'm going to buy twelve of these Playboxes." Phil picked up one of the powerful gaming consoles packaged in a colorful box. There were only three on the shelf.

Eugene looked like his endorphins were firing at full throttle. "Did you say twelve?"

"Yep, but I need some help getting them to my car. How many do you have in the back room?"

Eugene scratched his belly between two shirt buttons straining to their operational limit and adjusted his smudged glasses. "I dunno, maybe twenty or thirty."

"Do you think you can you help me check out discreetly without making a big scene and help me load them into my car from the back dock?"

"Can I? Hey, man, I'll come over to your house tonight and help you set them up!" Gene said loudly.

"Great," said Phil, trying to quiet Gene down. He wondered whether he would really want this guy at his house. "Let's get checked out, and I'll drive around to the back of the store."

■ ■ ■ ■

The bill came to ninety-eight hundred dollars. Phil was glad he had saved an unexpected two hundred—it could buy a few dinners once salt and MSG had nearly killed him. His car was packed to the gills with Playboxes and networking equipment. The only window he could see out of was the front. He hoped he could make it back to the office without being pulled over. He looked like he had just stolen the entire electronics section of Anystore, USA.

Just one more stop to make, he thought. *I can't very well move all this stuff into the office and get everything cleaned up wearing business casual. I might get caught, or worse . . . get a union grievance slapped against me.*

Phil pulled into a strip mall directly across the street from the sprawling campus of Axcess Energy. The mall had the prerequisite Chinese takeout, a dry cleaner, a pizzeria, and a newly refurbished package delivery store, Ship-n-Go, that had succeeded a video rental store left for dead by Internet streaming movie services.

Phil walked into the cramped store and purchased three moving boxes, packing peanuts, packing tape, and some labels. "I'll be right back," he said to the confused clerk. "Can I borrow this?" Phil asked, grabbing a hand truck by the door. Before the clerk could answer, he was out the door.

After placing the Playboxes and network equipment into the shipping boxes, Phil ran them back into the store. "Where's it going?" asked the clerk.

"Over there," said Phil, pointing at the corporate campus through the window of the store and beyond the busy intersection as he filled out the package delivery form.

The clerk shrugged. "Whatever."

"When will this go out?" asked Phil.

The worker looked at the clock on the wall. "You're in luck. The truck gets here in thirty minutes. I'll make sure the driver just takes it right across the street."

"Cool, thanks," said Phil, paying the bill. "So it'll be over there this afternoon, right?"

"Should be."

I'll start building it tonight.

Chapter Eleven
The Grid

P hil grunted, holding the small flashlight in his mouth and training it on a zip tie as he lashed a bundle of cables together.

Somehow this was not the vision he'd cherished of working in corporate America. He had spent the last hour collapsing the cardboard maze into smaller parts, binding the parts together with duct tape, and making multiple trips down the hallway at two o'clock in the morning to the trash depot. He was dressed like the maintenance man and wore a baseball cap to cover his face and eyes from surveillance cameras in the hallways. Now he was lying on his back on the dusty concrete floor, fishing Ethernet cables under a long table. His eyes were burning from particles of dust, mixed with whatever toxic cleaning solution had been used on the concrete an eon ago. The blowing air from the HVAC equipment rumbled nearby.

The good news was that it was cool down here in the basement, or the dungeon, as he had begun referring to floor B2. This was good, because the grid of Playboxes would generate an enormous amount of heat.

He finished working on the zip tie and slid out from under the table. The work was done.

Phil stood up and stretched his back, sore from lying on the concrete floor. His outfit was drenched in sweat. He walked over to the colorfully packaged Playboxes and began to open up the game consoles methodically.

Each game console went to the top of the table, followed by its power cord, fully unwrapped and snaking across the table before terminating in the large brick-shaped power supply. Phil unpacked two power-supply bars and quickly plugged them into their outlets.

In a conscious sequence of nerd-dom, he pressed the "on" buttons and brought the twelve consoles to life. A utopian start-up chime sounded a dozen times, and flickering green and blue lights danced and jittered on each Playbox's shiny black plastic shell.

If only Eugene could see me now, Phil thought. *He'd probably want to have my baby.*

Next, Phil began working on the network aspect of the project: he tied all the game consoles together with a network router so they could talk with one another and finally connected the last open port to a vacant Ethernet port, supposedly reserved for any new employees who might arrive in the dungeon.

Phil did a quick network test before powering the whole thing down.

He looked at the clock on the wall: 3:30 a.m. He was almost done with the hardware portion. The software would just take time to load and configure.

Once the software was loading, he stepped back and looked at his handiwork. The grid—commodity machines ganged together cheaply to solve ridiculously complex problems. Most grids were built with grants and corporate-supported funds. His was built with his signing bonus and some help from a super-friendly electronics store associate. Suddenly, a mental image of Lisa scolding him for doing something so stupid appeared before him like some sort of strange technological version of Charles Dickens's *The Christmas Carol.*

Phil muttered in the dark, talking to the mental apparition of Lisa. "Hey, Dr. Chambers said to do whatever it takes."

He glanced at his watch: 4:30. The morning security change would happen soon. He quickly collapsed the boxes that had contained the guts of his equipment and ran them to the dumpster.

Ooof. He smelled like old cardboard boxes and bad body odor.

By 5:30, he was in the corporate gym, showering.

Today was a special day.

Chapter Twelve
Above It All

What in the world is that sound? Lisa rolled over in bed, getting tangled in a sea of blankets to find her cell phone vibrating on her nightstand. She looked at the alarm clock near the charging cradle that held the obnoxious device. Six. It was still dark out; only the red-orange glow of the sun on the horizon was peeking through her window blinds.

"Saturday—the only day I can sleep in," she grumbled, propping herself up on one elbow and taking the call groggily. *This better be a national emergency, Governor!*

"Hello?" Her voice cracked halfway through the greeting.

"Hi, honey. Good morning!" It was Phil's voice, and he actually seemed happy to be up.

"Phil?" *I'm going to kill him!* "Phil, you woke me up. I was working late last night on an appearance that the governor will be making at Axcess. Did you know he's coming there next week? He's going to be making—"

Phil interrupted her. "You'll like this. Get dressed and come out front."

Come out front? Lisa hopped out of bed, walked to the front window of her apartment, and parted the curtains to stare down at the parking lot. Phil waved while sitting on the hood of the worst-looking car in the parking lot.

Lisa waved back, sure she was trapped in a surreal dream. She cut her wave short when she realized her hair looked like a lion's mane, tangled and bushing around her head.

"Come on," Phil said. "We have to be there by 6:45."

"Be where, Phil?"

"It's a surprise. Come on!"

Lisa glared at the cell phone. She hated surprises. In professional life, in personal life, the motto of the business world and the world of politics was "NO SURPRISES."

She ran to the bathroom and gargled half a bottle of mouthwash before brushing her teeth to a gleaming white. Quickly she ran a brush through her brunette hair, pulled it into a ponytail, threw a handful of hot water on her face, and wiped her face off with a washcloth. She took one last look in the mirror before grabbing a college sweatshirt from the nightstand and snatching up her running shoes and handbag as she made for the door.

Phil glanced at his watch as Lisa appeared at the front door. He watched her pull the door closed quietly and run toward him on the sidewalk in her white socks, running shoes in hand.

She didn't look mad, but she did look curious.

"Still mad at me?" Phil asked.

"That depends on what the surprise is," she said, pulling the door of the death trap closed. The hinges screeched like a caterwauling feline. "If it's a vacation time-share meeting, you might as well roll up the windows and asphyxiate yourself with your car's exhaust."

"It won't be a time-share meeting," said Phil, trying each jean pocket to find the car key.

After three half-starts, the beater came to life like a fire-breathing dragon, backfiring twice before they exited the parking lot and headed for the expressway out of town. Lisa scrunched down in the passenger seat, trying to hide from the angry neighbors who were undoubtedly standing at their windows cursing the foreign-made piece of junk.

Lisa looked over at Phil. He seemed happy—happier than she had seen him in a long time. The stress of finding a good job and living up to her parents' approval seemed to be fading into the background, and the happy-go-lucky boy she had fallen in love with in Toronto was reappearing.

"I'm really proud of you." She put her hand on his shoulder and rubbed his neck. "Did you know that?"

Phil laughed. "Why? 'Cause I got up early on a Saturday for once?"

"Nope. Because you landed a great job with a great company and you're doing what you love. I can tell you really believe in what you're doing over there."

Phil looked at her sarcastically. "So you only love me because I have this great job and this fantastic sports car?" The car backfired, and they both burst into laughter as they flew down the highway together.

Twenty minutes later, Phil pulled off the highway and onto a gravel road. A white fence ran along the perimeter of five acres of grass that looked like it hadn't been mowed in weeks. In the center of the field, surrounded by two cars, was a hot-air balloon preparing for flight.

Phil looked over at Lisa. "Surprise!"

Lisa was glowing. She had always wanted to take a sunrise balloon ride, but work and school had always interfered. She leaned over and kissed him. "Thank you," she whispered in his ear.

They stepped out of the car and walked toward the gondola. The dew from early morning quickly soaked Lisa's navy sweatpants. The pilot came over, shook their hands, and explained a few things about the balloon. A large fan running off a gasoline generator was blowing air into the gaping black nylon mouth at the base of the balloon, and the top portion writhed and inflated slowly as the sun peeked over the rolling hills of South Texas. The balloon's canopy was a quilt work of brilliant colors—all the hues of the rainbow arranged in seemingly random positions. It was beautiful.

The canopy of the balloon began to angle upward, slowly rising into the air, leaving the dewy grass behind. As the nylon envelope moved past thirty degrees, the pilot helped Lisa and Phil into the gondola and fired a propane flame deep into the volume of air welling up in the canopy.

As the patchwork canopy reached the ninety-degree mark, Phil and Lisa felt it pulling on the anchors still holding the gondola to the field. The basket bounced as it deliberated between flying and remaining tethered to the wet sod. Finally, after another burst of flame, the pilot released the anchors, and the balloon began to rise slowly upward.

Lisa looked over the edge and watched Phil's car become smaller and smaller in the middle of the five acres. The grass where the balloon had been inflated was a mere shadow of what it had looked like just twenty minutes before.

"That's strange," she said.

"What's that?"

"Your car looks perfectly normal from up here."

Phil pinched her on the arm teasingly. "Nice," he said, glancing at the pilot, who cracked a smile as he pulled the lever to send the flame up into the throat of the balloon. A joke about Phil's crummy car was funny even to people he didn't know.

The balloon crossed over the tree line and was bathed in the early morning sunlight. The sun was sitting on the eastern horizon, preparing for its circuit for the day, and the sky was deep blue overhead. The panels of bright nylon lit up like a stained glass chapel in the sky.

"It's so beautiful!" Lisa gasped.

Fields adjoining the one that they had just left came into view, looking like green-and-yellow tinted rectangles outlined with gravel and asphalt roads. In the far distance the downtown skyscrapers and skyline of Austin were visible, glinting in the morning light.

The breeze began to pick up a bit as they got higher, and the balloon went along for the ride. Lisa and Phil looked over the edge and watched the dark shadow of the balloon's canopy traveling over the fields below them. Dogs at nearby farms began to go crazy as the large nylon monster soared overhead, hissing at them with its propane breath.

Lisa shivered. As the early morning shed its last cool moments before the sun began to warm the air, Phil put his arm around her. They gazed out over the edge of the basket to the world curving beneath them.

"Lisa, being up here is like life. We go where the wind takes us—where God moves us. Sometimes it's in our control to get into a balloon like this, but life has its way of changing where we are and where we are going. Sometimes we have to make a decision, right here and right now."

Lisa was a bit shocked. Phil was no poet—he didn't even cry at sad movies—but this was heartfelt. She looked down to see him pull a small blue box from his jeans pocket.

"I want us to travel together on this journey . . . wherever it takes us . . . I want to be with you." He opened the blue box to reveal a platinum engagement ring with a one-karat diamond. Its emerald-cut stone glittered in the morning sunlight. Lisa's hands went to her mouth as she stared at the beautiful ring.

Phil knelt on one knee. "Lisa, will you marry me?"

There was silence for a moment before Lisa returned her answer.

"Yes. A hundred times, yes," she whispered with tears in her eyes as he slipped the ring onto her finger. She threw her arms around his neck and kissed him for a long time as the sunlit balloon sailed over the landscape.

Chapter Thirteen
Meet the Parents

Phil pulled into the Batons' long driveway and announced his and Lisa's arrival with a backfire and a puff of asphyxiating black smoke. The curtains of the family room parted, and Mr. Baton's frowning face was framed by a large bay window. Lisa started to giggle, and Phil instantly regretted buying thousands of dollars worth of computer equipment instead of a new car.

The couple headed up the walkway to the huge house and were greeted halfway by Lisa's parents, who were standing in the doorway of the mansion.

"I didn't know you were coming over this afternoon," said Mrs. Baton, holding a dolled-up, black miniature poodle.

"Well, we're sorry we didn't call. It's been a busy morning," said Lisa. Her body was shaking, as if the containment of the coming announcement was going to burst out of her. She grinned.

"Surprise!" she said, holding up her left hand. The diamond gleamed in the light. "We got engaged this morning. We're getting married!"

Mrs. Baton's head pushed back, and she fished in her jacket pocket for a pair of reading glasses. Propping them on her nose, she looked down over the lenses that were sliding down her nose and replied, "Oh."

That wasn't exactly the reaction Phil had hoped for.

Silence seemed to fill up the distance between the parents and the newly engaged couple. Phil decided to break the awkward tension. He reached over to pet the small dog that was coddled in Mrs. Baton's arms.

"Aroof!" yelped the spoiled poodle. Phil drew his hand back in just enough time to avoid a fistful of punctures from the annoying little beast.

"Phoebe!" said Mrs. Baton. Phil had always thought that "Phoebe" was a dumb name for a dog, but he kept his opinion to himself.

Mr. Baton stepped forward and kissed Lisa on the cheek. "I'm happy that you're happy, Peaches. Why don't you come in and tell your mother all about it, and Phil and I will go for a walk."

Uh-oh, thought Phil. *The infamous father-in-law walk is now commencing.*

Lisa tried to rescue Phil, but Mr. Baton was already to the driveway and coughing from the cloud of carbon monoxide Phil's car had spewed into the atmosphere.

"Bye, Phil. See you in a few minutes," said Lisa. Her voice was full of apology and embarrassment. Phil looked over his shoulder at his fiancée, smiled, and turned to say good-bye, but the door slammed shut. Only the yelping poodle could be heard through it. Phil hurried down the walkway toward his future father-in-law.

"Have you set a date yet?" asked Mr. Baton, kicking a stray pebble into the street.

"Not yet, but we have plenty of time for that," said Phil. He looked through the dappled sunlight coming through the large oak trees that lined the street and tried to keep up with Mr. Baton, who was double-timing it.

"Not really. The golf club always has at least a year's wait for reservations."

Phil lifted an eyebrow, knowing he was far enough back that his expression wouldn't be seen. *Who says we're having our reception at the golf club? Or did he mean the ceremony?* Phil knew better than to let his inner monologue become audible.

They reached the end of the road and crossed the street to the other side of the opulent neighborhood. Million-dollar houses lined the road.

"I know Lisa is happy, and I know she loves you," said Mr. Baton. Phil smiled. He was unaccustomed to this kind of sentiment—especially from a man.

Mr. Baton returned the smile and just as quickly returned his face to the blank look that always accompanied a conversation with Phil. "But Lisa's still my daughter, and I still want to take care of her."

Phil didn't know what to say. Getting married didn't change the fact that Lisa was Mr. Baton's daughter, but it would change his charge and responsibility for her. What was Lisa's father getting at? And why did Phil feel like it was going to be trouble?

Mr. Baton cleared his throat. "I've been waiting for this since you asked my permission a few months back on the phone. I deeply appreciate your asking. I know that nowadays not every guy would do that."

And then the shoe dropped.

"Lisa's mother and I want to give you a gift." Mr. Baton pulled a folded check from his wallet and handed it to Phil.

Phil's heart bulged in his throat as he opened the check and looked at the amount.

Seventy-five thousand dollars. He burst into a cold sweat.

The other shoe dropped.

"That's for a down payment on a house. There's a nice neighborhood that we really like just a few miles away. It's full of young families—"

"Mr. Baton, thank you. I truly appreciate this, but I can't accept it."

The walking stopped, and Mr. Baton turned and stared at Phil with eyes that bored into his soul. "What do you mean?" He sounded more shocked than offended. As if he was talking to someone with a serious mental illness.

"Lisa and I are starting out our life together. We want to make it our own way, with our own resources. Marriage is probably hard enough without worrying whether we've spent your money the way you expect us to."

Phil passed the check back to Mr. Baton, who remained dumbfounded.

Not sure of what to do, Phil walked back to the Batons' house and left his future father-in-law reeling over being politely told no.

Chapter Fourteen
The Discovery

T he chime on Phil's cell phone had been going off for over a minute when he finally opened his eyes. He lifted his head from the top of his desk and fumbled for the electronic leash. He rubbed his eyes drowsily and looked at the time: 2:30 a.m.

With these kinds of hours I should just become a vampire and be done with it.

Foggy memories of giving up seventy-five thousand dollars and a beautiful home in a posh neighborhood filtered into his tired brain, and he contemplated joining the undead for a few moments more before opening a window on his workstation and typing a command.

? STATUS DATALOAD ATLMASSV5681

A fraction of a second later, the result appeared on the screen.

LOAD SUCCESSFUL
TOTAL RECORDS: 10,578,854,259
NO ERRORS FOUND

Finally! Phil smiled. *Now I can get something done.* His fingers flashed over the keyboard initializing processes, firing up the program he had been working on for over a week. The four projectors in the adjoining room flickered to life, bathing the walls in blue light as they synchronized their outputs with the powerful grid of Playboxes sitting above them.

Phil picked up a long white remote from his desk and walked to the center of the vacant space. The projectors blinked for an instant before displaying a huge blue rectangle floating below him and heading off to the horizon, in front of him, to the left, and to the right. The blue rectangle's huge grid rolled and rippled like the ocean beneath him. The rocking motion gave Phil a moment of nausea. He closed his eyes tightly and spread his feet a few more inches to steady himself. As he opened his eyes, the grid had caught up with the massive data set being projected. The water looked semi-realistic, with white caps and wave trains moving across its surface.

Okay, let's see what we can see.

Phil moved the remote slowly downward, and the perspective began to change. The ocean surface moved toward him from below as if he were falling into the water. The motion was confusing but exhilarating. As Phil passed through the undulating virtual surface, he felt an incredible desire to take a deep breath as if he were diving into the deep blue. He moved the remote further toward the ninety-degree mark, and the drop accelerated. The ocean surface zoomed up his body and continued up the screen before disappearing.

Phil pressed a button on the remote, and a dashboard slid into view at the top of the screen, superimposing his position in latitude and longitude along with his depth. The depth measurement clicked off quickly as he pushed the remote past ninety degrees, accelerating his dive to the bottom. The normal one-hour dive on Atlantis Massif was compressed into mere moments, and Phil looked down to see a rugged mountain range quickly rising from the floor. As he got closer, the mountains, valleys, and ridges began to show more and more features, drawn in different color gradients representing height from the ocean floor. Phil had a flashback to the *Deep Pathfinder* projection room and felt like he was rappelling down the side of an enormous mountain as its features slipped up the wall in front and to the sides of him.

The craggy ocean floor appeared, and Phil brought the remote to a full straight-up position. His descent stopped immediately. He looked left and right, examining the topology from the satellite data he had digitally stitched to the acoustic signatures Gorin had laid down with THEO. He could see seams in the data, virtual rips in the earth where things didn't meet up exactly, but by and large the data was enough to see the underground mountain range in astounding detail.

Phil beamed. *Not bad for a first pass.*

He could see additional tearing in the surface as he turned his head left and right and scrutinized the virtual surface—probably from bad acoustic data. He thought about sending Gorin an e-mail and giving him a hard time about it. He could almost hear the rationalizations coming from the proud Russian.

Phil decided to move downward, beneath the ocean floor. He pressed the remote forward again slowly. The trench of the Mid-Atlantic Ridge began to move upward. He pressed another button on the remote, engaging a different rendering technique for the sonar data. The screen turned into a series of colored ranges.

At first, Phil was confused by what he was seeing, but then he remembered that this wasn't what a human would actually see. It was what the sound waves "saw" as they reflected from material that was denser than air. He was looking at enormous fields of rock that had reflected the sound waves from each sonar mine THEO had dropped along the undersea mountain range.

Yellow and orange hues were in abundance. Basalt, *just as you'd expect to see.*

He pressed the remote down, and the hues began to get warmer. Reds appeared prominently against the orange and yellow fields.

Peridotite, just like Dr. Chambers said.

Then the display did something Phil hadn't expected. Black spheres began to appear. Some intersected one another, looking like strange organic vegetables, and others were isolated and alone in the three-dimensional space. Phil moved closer to one of them by pointing the remote at it and clicking a button. The display moved around him as if he were walking toward the feature. He positioned himself inside the void and pressed another button on the remote. A shell, like the candy coating on a chocolate, seemed to wrap itself around the negative space.

Finally, Phil realized what he was seeing. *It's a gas pocket!*

Phil flicked the remote to the right and zoomed back to his original position, looking at all the voids on the display.

But not just one pocket. It's an entire field of gas pockets.

Phil was sweating and shaking with excitement, and he smiled, thinking about the strange formations in front of him. *Gas pockets are huge predictors for oil reserves; they're typically found in close proximity to pools of oil that could be pumped out of the earth. So if a gas pocket predicts a supply of petroleum is nearby, what does an entire field of them mean?*

He looked at the depth gauge.

Nine miles below the surface.

His smile disappeared. The deepest anyone had ever drilled was around seven miles. And he was starting at one of the deepest parts of the Atlantic Ocean. Frowning, he decided to push further into the virtual landscape. He slowly moved the remote past ninety degrees again and watched multicolored strata appear on all three walls as he descended lower.

More basalt, chrysotile, and peridotite showed up in their respective warm colors.

Suddenly, the basalt and other rocks seemed to disappear, and a strange gray haze appeared. There was an absolute void—not even rock. Phil clicked a button on the remote to increase the zoom factor. The haze became like a swirling blizzard, like snow on an old television.

That's weird, he thought. *Maybe the data fields are corrupted.* He reduced the zoom factor, moved back to his original position, and pushed further down, watching the depth meter continue to increase.

10.5
10.6
10.7
10.8
10.9
11 miles

Suddenly the snow effect ended, and the display filled with more mantle rock colors, mostly peridotite.

"Whoa!" Phil said. He spun around in surprise, and the display altered itself, but the colors were still a wall of solid rock. He decided to run a quick experiment. He brought the remote straight up and flew back up through the mantle, returning to the blizzard of gray.

Phil made a mental note of the space's coloration, or lack thereof, and its depth and position. *So this area is empty and sitting beneath a huge network of gas pockets. Let's go back down.*

He pressed the remote full forward, passing the ninety-degree mark. The gray sea flowed around him, and the multicolor rock strata appeared again, just as it had before.

Okay, so he was looking at gas pockets above, a sea of nothingness, and a solid rock floor, deep in the mantle. He pressed the remote further down, heading toward the core of the earth at a thousand miles an hour. Blurs of red, orange, and yellow blazed by for a few seconds before the screen showed a line of text.

DATA FIELD EXCEEDED. POSITION IS BEYOND THE DATA COLLECTED.

Phil stood in the dark with the white letters adorning the centers of all three walls, letting the results of what he had just flown through seep into him. *That static field is not a void. It's a defined space—but it's not filled with rock.*

Phil threw his hands in the air like he had just completed a marathon and let out a howl as the pieces clicked together. "It's an oil reserve!"

He ran back to his workstation and changed some settings for the program, mapping the gray static field to deep blue and purple hues. Phil ran the program again, and the Atlantic Ocean appeared once more, lapping up to the displays. He took a quick drink from a bottle of water before running back to the center of the room.

Again he plunged into the depths of the data, but this time not tentatively. He knew exactly where he was going. He zoomed past the Mid-Atlantic Ridge, leaving the rounded dome of Atlantis Massif behind, into a sea of basalt and peridotite. He watched the mile marker approach 10.35 miles, and suddenly the yellow and orange barrier rocks parted. A deep blue river appeared before Phil.

It was vast—huge in scope, heading beyond his vision in all three directions.

He shook his head in wonder.

He moved the remote downward, and the blue expanse covered the screens. As Phil fell through the swell of dark blue hues, checking for the oil field's depth, he began to get dizzy with excitement. He watched the mile marker click by until the yellow floor appeared again. The dark blue sea of oil was now on the top of the display, and the floor of the reserve was laid out ahead of him like a roadway.

All right; it's half a mile deep right here. Let's see how wide and long it is.

Phil pressed a button on the remote and flew up half a mile in the data field to the position above the oil. It stretched out ahead of him and seemed to beckon him to follow it. Phil noted his position and pointed the remote toward the wall. The blue stream began to move around him as he traveled forward. He wasn't sure what to expect, but he was surprised as the blue and indigo sea began to widen, and every once in a while the surface would jump up and he would travel through it. Apparently the reserve was shallower in some parts than at the point of origination. The blue would then flee away, and again a comforting ceiling of orange and yellow rock strata would appear, with the blue leading away.

Phil stopped and looked at the latitude and longitude: 31.92° N, 5.85° W. *I'm in the middle of Morocco on the western side of Africa.* A wave of euphoria flashed through his body.

This was big—huge. Call-a-news-network huge.

He decided to follow the blue forward and again pointed the remote. The display continued for a while, but the colors were getting lighter the farther he moved along the reserve.

The acoustic signature was fading. A few moments later the screens turned black and the message appeared again.

DATA FIELD EXCEEDED. POSITION IS BEYOND THE DATA COLLECTED.

Phil walked over to his desk and sat down. A strange mixture of excitement, exhaustion, and accomplishment swirled around him. Not that he was finished yet. How could he complete the whole picture?

He turned to his computer display and tapped a few keys. The display showed a bird's-eye view of the oil reserve, or as much of it as his data could reveal. There were huge rips in the model, empty voids and gaps, but the outline was there. The size of the find was undeniable.

He exhaled loudly and rocked back in his chair. He looked over at Gorin's vacant desk, where a stack of old data tapes were piled up like a digital version of Stonehenge. Phil walked over and looked at the label on the first tape.

PROPERTY OF US NAVY
ANOLOMOUS SEAFLOOR READINGS
JUNE 1964—AUG 1965
CONFIDENTIAL—RELEASED TO PUBLIC DOMAIN VIA
FOIA 2008

FOIA—the Freedom of Information Act—did Gorin actually request these tapes to be released? And why are they here on his desk?

Phil wandered over to his desk and loaded the file. After half an hour of wrangling with the ancient data, a chunk of imagery appeared on his display.

Phil studied the coordinates and compared them to his map of the reserve. It matched the gap almost perfectly. It seemed that the data collected during the Cold War had been categorized as strange and irrelevant by the navy, but they had saved all the measurements and locked them up. Now the technology existed to take the navy's sonar readings and add the context that had been missing for forty years.

These were the puzzle pieces!

Phil wondered momentarily how the Russian knew about these pieces and what else he might know, but then he was swept into the excitement of loading the rest of the missing pieces from the files on Gorin's desk into the larger model.

Phil typed and worked through the night, oblivious to time—caught up in the singularity of the moment.

His moment.

Chapter Fifteen

E-mail from Beyond

Aline of empty, ultra-caffeinated-beverage cans were placed in a perfect line on the bookshelf behind Phil as if he was marking time with aluminum containers like marks on a prison wall. His fingers flew across the keyboard as he gave specific instructions for untangling the vast web of seismic data contained in the growing stacks of tapes on his desk to the grid, which was running on the folding table in front of him.

Binders and manila folders littered the floor. Master's and doctoral theses from friends, along with his own on "Visualization of Seismic Data Using Animated Displays," were scattered about. A chalkboard he had "borrowed" from a conference room three floors up was covered on both sides in obscure equations.

He was exhausted and exhilarated at the same time. He could see the finish line.

After typing an exceptionally long command, he pushed back from the desk and stretched his back muscles, reaching high into the air and then cracking his lower back. He reached for a can of soda but found he had already finished it. He looked around, desperate for a caffeine pick-me-up. No full cans.

Phil grumbled and headed for the elevator with a crumpled twenty-dollar bill.

When he returned and plopped into his chair, popping the seal on the soda can, he saw that he had received an e-mail. He rolled his eyes and clicked on the mail icon. *Probably Chambers badgering me for a status report. At least I can tell him I'm almost . . .*

His thoughts trailed away as the message came up.

He hadn't been expecting the author of the e-mail to be *dead.*

Jackson "Jack" Sanders
Subject: You gotta check this out!
Sent Today at 1200 EST

Phil's hand pulled back from the mouse as if clicking on the message might somehow violate an ancient crypt and activate a curse. He looked over his shoulder for a prankster, but hardly anyone knew he was here. He mentally made a list of people who knew where he worked: Lisa, her parents, the security guard, Chambers, Ward, Gorin.

The list wasn't long. Jack hadn't even known he was interviewing here. Slowly, his courage was reinforced, and he double-clicked on the message.

It was short—really short.

Hey! I really got *into* this song. Thought you might like it—especially the ending.
Shalom!
Jack.

What in the world? Phil reread the message.

Shalom? Jack's not Jewish. That's a really weird way to sign off on so short a message— or a message of any size, for that matter.

At the bottom of the e-mail was a line of legal copy that trailed the message. That was unlike Jack. He hated anything legal: copyrights, intellectual property, digital rights on music—he was a raging digital anarchist. It took Phil a moment to get past the incongruity and focus on the words.

This message was sent on behalf of the sender through Immor-
talMe.com—the postmortem message service.

ImmortalMe? The small, controversial company had recently been in the
news with its radical business plan and ridiculously high IPO stock price. The
service allowed anyone to prerecord an e-mail message, designate recipients,
and set a wait time before delivering it—a duration measured from the sender's
death. The service scanned public death records, and upon finding the death of
a customer, obediently fired the messages to the recipients.

The idea itself was novel and even useful. Imagine someone sending a special message to a son or daughter on high-school or college graduation, fully
expecting to be there, but being taken suddenly by a heart attack when the kids
were still in grade school. Taken to the extreme, it could be mind-bending in
its implication and impact—sending an e-mail to a great-great-great grandson
a hundred years from now or stalking an ex-girlfriend every day for the rest of
her life.

Phil returned to the main message and found an attachment, apparently of
the song Jack had referred to in the body of the e-mail. A music player popped
up on his display. As soon as the first note hit, Phil smiled, remembering his
friend's taste in head-banging music. Jack's favorite artists, the Dead Scare-
crows, blasted from his speakers. It wasn't Phil's cup of tea. It was heavy, mind-
melting metal, virtually indistinguishable from the sound of a jet engine.

The notes skipped, and Phil winced. *Ugh, terrible sample quality.* There was
something wrong with this song.

Phil could hear a skip in the digital data every few seconds, like a scratched,
ancient vinyl record playing on a record player at his grandparents' house. It reminded Phil of a cat being swung through the air by the tail. He quickly grew
bored of the lyrics, the same lines repeated over and over, about parents being disappointed and school being oppressive, and beautiful teenage girls who
didn't find goth boys attractive.

Typical teen angst, thought Phil as he fast-forwarded to the ending. The song
ended in a hail of electric guitars squealing and roaring and a drum solo that
melted Phil's monitor. Then silence, and finally two beeps gurgled at the end.

That's the part he likes the best? Two bleeps? Maybe Jack was doing drugs?
Phil reread the message. *I really got *into* this song.*

Phil had first met Jack in Cryptography, his sophomore year at the University of Toronto.

Cryptography?

Phil listened to the song again: the abrupt skips in the music were now much more interesting to him. He made a quick copy of the original and then fired up the program he had been laboring over for the last few days. He opened the song and displayed it visually against a black background.

In visual form, the song looked like a madras sheet, multicolored squares and bars nested together in regular intervals—but something was different. Interwoven in the visual fabric of the song were intervals of the same length and width, like gray lines running in warp and weft through the song.

Phil ran a filter and dropped the song off the display, leaving only the skips, the strange gray grid. He zoomed into it. The grid was incoherent. Nothing made sense—almost like it was scrambled.

Phil thought about the class from many years ago and remembered an assignment where data had been embedded in a picture and mailed. The message was the picture, but only to people who had the means to look beyond the colorful pixels.

He riffled through his manila folders and binders, going back to his notes from the class he had taken with Jack and finding a memory stick with that semester's syllabus and programs he had written still intact.

Phil's hand was shaking as he pushed the memory stick into the USB slot on his workstation. He hunted through the directory and fired up the cryptography program, which simply asked him for the file name of the song and a password.

Phil sat for a moment and then typed the obvious: S-H-A-L-O-M

*** ERROR: PASSWORD CAN ONLY BE NUMERIC, NO ALPHA-CHARS ***

Oh, yeah, this program only likes numbers for passwords.

Phil pursed his lips and strummed his fingers on the desk.

What if "Shalom" is the password, but in numbers that only a computer would see instead of humans?

Again, Phil went through his things until he found the programming book he had used in his undergraduate years. He flipped to the back pages and stopped at a table with letters and corresponding numbers next to each. He grabbed a yellow sticky note and ran his finger down the chart, matching up each letter of the Jewish greeting with its numerical representation. He quickly typed the sequence into the password: 83, 72, 65, 76, 79, 77.

He closed his eyes as he pressed "Enter."

This time the program accepted the password and sprayed out a zillion numbers, all in sets of three:

125.6	67.8	98.5
126.7	75.2	99.4
125.3	38.4	109.6

The numbers marched down the computer screen—page after page filled it. Phil scratched his head as he watched the information scroll by. *Sets of three numbers in a sequence. Jack would've known I'm a visual person—I would see these numbers as three-dimensional data, not as a spreadsheet or even a song.*

Phil decided to take the message from his friend personally. He loaded the series of numbers into his new grid visualization program, and a few moments later, a strange shape appeared. It was odd-looking—actually, it was beyond odd. It looked like the roots of a legume plant. Oblong tubes jutted out, and a single long tube gnarled its way downward.

The last two numbers in the long data set seemed very out of place, incongruous with the combinations of three numbers. Phil grabbed another yellow sticky note and scribbled the numbers onto it with a pencil that had his bite marks all over it:

31.193192

35.210985

As he stuffed the note into his wallet, his cell phone chimed with a text message. Phil looked at the message glowing on the display. It was from Lisa.

"Don't be late for church—punctuality is a pet peeve of my parents. Luv Ya."

He looked at the clock and gulped as he grabbed his best suit, still sealed in the dry cleaners' thin plastic, and headed for the gym and the warm water of a needed shower. It was Sunday morning, and he barely had enough time to meet Lisa for church.

Chapter Sixteen
The Prophecy

P hil had just stepped into the lobby of the church when he heard the song leader announce the opening hymn number, and the organ and piano came to life.

Oh, man! I'm late—again.

Phil scooted into the sanctuary just as the big doors were being closed by the ushers. He saw Lisa and her family sitting five rows from the back on the left—where they always sat. Lisa smiled and pushed her Bible and purse out of the way, making room for Phil. Just to the right of Lisa, her mom looked over and shot a dagger in Phil's general direction.

Phil begged forgiveness from the overdressed and over-perfumed church lady blocking the pew entrance and squeezed past her to Lisa's side, where she was waiting with an open hymnal.

She moved close to his ear and whispered, "Where in the world were you?"

Lisa smelled wonderful, an intoxicating combination of light perfume and shampoo. "Um, I was working on something," said Phil between words of the hymn.

"This morning?" She looked at Phil's face. Small facial stubble was in abundance, but his hair was still slightly wet from his abbreviated shower.

"Were you at work before coming here?" Lisa was clearly annoyed. She knew the truth without him needing to respond.

Phil tried to pretend he was singing along with the rest of the congregation as Lisa peppered him with questions. "Were you there all night long?"

"Uh-huh," said Phil, yawning and sitting down with the rest of the congregation as the hymn came to an end. His fiancée, he reflected, was too smart.

The pastor stood up, welcomed visitors, and then began running through the upcoming week's events. The lady on Phil's right turned her church bulletin into a Chinese fan and began a wind-tunnel test on Phil's face.

Lisa smiled as she watched Phil's I'm-so-annoyed meter climb into the red zone while the tempo of the newly christened "Crazy Fan Lady" increased.

The song leader finally came back up to the pulpit and announced the choir special. As the heavenly words and music soared and lifted spirits, Phil zoned out, thinking about Jack. A dozen questions flooded his brain, squishing the meaningful special music into the back room of his mind.

Why would Jack send me a crazy 3-D data set using a service that would only be tripped by his own death?

If Jack did use ImmortalMe.com, what did he stumble upon that inspired him to do it? Did he know he was going to die?

What data would be so valuable that Jack's life would be in danger?

The choir finished, and the pastor reclaimed the pulpit.

"Please open your Bibles to Ezekiel 38. Today, we are going to discuss a mysterious set of verses that many believe are on the verge of becoming reality." Phil, exhausted from the long night in the lab, flipped through his Bible to the book of the major prophet.

The pastor continued his introduction. "These are the verses that some refer to as the "Ezekiel Option"—the coming battle between a nearly innumerable military coalition of forces headed by Russia, Iran, Germany, Austria, Saudi Arabia, Syria, and Turkey against the small nation of Israel."

The synopsis of the message caused Phil to straighten up, and he pulled out a pen and began jotting down notes. He loved hearing about prophecy, although as a child things like the Rapture had scared the willies out of him. For years, every time his mom was late to pick him up from soccer practice, he wondered if she'd been raptured and himself left there on the soccer field for the next seven years. Those weren't fun memories.

The pastor had a good speaking voice and a great style. Phil always enjoyed his messages, and it was clear the man spent many hours researching and thinking about the way he was going to explain his conclusions to the congregation.

"What would cause such an incredible military force to descend upon the nation of Israel?" asked the pastor.

The question seemed rhetorical, and the audience shifted a bit uneasily.

"There are many who think that in the last days, an enormous mineral deposit, or possibly even an oil field of amazing bounty, will be discovered in Israel. The forces of the coalition will attempt to take this land to grab that strategic resource for their own uses."

An oil field of amazing bounty. The phrase echoed in Phil's mind.

The pastor continued. "When might this invasion take place? Ezekiel 38, verses 8 and 10 through 12, speak of a time when the Jews are secure and prospering in their land just after coming out of exile. While many of us would immediately think of contemporary Israel, there is another time in history that scholars sometimes point to as fulfilling this prophecy—but these are not scholars that I would listen to."

A chuckle rumbled through the audience as the pastor tipped his hand.

"There was a time in Jewish history, 536 BC, to be exact, when the Jews were released from the iron grip of Babylon after Cyrus conquered that nation. However, in reading the rest of the chapter of Ezekiel, it would seem that this is where the similarity ends.

"So it would seem that the true time period spoken of here is the end of the second exile, or the establishment of the independent Jewish state on May 14, 1948. That establishes the notion of the end times or last days. Brothers and sisters, we are living in the last days."

A few "amens" boomed from the congregation. Phil agreed with the pastor, but he just wasn't an audible "amen" kind of guy. Even so, he was captivated by this message. For whatever reason, it seemed very relevant to him.

"This invasion will be led by an individual referred to as 'Gog'—apparently a leader from the country called Magog. *Gog* is a baffling word, but many think it is a title, like *czar*, *pharaoh*, or *prince*. Magog, or Russia, will lead the invasion of Israel with other countries identified in Ezekiel by their ancient tribal names: Rosh, Meshech, Tubal, Persia, Ethiopia, Libya, Gomer, and the house of Togarmah."

The pastor paused for a moment. "These are the offspring of Noah's sons. In particular, four or five of the seven sons of Japheth and two of the four sons of Ham. The modern names for these counties are Iran, Germany, Austria, Saudi Arabia, Syria, and Turkey, and possibly even Spain and France."

A titter of whispers sounded through the audience. It was clear the congregation was engaged.

"You might wonder where the United States is in this whole confrontation. Perhaps one of the most frightening aspects of biblical prophecy is the absolute silence regarding our country. The United States has been, and continues to be, the greatest ally and supporter of the state of Israel. This political and strategic stance has cost us in the eyes of the world at large, and we are regularly condemned for it. I believe that one of the major reasons our country has enjoyed prosperity and relative peace is because it has supported God's chosen people. God has promised that He will bless the countries that bless Israel and will curse the countries that curse Israel.

"As you read through the nations that form this coalition, it reads like a who's who of this principle. And while our support stands out in contrast to Europe and the Middle East, we can see rising anti-Semitism and anti-Israeli sentiment everywhere in our culture."

Phil agreed. He had noticed the increase in anti-Semitic comments on the university campus as well as everywhere else.

"Rockwell Schnabel, our ambassador to the European Union, spoke at a dinner of the American Jewish Committee in Brussels in 2004 and said, 'Anti-Semitism in Europe is as bad as it was in the 1930s.'"

A gasp was audible in the sanctuary as the horrors of Nazi Germany and the Final Solution flashed through the congregation's memory. The pastor paused for a moment before continuing. "The 1930s may seem like a long time ago for some of us, but how many of you, in your daily conversations with coworkers or family members, have heard this: 'Let the Jews fight their own battles. The only reason we as Americans are getting attacked by Muslims is because we support Israel—the sooner we stop, the sooner there will be peace.'"

Hundreds of hands shot into the air. Phil nodded; it was certainly a common sentiment among many of his own friends.

"You see friends, history may not repeat itself, but it does rhyme." The congregation chuckled at the familiar Mark Twain quote.

"The good news," said the pastor with a smile and a confident tone, "is that it really doesn't matter during the dark days that Ezekiel speaks of if the U.S. supports Israel or not, for Israel's ally is the greatest ally that anyone can ask for: the Lord God."

Again, "amens" sounded from the floor of the auditorium.

"In closing, what will happen to this enormous army arrayed against the tiny country of Israel? In short, they will be utterly destroyed. Not by Israel's weapons and prowess as an army. Ezekiel 38:19–20 states that there will be an enormous earthquake with the epicenter in Jerusalem, but instead of the damage being to the city of Jerusalem, the quake will be felt all over the globe, on land, in the sea, and even in the air. Then God will destroy these armies on the mountains of Israel with fire from heaven. Some have called this a nuclear war, but I don't think that's in keeping with the context of these verses. This is God telling the planet, 'These are my people, and I will protect them.' These armies are absolutely decimated, and it takes seven months to bury the corpses. This is not one country defeating another country, and it's not a country defending itself against an impossible force. It is in fact God showing Himself faithful to His people and protecting them to the glory of Himself."

As the pastor finished, Phil's mind was in overdrive.

If Saudi Arabia and Iran are essentially nuked, then what of the enormous oil reserves that those countries control? If Israel finds an enormous oil field or mineral deposit, it would literally precipitate a world war! It would shift the balance of power and finance globally.

He glanced back at the map of Israel projected against the white wall. For whatever reason, his eyes went to the legends of the map, the scale, and finally the latitude and longitude.

His breathing stopped for a second. *Wait a minute! The longitudes!*

They ran roughly from 34.2 to 35.4.

Phil scanned the vertical latitude: 29 to 32.

He was sweating now, his heart going like a jackhammer in his chest. He pulled out the sticky note containing the cryptic numbers at the end of Jack's encrypted message. He fished out the crinkled note and looked at the numbers again.

92   Sam Batterman

31.193192

35.210985

Earlier that morning, these two numbers had seemed random. Now they seemed almost too incredible to be true. Phil scrutinized the map, trying mentally to match up the coordinates on the note with the map projected before him.

Just southwest of the Dead Sea—right on the tip, just above . . .

Suddenly, the map disappeared as the projector was shut down by the sound and video booth as the song leader began the invocation.

D'oh!

Phil grabbed the hymnal, flipped nervously to the song, and tried to sing along. He was sweating. Lisa noticed the trembling hymnal and looked at Phil. He looked awful—pale and glistening in the bright lights of the auditorium. She leaned close to him and whispered, "Hey, are you okay? You don't look so good."

Phil didn't respond. He didn't know what to say—this was something she would have to see too.

As the pastor said the final prayer and the organist starting playing lively music to disperse the congregation, Phil turned and smiled at the heavy fan lady. His face was pale, wet with sweat, and covered with stubble from thirty-six hours of beard growth. The lady handed him a tract. "Drugs will end you, son; read this. I used to be addicted to Nyquil until I went to our support group."

Phil looked at the title of the small colorful tract: *Living with Drug Addiction.*

Caught off guard, it took him a minute to remember his own reactions to the sermon: trembling, paleness, constant licking of lips. He managed to blurt out, "Thank you, ma'am."

Lisa started to giggle. She grabbed his hand, and they followed her parents out of the pew. "Come on, you'll feel better after you eat something at brunch."

Phil froze. *Brunch with the parents? I'd rather stick a fork in my eye.* The Batons had a family tradition of going to the golf club every Sunday after the service. Phil wanted to get back to the office and work on the computer model of the reserve.

"Okay, but after that Lisa, I have to show you something at work," said Phil with determination. His mind kept going over the pastor's message and the coordinates of the strange object that Jack had sent him.

"Work?" Lisa reached up and felt Phil's face. "You're burning up! Are you okay?"

"No, I don't think I am. Let's get this brunch thing over with."

Phil briefly considered making a comparison of the coming buffet with the Bataan Death March, but decided against it.

He would already be in trouble with Lisa for keeping the oil reserve a secret for this long.

Chapter Seventeen
Death by Brunch

P hil drove with Lisa behind the beautiful golden Cadillac carrying the Batons to brunch at the golf club. The white gables and huge bay windows of the exclusive club soared above the perfectly manicured lawns, welcoming all the socialites in the area. Phil pulled into the parking lot, found a spot next to the Caddy, and jumped out of the car. He ran to Lisa's side, opening the door for her.

Lisa smiled and stepped out. Phil looked over to see if Mrs. Baton had noticed the gentlemanly gesture. Phil frowned—the Mrs. was putting on a fresh coat of fire-engine-red lipstick and had completely missed his wonderful treatment of her daughter.

"Well, I appreciate it," said Lisa, noticing Phil's defeated face. She gave him a nice peck on the cheek.

Mr. Baton walked over and stood behind Phil's piece of junk, examining it as if he were looking at the skeleton of a brontosaurus at the Smithsonian. Rust seemed to be overtaking the car, and the bottom of the doors looked like a coral reef. With Lisa free of the death trap, Phil closed the door of the passenger's side. A loud creaking and groaning came from the hinges. *Embarrassed* wasn't a big enough word for how Phil felt. An orange-red dusting of car powder made a line across the black pavement, the remains of the lower part of the door.

"How many miles do you have on this, um, thing?" asked Mr. Baton, staring at the eyesore and resting his hands on his hips.

"Two hundred and eighty thousand," Phil said, looking at the pavement and then looking up and pointing at the gleaming car. "How many on Goldie here?"

Phil meant the Cadillac, but too late to stop his gesture, he noticed that Mrs. Baton had just stepped out of the golden Cadillac and was standing in the line of fire. Mr. Baton looked at Phil for a moment, trying to decide if he was simply making conversation about his beautiful car or if he had, in fact, just insulted his newly lipsticked wife.

"I honestly don't know, Phil; I've had it only six months. I guess I've never really looked at the odometer on any car in recent history." Phil smiled humbly and looked at the Batons' car. It looked like something from Mount Olympus parked next to his rubbish heap, a souvenir from downtown Greece.

Mr. Baton smiled at Phil's admiration of the Cadillac and put a hand on his shoulder. "Don't worry Phil; your luck is bound to change one of these days."

Phil and Lisa followed the Batons up the cobblestone sidewalk to the entryway to the restaurant. *One of these days?*

As they waited in line for the host to seat them, Phil turned to Lisa and her parents. "I'll be right back. Go ahead and grab a seat," he said, and headed for the men's restroom.

Phil disappeared from view, and Lisa's countenance changed from pleasant to annoyed. "Daddy, what a rotten thing to say back there. Please don't make Phil feel like a second-class citizen."

Mr. Baton shrugged. "Honey, he needs a new car. That thing is an embarrassment to the automotive establishment."

Mrs. Baton pulled out a compact mirror and checked her bright red lips. "He looks terrible today—almost like he was up all night long."

"That's because he was up all night long working at Axcess," Lisa said.

Mr. Baton scowled. "Working on a Saturday night? He's not using his time wisely. When I was working, I would arrive precisely at 7:00 a.m. and leave at

5:30 p.m., Monday through Friday, every week of the year. I never had to work a weekend or overtime."

"Dad, the company you worked for doesn't exist anymore. Everyone everywhere works sixty to eighty hours a week now, especially at our age. You should just be happy he has a job at a great company like Axcess and leave it at that."

Phil came back from the restroom as the host came over. "What'd I miss?"

"Nothing—nothing at all," snapped Lisa, glaring at her parents.

Lisa thought Phil looked better now, less pale. After a quick drink order, the table of four scattered to the various stations of the buffet before regrouping at the table with coffee and fruit juice newly poured.

Phil's plate was stacked high with a sausage omelet smothered in cheddar cheese, hash browns, a doughnut, lemon chicken, and a stack of crispy bacon. Lisa had a nice plate of beautiful fruit, and Mr. and Mrs. Baton had their normal half-serving of bagel with strawberry cream cheese and a bowl of oatmeal.

They're paying full price for the buffet and all they get is oatmeal and half a bagel?

Phil looked at his plate stacked high with calories, fat, and yummy goodness and was happy he'd taken advantage of the buffet's offerings. He dug in with purpose.

Mrs. Baton watched Phil scooping mouthful after mouthful down his gullet. "Good heavens," said Mrs. Baton. "Haven't you eaten anything in the last week?"

Lisa scowled at her mother.

"Not really, only Ramen noodles and crackers," said Phil with a mouthful of cheese, egg, and sausage.

Mrs. Baton tried to classify the food that Phil had mentioned into one of the basic food groups. "Oh," she said.

Phil was certain that Lisa's mom and dad had never eaten Ramen noodles in their entire lives, and he wondered about crackers.

There was an awkward silence for a few minutes as Phil rounded the plate and headed for the golden hash browns. The clinking of silverware and glasses marked time.

"What's going on at work that is keeping you there at such ungodly hours?" asked Mr. Baton, carefully prepping his oatmeal with raisins and brown sugar. He hadn't taken a single bite yet, and Phil was nearly ready for seconds.

"I keep getting data tapes from the crew out at the Atlantis Massif formation at the Mid-Atlantic Ridge. I have to load the seismic data into geophysical models to look for possible deposits of petroleum."

The retired banker and his wife looked at Phil as if he was from Mars and had uttered some long-lost ancient dialect. It seemed like all the noise in the restaurant ceased at that moment.

Lisa gulped down her kiwi and translated. "Mom and Dad, Phil is helping Axcess Energy look for a new oil field."

Clarity returned to the parents.

"Well, why didn't you say so instead of the technical gobbledygook?" asked Mrs. Baton. She rolled her eyes and muttered "For goodness sake . . ." while adding creamer to her coffee with a pinky hanging daintily in the rarefied air of the restaurant.

Phil started to say something he was sure to regret when Lisa kicked him in the shins.

"Phil's going to bring me home later this afternoon, okay?" She took his arm to urge him up before the parents could protest.

"I wasn't done yet," said Phil, still chewing.

Lisa grabbed Phil's sport coat and escorted him to the door. "Yes, you are. Now show me what's making you crazy at work before World War III erupts right here in the golf club."

Chapter Eighteen
Recovery Method

Phil pulled into the parking garage of the Axcess Energy Company and helped Lisa out of the car. The place was deserted because it was Sunday, and Phil was able to park right by the entrance to the lobby. Phil held the door for Lisa as she stepped through the revolving glass door into the corporate lobby. She gasped at the opulence of the place: beautiful marble floors, oil paintings—all the things that had initially impressed Phil and were now commonplace for him.

Phil walked up to the young, red-headed security guard who was buried in the comics section of the weekend edition of *The Austin Chronicle*. A stack of *Sports Illustrated* and *Road & Track* stood ready to break his boredom should the newspaper lose its potency.

"Sheesh, Phil, don't you ever take a day off?" asked the security guard.

Phil smiled as he signed Lisa into the guest registry. "Hey, you know what? I did take a day off. I think it was Saturday. It felt . . . boring."

"You need a hobby, my friend," said the security guard.

Lisa made a mental note. *He's only been working here about a week, and the security guard already knows him by name—not a good work-life balance.*

"What floors will you be on today, Phil?" the guard asked.

"Only B2—no high-clearance floors today," answered Phil.

"Okay, young lady," said the security guard, winking at Lisa. "Can I see your driver's license?"

Phil frowned. *He's flirting with my girl right in front of me?*

Lisa blushed and handed the glossy plastic card to the guard. "You're a citizen of the United States?" he asked.

Lisa nodded. "Uh-huh." Her card was returned along with a black-and-white badge that hung from a lanyard. Her ID badge had a red tab that said ESCORT REQUIRED.

"Have a good day," said the security guard, returning to his duties in the pages of the funnies.

Phil and Lisa walked to the elevator and descended to the data lab.

When the doors opened, Lisa stepped into the dirty, dusty concrete hallway and peered through the poor lighting. "What happened to the beautiful marble and oil paintings?" asked Lisa.

Phil shrugged and zipped his badge through the card reader to enter the lab.

Lisa stepped through the door and was greeted by the vacant cubicles that belonged to John Chambers, Scott Ward, and Gorin Vladofsky. Each desk was piled high with papers, folders, and small packages. The active screen savers on their monitors were the only clue that anyone even worked there.

"This is my desk over here," said Phil proudly. The desk looked like Phil had been living there around the clock. The floor was a hopscotch pattern of papers and binders.

"If only my dad could see you now," joked Lisa.

Phil groaned. "That probably wouldn't be the best idea right now. Go stand over there." He pointed to the center of the room between the three white walls. Lisa stepped to the middle of the space, and Phil turned on the projectors, grabbed the remote, and walked over to join her.

Phil stood behind Lisa and put his arms around her, pressing a button on the remote. The displays all synchronized, and the blue, virtual ocean began rolling beneath them.

"Where—where are we?" Lisa stuttered, shocked by the beauty and realism of the display.

"The Mid-Atlantic Ridge," said Phil, pressing a button on the remote. A map of Africa, Europe, and the Atlantic Ocean appeared translucently over the top of the rolling display to give Lisa some appreciation for its location. A moment later the superimposed map faded away.

Phil smiled. "Now hold on, because we're going swimming." He pressed the remote downward, slowly at first, and the ocean moved up the screen as the depth began to increase.

"We're underwater?"

"Yep. Next stop, Atlantis Massif." Phil turned the remote further down, and within moments the giant domed mountain was standing before them. "This is what I saw on the business trip, Lisa. They hired me to figure out why it's bulged up like that."

Lisa noticed markers all around the mountain's base. "What are those?"

"Those are hydrothermal vents. Like the exhaust pipe for a car, but in this case, the planet. There's evidence of petroleum bubbling up from there."

"So?" asked Lisa.

"So what?"

"Did you find what makes the mountain bulge up?"

Phil laughed. "Oh yeah, I think I know what's causing it."

He pressed the remote further down, and the display changed to warm colors. Phil smiled as the images slipped by. Lisa was such a great balance to him. He loved the details, the boring, minute descriptions. All Lisa wanted was to cut through it all and simplify. He squeezed her hand.

"Now, what you need to understand is that the display you saw above the ground was done with radar from a satellite, so it's exactly what it would look like without the ocean water. This is different. This is the reflection of sound waves from the rock formations in the earth. You're literally seeing what the rock sounds like."

Lisa studied the winding strata of yellow, orange, and red. "What's with the different colors?"

"The colors represent different kinds of rock—granite and basalt, mostly." Phil kept the remote pointed downward, and the strata slowly moved up the screen. "Are you ready to see what's making me crazy?"

Lisa nodded, a smile playing on her face. She had to admit this was exciting.

Suddenly, the black pockets and bubbles appeared. "These are gas pockets. Gas pockets usually mean that petroleum is nearby."

"You're saying you found an oil field?"

"Wait for it," smiled Phil, pressing the remote further. The blue of the reserve filled the display, with the yellow basalt ceiling leading away in all directions.

Lisa literally lost her breath. She felt like she was swimming in oil.

"H-how big is it?"

"I can't really tell exactly, but it's already the biggest oil find in the history of the world. It's far larger than anything in Saudi Arabia."

Lisa was smiling from ear to ear, exuding pride in Phil. He grinned back. As the journey through the oil reserve continued without any end in sight, her smile began to disappear, and her internal alarm bells started to go off. Working in the governor's office had sharpened her skills in seeing things that had political ramifications.

This *definitely* had political ramifications.

Phil pressed a button on the remote, and the scene began to grow smaller and tilt on its axis as if they were looking at a side view. The slowly curving surface of the earth came into view, with the African continent sitting on top of the curve. The reserve seemed to start just under the Mid-Atlantic Ridge and snake under the continent of Africa, reaching further and further to the east until it disappeared under Egypt.

"Do sound waves really travel that far?" asked Lisa, stunned by the sheer size of the reserve.

"You're smart," said Phil admiringly. "No, I've had to piece this together like a giant puzzle. Most of what you're seeing are naval seismic studies from years ago during the Cold War. Submarines got strange readings in these areas, so they stored them, decades ago."

"They had all this detail in the 1960s?" asked Lisa.

"No, far from it—I had to amplify the signals digitally and do some prediction. You know, all that stuff I worked on in graduate school."

"This must be why they needed you so badly, Phil. They must be thrilled."

"Lisa, nobody knows about this yet—only you and me."

Lisa looked at him, stunned. "You haven't shared this with Dr. Chambers yet?"

Phil shook his head.

"Why on earth not?"

"Because it's way too deep to recover the oil. I'm still trying to find a place where it gets close enough to the surface to drill for it using contemporary drilling techniques. Look here."

Phil pressed another button on the remote, and small silver cylinders stretched down from the surface of the continent. The massive reserve curved beneath it, always out of reach of the silver straws. "These marks are just placed randomly, but they represent the deepest we've ever been able to drill—around seven miles. This entire reserve is just over eight miles deep, even in its most shallow areas, which seem to be over here." Phil scrolled the display toward Egypt. The oil reserve became shallower as it approached the Middle East.

"Do you think this huge reserve is actually feeding into the oil fields the Middle East is pulling from?" asked Lisa.

"That thought occurred to me, but that data is so closely guarded, I don't know how I'd ever get my hands on it."

Phil looked at the latitude and longitudes, and remembered the sermon from that morning.

"Wait a minute, here. Did I tell you that I got an e-mail last night from Jack?"

"Jack Sanders?" Lisa looked at Phil as if he had lost his mind. "Phil, Jack's dead."

"I know." He handed Lisa a printout of the letter. Lisa immediately recognized the ImmortalMe.com legal tag line.

Lisa held the ghostly note and read the cryptic words. "This is a very strange note to send postmortem."

"Or anytime. Check this out."

Lisa walked over to Phil's workstation and watched over his shoulder as he typed strange commands into the computer. A shape appeared on the screen. It reminded Lisa of a root system—a big, central, tapering tube with small off-shoots dominated the screen.

"What's that?" she asked.

"I'm not sure. It was embedded and hidden in the song Jack attached to his e-mail. At the end of it were two numbers that I couldn't figure out. Now, I think I know what they are." He typed while he talked. "I think they are the originating points of where to locate this thing."

"Where to locate it? You mean this is a place?"

"It looks that way—somewhere in Israel." Phil typed some more commands and overlaid the shape onto a map of the small country of Israel. "If this is right, it's southwest of the Dead Sea."

The shape was odd and out of place. "That doesn't look right to me," said Lisa. "There's nothing like that in Israel or anywhere else in the world."

"Wait a minute . . ." Phil typed some more. "What if that isn't above ground? What if it's underground at that location?" His fingers flashed over the keyboard, and the projectors blinked and displayed the strange shape.

Phil again stood in the center of the room, and Lisa joined him. He pointed the remote toward the strange root shape and felt himself rising out of the blue and purple hues of the oil reserve back toward the surface. As the bright yellow and orange colors of the ceiling of the reserve appeared, a bulbous shape appeared directly above them—part of the strange shape Jack had sent to him.

Phil gasped. "This could be a salt dome!"

"What's a salt dome?" asked Lisa.

"When water flows over a rocky basin over a long period of time, the water evaporates and leaves behind salts and other evaporates. The salt is really hard—almost impermeable. As the salt moves up toward the surface it can break and even bend the existing rock around it. The bending usually creates this shape." Phil pointed at the curving dome shape at the top of the structure. "Anyway, these things are usually important because pockets that form between the rock and salt layers can collect natural gas and petroleum."

Lisa got it. "So, just like the gas pockets, this big salt dome might be telling you that there's petroleum underneath it?"

"That's why I'm so excited. Look at this over here," Phil pointed at the screen where a long, root-shaped tube seemed to angle upward to the surface, just southwest of the Dead Sea. Phil rotated the object on the screen. The tube pointed directly into the earth—deep, deep into the earth. He clicked a button on the remote and measured the strange protrusion.

Fifteen miles.

Phil stood with Lisa in the silence of the room for a second, staring at the bizarre formation.

"Phil, what is it?"

"I think it's a lava tube, probably from a long-extinct volcano system."

The lava tube looked like a subway tunnel standing on end—a tunnel pointing directly at the largest oil reserve in human history.

Lisa put it together, vocalizing what they both were thinking.

"Israel might be able to get to it, mightn't they?"

Chapter Nineteen
Deep Biosphere

Monday morning arrived across Texas with a brilliant sunrise, but Phil missed it. He was already exploring the oil reserve by the time the first rays of light were fanning across the landscape. The door to Discovery & Development clicked and swung open, and a man stood in the dark room watching Phil and the animated display that wrapped around the three far walls of the room.

"I knew you wouldn't waste any time tackling this problem," he said. The timbre of his voice rumbled through the dark room.

Phil spun around, startled, and saw the silhouette of a thin man standing in the door. He dropped the remote control that he was using to move around the virtual environment, but in a moment his startled expression was replaced by a big smile as he recognized the man, even in dark silhouette. "You scared me to death!"

The newcomer flicked the overhead lights on, illuminating his face with its black beard and wire-rimmed glasses. The lights flickered and came up to full brightness.

Phil ran across the room and embraced Caleb Mosha. "Caleb, it's great to see you."

Caleb smiled and patted Phil on the back, glad that his long journey of recruiting Phil from graduate school to work for Axcess had born fruit. "I'm glad you're on board here at Axcess. We need you more than you know. You heard about Jack?"

"Yes. Have you spoken to Aliya recently?" asked Phil.

"Not since the funeral, but I know she's going to Israel for some downtime. I guess Toronto has too many memories of Jack."

Phil nodded. "Yeah—there are way too many good memories there. I can understand why she wants to get away."

Silence filled the space between the men before Caleb walked toward the animated display. "Show me what you've developed."

Phil and Caleb stepped to the center of the room, and Phil gave his colleague a tour of the most valuable discovery in human history. After only a few minutes of flying through the oil reserve and understanding its enormous size, the Israeli grasped the implications of the high-tech display that surrounded him.

After a quick lesson on how to navigate the virtual environment with the controller, Phil left Caleb in the center of the room and let him explore the data. Standing back and watching his friend navigate the dense data like some sort of astronaut brought enormous satisfaction to Phil.

As Caleb reached the lava tube in Israel, Phil smiled.

This one's for you, Jack.

Fifteen minutes later, the display finally came to a standstill, and Caleb turned and faced Phil. "Who knows about this?" he asked.

"Just you and I. Oh, and I showed it to Lisa too."

"Don't show anyone else outside the team." Caleb turned back to Phil. "Do you have the ability to add more to this display?"

Phil shrugged, curiosity mingled with excitement. Finally, someone who could challenge him and add to what he had brought to the problem! He was tired of working in the dungeon by himself with no one else to share the excitement of the discovery of the greatest expanse of petroleum on the planet. Still, Caleb's warning shook him. "What are you nervous about?"

"This is explosive stuff, Phil. There are people here at Axcess and in the oil industry that won't want this to see the light of day."

Caleb walked over to his messenger bag, pulled out a USB hard drive, and handed it to Phil. "Have a look at this."

Phil took the drive from his friend and plugged it into his workstation. He double-clicked on the data file containing the survey, and an hourglass appeared on the display as the computer dug into the file. Caleb stood behind him as the rows of data appeared on the screen.

LAT	LONG	DEPTH KM	HELIUM PARTS PER MILLION
30.02.37.16	42.03.27.72	-3916	350.1
29.55.58.72	42.02.59.16	-3304	389.9
30.03.04.64	41.56.53.93	-3727	325.5
29.57.52.03	41.58.41.13	-3446	276.4

"Can you superimpose this data over the reserve?" asked Caleb.

"Yeah, just a second." Phil's fingers flashed across the keyboard. Moments later, an image appeared on the screen.

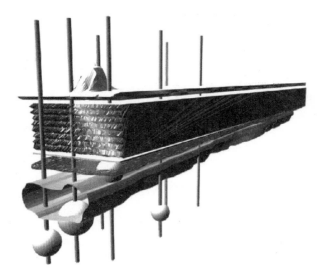

"I mapped the amounts of helium to these spheres. The size of each sphere is the amount of helium that was measured by the instruments that drilled into the earth," said Phil, pointing to four balloon shapes on the display.

He clicked on the lowest balloon shape and measured its distance to the surface. "This one is over nine miles below surface, and it's below the actual petroleum reserve."

He tapped the monitor with his finger. "Wait a minute—the amounts of helium you're showing here are far above the amounts of helium the sediment layers produce. So that means the helium is coming from far below the area that's supposed to be the origin for petroleum."

"Bingo," said Caleb. "That's why helium evidence is one of the most important first steps in proving the abiogenic theory. I'm assuming Chambers briefed you on that?"

Phil nodded, remembering the explosive theories Ward, Gorin, and Chambers had shared with him on the *Deep Pathfinder*. Caleb continued. "The helium must have been in the rocks far below the sediment layers, and in a fairly optimized ration with both methane and nitrogen."

"Optimized? You're saying that it's designed to be that way?" asked Phil

Caleb leaned against the table where the grid was humming. "If helium and methane are found below the layer of biology thought to produce petroleum, then world markets and strategic interests are threatened—not to mention the basic explanation we've been teaching everyone for the last hundred years about how coal and petroleum were produced. The basic framework for how the typical American thinks about energy would be overturned."

Phil leaned back in his chair, placing both hands behind his head. "Layer of biology—you mean the plant and animal life that is generally considered to be the source of oil and coal?"

"Exactly. If helium and hydrocarbons are actually found much farther down in the earth, and they are upwelling through the pores of the earth's mantle, then petroleum was *not* created in a single geological instant."

"Meaning?" asked Phil.

Caleb stroked his beard. "Helium is produced by the radioactive decay of uranium and thorium. The amount of helium produced in the rocks of sediment is not enough for the amounts that we are seeing. So it must be coming from farther below in the earth. And if the earth produces petroleum and it really is not a function of oil being in specific reserves in special locales, then that means that anyone could drill deeply into the earth and find oil."

"That would prove that petroleum is not a scarce commodity," said Phil. The realization of this theory's implications hit him like a ton of bricks. World markets, stocks based on futures—this would affect everything.

Caleb nodded. "That's why this data—not the data—your *picture* of this data is so dangerous. You've made this information digestible to the public."

"When did you start to learn about this theory?" asked Phil.

"When I first came out of school I worked on an exchange project at the Jet Propulsion Labs in Pasadena with Scott Ward."

"You worked with Dr. Ward at JPL before this project?" Phil was surprised. This was an even closer-knit group than he had realized initially.

"Yes. He was the one who recruited me to the Planetary Sciences Division there. We worked on a project there in the mid-1980s that measured primordial hydrocarbons in the large planets in our solar system. Most people don't realize this, but the ingredients we think of as being special for oil, coal, and natural gas to form here on Earth are abundant in the universe."

"Like how abundant?" asked Phil.

"Carbon is the fourth most abundant element in the universe, just behind hydrogen, helium, and oxygen. Carbon is found most of the time in combination with various proportions of hydrogen. That's actually where we get the term *hydrocarbon*."

Phil held out his hand, struggling to come to grips with Caleb's statement. "Wait a minute. You're saying that there might be oil on other planets?"

"Without a doubt. Spectrographic analyses of the largest planets in our solar system have shown that the wavelengths that we associate with hydrocarbons, especially in gaseous form, are major components of these planets' atmospheres."

"Gaseous form of hydrocarbons—you mean natural gas?"

Caleb smirked. "The most natural of all gases: methane."

Phil laughed out loud.

Caleb put his hands up and tried to reel the conversation away from sixth-grade jokes. "No, seriously: Jupiter, Neptune, Uranus, and Saturn all have huge signatures of methane in their atmospheres. At JPL, Scott Ward and I studied Titan, one of Saturn's moons, for over a year. Titan has methane and ethane as its atmosphere. It rains a toxic combination of these elements onto its surface every hour."

Phil was starting to put the pieces together. "Methane is another predictor of petroleum deposits. So if our major theories are that the hydrocarbons on this planet were formed by buried vegetation and animal matter that was compressed for long geologic periods of time, and then we discover that other planets have methane, we have a serious paradox."

Caleb pointed at Phil. "You got it. I don't think there were any dinosaurs or swamps on Titan a million years ago. Planets aren't the only factor either. Asteroids, especially those originating in the asteroid belt between Mars and Jupiter, have been observed to have hydrocarbons on their surfaces and in their interiors."

"All right, I get the point that oil's source can't be buried vegetation, but you still haven't explained how a process—a deep planetary process—might create petroleum. You must have a theory."

"We do. Dr. Chambers and I have been working on this for a very long time. One of the basic ideas that must be overturned initially is the idea that the earth was formed by colliding and coalescing debris after the Big Bang. Carbon is an element; it can't be created by any man-made process with the possible exception of a nuclear reactor. These hydrocarbons we're talking about are buried deep in the earth. If they were on the surface, they would have turned into CO_2 over time. They would simply have oxidized away. So they were either buried rapidly or they were formed in the internals of the earth."

Formed? Now Phil was really confused. "What do you mean by formed?"

"Created is what I mean, by God—the Galactic Architect. The average geology textbook says that the early earth was molten—a collection of coalescing elements that remained from the Big Bang—and gravity began to pull these granules together and pack them together into a planet." Caleb waved his hands all around him. "So this whole place was hot—super-hot—completely molten—right?"

Phil shrugged and pursed his lips. "That's what the textbooks say."

"If hydrocarbons come into contact with heat, even at relatively low temperatures, they burn—that's kind of the whole point of hydrocarbons. So here we have a major problem. There are hydrocarbons on the earth and throughout the universe, but they don't have biogenic origins. They were not formed over millions of years by buried vegetation and dead animals. But if they were part of the planets when they were formed, and it was hot, then they simply would have been consumed by the immense heat."

"Okay, so I agree with you. You know I believe the earth was created, along with everything else, but I've always been confused by petroleum—it seemed to either lend credence to the theory of evolution or be explained by the Great Flood. But now you're saying that petroleum may be more of a function of how God designed the earth."

"I'm not saying that some of what we find might not be attributable to the flood and the vegetation it would have buried, but there are still other things that even the flood doesn't explain—metal deposits in collections with one another and deep petroleum reserves are just a few examples. There must be a tremendous amount of hydrocarbons seated very deeply in the earth, and over time these hydrocarbons leach through the pores of the mantle, arrive in basins, and form oil reserves."

Phil leaned forward. "Just what depth do you think these hydrocarbons are emerging from?"

"Probably at least 186 miles; maybe much farther."

Phil began to open his mouth for debate, but the Israeli plowed on. "Now, scientists in the West will tell you that hydrocarbons can't survive in the presence of high temperatures, which of course increase as you get closer to the molten core of the earth."

"I was just going to mention the temperature problem. How do you get around that?" asked Phil.

"In Western institutions of higher learning, geologists are taught that at temperatures above 1112° F, even the most resistant hydrocarbons will dissociate and fall apart. But—and this is a big *but*—no one has proven this assumption in the West, and in Russia they are actually drilling wells that fly in the face of it. At these depths and under these pressures—some fifty thousand times the pressure of our atmosphere—molecules will form in ways that are impossible at the surface. Western energy companies don't see that drilling below six or seven miles is worthwhile, but Russia is another story."

"Has Russia actually found oil at depths below seven miles?" asked Phil.

"Yes, they have. They've found huge reserves in the form of the White Tiger and Black Leopard Reserves. What they've discovered is that there is evidence that the enormous pressures in the earth actually *stabilize* hydrocarbons regardless of temperature. A Russian journal in 1980 was written that claimed methane would not fall apart, or dissociate, down to a depth of 185 miles. The writer even concluded it could exist deeper than that—perhaps as deep as 372 miles."

Phil blew out the air in his cheeks. "So the assumption that molecules behave like they do on the surface was simply applied to an environment that has pressures that are fifty thousand times what we have on the surface?"

Caleb nodded. "That was a pretty bad assumption, but it has become dogma in universities. And this basic assumption controls so much of the world's balance of power and strategy that overturning it is very dangerous."

"What made you start down this road? I mean, you've been looking for an alternative to a theory that virtually every Western university holds!" said Phil.

Caleb smiled. "It started for me when I was ten years old. I remember going to temple and hearing stories about Noah's Ark. The rabbi would talk about the gopher wood and the pitch that Noah used to build the ark. I asked the teacher what pitch was. He said it was like tar. It was a form of waterproofing."

"Most waterproofing is made up of components of petroleum," said Phil.

"You got it. So if Noah's using petroleum to seal the ark from water, then where did the petroleum come from? Even creation scientists would have difficulty with this, because they assume there was no sediment at this point, and obviously nothing buried—yet."

Phil laughed. "I'll bet you were a real pain to your teachers at temple."

"I was. I wanted to know the reasons for the existence of this material that God described so specifically, and I've spent my entire adulthood pursuing the answer. I continued researching the theory all through college and graduate school. Being Jewish and nose to nose with countries that are loaded with oil and are only miles away from the Promised Land compelled me forward."

Phil laughed and opened a can of warm soda that was sitting on his desk. "Yeah, I guess Moses should have hung a right when he crossed the Red Sea."

After offering Caleb a can, he continued with his questions. "So you think that the petroleum upwelling process was designed into the very fabric of the planet? And in the case of the ark, that it was actually upwelling nearby and being used before the flood created the sediments that the average creation scientist would attribute to petroleum reserves?"

"Well, it could have been upwelling, or perhaps ancient men discovered ways to exploit petroleum just as we do—perhaps not with sophisticated oil wells, but with other technology. The theory answers a lot of things that existing evolution-based theories can only answer in contradictory and piecemeal fashion and in some cases are difficult to explain just with the Great Flood."

"For instance?"

"A really big one is the collection of metal deposits found in the earth and the association of petroleum with organic molecules."

Phil stared at the ceiling and thought through the common theories he had learned in school. "The organic angle is a tricky one. As I remember it, scientists have always assumed that the organic properties found in petroleum are there because of its origination with buried plant and animal matter."

Caleb took off his glasses, wiped them with a cloth, and held them up to the light for a quick inspection. "It's not as tricky as you think, but it does require a change of assumption. This organic signature in petroleum can come from things other than buried plants and decaying animals."

"So how do you and Dr. Chambers explain the biology?" asked Phil. "Most theories say the presence of organic molecules in petroleum mean that only life can create hydrocarbons."

"If you drill down five or six miles, you will always find these microbes contained in the oil—but even in our deepest wells we find cultures of bacteria that defy the general considerations of how deep life can exist on our planet. Our deepest boreholes have found these organic molecules at depths of up to seven and eight miles."

Phil put his hands to his head and rubbed his temples. "Wait. It's the same problem as the helium. You're drilling beyond the sediments that are supposed to be the source of the organic material, so the petroleum is further down in the earth and it's moving up. It's upwelling through the crust and accumulating in reserves. But it also has an organic tint to it, so that means it's coming into contact with life—maybe not life like we see on the surface, but microbial life nonetheless."

"You got it. So that means there is life deep in the earth. The petroleum is being transported to the surface through the pores of the earth, and along the way it is picking up biological molecules, helium, and upwelling nitrogen and methane—while at the same time picking up traces of iridium, which are deep in the earth. Petroleum doesn't contain organic molecules because it originated with them; it contains them because it's passing through an enormous body of them."

Phil did some calculations in his head. "If petroleum can be recovered outside of sediments and you can drill deep to get to it, this underground bio-sphere must be immense."

"Dr. Chambers agrees with you. His estimate is that there are at least 1013 to 1014 tons of these microbes in the deep biosphere. That's more than the flora and fauna on the surface. If you took those microbes and spread them out over the face of the earth, they would be nine feet deep."

Caleb smiled wryly at the look on Phil's face as he tried to comprehend the estimate. "Dr. Chambers says the deep-earth microbial world must be feeding on this petroleum as it upwells—at least in part—and they must also be hyper-thermophilic, living in temperatures of up to 300° F. They are also living under immense pressures, and just like the tube worms scientists found in the late 1970s around oceanic vents and black smokers, they exist in a pressure bath."

Phil nodded slowly. This, he was familiar with: the pressures down at the bottom of the ocean were two hundred times greater than those on the surface. Yet, tube worms were fragile—even more fragile than many species that thrive on the surface. Scientists called the phenomenon a pressure bath, as everything around the tube worms was immersed in common pressure.

"Okay," Phil said, "I see where you're going with this. Rocks at the surface and deeper, say to a depth of six to eighteen miles, keep their mechanical prop-erties under pressure and seem to close up, precluding an upward flowing of internal hydrocarbons. But actually, as the temperature increases and you go deeper, you believe the rocks begin to melt or plasticize and lose the mechani-cal properties that keep the upwelling hydrocarbons at bay."

"You got it. And here's another piece of interesting evidence: petroleum reserves we thought we had completely drained are refilling."

"Excuse me?" Phil said.

"They haven't refilled completely, but there are numerous examples in the Middle East and also along the Gulf Coast of reserves that continue to mea-sure increasing volumes of petroleum when we thought they were completely exhausted. It's great evidence of the theory."

Caleb glanced at a plotter that was standing against the wall. It was brand-new and had yet to be used by the team. Plotters were normally used by ar-chitects to print out enormous blueprints, but now this one would be used to document a new blueprint—a blueprint of energy independence. "We need a printout of this thing. Phil, reposition the viewpoint so we are looking at the entire reserve in a plan view."

Phil flicked the controller to the right, and the oil reserve shrank on the screen and moved away so that its entire length was visible. From this angle it looked like the world's longest subway tunnel.

Caleb's fingers tapped across a keyboard, and the high-end plotter began to hum as it sketched out the massive data set. The edge of the forty-two-inch sheet of paper began to slowly appear and then drop to the floor as the plotter transferred the digital information to the glossy white paper.

"So I get the biology explanation," Phil said. "Let's go back to the point you made about metal deposits. If this theory is true, then why do huge bodies of similar metals seem to stick together in the rock strata? It's true about silver and gold and lead and zinc," said Phil. "I've heard theories that the deposits are laid down as layers of sediment or that they're leeched into cracks in the rock by hot water after the rock is already formed."

"Metal deposits are one of the most important evidences that the crazy pressures in the earth allow molecules to form in ways that are different from how they form here at the surface," Caleb answered. "They are also great evidence that nitrogen, methane, and other gases are upwelling to the surface. The hot-water theory you mentioned goes by the name of *epigenetic processes*—and it definitely tips its hat to the abiogenic theory. Strong hydrothermal forces deep in the internals of the earth form the metal deposits: hot water circulating through the cracks and fractures of the rock leeches these minerals into veins. In the past few years, the epigenetic process theory is winning more arguments because of the minerals we find near things like gold—minerals that are probably formed by reactions."

"You mean the water that's leeching the ore upward reacts with something else, like another type of rock?"

"Exactly. Gold is almost always juxtaposed with quartz, carbonate, and mica, and we also find a lot of carbon in gold veins. There's a class of molecules called porphyrins that contain nitrogen, hydrogen, and carbon. You know about two of the molecules in this family right now," said Caleb.

"I do?" Phil was watching the long diagram of the oil reserve slowly emerge from the plotter.

"You do: hemoglobin in our blood contains a single iron atom at its core, and chlorophyll has a magnesium atom at its center."

"Those are both metals," said Phil.

"Right, so you can easily imagine organic molecules at pressure binding to atoms of metal and flowing upward through the pores in the rocks—pulling them toward the surface. Now here's the trick. We constantly find nickel and vanadium in petroleum, but there's not a case of magnesium or iron in the form of these specialized molecules in oil."

"Exactly how would plant debris generate nickel and vanadium?" asked Phil.

"That's the real issue. It's coming from beneath the sediments. I don't think that nickel and vanadium are the only metal atoms that are being upwelled, but they might be the ones that last the longest in a molecular bond," said Caleb.

"Last? You mean that as these molecules approach the surface, the pressure drops and they can't keep their grip on the metal atom—so they lose it in the rock?"

Caleb snapped his finger at Phil. "You got it. This might explain why we see elements that are closely associated on the periodic table closely positioned in the rock. Lead and zinc are typically found together, and so is gold with silver."

"There's actually historical evidence of this in England. The ancient tin mines in Cornwall that supplied ancient Rome had oil dripping down on the miners," said Phil, his excitement growing. The abiogenic theory had sounded crazy when Chambers first brought it up. But Caleb was doing a great job of fitting all the pieces together.

"There are also modern examples. Miners in Wyoming, Alaska, and the Urals find evidence of this phenomenon in their mines as well."

A growl came from Phil's stomach, and he blushed as he put his hand over his torso. "Sorry, I skipped breakfast."

Caleb glanced at his watch: 12:50 p.m. "There's just enough time to catch the tail end of lunch. I'm buying. Just one more point about the abiogenic theory, and then I'll stop blowing your mind."

"I think you've pretty much convinced me," said Phil.

The plotter beeped, informing them that the job was complete.

"Deep microbial life might even be involved with metal production in the earth," said Caleb with a smile. He picked up the ten-foot-long, curled diagram of the reserve and smoothed it out on Gorin's vacant desk.

"Microbes might be creating the atoms of metal?" asked Phil, digging through his desk drawer for pushpins to hang the diagram on the wall.

Caleb held a corner up to the wall, and Phil followed him around the perimeter of the diagram, pinning the strange picture to the stark white wall.

"Bacteria and microbes are well-known for reworking their geologic surroundings. There's even a bacterium, *Desulfovibrio*, that produces pyrite, sphalerite, and galena. Some bacteria produce magnetite, which we find in the boreholes of oil wells."

"That is blowing my mind," said Phil with a laugh. His head hurt with all the information Caleb had downloaded into it.

The men stood back and surveyed their new artwork.

Caleb stroked his beard. "It needs a name. Since you discovered it, why don't you give it a name?"

Phil laughed. "You mean like Phil's Oil Reserve?"

"No, something more befitting, more grand," said Caleb, still stroking his beard as he always did when he was thinking. "A name that carries the idea of its size and importance—maximum, optimum, optimal."

Phil thought through numerous mathematical terms describing high-end boundaries and manifolds. He smiled, bent over his desk, and scribbled the name on a yellow sticky note. Caleb laughed. "That's it," he said.

On the way out to lunch, Phil slapped the note on the bottom of the newly printed side view of the oil reserve, which was hanging on the wall of the department of Discovery & Development.

The note read, "Maximal Reserve."

Chapter Twenty

Drill Platform

The steel grates that lined the catwalks rattled beneath the work boots of Wayne Harrison. He walked through the oil-gas-separation structure—the Christmas Tree, as it was known—a vast and monstrous array of thick steel pipes fastened together with nuts and bolts the size of a man's hand. The paint of the pipes varied widely from rust-colored orange to white to yellow, all designating various processes and flows of the oil as it was extracted from dirt, grit, and water.

He stopped and tapped a glass pressure gauge, taking stock of its reading. *This isn't right.*

The ever-present hissing of gas from the Christmas Tree spoke to him like an old friend. While the noise would have frightened others, Harrison could tell from the sound that something was slightly off.

He closed off the gas valve with a strong pull of his muscular, tattooed arms and double-checked the gauge for a pressure reading. The hissing changed pitch imperceptibly, but somehow Harrison could sense a difference.

That's better.

Unable to sleep and suffering from jet lag, the native of Mobile, Alabama, and third-generation oil hound was taking a midnight patrol of the oil rig.

The rig belonged to Parezim Petroleum, which wasn't the biggest oil and gas company on the planet—far from it. But they treated their people right, something that Harrison appreciated more than money the older he got.

He ran up a floor of steel gantry steps and leaned over the edge, looking into the night sky. Out here, away from the major population centers, there weren't any city lights to dampen the effect of the massive star field that stretched above him. Seeing the stars—millions of them—reminded the roughneck of the crazy goal of the owner of Parezim Petroleum, or P2 as it was known by the oil wranglers.

Ross Valor, a onetime hell-raiser and alcoholic, had abruptly changed course in his life some twenty years ago. The Texas oilman was already a multimillionaire when his self-confessed "meeting with Jesus" changed his life goals. Within a year he had founded Parezim Petroleum and begun assembling his closest friends, who shared the same goal: finding oil in Israel and making the nation geopolitically self-sufficient and stable enough to do whatever it wanted.

Harrison snorted out loud as he thought of how absurd the business plan was: find oil in another country, spending millions and millions of your own money and funds from others, only to take the find and turn over a large percentage of it to the state of Israel.

Through some tricky negotiations and cashing of political chips with a few people in the State Department, Valor had been able to secure petroleum exploration licenses and drilling rights at three sites in the Holy Land. Two in the north, the Manasseh Project and the Joseph Project, abutting one another only a few miles south of the Syrian border; and Selah in the southernmost part of Israel near the Dead Sea.

The northern sites were not the best spots to drill for oil, especially when Hamas and the Israeli Defense Ministry exchanged volleys of rockets and tank shells across the short expanse of desert. The southern site had been recently purchased for a song from a mineral mine that was going bankrupt and had shown great promise before a seismic study at the northern sites had convinced Valor to begin his work there.

Valor was that kind of guy—tenacious, dedicated, and frugal, while at the same time making sure his men had the very best equipment. It was not uncommon to see Ross Valor on the rigs, shaking hands and talking with the oil hands. Not in a shirt and tie, either. In jeans and a hard hat. Harrison liked that part of the man—he liked it very much, and so did his coworkers, most of whom were from the Gulf Coast of the United States, just like him.

An oil flare at the top of the rig burned with a clean orange flame in the slight breeze from the Mediterranean Sea just a few miles away. This rig had been the one to find oil in Israel, and now the old man was reinvigorated, pushing forward at breakneck speed.

Other than the long flight over from Mobile, Wayne really didn't mind the travel and distance from America. He was working with the best, and as kooky as Valor seemed to the news media, he was a good, honest man to work for.

■ ■ ■ ■

A mile away, two men dressed in camouflage, lying near a cluster of scrub, looked through the FLIR binoculars at the oil well. The bright green images of amplified light made the night nearly as clear as midday to the two men. They pressed the talk button on a satellite phone and relayed what they were seeing.

A moment later a command came back, and one of the men pulled a black box from his pack and clicked a switch that was labeled ARM.

A red glow illuminated the men's sharp facial features.

■ ■ ■ ■

The oilman began to feel tired as he watched a shooting star fire across the dark blue expanse of the heavens. The exhaustion from the trip and the time-zone change was finally taking its toll. He began to head down the stairwell that ran around the rig when a vibration shook the entire platform. Harrison nearly lost his balance before reaching out and grabbing the handrail.

Whoa! What was—?

The rail began to rattle until Harrison thought it would fly apart from the vibration. Suddenly the metal casings of the rig fired up through the top of the derrick, crashing around the metal support and nearly taking his head off.

The vibration continued, and then came a loud hissing sound, followed by a huge spray of oil that fired high into the sky with such pressure that Harrison was blown onto his back.

Harrison pulled himself to his feet and wiped his eyes with his meaty palm, trying to clear them of the black rain that was pouring around him. A rumble blew him off of his feet again as a second explosion rocked the rig, and a bright orange-and-yellow flash started at the bottom of the rig and rolled up through the center, setting steel, oil, and equipment on fire. He looked down in horror to see the entire base of the platform in flames.

Why wasn't the suppression system activating?

Harrison ran down the stairs, dodging columns of fire and burning oil on the steel columns of the rig before reaching one of the fire suppression stations, which were positioned in a dozen locations all over the rig. He broke the glass cover with his fist and mashed down on the activation button. He looked at the nearest nozzle, expecting to see a fountain of foam and water spraying from its opening.

Nothing.

The fire moved up two floors, and a can of gas sitting by a generator exploded like a grenade. *Impossible!* He punched the button again. *Someone's turned the suppression system off!*

Harrison looked down through the smoke and coughed as the fumes from oil and grease mixed into a toxic killer. His eyes were watering—stinging from the roiling smoke and particles of petroleum that were floating in the air like a vapor.

And then he saw it.

The pipes containing natural gas lines a few meters from the rig were on fire. The placard stickers with warning signs of EXPLOSION and NO SMOKING could barely be made out against the yellow and orange licking tongues of flame.

A moment later the gas ignited, and a fireball a hundred meters in diameter engulfed the rig, the ruptured gas lines, and the desert all around. The oil in the drill pit ignited and shot two hundred feet into the air, creating a funeral pyre for Wayne Harrison and the dozen unknowing oil hands who had been asleep in the trailers around the site.

Chapter Twenty-One
The Announcement

The auditorium at Axcess Energy was buzzing. Bright TV lights and cameras from the financial networks and local affiliates looked like bazookas, ready to blow the high-tech stage away. Cameramen from newspapers and business periodicals were sitting on the floor, just in front of the first row of dignitaries. The cameras around their necks sported long telephoto lenses and expensive flashes. Teleprompters were being tested, and audio checks were underway for the live broadcast.

Lisa, dressed in a conservative navy suit and wearing her brunette hair in a sophisticated updo, checked her phone for messages as she waited for the governor to arrive.

She greeted lobbyists for the oil and energy companies and environmental activists alike, seating them in the front row, which was reserved for VIPs. Lisa had been preparing for this hour for over two months. It was an important meeting: for Axcess, for the governor, for the local economy, and for the people of Texas.

She hoped she could get through it without having a nervous break-down.

Lisa looked up the steep stairs of the auditorium, which was arranged in stadium seating like an IMAX theater. There were no bad seats. She was thankful she didn't have to walk up and down the stairs and was almost certain she would have performed a Gerald Ford if she had. An image of the thirty-eighth president waving to a crowd from the top of the stairs of Air Force One and then tripping and falling down the steps in front of all the media of the Western world flashed through her mind.

The governor, flanked by security and handlers, finally arrived. Lisa quickly briefed him on last-minute changes while a makeup artist patted his head with powder to knock the shine down. It wasn't his turn to be on stage yet. That was the Axcess Energy CEO's privilege.

The overhead lights dimmed, and the rumble of the audience's networking and cross talk faded with them.

The screen on the wall behind the stage came alive. A deep rust-orange Texas sunset with a pump jack nodding relentlessly at the scrub-covered ground filled the screen. A soundtrack filled the air: instrumental ambiance, but with a thoughtful, almost mournful theme.

The camera panned to focus on the pump jack. It looked like an iron dinosaur. The symbology of the sunset, the dinosaur-like pump jack, and the slow up-and-down motion was powerful and clear: the oil industry was in its sunset years.

The voice-over began, a deep, production-heavy bass that spoke over the creaking pump jack as it continued to nod its head.

"Oil, the blood of the Earth, once thought to be abundant and nearly inexhaustible in supply, is now nearing its end."

A rumble filled the room as executives and reporters buzzed among themselves. This was not a good advertisement for an oil company to run.

The deep voice of the moderator continued. *"We are moving from an era of abundant, cheap energy to scarce, expensive, and hard-to-acquire energy. This change will alter our society in ways that are difficult to fathom."*

The crowd of financial analysts and oil lobbyists nervously shifted in their seats.

"One company is preparing to lead the way into a new era of energy generation."
A large white title filled the screen:

Axcess Energy Corporation
We power your life.

"Ladies and gentleman, please welcome the CEO of Axcess Energy Corporation: Mr. Glenn Martin!"
A round of applause broke out as Martin strode onto the stage in an elegant dark gray suit, black wingtips shining like mirrors, sporting salt-and-pepper "executive" hair that any TV evangelist would covet.

Martin flashed a set of perfect white teeth and waved to the audience as he took the podium.

"Thank you for coming. This is an exciting time for the energy market. It's a time for reflection on what we have done, both as a company and as an industry. Oil is the bloodstream of the world economy. It's what moves the world, and we use it for *everything.*"

He paused for a moment to let that word hang in the air.

"We tend to think of oil and gasoline only as the fuel that propels our cars and trucks across the interstates, but the reality is that petroleum is in nearly everything we use. It allows us to make plastics, for preserving meat during transport and fashioning trivial things like ice-cube trays. It's used in wax sealers for packaging and in fertilizers for the fields in the Midwest that feed tens of millions of people here and around the world. Petroleum is even used in cosmetics, and in pharmaceutical products that extend our very lives."

Lisa smiled; the man could give a good speech. She scanned the audience and saw they were hooked, completely mesmerized, hanging on every word Glenn Martin conjured up.

Photos dissolved and appeared on the screen behind the CEO: cities expanding, men working on high steel and guiding I-beams into place—the nostalgic images of American progress.

"Axcess has been a part of American progress since the beginning. We helped the United States win World War II; we helped propel the U.S. ahead of all other nations with industrial might as we expanded our nation's highways and cities in the 1960s and '70s."

As he finished, a new set of photos stepped across the projection screen, covering up the black-and-white pictures of America's progress. These were in color: a bustling street in Shanghai, downtown Mumbai, and the instantly recognizable Dubai skyline—globalism on its unrelenting march across the business world.

"But—" the executive let the pause do the work for him. "We are not alone. The world has seen our prosperity and what energy has done for us, and they want it too."

Lisa looked down at her script. *Those aren't the words he's supposed to say.*

Martin continued. "And why shouldn't they want it? Energy has helped us all live better, happier, more productive lives. Energy is not an American 'thing'—it's a human thing. It's a gift to the world population from the Mother of us all."

He was off message. He was using different words and a different tactic. A tactic that was unusual for a businessman to exploit, though not uncommon territory for a politician. He was playing with the audience's emotions and prejudices.

More photos arrived on the screen. An empty oil field abandoned near the Caspian Sea. Pictures of the "Bust" portion of the "Boom and Bust" cycle filled the screen: "Out of Work" signs, soup lines, and shanty towns—images of the Great Depression.

"There's a problem with this precious gift from our Mother, though, and that problem is that petroleum is nonrenewable. We cannot grow petroleum. It's not like the nearly endless wheat and cornfields you see as you drive across I-70 in Kansas and Indiana. Yet we have pulled it out of the ground and processed it as if it will never end. The petroleum we are pumping out of the ground was created in a single instant in geological time, 90 to 130 million years ago by ancient vegetation and prehistoric animals that were buried some two thousand meters below our feet and transformed by a chemical reaction into black gold. The demand for oil is beginning to strip its supply clean."

Again, the crowd shifted nervously. Scarcity was not a common topic of conversation for a business meeting about petroleum.

Martin drew himself up for the final blow. "Ladies and gentlemen, this supply is running out. It may be ten years or fifty years, but we will, as a nation, as a continent, as a planet, run out of the energy source we have come to rely so heavily upon. We have passed the peak of oil production and are beginning to slip past the summit of this great mountain of prosperity that has helped us in innumerable ways. The view from the other side is, in a word, frightening."

Lisa looked at an alert that chirped across her mobile phone. Axcess's stock price was down sharply. Other cell phones in the audience dinged and chirped with news alerts to analysts and lobbyists.

Martin plowed on with his speech.

"We use ten calories of fossil fuel for every one calorie of food we produce. In just two hundred years, we have gone from a world population of two billion people to over six billion. How do we feed these people when fossil fuels are gone and we can't run our farming equipment? How can we produce fertilizers and pesticides to produce quality crops when we use fossil fuels to make them?"

Photos of famine in Africa tiled the screen. Some of the audience members were beginning to look a little green.

"What about hydrogen? Is that our escape from this desperate future? No, it isn't. Our modern life is based completely on electricity. Virtually every megawatt is generated using oil, coal, and gas. If we were to switch all of our cars from fossil fuels to hydrogen, we would need to generate four times more electricity than we are now to power its systems."

Lisa looked around at somber faces, looking like the audience had received a mass diagnosis of terminal illness. The CEO looked at one of his handlers as if on cue.

"Are we down ten percent yet?" he asked, playing up the moment, glowing in his unique ability to influence the wealth of so many others. Lisa shook her head, impressed despite herself. This guy knew exactly what he was doing. The handler gave a nervous nod and returned to the flurry of e-mails pounding his inbox from news agencies demanding interviews.

"Good," Martin said, "because it's not all bad news. This is the challenge that faces us, my friends. This is beyond simple economics and business. This is security—security for this company, security for this country, and security for the world at large. We are no longer sovereign nations. We are united in our demand and need for energy. Axcess Energy will be that uniting force across all these dimensions."

Lisa frowned. This was quickly moving beyond cold business and into the realm of exploitative politics—and not just local or state government politics, either.

A slide title filled the screen behind the CEO:

Phase One: KAVENDISH

Martin beamed. "That's why today we are announcing a new joint venture with the Chinese and Cuban governments to develop the newly discovered Kavendish Oil Field. This giant reserve will boost the company's supply by as much as fifty percent. This reserve is located two hundred and fifty miles southwest of New Orleans, and our scientists estimate that it holds as much as fifteen *billion* barrels of oil."

The audience exploded into applause as if the profits this oil field represented were being piped directly into the pockets of those watching the briefing.

The turnaround in emotions jolted Lisa. Had they all forgotten what the CEO had said just moments before about the precarious position of the nations of the world and their reliance on petroleum?

Again cell phones chirped and bleeped across the audience. Lisa glanced at her phone. Axcess's stock price had zoomed up thirty percent. She noticed Glenn Martin glancing over at his handler again. The man simply nodded as he watched the stock's trajectory go ballistic. Such a volatile change in so short a period of time was sure to make the national evening news.

Lisa watched the row of news reporters waving their hands in the air, jockeying for questions. Martin had gambled billions of shareholder value. Why? It had been completely unnecessary—total drama when objectivity would have accomplished the same thing.

Lisa moved close to the governor. He was scheduled to take the stage next with Martin.

The next slide flashed onto the screen.

Phase Two: MANHATTAN

Again the deep bass voice of the announcer rolled across the audience. *"Ladies and gentlemen, please stand for the governor of Texas, the honorable Mr. Roger Wyngate!"*

The audience took to its feet and cordially applauded as Wyngate strode across the stage to take his place to the right of Glenn Martin. Martin beamed. "The second initiative we are announcing today is the Manhattan Project."

The name was so loaded with meaning that the audience began buzzing immediately. "No," smiled the CEO, "we are not going to start building an atomic bomb." The crowd laughed dutifully. "Manhattan is a partnership with the great state of Texas and the city of Austin in particular. Governor . . ."

"Thank you, Mr. Martin," said Wyngate, stepping forward and away from the glamorous chief executive. "Today we are announcing a ten-billion-dollar cash initiative into alternative energy to research and deploy alternatives to oil. With Axcess, we will work to advance basic and applied research in hydrogen fuel cells, solar energy, biofuels, wind power, and geothermal energy sources. While the Kavendish Field will keep the company in great shape for decades, we will push forward together to form a bridge to this new world of energy."

The environmental lobbyists seated up front burst from their haunches and applauded wildly. Some even whistled.

The mayor of Austin came onstage and shook the CEO's hand before speaking to the audience. "The proud city of Austin will build an energy science park just four miles from here that will be viewed the same way the Research Triangle Park is viewed in North Carolina for biotech and life sciences. This will be the magnet for the energy researchers of the world."

An architectural rendering of an enormous complex of glass-and-steel buildings, looking very collegiate, flashed to the screen. The audience was applauding madly. The stock was up forty percent.

Lisa felt sick again as the stack of photos that Sheridan Preston had shown her in the ladies' room came back to her—clicking through her mind like a camera shutter.

The CEO shook the hands of the governor and the mayor, and the two men moved to the right side of the platform. "And now for the final phase," said Martin. "We mentioned that oil is an international issue, a problem that causes conflict and war. We can be an important part of resolving this conflict."

A new slide filled the screen with a quilt work of national flags: United States, Russia, Syria, Turkey, Israel.

Lisa's stomach tumbled. Seeing the white flag with the Star of David juxtaposed with the flags of nations that blatantly despised Israel's very existence made her anxious. She thought about the salt dome and the lava tubes over Phil's newly discovered reserve.

Suddenly the conference felt very personal. Phil's carefree, almost naïve personality was a serious risk. *Phil needs to be very careful who he shows that data to.*

Phase Three: ANKARA

Glenn Martin licked his lips as if he couldn't deliver this next phase fast enough. "Today we are also announcing our new relationship with LukZag Petroleum, Russia's largest petroleum producer."

No, not LukZag! The incident with the reporter was now beyond a curiosity. Sheridan Preston was right about her boss. On the surface, maybe there was nothing wrong with Axcess and the governor working together—but why keep it a secret so long, a secret from their own people? But then there was the connection to the Russian crime lords. And how exactly did David Rohm fit in? Desperately, Lisa wished she could see this conference as a good thing. But something felt all wrong.

The audience applauded lightly—a tentative response. They wanted to know more.

"Axcess Energy doesn't always have to be the explorer, or even the one who produces the recoverable oil—we can also be the engineering partner to help bring it to the world. It is my pleasure to announce that Axcess Energy will be paid $20.6 billion dollars for helping LukZag build a natural-gas pipeline that will run over five hundred and sixty miles under the Black Sea, through Bulgaria, traveling through Turkey, and ending in Syria. This will reduce Israel's dependence on Egypt's energy supply. This pipeline will carry over sixty-three billion cubic meters of natural gas annually to our friends in the Middle East."

The crowd jumped to its feet, caught up in the hype—in a joke, Lisa thought. No one on earth could hope to deliver on this promise. The applause was extended as a map of the pipeline project overlaid the projection screen. Martin raised his hands to quiet the crowd. The applauding reduced in volume and tempo, and the crowd retook their seats.

"This is the part I really like," said Martin, flashing his million-dollar grin. "We aren't just another greedy corporation or energy company exploiting the land. We are doing something new here—something bigger—something that is larger than Axcess Energy and LukZag Petroleum. We are bringing the world together in spite of its differences. Over four billion cubic meters of this natural gas will be sold to Israel starting in the first year of production, and that amount will more than triple over the next decade. We are the vehicle that will bring prosperity and peace to the Middle East. We are the real peacemakers."

Lisa felt sick to her stomach. This was over the top—an energy company transcending business and becoming a world peacemaker? The pompous arrogance of the man was obscene.

Lisa glanced at the invited guests who were lined up off the stage. The Israeli national infrastructure minister, Benjamin Ben-Eliezer, looked mesmerized—taken in by Martin's every word.

Lisa's phone chirped with a text message from Phil. Lisa flipped her phone open and read it quickly.

"What a windbag . . . can you believe the nerve of this guy? He really thinks he's a politician, or maybe the messiah—lowercase m."

Lisa didn't disagree. Even so, she looked over both shoulders and quickly deleted the message. Phil had to be more careful!

This was not how the meeting was supposed to go. It wasn't what they had planned and rehearsed for months. It wasn't just that Martin and Wyngate had deviated from the script—a huge risk in public relations that bothered her. It was the fact that Rohm, and apparently the governor, were keeping secrets from her—*huge* secrets.

She looked over at David Rohm and watched him schmooze the power brokers of the Texas energy sector in the shadows of the auditorium. She looked out at the reporters who were jotting down their notes and typing on their laptops. One journalist wasn't writing anything down. She was staring directly at Lisa.

Sheridan Preston.

Their eyes locked, and Ms. Preston smiled grimly at Lisa before the reporter looked down at her notepad and continued her job. Lisa's mind flashed back to the ladies' room and all Preston had disclosed.

The photos, the secret meetings, the flights to the Middle East—it was starting to corroborate Preston's observations.

I have to find out more.

Chapter Twenty-Two
The Accident

Ross Valor, founder and president of Parezim Petroleum, looked through the window of thick-paned glass out at the Gulf of Mexico, which glistened in the sunlight. Two enormous oil tankers were moored just off shore, taking on oil for trade with other nations.

It wasn't his oil, but he knew someday it could be.

His gaze and fantasy were sheared back to reality by the ringing phone on his desk. Valor grabbed the phone with his hands—bear-like in size. The small receiver disappeared into his fleshy mitts.

He turned away from the window and stared at the dark wood of his executive desk. His tone was somber.

"When?"

Tobias Levy, Ross Valor's VP of Exploration, looked up from his laptop. He sensed bad news. He set his e-mail-laden machine on the plush couch and approached Valor.

Valor snapped his fingers and pointed at a flat-screen television mounted on the wall. The financial markets marched across the ticker, and a large graph of commodities being traded glowed on the display.

Tobias clicked to a cable news show. The display showed a raging inferno. A tower of flame fired high into the night sky. Remains of a metal oil platform could be seen intermittently through the flickering tongues of orange flame.

Another camera angle appeared, and a helicopter orbited the fire. Oil shooting out of the ground instantly ignited. Black smoke rose from the drilling station like a flare as it drifted high into the atmosphere.

Ross Valor glanced at the television and ran his hand over his forehead, continuing the motion to the back of his head. "How many men?"

Tobias gulped and turned back to the newscast.

The muffled dialog streaming from the phone was unintelligible to Tobias, but he could see the weight of information pounding on the president of the oil company like a heavyweight boxer. Valor sighed before giving an order to the person on the other side of the world. "Make sure you get the life insurance process started. Those families are going to need as much as we can give them."

Ross placed the receiver slowly into its cradle and exhaled deeply. "We lost twelve men." His voice softened. "Good men."

The rusty orange color of the sun enveloped Ross as he looked through the window. Ross Valor was well acquainted with loss and grief. He had been a marine sergeant in Vietnam and had lost dozens of men under his command.

Tobias thought of the other griefs Ross had known. Tobias had still been fresh from his doctorate at MIT when he met Ross at an exploration convention. Valor's wife was in the final stages of breast cancer then, and Ross had spent every night at the hospital watching his soul mate slowly disappear as the disease ran its course.

Tobias looked out the window and let a full minute of silence pass by before asking the question that was paramount in both men's minds.

"Do you think it was an accident?"

Ross harrumphed. "No—no way."

"Should we form an investigation?"

"Yes, but quietly. We need to get to the bottom of why the fire happened just in case it really was an accident, but—"

Tobias looked up from a pencil he was nudging across the desk.

"We both know it was sabotage." Ross walked over to a large map of Israel mounted on the wall. Three regions were marked with small drilling-rig graphics, and the map was colored with gradations of rainbow colors: predictions of oil saturation.

"This should be a joyous day, Tobias. Despite the tragedy of the oil fire and the loss of twelve men, there's oil under Israeli sand. We've proved that now. Once we get that drilling station blown out, we can begin recovering oil and fulfill our promise to the state of Israel."

His attention moved from the north end of the map where the Manasseh and Joseph Projects were outlined to the drill diagram at the extreme southern end of the country, just below the Dead Sea. "Maybe we should hedge our bets a bit," he said, tapping the map with his finger.

Tobias raised his eyebrows. "You want to return to the southern site?"

He tried to suppress his surprise. Ross had pulled the plug on the southern site two years before, simply capping the well they had begun, and moved all of his interests and assets to the north of Israel, which he felt held bigger promise.

Ross was deep in thought and didn't answer. Tobias headed for the door and a day that promised to be insanely busy. As his hand touched the handle, his boss's request changed, and his tone became urgent. "Let's give these guys more than one target. Let's put out that oil fire and get the oil out of the ground as soon as possible. With Axcess Energy's announcement about the pipeline, the press and analysts are going to descend on us. Don't be too surprised if Axcess starts to put the screws to us. They will be under tremendous pressure to find a problem with our production capabilities."

"Should we be in a press blackout until after we put the fire out?" asked Tobias.

Ross Valor's thick fingers began to mash the buttons of his speakerphone.

"Who are you calling?" asked Tobias.

"Everyone! The press will be all over Axcess Energy too. That can work to our advantage."

Tobias smiled. "David versus Goliath?"

"Exactly. Let me know if you need anything. Good luck."

Urgency hung in the office like a fog. Parezim Petroleum was running out of time and money.

Chapter Twenty-Three
Saturday at the Office

L isa walked into the dark office of the Department of Commerce, located north of the city and nestled among other nondescript office parks.
She flicked on the lights while juggling a large cup of coffee in one hand
and a stack of manila folders stuffed with papers under her other arm. The sun
was just starting to peek through the overcast and humid Texas sky, and the
pattern from the blinds obscuring the sunlight cast a horizontal series of alternating bands of light and shadow on the wall.

The room was eerily silent, the only sounds coming from the workstation
fans in vacant cubicles and the hum of warming fluorescent lights.

First executive decision of the day.

She flicked the lights back to the *off* position, and the sound of the fluorescent lights stopped. Lisa liked to work in a darkened room with just the light
from the computer display—an old college-study preference. The computer

fans continued, but they didn't bother her. They added enough white noise that she could focus on her tasks.

The newly recovered silence caused her to close her eyes and sigh, comfortable in jeans and a T-shirt. She smiled. *I love Saturdays.* They reminded her of the good times in college, times that were fun and stressful at the same time. *A bit like now,* she thought. With Phil burning the midnight oil at Axcess Energy and her questions about the conference unable to be resolved—for now—she had decided to catch up on some work that had been piling up.

She walked into her office and logged into her computer, then began to riffle through papers and pink and yellow "While You Were Out" sheets. The words on all the little sticky notes were annoyingly similar: *urgent this, urgent that, call me back soon, looking forward to meeting you.*

She was happy when her e-mail finally sprang up on the display—until she read the status on the screen.

Two hundred and five new messages—*holy cow!*

She had cleaned up her inbox just last night while watching the evening news and eating a cup of soup for dinner. E-mail was the part of her job that never ended.

With a sigh, she began to triage the inbox while sipping the wonderfully large cup of coffee she had purchased at the local bakery. She had considered buying a doughnut or a croissant for breakfast, but the beautiful sparkle on her left hand reminded her that in less than a year she would have to squeeze into a wedding dress.

She looked at the ring on her finger and thought of the hot-air-balloon ride with Phil. The planning he must have gone through, especially given how busy he was. The way he proposed. The words he used. The way he looked at her. It replayed like a movie.

She moved her left hand into the brightness of the sunlight and watched the prismatic points of refracted light dance on the walls of her office.

Work pulled her back from her daydream, and she began to delete messages that were clearly spam. She loved blowing away e-mail, and her index finger hit delete as she rapidly scanned the unknown names and looked at the subject lines for obvious hints of promises no one could ever deliver.

A message from Audrey Busher, the secretary for David Rohm, broke up her love affair with the delete key.

Lisa—

Mr. Rohm would like a list of the scheduled meetings with energy companies in the next two months. Just dates, contact names,
and numbers will be fine. Can you put some urgency on this?

Also, I sent a hard copy of some notes made in a meeting a few
weeks ago regarding energy companies he would like to add to the
list. Can you take a look at that list and go through your contacts to
see what we can pull together?

Thanks,

Audrey Busher

Administrative Assistant to David Rohm

Governor's Office

Lisa pushed back in her chair and looked at the ceiling. *More energy companies? What are you up to, Rohm?*

Grabbing her half-empty coffee cup, she walked over to the ghastly sage
mailbox corral, a true relic of the early 1990s. A stack of papers stuck out of her
box, and she groaned as she pulled out the hard-copy equivalent of the spam
she had been killing electronically a few minutes before. She found the notes
Audrey had routed to her and instantly recognized David Rohm's scrawl. She
squinted at the scribbles and held the page closer, attempting to divine names
from the unreadable writing.

What is this, a doctor's prescription? The writing was virtually undecipher-
able. She put the scribbled page in a separate pile on the counter and continued
thumbing through the papers. Lisa picked up the keeper pile and started back
to her office—but not before another name on the mail corral caught her attention: *David K. Rohm.*

A bouquet of multicolored pages jutted out from his mailbox, like the rip-
ened fruit dangling from the Tree of the Knowledge of Good and Evil.

She looked up from the alcove containing the copier, fax machine, and
mail corral and across the empty office space. The office in the corner, the largest, was Rohm's. The door was closed, and the frosted sidelights around the
door were neutral, unlit by the office's fluorescent lights or even the sunlight
invading the Texas landscape outside.

She looked back at the mail bin and bit her lower lip. *I really shouldn't do this.*

She disliked Rohm in a deep way. It wasn't just that he was rude and inconsiderate. There was more there: a deep-seated ambition and viciousness that would stomp anything that got in his way. David Rohm cared for no one else on the planet other than David Rohm.

She craned her neck and looked into the mail bin, scanning the words across the first visible page. Her eyes flicked across the office space again, and she scanned the ceiling for any surveillance cameras. None.

She bit the fruit.

Lisa pulled the papers from the mail bin and scanned through them. Some of the papers were mundane office memos, others were interoffice communications sent by people in the government who still didn't understand or trust e-mail.

She flipped to the last page, which was different from the other mundane pages. It had a bright orange sticky note plastered on the front with a rapidly written note:

ROHM—
HERE'S THE LIST YOU ASKED FOR. TWO ARE GONE.
I'M WORKING ON THE LAST.
—G

A paperclip held an open envelope to the paper. The envelope's return address was a corporation: an energy company in Russia.

Lisa gasped and sat against the counter in the mail room. LukZag Petroleum—there it was again, staring her right in the face. *Sheridan was right about the connection of the oil company to David Rohm.* It was right there in her hands.

Lisa's heart raced, and she turned her attention back to the letter and peeled the sticky note back to look at the letter beneath it.

The paper was expensive stock and had an official look to it. It was a research grant from the Department of Energy.

Lisa scanned the text.

Department of Accounting

United States Department of Energy

Office of Fusion Energy Research Sciences, SC-24.2/GTN
19901 Germantown Road
Germantown, MD 20874-1207
ATTN: Program Announcement LAB DOEENGY-P452

Blah, blah, blah. The words on the document were written in bureaucratic style—aka boringly. She tried to comprehend the obtuse memo and immediately began to see words that alarmed her: *anomaly, Atlantis Massif, petroleum emissions, strategic interest.*
Lisa skipped down.

Funding
Abstract (one page)
Literature Cited
Biographical Sketch(es)
Description of Facilities and Resources

Wait a minute—biographical sketches. She flipped through the document until she reached a section that described the members of the research team. Three researchers and the universities where they worked were listed on the letter:

DR. SCOTT WARD—CORNELL THEORY CENTER, ITHICA, NY, USA
DR. LE WU NING—MIT SEISMIC STUDIES, CAMBRIDGE, MA, USA
JACKSON SANDERS (DOCTORAL CANDIDATE)—UNIVERSITY OF WATERLOO AT TORONTO, TORONTO, ONTARIO, CANADA

Lisa's heart skipped a beat. She slumped against the edge of the counter, her hands trembling. Her eyes flew across the last name again.
Jack?
Her heart was racing now. *What did David Rohm want with a research grant from the Department of Energy, and how was poor Jack involved?*

Lisa flipped back to the envelope with the sticky note: *"Two are gone. I'm working on the last."*

Gone? What does that mean? Jack is dead. Is that what it means? Two what? People. Does it mean people?

Resolve set in. *I have to show this to Phil.* The 3-D model of the salt dome that Jack had mysteriously sent flashed through her mind.

Lisa rushed to the copy machine to make two copies of the document. The machine hadn't warmed up for the day, and it clicked and whirred while displaying annoying messages on its front display panel.

Come on! Hurry up, you stupid copier!

The copier sounded a tone as it finished its warm-up process. *Finally!* She put the original facedown on the glass and pressed the copy button.

The overhead lights of the office flickered on, and Lisa's body flared with adrenaline. Someone else was in the office!

Startled by the buzzing fluorescent tubes, Lisa looked up, threw open the copier cover, grabbed the original, and stuffed it back into Rohm's mail bin. She turned back to the copier and grabbed the two copies that were sitting in the collating tray.

"Well, hello there, Miss Baton," came a smooth voice.

Lisa shrieked and dropped the stack of papers all over the floor of the copy room.

It was David Rohm. His dark, bag-laden eyes stared at her.

"Oh, I'm sorry. I didn't mean to scare you." Rohm squatted down and began to pick up Lisa's mail. Lisa was holding her chest, feeling her heart pounding like a jackhammer, when she realized that the research grant was laying at her feet—face up.

Lisa threw herself on top of the research grant. "Oh! You don't have to do that," she said, scooping up the rest of the papers.

"What are you talking about? I scared you. Of course I need to help," he said.

She swore he had a lisp like a snake. Lisa forced a smile and grabbed the papers that were scattered further out. She stood up and met Rohm's gaze, which seemed to bore into her.

"I'm glad to see someone else doesn't have a life, but I thought you had a boyfriend."

"Fiancé," Lisa corrected him, flashing the ring at him.

Rohm's sunken eyes seemed to bulge from his sockets as he saw the diamond. "Wow, that announcement hasn't made interpersonal mail yet." He grabbed Lisa's hand and looked at the glittering diamond.

Lisa's hand trembled and began to sweat as the examination of the ring went from a simple look to a lingering and inappropriate holding.

"That's quite a ring. He must care for you very much. What does he do for a living?"

Lisa pulled her sweaty hand from Rohm's meat hooks. "He's a petroleum exploration scientist at Axcess Energy." *And you would know that if you had showed any interest at all at the restaurant the night I introduced you to him,* she thought to herself in disgust.

"Ah . . . well that explains the size of the stone. Axcess is a great company. It's a shame about all the accidents they keep having."

"What accidents?"

Rohm's normally cold, calculating exterior was shattered for a brief moment. "Oh, you said Axcess. I must've been thinking of another company." His unreadable eyes glanced upward to the left.

He's lying . . . but why?

Rohm handed the rest of the papers to Lisa. "Thank you," she replied, as polite as possible while being as distant as she could be.

"Have a good day," he said, turning to his mail bin.

As Lisa walked away, she could still feel his sunken eyes crawling over her body. She didn't look back as she headed to her office and closed the door.

She glanced toward the sidelight, a narrow window between the wall and her closed door that looked out into the office space. Rohm walked by on his way to his office, glancing in her direction with a sly smile.

Lisa returned the courtesy coldly.

The words on the sticky note played over and over in her head. *Two are gone. Working on the last.*

She pulled the grant from the stack of papers and typed Jack's full legal name into a search engine. Academic papers, research organizations and associations, and his obituary.

She pulled out a red pen and placed a check mark next to Jack's name on the grant. She stopped, looked at the cold annotation, and shivered.

Sorry, Jack; maybe I can save someone else's life.

She looked at the next name in the list: Dr. Le Wu Ning. The search results for the scientist flashed across her screen. Again, numerous research papers and associations filled the browser—too many to work with.

Lisa modified the search. *Only show me the newest stuff.*

Two results came back, both newspaper articles. The title of the most relevant find was ominous: "Accident in the Rockies Claims Seismologist's Life."

Lisa's finger trembled as she clicked the link.

The article described the emergency crew in Colorado finding the shattered remains of a car that had broken through a guardrail on Vail Pass and plummeted hundreds of feet down the canyon. She looked at the date of the article—one month ago, right before Jack's death. Lisa put a grim red check mark next to Dr. Ning's name.

Lisa tapped her pen on the desk while she thought about the similarities between the two men. *Jack was a computational geologist; this guy was a seismologist. Both were working on a grant for the Department of Energy involving some anomaly at the Atlantis Massif and a possible petroleum reserve.*

Lisa began to get a pain in the pit of her stomach.

She looked up the last name on the list: Dr. Scott Ward. The results were the same as the others, more boring research papers and organizations, but one result caught her attention. An announcement from Cornell describing a joint venture between the Theory Center, where Ward worked, and Axcess Energy's exploration team and their work in the Mid-Atlantic.

That's Phil's department! Lisa remembered Phil's excitement as he described his trip to the Mid-Atlantic Ridge and how that excitement had translated into all the hours he was now pouring into the research project—with incredible results that could be dangerous to him, as she was more aware every second.

Lisa modified the search, this time adding the words "obituary" and "death" to Ward's name. No results came back.

Was this the remaining "one" the anonymous sticky note referred to? She had to talk to Phil about this.

Lisa logged out, stuffed the papers into a folder, and slid it into her backpack. On the way out of the office, she heard Rohm's monotone voice call out to her.

"Leaving so soon?"

"I have some errands to do, but I'll be working this afternoon. I'll have that list Audrey requested by tomorrow morning."

"Excellent," he said. "Are we all set for the meeting at the Four Seasons on Monday afternoon?"

"All set." Lisa surprised herself with her ability to cover her suspicions and distrust for the man she was talking to. Was she becoming like him?

"Great! Enjoy the rest of your weekend, Lisa." Rohm went back to reading his e-mail, and Lisa bolted out the door feeling like she needed a shower to cleanse herself from the slime that Rohm felt so at home in.

Chapter Twenty-Four
Dilemma

Lisa drove through the light weekend traffic, but her mind was not on the drive or the numerous minivans full of screaming kids and dads with five o'clock shadows that boxed her in from all sides. She was reeling with what she had just discovered: the grant, the list of researchers, the two obituaries describing violent deaths. They were disjointed facts, puzzle pieces without the box cover to show how they all fit together—but disturbing enough even without that.

Lisa bit her nails and tapped her left foot nervously.

She dialed Phil's cell number.

"Hey there, beautiful! How was work?"

Lisa ignored the platitude. "I—I found out something today at the office. There was a memo—"

"Lisa, slow down. Go slow, honey. What happened?"

She took a deep breath. "I found a memo in David Rohm's box. It's a grant, a research grant from the DOE, something to do with a petroleum anomaly in the Mid-Atlantic."

In his office, Phil switched the cell phone to his other ear and tried to focus on the conversation. It was unusual for Lisa not to make sense in a discussion. He was logical, but she raised logic from a science to a true art form.

"What kind of anomaly?"

"I don't know. I didn't really understand all the technical descriptions, but there was a list, Phil, a list of researchers who were working on this project. Phil, Jack was on the list."

A pregnant pause filled the space between Lisa and Phil as he processed her words. "Jack Sanders?"

"There were two other researchers on the list too. Some guy named Le Wu Ning from MIT and Scott Ward from Cornell. Do you know these guys?"

"Yeah, I work with Scott Ward. He's on the team out at Atlantis Massif. He was there when I went out two weeks ago. I met Le Wu Ning at a conference last year. He and I—"

Lisa cut him off mid-sentence. "He's dead."

"What?"

"Le Wu Ning is dead. I saw his obituary on the Web this morning. His car flew off a mountain pass in Colorado, and he was killed."

"When?"

"A few weeks before Jack."

Phil felt his legs go weak. He sat down in his office chair and stared across the room at the plotter's printout of the reserve.

"There's more, Phil. There was a sticky note on top of the grant, and it was scary. It said something like two of the three were gone and they were going to finish the list off."

"Gone? Are you saying that the same people who killed Jack killed Dr. Ning?"

"Maybe. I don't know," said Lisa.

"I have to warn Scott," said Phil. "Where are you?"

"I'm on 35, heading over the river. I'll be at my apartment in about an hour."

"Okay, I'll call you back. Don't talk to anyone. Let's sit on this until I understand what it all means."

Lisa wiped the tears from her eyes as she sped down the road. "Okay. I love you, Phil. Please be careful."

"I love you too, honey."

Phil got on the phone again right away, calling and calling again, leaving two messages on Ward's voice mail. His right leg jittered up and down as he called the third time and waited for Scott Ward to pick up his phone.

Where could he be?

■ ■ ■ ■

Scott Ward's cell phone buzzed incessantly, rattling and vibrating on the wraparound desk of the control room. Its chime was set to silent, but it was doing its best to inform its owner of the incoming call. The device's small color screen glowed white, illuminating the dark ambiance of the spherical room.

The phone was picked up off the desk, and the man looking at the number recognized the area code for Austin.

The thick steel hatch to the outside swung open, and the man ran up the steel stairs to the main deck.

He moved quickly to the back of the research ship and took another set of stairs to the lowest deck on the *Deep Pathfinder*. A small orange dinghy with an outboard motor was moored to the railing and bouncing in the waves, providing a challenging boarding. Another man, sitting at the back of the small craft, did the best he could to steady the bobbing boat and cast off from the moorings. The motor of the small boat fired up, and the dinghy swept around the bow of the large research ship, speeding toward the support vessel.

The cell phone began to vibrate again, and the man sitting in the front of the boat hurled it into the gray waves of the sea.

Chapter Twenty-Five
The Chimney

A hundred thousand miniature bubbles shimmered and morphed in the sunlight as the robotic arm of the *Deep Pathfinder* slowly lowered the manned submersible into the waves of the Atlantic. Scott Ward watched as the blue, sunlight-drenched water lapped against the five-inch-thick acrylic bubble. The shell allowed them three hundred and forty degrees of obstacle-free visibility and also protected the passengers from the crushing pressure of the ocean depths.

The ambient light that cocooned the two men seated in the vehicle began to noticeably darken as the waves covered the top of the bubble, marking the beginning of the long dive.

"Preparing to vent," said Dr. Chambers.

"Roger that," came a response from the *Pathfinder's* control room.

Chambers's fingers worked a series of switches and breakers, and a plume of bubbles streamed from the ballast tanks of the submersible as the vehicle began its long fall into the abyss.

A school of silver, iridescent fish swarmed around the sub as it descended. Scott Ward's thumb twitched on the joystick as he maneuvered the deep-sea submersible, Deep Rover 2, or DR-2 as the crew called it.

"It's just like a video game," grinned Ward, glancing at his copilot.

"Yeah, a really, really expensive video game," responded Dr. Chambers, clicking a few switches on the overhead control panel.

Green oxygen tanks were slung under the acrylic bubble, doubling as skids. Two large, black robotic arms jutted from the front of the craft, their grappling fingers wide open. A spotlight was positioned on a small articulating arm, connected to a yellow spine that housed the electronics for the smart little sub.

For over ninety minutes, the submersible dropped through the depths until a craggy, moonlike terrain of desolation appeared under the sub's floodlights. Here, far below the photic zone—the area where the light of the sun powers the critical process of photosynthesis—was something that seemed out of place. Life was here, and it was thriving.

The rocks of the ocean floor were covered with yellow mats of microbes, and sparse fronds of coral waved in the deep current as if welcoming the men to another world. Small particles of plant and other biological material finished their long fall like snowflakes from the surface, glittering briefly in the spotlight of DR-2 before being gulped by a whitefish perfectly camouflaged against the ocean floor. The fish swerved away from the sub at the last second, causing Ward to flinch.

The two men floated over the carbonate-covered ocean floor like an airplane following the terrain of the earth. The grade of the slope began to increase, and the populations of coral and microbes to diminish. The ocean floor was marbled with tendrils of minerals, glittering in the brilliance of the sub's floodlights.

As the submersible came over a small hill, a reminder that life was still present greeted Chambers and Ward. A crinoid, a delicate particle-feeder whose crown resembled a parasol, danced in the deep ocean current, constrained only by a single stalk that connected it to the underlying rock face.

Chambers pushed the joystick forward, and the rear thruster of the sub burst into activity, propelling the vehicle a little closer to the chimney—a black smoker. A swarm of shrimp flew in and out of the venting water and the billowing black smoke. Miniature embers, evidence of incomprehensibly hot geologic processes deep in the earth, flew up through the blast before being extinguished by the near-freezing water surrounding the superheated blowtorch.

The biomass surrounding the chimney was mesmerizing. Millions of shrimp clung to one another and crawled in and through the hot water. It was like the entire chimney was alive.

"That's amazing!" said Ward.

"Yeah, and it's also dangerous," said Chambers, checking the ambient temperature meter on the panel above him. "That vent is registering in at 750° F. We'd better get busy; we don't have time for sightseeing."

Chambers clicked a switch and spoke into his headset. "*Deep Pathfinder,* this is DR-2, come back."

A second of silence seemed to drag longer before the speakers in the sub came to life. "DR-2, we read you five-by-five."

"Tell Gorin we've reached the black smoker north of the vent field and are laying down the final grid of acoustic beacons now. We'll be done within the hour."

"Roger that, DR-2, but Gorin isn't on board." The captain's voice was muffled like he had marbles in his mouth.

"Are you eating another sandwich?" asked Scott, clicking the intercom.

"Um . . . no," came the reply between sandwich bites, barely intelligible. John Chambers rolled his eyes.

"Do you have any idea where Gorin might be?" asked Ward.

The topside pilot's voice sounded unsure. "I think I saw him taking a dinghy over to the support ship. I thought you knew he was going over there."

Chambers forced his voice to an even keel. "I have no idea what he's doing, but he should be monitoring our progress." Chambers contemplated going ballistic about the Russian's absence, but decided against it.

"Don't bother him," he said, biting his lip, "we'll get these laid down and be back up soon."

"Roger that, DR-2."

Chambers clicked off the transmission button. "What is Gorin thinking? This is extraordinarily expensive. He should be in the projection room helping us."

Ward said nothing as he watched the chimney continue its unabated venting, just as it had for hundreds of years.

■ ■ ■

Ping. Ping. Ping.

Roger Shubert, the skipper of the *Deep Pathfinder,* looked down at the sonar, which was now registering three contacts. The green, concentric circles of the instrument screen showed a blip to the southeast that he recognized as the supply ship, but the new clip was bearing 220—there was no one in that position that he knew about. He picked up a pair of binoculars, stepped over to the bay of windows, and looked out across the waves.

He squinted at a strange disturbance that most seafaring men wouldn't have noticed: a thin pole poking up through the rolling surface with a spray of sea foam ricocheting off it.

What the . . . a submarine? Here? He scratched his red beard and continued to study it.

Shubert picked up the radio and clicked on the intercom, but just as he was about to alert the crew to the presence of the uninvited guest, he saw three lines of bubbles fan across the surface of the waves between the periscope and his ship.

He recognized them instantly and hit a large red button on the console that sounded a collision siren throughout the ship.

A moment later, three explosions, one right after another, burst into the sky as the torpedoes slammed into the hull. The *Deep Pathfinder* trembled and jerked into the air as the torpedoes ripped open its hull. The skipper was blasted through the control room by the concussion wave, and he smashed into the far wall like a rag doll. Water poured into the hull, killing some crewmen and trapping others in watertight compartments as the vessel snapped into three ragged pieces and began to sink under the water.

Another line of bubbles passed over the research vessel's remains as they began their long fall to the bottom of the ocean, and more torpedoes slammed into the support ship. An orange mushroom cloud erupted, and the bow of the ship tilted high in the air as it sank and followed its sister to the bottom of the Atlantic.

The sea foam bubbling around the periscope settled down as the submarine disappeared from view.

■ ■ ■

Three miles below the descending remains of the *Deep Pathfinder*, the telemetry screens on Deep Rover 2 went blank, and red warning lights began to appear on the overhead console.

"That's impossible," said Ward. "We just lost all the topside feeds."

Frowning, Chambers reset the breakers and reinitialized the sub's computer.

Nothing.

As the two men struggled to diagnose what was wrong, a small black box connected to the underside of the propulsion unit of DR-2 exploded with a muffled sound. It was a small charge, just enough to destroy the steering ability of the submersible.

The floodlights on the front of the sub went out. Total darkness enveloped the men in the sub. Deep Rover 2 began to list in the deep current, turning onto its side and heading downward toward the ocean floor.

Ward tried to counteract the motion by moving the control joystick, but nothing happened.

Then the sound of a million air bubbles glancing off of the acrylic protector filled their ears.

The chimney!

The hiss of melting acrylic against the superheated venting gases began to get louder and louder.

In the dark, with the inevitable just moments away, Ward's voice broke the darkness. "Well, at least it will be fast, my friend."

Ward reached out and touched Chambers on the shoulder. "John, it's been an honor working with you." His voice was shaking, but full of sincerity.

"Likewise," said Chambers.

The bubble began to shriek and crack as the water pressure pushed against it and probed for weaknesses. The hiss became so loud that Ward barely heard the last words from Chambers.

"Good-bye, Scott."

A moment later the protective bubble could no longer hold the outside titan from invading, and the acrylic and aluminum portions of the submersible melded with human tissue and bone, crushing both into the size of a softball at the bottom of the Atlantic.

Chapter Twenty-Six
Eavesdropper

Lisa nervously smoothed the lapel of her jacket and double-checked her shoes, making sure they were shined and reflected the environment with perfection. The flags in the courtyard of the Four Seasons snapped in the slight breeze. Lisa looked behind her at the glass, steel, and concrete climbing into the sky. This was the right spot for the meeting. It was easily the most opulent hotel in center-city Austin.

"We're all set, right?"

Lisa didn't have to turn around. David Rohm's voice was unmistakable, with a tone that was at once threatening and reassuring. Such was the duplicity that her boss enjoyed wielding over her.

Lisa ignored the threat as she always did. She was confident in her work and her methods. "All set; everything's ready. I've double-checked everything."

Rohm's cell rang, and after a very brief, one-sided conversation, he turned and smiled at Lisa. "They're here."

A convoy of black Suburbans pulled into the hotel's courtyard, and men with dark sunglasses and serious expressions took positions up and down the sidewalk. There were no bellmen, gardeners, or anyone else who would normally be seen around the outside of a hotel. The governor had reserved the entire building.

A moment later, a Mercedes-Benz with tinted windows pulled around. The security detail did one last check of the environment and then pulled the passenger doors open. Two men stepped out, dressed impeccably in dark suits. One was Hui-Ben Hong from the Chinese government's Ministry of Energy; the other was Sven Gorsky, the arrogant Russian oil baron from Siberia.

Lisa and Rohm greeted the men and guided them into the hotel lobby. The men's shoes clacked on the rare marble floor as they headed for the elevators.

The trip to the top floor was awkward, with few pleasantries. The language and accent barriers were landmines. The elevator dinged, and the polished brass doors slid open, exposing a large room with windows all around. Wainscoting accented the walls, and a massive conference table dominated the center of the room.

Senator Camran, Governor Wyngate, and Glenn Martin, fresh from the Axcess press conference a few days before, had all arrived earlier. They rose from their seats, greeting the foreign dignitaries. Lisa stepped onto her tiptoes and saw a man with an olive complexion wearing a full dress military uniform. She shifted behind the security detail and barely made out stars on his shoulder.

Who in the world is that?

Lisa ran through the attendee list—a list she had memorized—but she came up blank on this man. Certainly no one from any military organization was on the list. Her stomach sank—not that she hadn't been expecting something strange after her discovery in Rohm's office. Now she wondered if she even knew what this meeting was all about.

The meeting had been arranged hastily, and she knew only a few of the specifics. It had something to do with engineering and work contacts, Axcess Energy's newly announced joint venture, and the governor, whom she assumed would take credit for arranging the whole thing. Rohm had guarded the agenda carefully, delegating only a few things to her—securing the location, the meals and dietary restrictions, security details—the basic things a venue like this required.

Lisa was about to ask Rohm where he wanted her to sit in the meeting, but as if he sensed her anticipation and hope for some of the credit for pulling the meeting together in record time, he met her eyes first. His face was cold and hard, showing zero emotion.

"You won't be needed here today," he said flatly.

"You don't want me in there?" asked Lisa. The governor had always let her sit in on meetings, especially those dealing with commerce. It was her job, for crying out loud.

Rohm refused to get into a debate. "We're not going to talk about it right now. Just take your laptop into one of the conference rooms, do e-mail, and prep for next week's staff meeting."

Lisa was fuming, but somehow she found the strength to camouflage her anger as she grabbed her computer bag and handbag and headed for the nearest anteroom twenty feet away.

Her hands trembled as she booted up her laptop.

How can I get into that meeting? I know something is wrong here. I have to find out more about Rohm and his intentions.

As she was typing in her password, one of the female hotel staff wheeled a large rolling table up to the wooden door of the conference room and adjusted the plates of breakfast foods. The silver plates clinked and rang as she arranged muffins, croissants, and pastries. The spread even included hot blueberry compote for topping waffles and French toast.

Lisa watched the lady struggle to light a Sterno fuel cell under the fruit compote three times. The canister remained unlit, and the woman muttered something in Spanish under her breath and walked away with the malfunctioning food warmer.

Two security guards came out of the room. "I'm going to check the bathrooms and the hall." The one in charge glanced at the breakfast cart. "Make sure you check that thing out before it goes in there."

The men separated. Lisa watched the remaining security officer lift up the linen sheet and look under the cart. There was a metal shelf—completely empty—that ran the length of the breakfast cart. The security guard dropped the covering, and it settled back over the height of the cart, concealing the metal frame and shelf.

The door reopened, and another security guard asked the cart checker to come inside.

The hall was empty, but Lisa was sure it wouldn't remain that way for long. She slipped off her dress flats, stuffed them into her already bulging computer bag, stepped to the threshold of the anteroom door, and looked down the hallway. It was empty in all directions. She moved to the breakfast cart, her heart beating a million times a minute.

Standing there in the hallway in her stocking feet, she felt the moment come. She had to make up her mind.

Lisa, what are you doing?

She hiked up her skirt to mid-thigh and awkwardly crawled under the rolling table and lay down on her right side on the shelf. She barely fit, but her whole body was cradled and suspended about four inches from the ground. She looked around the grimy undercarriage of the breakfast table and hoped she wouldn't ruin her skirt or blouse. *Ha*, she thought. The condition of her clothing was the least of her worries now.

Her pocket rattled with an e-mail reminder emanating from her cell phone.

Oh, man. I'd better turn this thing off. She had a vision of someone lifting the linen during the meeting because of a rambunctious ringtone coming from the muffins.

As Lisa set the phone to silent, a set of shoes appeared in front of her, scuffed but feminine. The hotel lady had returned. She heard clinking above her as the hostess replaced the canister, and a few moments later, the unmistakable smell of burning fuel filled the hallway. Lisa watched the shoes glide up and down along the sheet as the woman prepped the breakfast cart. She wondered if the woman would look under the linen for any reason and what in the world Lisa would say to her if she did.

The wooden doors to the conference room swung open, and the hotel lady pushed the table loaded with breakfast into the room. Lisa watched the carpet change from the high-traffic hallway pattern to the more expensive style of the conference room. The ambiance changed from the quiet of the hallway to a high-powered, stress-filled environment where trust was scarce.

"Feel free to get something for breakfast, and then we'll get started." Lisa recognized the governor's voice, and she heard people pushing back their chairs from the table.

A parade of shoes marched by Lisa, and the clinking and thumping on the table above her was disconcerting. A particularly shiny pair of black wingtips strode by, and Lisa picked them out as belonging to David Rohm.

The noises above her stopped as the men made it back to the table with their breakfast. The security guards closed the wooden doors, and the meeting began.

Lisa licked her lips anxiously as she heard Rohm's voice welcome the visiting dignitaries.

"You have all heard the announcement that Mr. Martin made at Axcess Energy a few days ago. You can think of that meeting as—shall we say—the cover story. This meeting is about what we really need to do to succeed in our plans."

Well, that's an ominous way to start a meeting. The knot in her stomach tightened. She was right: something was very wrong here.

Glenn Martin's voice came next. "The key to this plan is to secure the endpoint of the pipeline inside of Syria with access to Israeli roads and infrastructure. Once we have that point established, we can control energy prices and supply to the Israelis and even into Africa."

The Russian oil baron spoke up, his accent thick and hard to decipher. "We have general agreement from Syria. The terms of the agreement are . . ." The Russian worked through both languages to match up the word that best described his intent. "Sensitive."

The Syrian general cleared his voice. "The package we require is necessary for our future plans. These plans do not include an Israeli state—with the delivery of this term of the agreement, you will have your endpoint."

Lisa struggled to follow the conversation. *Endpoints? Packages? Why the vagueness around a natural-gas pipeline?*

"Exactly how will the package reach our country?" asked the Syrian general.

Governor Wyngate's suave voice rolled across the room. "David Rohm here has been working on this for over eight months. As you know, I formed a small company twenty years ago that designs and manufactures some pretty amazing things."

A chuckle rattled around the room at Martin's less-than-humble description of a ten-billion-dollar-a-year defense contractor.

Wyngate Corporation is the originator of the package? Wait a minute here . . .

Hui-Ben Hong, the Chinese industrial minister, finished Lisa's thought. "Syria is under serious economic sanctions right now, and failure to conceal this shipment could ignite an international investigation and perhaps even lead to indictments of everyone seated around this table. What fail-safes do you have in place for protecting all of us?"

Hong's English was incredible—very little hint of accent. He was the most articulate of the whole group.

Glenn Martin answered, "Senator Camran is on the Armed Services Committee and has the connections for us to get this shipment through customs on both sides. He can firewall all of us in the meantime."

Lisa thought back, working the pieces together. Senator Camran received endorsements and huge support from the governor's office. David Rohm was always working with the unions and other labor organizations to gain support for both men.

Even though she had only been working with Rohm for less than a year, she knew it wasn't the elected person sitting in the chair, but the apparatus—the connections—behind the scenes that really made policy. Rohm was a career politician, but not the one in the limelight. He was the real power, the man behind the curtain who made the puppet look alive to the simpletons watching the show.

Camran spoke up, and his confidence backed up every word like a levee. "We will use an outsourced security firm that augments our armed forces from time to time to guarantee safety of passage and completely firewall the operation from the United States."

"I hope for all of our sakes that your abilities are exactly what you say they are," came Hong's barely accented response. Lisa pushed up on her forearms and shifted her body to a new position. The steel shelf was uncomfortable, and her body ached.

"The Chinese government has another concern," said Hong. "Israel is now an oil nation with Parezim Petroleum's highly publicized discovery. If this small company continues to make inroads into the marketplace, it will eventually remove the need for your pipeline to deliver gas and oil."

Rohm laughed and waved dismissively. "I wouldn't worry about Parezim. They're zealots—fanatics. They don't—"

Hong interrupted the arrogant secretary of commerce. "Mr. Rohm, I'm not talking about Parezim so much as I am their benefactor. Their charter, indeed, their agreement with the nation of Israel, is that the Jews get a vast percentage of any petroleum discovered. If Israel becomes a power player in the Middle East, with the leverage of oil and the backing of the United States, they can export this energy—just as they attempt to export democracy throughout the region. This will be incredibly destabilizing for many of us around the table."

Rohm attempted to recover some dignity after Hong's rant. "We are already discrediting them. We are using their small size and their poor safety record against them. It won't be long before regulators are crawling all over their rigs and burying them in a blizzard of paperwork. They won't be able to fight a legal war and an exploration war. We will never let them commercialize their find."

Glenn Martin put his palms on the surface of the large table. "Rohm is heading to Turkey tonight with General Alhajal to conclude the negotiations around the package they are requesting."

Under the table, Lisa could barely hold herself still. *He's heading to Turkey—just like Sheridan said in the ladies room.* The pieces clicked together, the picture becoming clear. *It's an arms deal for a business move.*

The meeting broke up, and Lisa heard the large doors creak open to the hallway. Good-byes and pleasantries in multiple languages faded as the room emptied out.

Lisa waited another moment and then lifted the linen and peeked beneath it across the carpet of the conference room. No one was there. She crawled out from underneath the table and stood up, smoothing out her skirt and blouse.

Suddenly, she heard a bustle of noise coming from the hallway. She thought about climbing underneath the table again, but it was too late. There was no way out. A group of security guards came in, with Rohm right behind them.

Lisa looked down at the breakfast table and picked up a plate. She placed a cold slice of French toast on the china and added a few berries.

"Where have you been?" asked Rohm.

Lisa ignored his rudeness and continued adding to the plate. "Around." It wasn't a lie.

Rohm looked down at her feet and frowned. "Get your shoes on. We have a lot of work to do."

He turned and left the room, and Lisa's hand trembled as she set the china down.

Chapter Twenty-Seven
Weapons Demo

D avid Rohm yawned and sipped the tepid water from a canteen, wetting his lips as he looked out across the bleak terrain of Ankara, Turkey. The day before, he had been in the nicest hotel in Austin, and now his wingtips were coated with dust and scratched from tumbleweeds and rocks. He watched a dozen Syrian servicemen standing around a stolen Israeli radar station. The radar was originally designed by the United States for dealing with the Soviets in the Cold War, but the Israelis had improved the design, making it even more effective at spotting threats headed toward their small nation.

He took another swig of water and stepped out of the truck, adjusting his sunglasses. The scrub bushes and rocky hillsides reflected in the dark lenses.

"The Israeli Defense Force has hundreds of these radars across their country," said General Baltasar Alhajal. "When they combine this tool with their Arrow and Patriot missile batteries, they create a shield that makes their airspace literally impenetrable. Without neutralizing their air force and radar net, it would be suicide to attack the Jews."

A jet roared overhead, high in the azure sky. The general picked up a pair of binoculars and looked upward at the tip of the contrail forming across the sky.

"The Arab nations of the world cannot afford to do battle with the Jews. They are too well trained, too well equipped." The general lowered the high-powered binoculars. "Need I remind you, Mr. Rohm, that they are trained and equipped by *your* nation? So you'll forgive me if I'm a bit skeptical about whatever weapon you are planning to show me."

Rohm smiled at the man. "Relax, General. The weapon I'm about to show you will tilt the balance in your favor."

"Your confidence and arrogance concern me," said the general. "How are you able to elude the very people your government has in place to keep weapons like this out of our hands?"

Rohm didn't like this man and was sure that the feeling was mutual, but he submerged his considerable ego beneath the waves of his even larger ambitions. "General, some things are better left unknown. Suffice it to say that I work for a very powerful, very influential man. We can make almost anything possible."

"You speak of the governor of Texas?" asked the general.

"Among others," replied Rohm.

"Let's hope he is as shrewd and wise as a cobra, Mr. Rohm, for both of your sakes."

Another man, standing next to Rohm and dressed in the garb of a modern mercenary, received a message on his satellite phone. *Rhino Eight is en route.*

"Mr. Rohm, the music's about to start," he said.

Rohm nodded. "General, watch carefully. Your deliverance is at hand."

The mercenary gave the command. "You may commence your run, Rhino Eight."

The Syrian general raised the binoculars to his brow and adjusted the focus to wide angle.

■ ■ ■ ■

Thirty thousand feet above the high-desert terrain of Turkey, a lone F-18 Super Hornet cruised along at five hundred miles per hour. The pilot pushed the stick forward slightly, and the fly-by-wire system translated his expert, minute movements into electrical signals, causing the elevators on the fighter-bomber's wings to angle down slightly. The aircraft began to dive.

The plane broke through the cloud cover. The mountainous terrain north of Ankara lay before the pilot. To his left and in the far distance, he could see the dark waters of the Black Sea, dotted with white caps. The pilot turned from the panoramic view to the instrument panel in front of him and flipped a switch to the "on" position. A small display just above the switch began to feed back information.

AGM-136 INITIALIZED . . .
WEAPON ARMED.
WEAPON SEARCHING FOR GPS SATELLITES . . .
SATELLITES ACQUIRED.
SEARCHING FOR TARGET COORDINATES . . .
TARGET ACQUIRED.
WEAPON READY FOR RELEASE.

"Coming down," the pilot radioed to the mercenary on the ground. He pressed a button on the side of the control yoke while simultaneously pressing a trigger, and a large cylindrical pod slung under the belly of the Super Hornet was released from the craft and began to fall to earth.

The jet fighter, now free of hundreds of pounds of weaponry, streaked back into the blue sky and disappeared from view, leaving only a sonic boom in its wake.

The weapon wobbled at first as it left the jet, but a small rudder and stabilizing fins automatically expanded from its tail, and a thin wing snapped out from under the craft's fuselage in a scissor-like motion at its midsection.

The weapon didn't look like a missile—it looked more like a miniature airplane, eight feet long, with a snub nose and a jet intake hood running along its spine. An explosive charge inside of the weapon's airframe fired and kick-started a super-efficient turbine engine.

The device began to measure its position and its altitude, comparing these attributes with the target's location. The fins on the tail moved almost imperceptibly, adjusting the flight path of the weapon. The weapon made a tight turn and headed downward toward the fast-approaching rugged terrain.

■ ■ ■ ■

"Go ahead and turn on the radar for a moment," said the mercenary to the Syrian general. Alhajal simply nodded the order to his men, who were standing at his side. They typed a few commands on a laptop, and the radar-station antennas made a quick revolution. A soldier typed another command, and the radar went silent.

Rohm cleared his throat. "A typical anti-radiation missile looks for the radiation energy emanating from radar, and then the missile simply heads toward that location—but if the radar's off, then there's nothing to lock on to. The Israelis are experts at tuning their training to this vulnerability. They can turn on the radar, measure threats, and then relocate the radar while it's off to a safe location and repeat the procedure."

"This is not a new trick, Mr. Rohm," said Alhajal. "They are simply exploiting the fact that any missile can only burn fuel for a few seconds and can't change its trajectory after a certain point. We know all about this."

"You don't know about this," said Rohm. The general scowled.

The weapon screamed by overhead. General Alhajal ducked and then watched as it flew toward the radar and turned and banked away toward a mountain range to their north.

"It's called the Tacit Rainbow," said Rohm. "It's a combination of a cruise missile and an anti-radiation missile. Unlike the average missile, it doesn't fly for mere seconds, but up to twenty minutes over a preprogrammed route. It waits and it loiters for a radar station to come online."

The Syrian general watched the smart weapon fly a racetrack pattern across the Turkish sky, patrolling the area like an overzealous police officer. Its engine droned as it autonomously followed the terrain.

"Go ahead and turn the radar back on to see how good it is at its job," said Rohm.

■ ■ ■ ■

The Tacit Rainbow's internal sensors examined the landscape, adjusting its flight characteristics and continuing its flight path—hunting—seeking—untiring in its mission.

The craft immediately detected the stolen Israeli radar being turned back on and plotted the shortest flight path toward it. The weapon pulled up into a high G-turn and banked to the left until it was facing the radar. Its small elevators and flaps flicked precisely until it was perfectly lined up with the radar station.

Its engine increased to maximum speed, and it slammed into its target. An orange fireball exploded from the radar station, sending metal fragments flinging through the air. A black cloud formed and rose into the air.

There was nothing left of the radar station or the Tacit Rainbow.

■ ■ ■ ■

General Baltasar Alhajal stared at the flaming debris. David Rohm watched his Syrian business partner like a hawk, and a smile crept across his face as he saw that the high-tech demonstration had made its point.

The general continued to stare at the burning wreckage of the radar without saying a word. He was either amazed by the technology or was mentally doing arithmetic.

"I'll take it by your silence that we have a deal," said Rohm, glancing at the mercenary, who was smirking at the general's silence.

"Eighty of them; we will need eighty of these weapons," stuttered Alhajal. "You may bring your natural-gas pipeline to Damascus, but only if we get these weapons."

A feeling of success wrapped itself around Rohm like a warm blanket. "We will launder the weapons through Russia, and you can buy them through your normal channels. What you choose to do with them is your own business. Do we have a deal?"

Alhajal shook Rohm's hand and uttered a blessing for him.

Rohm stepped into the truck to head back to the airport and fired off a text message to the governor. *The deal is struck. Now we need to clean up the loose ends.*

Chapter Twenty-Eight
Assassins

Phil watched the blue progress line march across his display as the data backup proceeded. A chime sounded, and a digital tape ejected itself from the backup device. Phil grabbed a padded FedEx envelope from a stack on his desk and slipped the backup tape inside. He zipped the wax-paper backing off the sticky adhesive flap and sealed the package.

Phil ran his hands through his hair and looked at his watch: 2:15 a.m. He had sent numerous e-mails to the team at Atlantis Massif, but no responses had come back. He was worried for Ward and Chambers, especially after the call from Lisa.

He sent another text message to Ward's phone as concern whirled around him like a blizzard. Still no answer. They were probably just busy. He hoped. *I've had it—enough of this.*

He logged out and grabbed his backpack, heading for the elevator with the FedEx envelope tucked under his right arm.

When the elevator reached the lobby, Phil bounded through the check-point and past the security guard, Daniel O'Connell, a freckle-faced redhead and recent high-school grad who couldn't be more Irish if he tried. Everyone called him Danny, and he didn't seem to mind.

Danny looked at the clock on the wall from behind the sports section. "Working half days again, huh?" he asked with a smirk.

Phil laughed groggily and headed out the front door. It was an old joke.

The parking lot was empty and wet from a rare rainstorm. Phil had heard from someone in the cafeteria that it had occurred in the late afternoon.

That's really pathetic, he thought. *I have to get local weather reports from fellow employees because I work in the dungeon. Not to mention that I'm heads-down on this project.*

Phil trudged down the sidewalk to the FedEx mailbox on the corner and deposited the data tape, bound for the archive service that stored all the company's documents and data.

The only cars in the lot were those belonging to the night cleanup crew, Danny's hot red Mustang, and Phil's piece of junk. The overhead parking lot lights fired down cones of light onto the dark, wet asphalt. Swarms of insects clouded around the lights while particles of humidity and mist mixed together in a low fog that rolled across the asphalt, which was cooling off from the summer heat.

Finally, after half a mile, Phil reached the beater. When he had arrived at 9:00 yesterday morning, he had parked in the only vacant spot in the lot. Now the spot just seemed ridiculously far away and random. He fished his keys out of his pocket and unlocked the door, pulling it open with a squeak that would wake the dead. Even with no one around, he was embarrassed by the rusty college car.

I have got to get a new car! he thought.

He climbed inside and pushed his backpack onto the passenger seat. He pulled his seat belt around and buckled it, feeling it tighten uncomfortably around his torso. Turning back to the steering column, he fumbled drowsily and dropped the keys onto the floor. Phil sighed and bent down, fishing blindly across the floor mat for the keys. His fingers passed across an old coffee cup, a crinkly Pop-Tart wrapper, and something sticky. His fingers formed up around the object: rectangular, with a smooth surface.

Oh, a Jolly Rancher—disgusting!

He felt further back, groping until his fingertips found the cold metal of the key ring. *Eureka!*

The tight seat belt constrained him from getting the keys. Phil sat back up and pulled the nylon strap. The cincher released some slack, and Phil ducked back down, grabbing the keys.

Plink!

A waterfall of glass shards spilled over the cracked dashboard and scattered on the floor mat like diamonds. Phil pulled his head back up, more from reflex than from curiosity. The windshield was spiderwebbed with cracks, and a bullet hole the size of a quarter stared him straight in the face.

Confusion reigned for what seemed like minutes but in reality was only a fraction of a second. Shaking, Phil pushed the key into the ignition and fired up the car. Peering over the dashboard, he saw a muzzle flash.

Plink!

Another bullet hole decorated the passenger's side with cracks and a matching hole, and the headrest exploded in a cloud of maroon upholstery. The fabric particles floated momentarily in the air of the car like a ripe dandelion releasing its seeds in the summer heat.

Phil floored it.

The college car squealed its tires on the asphalt and took off, fishtailing on the wet pavement. Phil pulled the car into a tight right turn and aimed for the lobby of Axcess.

More bullets sparked off the black pavement, and the left rearview mirror exploded in a hail of glass and plastic. Phil scrunched down in the seat and looked in the rearview mirror on the passenger's side. A black SUV swerved from a dark recess in the shadows and approached at breakneck speed from behind, its halogen headlights beaming furiously through the cabin of Phil's clunker.

The motor from Phil's car was screaming so loudly in Phil's ears that he didn't hear the back window explode as another shot was fired.

Phil's foot mashed harder on the accelerator, taking it completely to the floor. He looked back from the shattered rearview mirror to see a steel light post directly in front of him. He pulled the steering wheel to the right. The car screeched and shuddered, swerving and missing the post by inches.

The SUV didn't make the move fast enough. The driver's view was obscured by bright headlights reflecting from the humid clouds of mist. The SUV slammed into the pole at eighty miles per hour, shearing the pole off from its base and bending to the ground. The light support rolled under the chassis, and the SUV pitched onto its side and rolled across the pavement. Fiberglass, carbon fiber, and composite plastic parts flew into the air as the vehicle rolled over and over into a ball of twisted debris. The assassin opposite the driver was ejected through the passenger window and slid to a grisly stop a hundred feet from the mashed hulk.

Phil reached the lobby entrance and shifted his foot to the brake pedal, pushing down with all his strength. The car slid as it drifted to a reckless stop in the courtyard, trailing a pair of black burnt-rubber marks on the pavement. Phil jumped from the beater and ran through the rotating glass door.

Danny ran toward the center of the lobby with his hand on his gun. "Phil! What's going on?"

"Run!" Phil gasped.

The security guard froze. "Why? What's going on?"

Phil looked behind him and saw the front headlights of another car.

"Get down!" he screamed at Danny, throwing himself flat on the marble expanse.

The glass door behind Phil exploded as more bullets were fired into the lobby.

When he looked up, Danny had fallen to his knees, staring straight ahead with a gaping red hole in his forehead. He fell on his face. His head hit the stone floor with a sickening thud.

Phil scrambled to his feet and bailed over the security checkpoint as another burst of gunfire riddled the lobby with bullet holes. Fragments of wood splintered from the guard station and began to shower around him. Phil crouched down and ran for the hallway ahead. As he made it to the elevator shaft, he looked over his left shoulder into the remains of the lobby. Two men were heading into the lobby dressed in black—complete with ski masks to hide their features.

As he ran past the elevator, Phil pressed the "up" button and hit the door for the stairway without pause. The door swung open and banged into the wall as Phil bounded down the stairs two and three at a time, swinging over the rail and landing on the next stairwell halfway down.

When he reached B2, he ran past the elevator to the door of his department. The elevator motor droned in the background. Phil watched the floor indicator change.

L . . .

B1 . . .

They're coming down to this floor!

Phil glanced around the dingy hallway. There was nothing he could use as a weapon. The only thing he could do was keep running, keep evading.

Think, Phil. Think.

Phil swiped his badge on the door, pulled it open as wide as the self-closing pneumatic arm would allow, and then released it, retreating back into the dark hallway past the elevator and into the janitor's alcove.

The noise of the motor in the elevator shaft stopped, and a ding rang out into the darkened hallway. Phil pressed up against the cinder-block wall and listened as keenly as he could. The fluorescent lights buzzed overhead, masking the noises in the hallway.

Are there one or two of them?

In his head, he could still hear the gunshots and see Danny being cut down right in front of him. He swallowed, feeling sweat drip down his face.

It won't matter; I'm dead any way you look at it.

He heard scuffles on the floor as the assassin's shoes moved over the dusty cement. Another ding rang out into the hall, and the door on the elevator slid shut. Phil could hear the motor through the wall to his back and feel the vibration of the shaft. They must have split up.

Just as the elevator started back up, Phil heard the door close and latch. The scuffing on the floor continued. The assassin had not taken the bait. He was still in the hallway, locked out of the only room on the floor.

Phil heard another card swipe at the lock. The latched clicked, and he heard the door swing back open.

These guys have access to the building!

The door latched behind the assassin as he headed into the room. Silence hung in the hallway like a cloud; only the buzzing overhead broke the quiet.

Phil looked around him for a weapon—anything would do. He willed the outline of a gun to magically appear. Instead, only a dozen flattened boxes stood against the far wall from him, the results of his cleaning exercise the week before. A broken floor scrubber that had to weigh a ton and a red hand truck were the only other items he could see.

The hand truck!

Phil looked at the handrail at the top of the hand truck: its height was configurable. A steel pin on either side was secured with a cotter pin. He squatted down and pulled the stubborn cotter pins free as quietly as possible, lifting the top of the steel rail free of the base. It looked like a giant U.

Phil gripped each side firmly as he slowly peered from his hiding place into the hallway.

No one was there.

Phil crept up to the department door; he could hear the man's footsteps inside the room. Phil glanced up at the elevator's floor indicator. A bright digital "2" was lit up. Suddenly, it changed to a "3" and kept going. The other assassin was going to the top floor.

The department door clicked. Phil pushed his back against the wall, getting as close to the hinges of the door as he could. The door opened, and Phil swung the rail with every ounce of strength he had. The attacker's mask-covered face stopped the blow, but not before the crunching sound of shattering teeth filled the air.

The assassin slumped to the floor, dropping his gun. It bounced on the concrete floor.

Phil started at him, heart pounding. *Did I kill him, or is he just unconscious?* He wanted to care, but he sure wasn't going to hang around and find out if the man liked walks along the beach at sunset when he came to.

He dropped the hand-truck railing to the ground and pulled the man's ski mask off. He was Caucasian with long, unruly blond hair and high cheekbones—very Eastern European in appearance, with one notable exception: his mouth. The man's lips were curled up in a sickening smile, bleeding and dusted with shattered tooth fragments. They were already puffing up from the close encounter with Phil's ad hoc weapon.

Phil's mind took an imprint of the man, a picture he was sure he would regret for the rest of his life. He reached down and pressed his fingers into the man's neck to feel for a pulse.

Nothing.

He's gone.

Phil picked up the man's pistol and held it clumsily: a black Glock with a long silencer screwed onto the muzzle. An accessory rail ran beneath the barrel and held a laser sight with a miniature flashlight.

These guys are professionals.

He checked the man's clothing and found another loaded magazine.

Phil stepped back into the stairwell and looked up through the steel railings all the way to the top, listening for anyone in the shaft. Hearing nothing, he ran up two flights to the lobby as quietly as possible.

Phil carefully pushed the door of the lobby level open and stepped out from the steel floor of the stairwell into the corporate lobby. Shattered glass littered the floor, and Danny's body lay facedown in the center of the large room. A crimson pool radiated out from his body and reflected the overhead lights.

Behind him, Phil heard the elevator ding. He sprinted for the revolving front door, or the remains of what used to be the portal to the lobby. As he passed through, he heard footsteps and gunshots. Glass exploded into the courtyard. Phil didn't look back; he just ran past the assassin's Town Car, past his own bullet-ridden car, into the wet parking lot, sprinting for all he was worth.

As Phil pumped his arms and ran across the lot, the sound of his footsteps was gobbled up by another sound. A black helicopter with a shrouded tail rotor descended sixty feet ahead of him. Its rotor wash blasted the sand and rain into a miniature tornado of mist and grit.

Phil's will to flee died.

Game over. He was dead.

The chopper rotated so that its right side faced Phil. The back doors of the sleek, teardrop-shaped cabin were removed, and Phil could see a man with a rifle aiming right at him. The red laser beam of the sniper's sight flashed onto Phil's chest and then moved up over his torso and finally over his head.

Phil saw the muzzle flash and clinched his eyes, expecting to feel the round hit his body. A fraction of a second later he opened one eye, followed by the other. He looked behind him. The assassin who had chased him through the lobby and across the parking lot was face down on the pavement, his gun still in his hand.

Phil looked back at the helicopter where the sniper was waving at him to get into the cockpit. Phil hesitated.

"Get in! We are not here to hurt you," came a quick burst from a loud-speaker. The accent was not American.

When Phil climbed up on the helicopter's metal skid, Caleb Mosha reached a hand out and helped him into the streamlined cabin.

"Caleb?" Phil climbed into the helicopter and yelled over the helicopter's deafening turbine. "What are you doing here?"

Caleb was dressed in all black, and he had a sleek headset attached to his ear. He patted Phil on the arm. "Well, what I told you was true. I do work for the Israeli government. I work for the Mossad."

The helicopter gained altitude and banked away. Phil could feel his heart hammering in his ears as he watched his car, the destruction in the parking lot, and the shattered lobby of Axcess Energy disappear from sight.

Assassins. Mossad. What have I gotten myself into?

Chapter Twenty-Nine
Clarity of Morning

The pink traces of dawn began to dissipate in the clear morning sky as Glenn Martin's black limousine pulled to the sidewalk outside of Axcess Energy's lobby. The driver got as close as he could before a swarm of uniformed policeman approached the car; each holding his hand out, telling the driver to stop.

Martin opened the back door himself, preempting the usual wait for the driver to do his lowly but status-providing job. As he stepped out onto the asphalt, his expensive shoes crunched on the glass shards that were sprayed all over the parking lot.

The parking lot was cordoned off with yellow police tape, which echoed the seriousness of its presence: CRIME SCENE—DO NOT CROSS. A dozen black-and-white police units were positioned all around the perimeter of the tape, and an ambulance was right in the middle of the action.

Rose Stanton, the Director of Human Resources, was waiting for Martin. She was standing next to a man who looked like he had rolled out of bed and come to the crime scene.

"What happened here?" asked Martin, approaching his HR director.

"Homicides—the plural form of the word," said the man in the rumpled clothes. "Four of them, to be exact. I'm Detective Mark Rizzo."

The detective had stubble that only amplified his Italian features, which included a thick black mustache, bushy eyebrows, and curly black hair—all mussed slightly. A toothpick was jammed in his mouth.

Martin grudgingly shook his hand.

The CEO watched as two coroners pushed a gurney containing a black body bag toward the ambulance. The area around the ambulance was covered with small numbered placards and a chalk outline of where the victim had fallen.

"Were any Axcess employees hurt?" asked the CEO.

Mark Rizzo studied the executive. Martin seemed concerned, but in a cold, clinical way. "A security guard," Rizzo said, flipping through his notes. He scanned his chicken scratch for the details of the fallen man. "A Mr. Danny O'Connell, nineteen years old."

Rose Stanton corrected the detective. "He's an Allied-Benton employee. We outsource security to them. He's not an Axcess employee. We haven't found any bodies belonging to our employees."

Martin let out a sigh of relief. "At least there's some good news here."

Rizzo raised his bushy eyebrows and scratched a note down in his notebook. *Cold and ambivalent—not a good set of qualities for an executive or an employer.*

"And these other men . . . you said there were three others?" asked Martin. The detective nodded with only his toothpick, an action that clearly annoyed the executive. "What do we know about them?"

"Not much; no identification was found on them. They have Eastern European physical traits, but that doesn't mean they aren't U.S. citizens. The guns we found on each of them were a little out of the ordinary for a typical robbery. We found a Scorpion—that's an assault rifle—and a pistol: a Glock, a favorite of terrorists everywhere."

The CEO's stoic face broke. "Terrorists? Now wait just a second here . . ."

Rizzo shifted the toothpick to the other side of his mouth. "Mr. Martin, these are the weapons of professional assassins. Do you have any idea why killers of this skill would be hanging out at the headquarters of an energy company?"

The chief executive looked past the detective as if his questions were an annoyance. "I don't have the first clue, Detective. That's why you're here—isn't it?"

"It certainly is," said Rizzo. "I just thought you might also have some curiosity in the matter."

"I don't like your tone," said Martin.

The detective ignored the CEO and began to walk across the parking lot toward a car that was riddled with bullets. It was an older car, much older. Its left rear tire was flat, punctured with multiple bullet holes. The back window was blown out, and the driver's door was wide open.

Martin followed along and pointed at the destroyed vehicle. "What do we know about this car?"

"We checked the license with your security department," said Rizzo. "You know—the one you outsourced?"

Martin ignored the sarcasm; he didn't expect this officer to understand the pressures of a business to reduce its expenses wherever possible. Security was not a core business concern for Axcess.

A smile broke through Rizzo's bushy mustache. His remark had hit a nerve. "It belongs to Philip Channing, one of your employees."

Martin turned to Rose Stanton, who chimed in. "He's a new employee who just started two weeks ago. I personally gave him his orientation. He was such a nice young man."

"No sign of his body?" asked Martin.

"Nope, but we have a lot of good surveillance video of him giving these guys a run for their money."

"The gunmen were after Channing?" Martin asked.

The detective nodded. "See all these skid marks out here?"

The accident reconstruction team was busy surveying and measuring equipment. Martin scanned the parking lot and saw dozens of skid marks that arced over the painted parking spots. He noticed a particularly intense set of marks by an overturned light post. Plastic and fiberglass remnants of a car bumper and glass from headlight lenses littered the pavement around the base of the light. Detective Rizzo pointed at the downed light and replayed the incident with his finger, pointing at various marks on the lot. "We think it started at the far end of the parking lot. Philip gets in his car, gets shot at, and makes for the lobby. The lot is empty, so he has lots of room to maneuver, but the bad guys turn Phil's car into Swiss cheese, so he tries to use this light post as a way to stop them. It works, and they hit the light. Phil swerves and runs inside the lobby."

"But where's the car that was chasing him? That light had to total the front end of whatever vehicle it was," asked the executive.

"That's a very good question, Mr. Martin," replied Rizzo. "But wherever the vehicle disappeared to, Philip's James Bond moves took out the passenger in the front seat." The detective pointed to a chalk outline forty feet away from the debris field. "That guy was ejected through the windshield and ended up over there."

"How fast were they going for the force of the impact to do that?" asked Martin.

Rizzo bobbed his toothpick at the reconstruction team. "These guys say Phil was doing about eighty miles per hour. No question that Phil was haulin'— of course, if someone was shooting at you, Mr. Martin, with the weapons that we found on these guys, you might be pressing on the gas pedal too." Rizzo flicked his toothpick to the opposite side of his mouth.

Martin looked across the parking lot toward the lobby and saw the chalk outline of a person sprawled toward them. "Was that man killed by Philip Channing as well?"

"No, I don't think so. That guy was popped in the head by a very high-powered rifle. We haven't recovered anything that even closely resembles the weapon that shot him."

Martin processed the statement. "So what are you saying? There are three parties involved?"

"Maybe." The detective studied the executive's face for any sign of concern, but he saw nothing. "If you like this, then you'll love what they did inside. Come on."

Rizzo led the way through the shattered glass and around bullet casings announced by numbered plastic placards standing off the pavement.

As they walked inside the shattered lobby, a FedEx truck roared into the parking lot and stopped at the purple-and-white drop box at the corner of the parking lot, just outside the police tape.

Chapter Thirty
Discovery of the Grid

Glenn Martin was aghast at the remains of his once-beautiful Axcess corporate lobby. The ornate space was a mess of splintered wood, bullet holes, and shattered glass. And in the center of its perfect Italian marble floor, a dark pool of drying blood marked the spot where the night security guard, Danny O'Connell, had died and bled out.

Some of the rare oil paintings and sculptures were victims of the violence—ripped oil canvases and shattered fragments of clay and bronze from the modern-art sculptures were silent sentinels over the violence that had enveloped the lobby earlier that morning.

A dozen crime-scene technicians were working with lasers mounted on tripods, making minute adjustments and running ballistic trajectories from the holes in the security station and turnstiles back toward the damaged frame of the rotating glass door of the entryway.

"We have some video of what happens next," said Detective Rizzo, walking over to the security desk. "Okay, go ahead and play it," he said to a tech who was working the playback controls.

A grainy black-and-white image with snowy feedback lines stabilized and played in a jerky manner. "Only a few frames a second are picked up by the cameras, so the details are a bit jarring," said the tech.

The images showed Phil casually walking out, backpack over his shoulder, waving toward the security desk.

Rizzo's eyes narrowed, studying the video footage. "Hmmm."

"What?" asked Martin.

"Nothing. We'll come back to it. Keep going."

Martin turned back to the video replay, annoyed and short of patience with the detective, who seemed to be playing games with him.

The video showed Daniel O'Connell jumping out from behind the security booth and running to the center of the lobby before Phil came flying through the door, and a moment passed before flashes of white appeared in the video like overexposed frames. "What was that?" asked the chief executive.

"Muzzle flashes. That's it for Danny boy," said the detective coldly. As if on cue, like Rizzo was the director in some bizarre Hollywood horror movie, O'Connell collapsed forward onto the marble.

Rose Stanton and Glenn Martin looked at the detective in disbelief, disgusted by his reaction.

The images of Phil athletically jumping over the security barricade as a hail of gunfire turned it into splinters ripped Stanton and Martin's attention back to the video playback.

Rizzo bit down harder on his toothpick. "Now watch, here come the bad guys."

"How do you know that Philip Channing isn't a bad guy?" asked Martin.

Rizzo ignored the executive's question long enough to raise Martin's blood pressure. Finally he said, "Experience, ballistics, and the crime lab will bear that out. Believe me; this kid's smarter than the average bear."

The video showed two men entering the lobby, both shooting across the security barricade. They were dressed in black and wearing ski masks. One of the men put another round in the back of the fallen security guard's head. Rose Stanton jumped at the silent flash as if she could hear the crack of the shot.

The images were interlaced with static as the men disappeared to the upper left of the frame. The only marker of time was the constant ticking of the superimposed digital click and a dark red disc under the security guard's head that slowly increased its radius.

"Go ahead and fast-forward," said Rizzo. The tech did, and the images jumped and shifted as the read head of the video player flew over the tape.

"Stop there!" said Rizzo. The tech pressed "play."

Phil came running through the scene again, breaking into a full sprint as one of the men in black chased him out of the lobby.

"Two bad guys went to look for Channing, but only one comes out chasing him. Interesting, huh?" said the detective, raising his bushy eyebrows at the CEO.

Before Martin could respond, Rizzo tapped the crime-scene tech on the shoulder. "Go back to the beginning of the sequence where Phil is walking out initially."

The images scrambled as the tech repositioned the tape to the beginning. Phil walked toward the revolving doors.

"Stop it right there," said the detective.

The grainy image froze.

"What's that under Phil's arm?" asked Rizzo, shifting the toothpick up and down.

Stanton and Martin both squinted, moving closer to the display.

"It looks like an envelope," said Stanton. "There's a FedEx mailbox at the corner of the sidewalk."

"That envelope does not reappear in the remainder of the video sequence. It's not sitting outside in the parking lot, and it's not in Phil's car," said Rizzo.

"He must have mailed it before all this happened," said Stanton.

"That's right. I wonder what was in that envelope?" asked Rizzo.

"The FedEx truck was here this morning. I saw it pull in while we were walking into the lobby, but I didn't think anything of it," said Martin.

Rizzo grabbed his walkie-talkie from his belt and pressed the talk button. "Get someone over to that FedEx mailbox and get it cordoned off. Get ahold of the local FedEx branch and put a stop on the mail."

"Roger that," came a response.

"Now, let's go see what happened with Phil downstairs," said the detective, trudging across the marble floor.

The elevator was stopped, and its doors were propped open, as was the door to the stairwell. The members of the crime lab were dusting for prints and working the scene.

Rizzo tapped the lead tech on the shoulder. "What's the story?"

"Philip Channing pressed the 'up' button for the elevator, but the only button with his print on the inside console is the top floor. That's not for the floor he works on."

Surprise bloomed on Rizzo's face. "What about prints for the other guys?"

"Nothing so far—they were wearing gloves."

"Of course they were," Rizzo said, chomping down on the toothpick as if he was expecting that answer.

"I don't understand," said Martin. "What's the significance of the 'up' button?"

"Smart move. He's got two guys on his tail, so he hits 'up' but takes the stairs down, splitting them up. Like I said, he's a smart kid."

Rizzo led the way down the stairwell until they reached the last floor, their feet clanging on the industrial steel of the stairs. As they exited the stairs, a dusty, musty basement smell filled their nostrils. Rizzo glanced at a stack of cardboard boxes leaning against the cinder-block wall and then turned his gaze upward toward the intermittent flashing of the overhead fluorescent lights.

"Only the best for your best and brightest, eh, Mr. Martin?"

Martin blushed, embarrassed by the conditions of the floor, and flashed a glare at Stanton. The Human Resources director shrugged and took a step back like a beaten dog. The three moved through a group of investigators working on a dead man who was wedged between the hallway wall and the door to the only department in the basement level. One of the techs held out a clipboard and asked the three to sign into the crime scene. Rizzo scribbled his name and handed the clipboard back to the CEO without even looking at him.

Rizzo looked at the label on the door's face. "Discovery & Development— I assume that was Phil's department."

Stanton nodded.

The crowd of techs and a coroner parted, briefly revealing the man's face. Rose Stanton gasped and turned away. It was contorted and blackened by a giant bruise, and shattered tooth fragments were sticking to the man's face in random positions. His eyes gazed out blankly and were beginning to cloud over as the process of decomposition took hold. The lower part of the man's body was already stuffed into a plastic body bag.

"Did Channing do this to him?" asked Martin. "He killed him?"

"Most likely," said the detective.

One of the investigators pointed to the top of the hand truck that was lying against the wall. "There's the weapon. We lifted prints from the hand truck's rail—a lot of them."

Rizzo studied the rail and then walked to the alcove past the stairwell. Two cotter pins were lying on the cement with evidence markers standing over them like little plastic tents.

"I'm not a betting man, but if I were, I would put all my money on Philip Channing being the owner of those prints. He caught this guy coming out of the room here and bashed him in the head—self-defense."

"How do you know it was self-defense?" asked Martin.

Rizzo held up a plastic ziplock bag marked with an evidence label. A black Glock 27 handgun was inside.

"Glocks versus hand trucks—seems pretty unfair to me," said Rizzo. "By the way, they all had similar guns."

Another tech entered the hallway and addressed Rizzo as he opened up a body bag in the hallway. "We just ran those prints on the hand truck. They belong to Philip Channing."

Rizzo looked at Martin with a smug smile. "See." The detective tilted the toothpick upward. Martin frowned.

"Look here." Rizzo knelt down and pointed to a plastic access card attached to the dead man's belt. "He has a corporate access card."

Rose Stanton gasped when she saw the card. That was her department's responsibility.

Glenn Martin's initial shock gave way to anger. "He had access to the campus? That's impossible!"

"Why is that so impossible, Mr. Martin?" asked Rizzo. "Don't you see who these guys are? They are professional killers. Frankly, I'm amazed that Phil's not lying here instead of this clown."

Another detective came down the stairs, and overhearing the conversation, interjected. "The two we found in the parking lot also had access cards. They don't have the same one, though—they're all different serial numbers."

Rizzo raised his bushy eyebrows. "So they were getting help—help from the inside."

"Now wait just a minute here," said the executive.

Rizzo ignored him. "May we go into the room?" Rizzo asked a crime-scene tech. The tech nodded, and Rizzo stepped over the dead man into the

Discovery & Development Department. Stanton and Martin followed behind, watching where they stepped.

"Which one is Phil's desk?" asked Rizzo. Stanton returned a blank expression.

"You guys don't come down here much, huh?"

The walls were covered in seismic analysis pictures, printed off of the huge plotter. Rizzo scanned the strange images and noted the print dates on the legends. "These were all printed in the last week. What exactly does the Discovery & Development Department do for Axcess Energy, Mr. Martin?"

"They collect seismic data and attempt to find oil deposits and natural-gas fields for Axcess to develop."

Rizzo stopped at the largest of the color printouts. It took up the entire wall. The colors, representing different rocks and densities, made the pale paper come alive.

Rizzo put on his reading glasses and phonetically pronounced the legend at the bottom of the large sheet of paper: "Atlantis Massif." He dropped his glasses down the bridge of his nose and looked over the top of them at Martin. "Does that mean anything to you?"

Martin's eyes shifted, and he coughed before answering. "It was a research project around the Mid-Atlantic Ridge. A joint exploration effort with a number of universities, if I remember right."

As Rizzo, Martin, and Stanton moved through the room, they ran into a table covered in a neat line of black game consoles. They were bound to one another by yellow cables that snaked in and around them.

Rizzo pointed at the table. "This seems strange, don't you think?" He didn't wait for an answer to his rhetorical question. The mounted projectors on each wall grabbed his attention. "Four projectors all pointed in different directions—one for each vacant wall and one pointed downward toward the floor—like a little home theater on steroids."

"I don't know anything about this project," said Martin.

"I'm not too surprised by that," said Rizzo, pulling a fresh toothpick from his pocket.

"How many of those things do you chew on a day?" asked Martin.

"You don't want to know. Can we get someone down here to power this thing up?" asked Rizzo.

Stanton nodded, walked to Gorin's desk, and dialed the internal help desk. A few minutes later, a young man appeared at the doorway. "Did someone here call for help-desk support?" he asked, his voice cracking in a prepubescent manner.

"Yes, come in here, young man," said Rizzo. "What's your name?"

"Ethan," said the young man as he gingerly stepped over the rubber body bag containing the remains of the assassin found in the hallway.

Rizzo walked Ethan to the table where the grid sat silently. "Can you turn this thing on?"

Ethan studied the setup. "Why does someone have this many video-game consoles hooked up?"

Rizzo raised his eyebrows and shrugged. "That's why we're here."

Ethan looked at the back of each console and found that the video outputs led to a multiplexor, which trailed a cable running up an iron support into the ceiling. His eyes followed the black cable till it reemerged on the ceiling where the projectors were mounted. He looked around the table for a remote that was branded like the projectors and finally found it sitting on Phil's desk. He pressed the "on" button, and the projectors blinked to life. A manufacturer's logo blazed across each of the walls and the floor.

Ethan smiled with satisfaction. "Okay, now we just need to fire up these things, I think."

He pressed the "on" button for each console and was greeted by a start-up chime each time. The lights on each console blinked incessantly as the grid plowed through millions of instructions per second. A digital progress bar appeared on the walls and floor and slowly began to fill in.

10%, 20%, 30% . . .

"No password protection. This is definitely not an IT project. He probably didn't use corporate funds to purchase it either. This is someone's pet project," said Ethan.

"Someone stupid," said Martin.

Rizzo corrected the CEO. "Or maybe just committed to finding something important at his own expense."

The progress bar finally reached one hundred percent, and the projectors synched up their displays with the high-speed computer grid Phil had constructed. The walls came alive with imagery.

Martin gasped, and Rizzo slowly walked forward to the center of the room. "Now we're getting somewhere," he muttered, staring at the three-walled display. The Atlantic Ocean swirled and undulated in front of the detective and headed off in the distance regardless of how he turned.

"Was this Phil's job? Building this . . . *thing?*"

"I've never seen anything like this," said Martin, dialing his cell phone.

"Who ya calling?" asked Rizzo.

"Legal. This may be highly confidential—even from you, detective." Martin turned and cupped his hand over the phone, ignoring the detective.

Rizzo shook his head, turning red. "Mr. Martin, I don't care *who* you are, or *what* this is," Rizzo pointed at the animated display, "but you're standing in the middle of a crime scene. All of this is evidence, and the DA will probably subpoena all of it. I don't know what's more sickening to me: your concern for corporate secrets or your lack of concern as to why one of your employees was being hunted by professional killers. People like you get lots of money and forget you're human."

Martin ignored the detective and continued talking in hushed tones. Rizzo bit through his toothpick in anger and cursed under his breath. He looked back at the display. The only text on the display was on the center display at the top of the screen:

LATITUDE: 29° 59′ 59.66″ N.

LONGITUDE: 41° 59′ 59.53″ W.

ELEVATION: 100 m.

Rizzo walked back over to the large sheet of paper hanging on the wall and looked at the brilliant swatch of colors that spanned the ten-foot-wide poster. A vertical axis caught his attention. It was in meters. A large dome-shaped mountain with a cutaway cross section dominated the top half of the poster.

A notation near the domed shape read, *Atlantis Massif: 4211 m.*

Martin glanced over at Rizzo, still cupping his hand over the phone. Rizzo sneered back at him in contempt.

Sick of Martin, Rizzo jogged back to the animated display. "So it's like a giant video game, except it's a map of a real place." Rizzo looked over Phil's desk for a joystick or something to control the display.

"Here, try this," said Ethan, handing Rizzo a motion controller from near Phil's keyboard.

"Thanks, Ethan. You know, my kids love video games. I just don't have the time or energy to play with them when I get home."

One of Ethan's beepers went off.

"I have to go. Someone else needs help," said Ethan.

The detective shook the young man's hand. "Thank you for your help."

Rizzo walked back to the center of the room again. He awkwardly held the controller in front of him and angled it back toward himself. Suddenly, he was flying upward, away from the ocean as the horizon arched away from him on all the walls.

"Oops, wrong direction."

He pressed the controller downward, and the ocean rushed back at his feet until he plunged beneath its wavy surface into the depths.

"There we go. Hey, this is kind of fun," he chuckled.

Rizzo looked back at Martin, who had hung up and was standing at the edge of the display with his mouth open, clearly astonished at the display.

Rizzo watched the elevation indicator continue to get deeper and deeper. At four thousand feet below the surface, the domed seamount appeared in amazing detail, like he was flying over the Rockies on a sunny day.

"Okay, so that colorful structure on the wall should be just below this mountain." Rizzo pressed the controller forward again, and the display filled with rock strata before a rainbow of brilliant layers broke through the floor and bathed Rizzo and the others in primary colors.

"Bingo!"

"Sir, I must ask that you stop what you are doing," said a new voice. "This is confidential property of Axcess Energy. Under the Federal Trade Secret Act, I must insist that you stop investigating this material. You may continue with the rest of your investigation."

Rizzo turned to find a tall, thin man dressed in a gray, pinstriped, three-piece suit. His hair was jet black and combed straight back—a cross between a financial wizard and mafia godson.

"Who are you? Gordon Gecko?" asked the detective.

"I'm Walton Hendricks, chief legal counsel for Axcess Energy, and you do not have the right to come into our departments and riffle through our corporate secrets without a warrant."

"You know, that could be mistaken for threatening an officer, and, Wally—can I call you Wally?—that's not something you want to do."

"It's Walton Hendricks," said the lawyer.

"Whatever." Rizzo put the motion controller back on Phil's desk and walked over to the chief counsel and the CEO.

"You and your chief executive friend here have some big problems," he said to the lawyer. "You have a dead security guard in your shot-up lobby. You have a dead professional killer without any identification except for a corporate access card to a department that is so important you have it in the basement that neither of you have ever visited. And you have a computer ignoramus— that's me—who found out that Phil has made an amazing discovery you now consider a trade secret."

The room was silent. "Have I missed anything?" asked the detective.

Rizzo's cell phone rang, and he pulled the device from his pocket, welcoming the interruption from the idiots in his sight. He didn't recognize the number on the phone's display.

"Rizzo."

The voice on the other end seemed to take the wind from the detective's sails. He looked over at the lawyer and then at Martin, who was standing erect and smug. The voice emanating from the phone seemed to be lecturing—it was definitely a one-sided conversation.

"Yes, sir." Rizzo terminated the call and turned to face the CEO, who had a knowing smirk on his face.

"Seems you have friends in high places, Mr. Martin. That was the commissioner; the 'thing' we just looked at is off limits."

The CEO smirked. "I'm glad we have some understanding, Detective. Now, if you don't mind, I have a company to run. Please keep me updated with any progress on the investigation." Martin walked out of the room and up the stairs. The chief legal counsel and HR director followed dutifully behind.

Rizzo watched them leave with his fists clenched, and then he stared at the cement floor. Why did he keep doing this thankless job, anyway? His anger disappeared as he looked in the trash can near Phil's desk. A small collection of crinkled clear-cellophane wrapping was at the top of the trash. Rizzo leaned down and studied the wrapper, then looked over Phil's desk. A stack of unused DLT tapes, still in their pristine wrapping, were nestled together in the manufacturer's shipping box. The cellophane wrappers seemed to match the general shape of the item in the trash can.

"Did you already process the evidence on this desk?" he asked the investigator still loitering over the dead assassin. The tech grunted back at him in the affirmative. Rizzo pulled a latex glove out of his pocket, snapped it on, and retrieved the torn cellophane wrapper from the trash.

He set the wrapper on the center of Phil's desk next to a piece of curled-up, narrow wax paper. Rizzo smoothed it out carefully with two pencils. The label read, REMOVE STRIP AND PUSH DOWN FLAP TO SEAL. A FedEx watermark was tiled in light gray ink across the wax strip. Rizzo saw a stack of FedEx envelopes lying on Phil's desk. Their wax strips were intact.

"So it was a shipping envelope. I wonder what was in it."

Rizzo yelled over at a tech still dusting for prints near the dead assassin. "Hey, do you know much about computers?"

"Some," said the technician, approaching Rizzo at Phil's desk, glad for a short break from the dead body.

Rizzo read the data capacity from the box containing the tapes to the tech. "How big is 1600 GB?"

"Big—huge. 'GB' is gigabytes, a billion bytes, so that's over a trillion bytes. It would take a long time to back up that much information," replied the tech.

"Yeah, a late night working . . ." said Rizzo. "I think we know what was in that FedEx envelope." Rizzo picked up the cellophane wrapper with a gloved hand and pointed at the wall, where the poster of the Atlantis Massif and the Maximal Reserve hung. "A backup tape— containing something huge and important."

The conversation was interrupted by the clanging of someone running down the stairwell. A moment later another detective jumped over the dead assassin's body and into the room.

"You're not going to believe this," rasped the man.

"Try me," said Rizzo.

"You know that FedEx mail drop outside?"

"Yeah."

"They haven't made their pick-up run yet," said the out-of-breath detective.

"What?"

"The FedEx truck that picked up the packages at that mailbox this morning wasn't theirs, or if it was, it was stolen. Want to hear something else?"

"Why not?" said Rizzo, sticking a fresh toothpick in his mouth.

"All the packages are still in the box. At least, the ones they didn't take this morning."

．．．．

On the fourth floor, in the executive wing, Martin marched to his office with his chief counsel in tow. As he reached his office, he looked back at Walton Hendricks. The chief legal counselor was on his cell phone with his legal team.

"Wait for me out here for a second," Martin said.

The lawyer nodded.

Martin closed the red oak door to his office and pulled out his cell phone, dialing a number.

"David Rohm here; how can I hel—"

Martin didn't wait for the commerce secretary to finish his greeting.

"You stupid idiot! Do you realize what your associates have done to my company? The lobby looks like Iwo Jima. This is not Istanbul or Damascus. You'd better get a leash on your dogs, because I've got about a hundred cops swarming the campus right now looking for evidence that would put you and me in prison for life—or in the electric chair."

"Martin, settle down. I've got everything under control."

"Listen, from my vantage point, it doesn't look like you have anything under control. You'd better get this thing turned around, because if this goes to court, I'm going to hang this whole mess around your neck."

Martin terminated the call and looked out the huge windows onto the courtyard. A dozen more police cars had shown up, and a satellite news van was pulling into the lot.

"Oh, great. The stinkin' press," he said, slumping into his desk chair.

Chapter Thirty-One

Delivery

"I still can't believe it . . . I can't believe I killed someone," Phil stammered, holding his head in his hands. Caleb walked over with a cup of water and placed it on the table Phil was bent over.

Phil looked through a large office window into an airplane hangar where a white Gulfstream 5 business jet was being fueled. The crew was busily crawling all over its aluminum surface—connecting the APU, checking control surfaces, closing access panels. Caleb sat quietly for a moment, adjusting his wire-rim glasses and absorbing Phil's emotion. "It was either you or him. You know that. You defended yourself."

Phil shut his eyes. "I keep seeing his face in my mind. I—I can't forget it."

"Drink some water, my friend. In time this will pass."

Phil ignored him and stared straight ahead.

Caleb's face reddened, and his voice went from calm to irate. "Snap out of it, Phil."

Phil's head snapped up, shocked. Caleb was through coddling him. "Did you think you could have a conversation or a debate with those men? They were there to kill you. They didn't care what you looked like or how good a person you were. All my life I've been around such men—men who have such a focus. It's like morality and conscience don't exist in them anymore. They are not like you and me. God has given them up to themselves—seared their consciences with a hot iron."

Phil nodded, remembering the verse from the New Testament, and finally drank some water. Caleb was right, of course, but it didn't make him feel any better.

A FedEx delivery truck pulled into the hangar and screeched its tires as it came to a stop. The man who got out was dressed like a deliveryman—perfect for the part in every way. He stepped off the truck with a single package. A crowd of others gathered around him and examined the package he handed to them.

Next to the muscular delivery guy, the other men were thin and geeky.

Scientists, thought Phil. The stereotype struck him as humorous for a moment before he was dragged back into reality.

Lisa—I have to call Lisa.

"I have to call Lisa," said Phil, looking around the room for a phone.

Caleb looked torn. "I wish I could allow that Phil, but, no, we can't let you do that. The NSA and the Echelon System are probably scanning the airwaves for you right now. It's best that no one else knows your condition or where you are."

"But if they know about me, how hard would it be to find Lisa?" Phil rebutted.

"Phil, the authorities in Austin will take care of Lisa. She'll be one of the first people they question."

Phil frowned, not liking the sound of that. He wanted nothing more than to reach out beyond this room to Lisa—but it looked like that was out of the question.

The deliveryman came into the room with Phil and Caleb and unzipped the delivery uniform. He stepped out of it, revealing camouflage pants with a dozen pockets and a tan T-shirt that fit over his muscular body like a second skin.

"Phil, this is Amir. He's the one who saved your life this morning."

Phil had a flashback to the laser sight running over the length of his body before a shot killed his pursuer in the Axcess parking lot. Had that only been a few hours before?

Phil was unsure of the exact etiquette of thanking someone for saving him from deadly assassins. He extended his hand, and Amir took it strongly and gave it a firm shake.

"Thank you," said Phil.

Amir said nothing. Phil wondered how many people the man standing before him had killed. Phil was glad for his technical career—or what used to be his career. It seemed so simple in comparison to the taking of human life for government security purposes.

The pack of scientists in the hangar waved at the trio, and Phil watched the men disappear through the corporate jet's door.

"Time to go, Phil," said Caleb. "Twelve hours to Tel Aviv."

The whine of the Gulfstream's turbines filled the hangar as Phil mouthed the words, "Tel Aviv?" His voice was drowned out by the powerful engines.

Phil climbed inside the jet, feeling like his life was out of control but knowing he had to trust these men. After all, they had saved his life. The roar of the turbine engines was dulled as the jet door closed.

The seats on the plane were situated lengthwise along the curved walls of the fuselage—each side facing the other. The scientists crowded onto the opposite side, and Caleb and Amir sat on each side of Phil.

Phil felt like he was being interviewed all over again.

As the white jet taxied down the runway, one of the scientists pulled a thick stack of papers from a manila folder and handed them to Phil. He accepted the papers with trepidation, like he was being handed the blueprints for a super-secret military project.

The engines came up to speed, and the jet charged down the runway. Phil thumbed through the stack of papers, dumbfounded. It was all of his work over the last few weeks at Axcess. Xeroxed copies of handwritten notes, scrawled in late-night moments of brilliance but unreadable to anyone but himself, in combination with diagrams and profiles of the reserve. Even the source code from his program to bring the data to life on the Playboxes was there.

Everything he had accomplished since his first moments at Axcess was in these papers.

Phil was stunned. He turned toward Caleb.

"What? Did you think I was actually working there?" asked Caleb, giving an extra tug to his lap belt.

A scientist across the way from Phil leaned forward. "Now, let's start from the beginning, Philip. Tell us about the size of the reserve, and tell us about the structure that was mailed to you by Jack Sanders last week."

Phil could tell this was going to be a very long trip.

Chapter Thirty-Two

Freeway

D avid Rohm walked out to his reserved parking spot and examined the shiny hood of his black Mercedes S-Class Sedan. The car was immaculate. Rohm was fanatical about having it washed three times a week and detailed at least twice a month.

He fished the keys out of his pocket and pressed the unlock button. The car flashed its lights and chirped obediently at him.

Rohm fired up the car and revved the engine, checking his e-mail messages one more time before placing his cell phone in its charging cradle. He pulled out of the lot of the corporate center and headed for the expressway and his fifteen-minute commute to downtown Austin and the high-priced skyscraper where he lived the good life.

He smiled. He liked being rich. He pressed the pedal down and felt the acceleration of the engine respond to his command.

A black van pulled out of the corporate park behind him, accelerating and matching the speed of the sleek sedan.

Rohm stopped at a red light just before the entrance to the expressway and dialed voice mail on his cell phone.

"Thirty-three new messages," said the robotic voice-mail attendant. Rohm groaned as the messages began their assault on his hearing.

Two cars back, a man sitting in the passenger's seat of the black van pulled a laptop from a padded box and attached a wireless device to the USB port. The driver glanced over at the man in the passenger's seat as he booted up the laptop and uttered something in Russian.

"Da," said the man, tapping on the keyboard. A light on the wireless device illuminated bright green as a schematic diagram of a car was drawn on the laptop's display.

The traffic light turned green, and Rohm raced toward the on-ramp to the expressway. The sun was already resting on the horizon. It was a nice evening. Rohm hung up on his voice mail and loosened his tie while putting his car window down. He rested his left arm on the door and let the evening breeze course through the cabin of the luxury car.

The traffic around Rohm got lighter, only a few cars on the expressway. He passed St. John's Park on his left and looked over to see families playing, couples walking, and singles mingling, all enjoying the evening. The overpass of 290 loomed ahead of him.

The man with the laptop dialed a number on his cell phone, and David Rohm's phone began to ring. The charging cradle passed the signal on to Rohm's Bluetooth headset.

"David Rohm."

"We warned you that we do not tolerate failure," came a response over the phone, with a heavy Ukrainian accent. "Your failure to keep the authorities at bay and your attracting them to our activities must now be paid for."

Rohm pulled his arm from the window and sat straight up, leaning forward. His heart rate increased with every word that came from the mysterious caller.

"Wait a minute! Who is this? I can fix this—no, don't hang up—I can fix everything!"

The call terminated.

"Hello? *Hello?*"

Rohm exhaled, exasperated. He needed a drink. He put on his right turn signal and headed for the exit, looking for signs stretching above the concrete thoroughfare that might point to temporary relief from the stress.

He turned the steering wheel slightly, aiming for the exit that was fast approaching.

The car didn't change course, but remained in the passing lane.

What the . . .

Rohm pressed on his brake pedal, but nothing happened. He mashed it to the floor.

The car accelerated.

Rohm watched in horror as the speedometer climbed higher and higher. *70, 75, 80, 85, 90 . . .*

The man in the black van, three cars back, slowly tapped on the keyboard and watched the sedan he was controlling like a puppeteer pull away from them.

Rohm eyes darted wide-eyed at the tachometer. It was buried in the right side of the gauge. The engine screamed for relief.

That was when Rohm saw it: the upright concrete support for 290 in the median. His car was gently angling directly for it. Rohm watched the centerline move farther and farther to the right and then felt the warning divots on the left side of the expressway began their machine-gun-like rat-a-tatting against the sedan's tires—first on the left and then on the right side of the car.

The whole environment around Rohm was a blur, a smear of light and shape and horror.

A light on the dash blinked on as the speedometer passed ninety-five miles per hour: "Driver Air Bag Disabled."

"Oh, no!"

The seat-belt tensioner on the driver's side failed. Rohm felt it release its secure grip on his body. For a brief instant he felt weightless.

No!

The windscreen filled up with the concrete-barrier base of the upright. The sedan slammed into the concrete at over a hundred miles an hour. The crumple zones absorbed the impact, and the ceramic supports holding the engine mount sheared off as designed, but the car was on top of it a microsecond later. The hood snapped up and bent in half before the forward fenders lost

194   Sam Batterman

their support, folding and crumpling like an accordion. Rohm's body flew forward from the sudden deceleration and formed around the steering column as if it was a medieval pike. His arms flew forward, dislocating from their sockets before being mashed in the metal, plastic, and composite materials of the car, which were going the opposite direction.

The gas tank split open, and the flammable vapor of the fuel ignited instantly. An orange fireball bloomed around the vehicle and rolled upward along the column, turning rust-orange and then into an oily, black, roiling column of smoke.

Cars behind swerved in their lanes as drivers slammed on their brakes and pulled over to the side of the road.

The black van continued under the overpass and disappeared into the coming night.

Chapter Thirty-Three
Disclosure

L isa squinted in the brilliant sunrise illuminating the Austin landscape. She put on her sunglasses, shifted from third gear to fourth, and cruised up the 35 expressway, her blue sedan slipping in and around slower traffic as she headed for the office.

She tried Phil's cell phone again. She had left three messages for him, with no response yet.

Maybe he had an early meeting. Or he forgot to charge his cell phone . . . again.

As she passed the 290 exchange, she looked in her rearview mirror to see a swarm of police cars and a flatbed truck on the other side of the expressway. The concrete upright that lifted 290 over the 35 was blackened like it was charred. A series of orange cones were forcing the left lane to merge and slowing the morning commute into Austin.

I wonder what happened there.

Lisa switched on her car radio and scanned for a local traffic station. As the radio scanned the band, it stopped at a news station and played for a moment.

" . . . while authorities refuse to admit that Axcess Energy was attacked by terrorists, the evidence in the parking lot of the corporate center seems to confirm it by the sheer carnage alone . . . "

The radio continued its scan, interrupting the news report and landing on a country station. Lisa dialed back.

She listened to the news report and pulled her foot off of the accelerator. She was ripped back to driving reality by the blowing horn of a red sports car behind her. She waved at the impatient driver, trying to express her apology in hand motions, and pulled over to the side of the expressway while turning up the radio's volume.

"The attack seems to have claimed at least four lives, including three of the attackers. A corporate security guard, a Mr. Daniel O'Connell, was killed in the attack. Detectives are also investigating an employee of Axcess Energy who was found on surveillance tapes to be fleeing the site. The employee's name is being withheld until his whereabouts can be determined. We will continue to update the story as more details emerge."

The radio station began to play car-dealer commercials, and Lisa turned the volume down. She tried Phil's cell one more time. No response.

Her mind spun in a million directions. What should she do? Should she go to Axcess?

As she was trying to formulate a plan, her cell rang. *Finally, Phil!* But when she looked at the display, it was a colleague calling: Miranda Bayes. Her cubicle was just outside of Lisa's office.

Lisa frowned with disappointment. "Hello," she said blankly, still focused on the news report.

Miranda was hysterical; skipping all pleasantries, she jumped directly to the point. "Did you hear the news?" she asked.

Lisa replayed the Axcess news report in her mind. *Was this about Phil?*

"What news?" she said, trying to prepare herself for something bad.

"He's dead!"

Lisa's heart sank. "What? Wait, Miranda, slow down. Who's dead?"

"Rohm—David Rohm was killed last night." Miranda was sobbing.

A strange feeling came over Lisa—a conflict of emotions. Loss and happiness—or rather, relief. This wasn't about Phil. But suddenly she had a premonition that she was in trouble.

"What? How? What happened?" she managed to stammer.

"Some sort of accident on the 35 expressway last night. He crashed his car into the concrete barrier near the 290 exchange."

Lisa looked into her side mirror. She could still see the flashing lights and slowing traffic trying to make their way around the blackened barrier.

"Are you coming into the office?" Miranda asked. Without waiting for an answer, she blathered on. "There are some policemen here who want to ask you questions about Mr. Rohm. Everyone's scared and confused. They're interviewing everyone in the office. I don't think they believe it was an accident."

Lisa thought for a moment. "I'll be there in an hour or so. Will they still be there?"

"Are you kidding? It's going to take them all day to talk to the entire office," replied Miranda. Her sarcasm was still intact, despite the tragedy.

"All right, I'll see you then. Are you okay, Miranda?"

"Yes. It's just such a shock. You never know . . . "

"I know what you mean. Hang in there. Bye." Lisa terminated the call and merged back into traffic heading for the next exit.

She had nothing to lose now. Rohm was dead.

■ ■ ■

Sheridan Preston was driving as fast as she could go in her sports car. The news reports were all centering on the overnight disturbance at Axcess Energy.

Her own mind was elsewhere, even though she was headed for Axcess. News from yesterday was more pertinent to her. *Too long,* she thought. *I waited too long to write the story. Too much research, too much snooping. I should have written the story on Rohm a week ago.*

She punched the scan button on her radio, jumping from news report to news report. In her mind she rehearsed the questions she would ask at Axcess. The questions a career as a newspaper reporter had prepared her for.

She popped down the sun visor and checked her hair and makeup in the mirror, using her nail to better define a sharp edge of the red lipstick.

Her cell phone chimed, and she glanced down from her breakneck pace to glance at the small display. She didn't recognize the number. Ahead, she could see the traffic building and knew she would get snarled up in it. As the car slowed down and the roadway became a parking lot, the phone continued its irritating ring.

Oh, why not?

"Hello, Sheridan Preston speaking."

"Miss Preston, this is Lisa Baton. I don't know if you remember me, but..."

"Of course I remember you, Lisa," Preston interrupted. "How can I help you?"

"Have you heard about what happened at Axcess overnight?"

"Yeah, I'm on my way there right now. Traffic is terrible. Why do you ask?"

"My boyfriend—I mean my fiancé—Phil Channing works there and was somehow involved in what happened. I can't get him on his cell, and he's not at home."

"Are you saying that Phil was one of the killers?"

"No. Never. I think they were after Phil. He found something—something amazing, but I can't talk about it on the phone. I also want to give you something that I think relates to what you discussed with me in the ladies' room at the River's Edge. Can you meet me?"

Preston looked at the traffic ahead and weighed the value of late interviews at a crime scene that was locked down or a lead on a story she had been working on for over a year. A story she'd thought she'd lost.

In her mind's ear, Preston could hear her editor telling her to follow the sure story, the hot story, the one that would sell papers today or tomorrow. She immediately dismissed the annoying specter. "Yes, I'll meet you—where?"

"Walter Long Park, off 290."

"I'm ten minutes away. See you there." *That is, if I can get out of this traffic.*

Sheridan glanced in her rearview mirror and pulled toward the median between the north and southbound lanes, escorted by horns and cursing from the other drivers waiting their turn in the queue. She cut across the tall grass of the median and up onto the side of the southbound lane. After looking for an opening in the traffic, she gunned it and merged quickly into traffic before taking the first exit for 290.

■ ■ ■ ■

Lisa pulled into the municipal park and stopped under a shade tree, turning her AC to full blast. She watched some high school kids struggling to get a Jet Ski into the lake and a new mother running along the walking path with her newborn bouncing along in her jogging stroller.

I can't believe I'm going to talk to a reporter. I'm about to give away information that will likely destroy the governor's career or worse.

The high-school kids miscalculated with the Jet Ski and dumped the expensive recreational toy on the gravel of the shoreline.

He might even end up in jail . . . and I'll be known as a whistle-blower for the rest of my life. But if these guys are killing people, then I can't stand by and let that happen. I can't.

Lisa saw Sheridan pull into the parking lot and waved at her.

God, give wisdom here, Lisa prayed as she walked toward the reporter.

"I'm sorry to hear about David Rohm," said Sheridan.

Lisa nodded, not exactly sure how to respond. Her emotions on the subject were complex and tangled.

A pregnant pause developed between the two women before Lisa finally broke the awkward silence.

"I think you were right," she said quietly. "I think the governor is up to something that's illegal. I don't know all the pieces yet. It's complicated, and lots of people are involved."

"What *do* you know, Lisa? Let's start there."

Lisa reached into her messenger bag and produced a folder. "This is probably the end of my career, but I feel like people are dying and I could have stopped it."

"Dying?" asked Sheridan, eyeing up the folder as if the secret tapes from Watergate were being handed to her.

Lisa handed Sheridan the folder, her hands trembling. "There's a paper in there. It was sent from someone at the LukZag Oil Company to David Rohm. It's a grant from the Department of Energy, but nearly everyone who was working on it is dead."

Sheridan rifled through the pages in the folder. She knew incriminating material when she saw it, and this was exactly that. "Why are you doing this, Lisa?"

Lisa's countenance went from fearful to despondent. "Phil's gone. He knew—knows—a lot of scientists who were working on that grant. I don't know where he is, or even it he's still alive, and the man I've worked for is somehow responsible. I just hope I'm not too late." Lisa's shoulders began to heave as she put her chin down and covered her face.

Sheridan was supposed to be a hardened reporter, but she broke the stereotype and gave Lisa a hug. "I'll do what I can to stop it, Lisa."

Lisa looked up, her eyes glossy with tears. "I have to go. The police want to talk with me about Rohm. I don't know what I'm going to say to them. Can I trust them?"

"I don't know, Lisa. Be careful. And thank you." Sheridan smiled empathetically and headed back for her car.

Lisa turned back to her vehicle and glanced out at the teenagers shouting and flirting in the waves. She didn't remember what that kind of frivolity was like now. She got into her car with a new resolve to find Phil and headed for the expressway.

■ ■ ■ ■

Across the lake, a black van sat idling while a man in the driver's seat clicked picture after picture with a digital camera outfitted with a telephoto zoom lens. A parabolic antenna was mounted on the top of the zoom lens, sucking in all the audio the camera was pointed at.

As both of the cars drove out of the parking lot, the man lowered the camera and rewound the tape that had recorded the conversation across the lake.

"... I'll do what I can to stop it, Lisa." The voice changed. "I have to go. The police want to talk ..."

The man pressed the stop button. "This is getting out of control. We have to stop this now."

The driver stowed the expensive camera and audio equipment and charged out of the parking lot, squealing the tires of the black van on the hot pavement.

Chapter Thirty-Four

Puzzle Pieces

*O*h *my word,* thought Lisa as she pulled her sedan into the parking lot in front of the corporate center. A dozen black-and-white police cars were parked in parallel up against the sidewalk, and another cruiser was pulled up across the entryway. The cruiser's lights were flashing and rotating, and an officer stood on the driver's side talking on his radio.

Lisa blinked as the oscillating lights blinded her over and over again. Slowly, she edged forward. The officer held his hand out and pulled the receiver away from his mouth.

"I'm sorry, ma'am. You can't park in here."

Lisa rolled her window down. "I'm Lisa Baton, assistant to the commerce secretary. I work here." Lisa fished through her handbag and produced an ID badge for verification.

The officer took her ID, walked back to the cruiser, and picked up the radio. A few moments later, he returned to the car and gave the badge back. "Detective Mark Rizzo is in the lobby and would like to speak with you, Miss Baton."

"Thank you."

The officer pulled the police car to the side and waved her through.

Lisa slowly pulled down the ramp and found an empty space. She thought about Phil and the discovery he had shown her in the basement of Axcess a few days before. A lump formed in her throat, and she fought past the urge to break down.

We were so naive, she thought. *Too naive . . .*

She pushed through the rotating door and entered the lobby, coming face-to-face with a tall man with a bushy black mustache. He was looking at a notepad that had seen better days. The worn, crumpled pages of past cases created a crinkled buffer between his large hands and the crisp piece of white paper he was reviewing. He looked up at her entrance.

"Miss Baton, I presume?"

"Yes. Who are you?" Lisa scanned the lobby. There were two other detectives and another officer.

"Name's Rizzo—Detective Mark Rizzo. Homicide." He swept his rumpled coat aside. Lisa glanced at his metal badge and got a brief glimpse of a gun in a leather holster.

"Homicide?"

"Yes. Your boss, David Rohm, was killed last night during his drive home. He ran head-on into one of the concrete supports for the 290 overpass." The detective studied Lisa's face for reaction. "It wasn't an accident."

She lowered her eyes. "I heard that this morning." Her emotions were a tangle. She was upset about Rohm, but what was happening with Phil?

"I got a call from Miranda that you wanted to speak with me."

Rizzo smiled. "Yes, Miranda." He flipped through his case pad. "She's a nice girl," he said before producing a small picture frame from his coat pocket and handing it to her. It was a picture of Lisa from college.

It was one of Phil's favorite pictures of her. She thought she looked different—younger, idealistic, less responsible—but still as deeply in love as she was now.

Her voice shook. "Where did you get this?"

"It was on Phil Channing's desk at Axcess Energy. He marked you on his HR paperwork as his emergency contact. What, exactly, is your relationship with Philip Channing?"

"He's my fiancé," she said.

Rizzo raised his eyebrows and scribbled in his notepad. "Fiancé. Congratulations."

Lisa noticed that the man was chewing on a toothpick, and from the looks of it he had a seriously bad habit.

"Do you know where Philip is right now?" asked the detective.

"No."

"Has he called you this morning?"

"No."

"May I see your phone?"

"You don't believe me?"

"Let's just say I trust but verify, to quote a past president of ours," replied Rizzo.

The other detective approached Lisa, and she handed him the cell phone.

"What does Phil have to do with David Rohm? Why are the two connected?" asked Lisa.

"We don't know yet, Miss Baton. We're still investigating," said Rizzo, scribbling in his casebook. His tone was unmistakably condescending.

Lisa resented the sarcasm. "May I go to my office?"

Maybe Phil left a message on my corporate voice mail. Lisa looked longingly at her cell phone, which was being placed in an evidence bag by another detective.

"How about later? I'd like to take you back to the precinct and go over some things."

"About Phil or David Rohm?" Lisa asked.

"Both, most likely," said Rizzo, heading out of the lobby. Lisa followed.

I'm already sick of these questions. What do they know about Phil?

Rizzo yelled over the policemen convened in the area. "Hey, Ron!" A tall blond man dressed in a pair of khakis and a tweed jacket jogged over. "I want you to take Lisa to the precinct and treat her well. Let's get a background workup and find out what was going on before last night."

Ron smiled at Lisa and shook her hand. Lisa began to feel at ease with him before it occurred to her that this might be the beginning of "good cop, bad cop."

"Is this all you have, Lisa?" Ron gestured to the messenger bag sitting at her feet. Lisa nodded, and Ron picked up the bag and walked toward an older, gray Crown Vic with municipal plates.

As Lisa walked away, she wondered if she should call her dad—or a lawyer—maybe both.

I have nothing to hide. I know Phil. Phil is innocent—whatever he's involved with.

Lisa did her best to convince herself that she didn't know what her fiancé was involved with, but she had a sinking feeling that she knew all too well.

The detective opened the back passenger door, and Lisa stepped in, slid across the leather seats, and buckled her seat belt. Ron handed her bag to her and climbed into the driver's seat.

"Want to sit up front?" he asked, sounding slightly embarrassed by the taxi driver role he had inadvertently created for himself.

"No. This is fine."

Ron smiled back. "I understand."

No, you don't.

The detective waved at the officer who had stopped Lisa earlier at the corporate entrance and pulled out onto the ramp for the expressway.

"How long have you known Phil?"

"Is this for the record or are you just making conversation?"

"Both."

"Phil and I met in college." Instead of continuing in short bursts, she decided to anticipate the next obvious question. "We both went to the University of Waterloo at Toronto."

"That's a great school—good math and engineering programs."

"Yes, that's correct."

The expressway was mostly empty, and the trip to center-city Austin went fast. The Crown Victoria swept down the concrete ramp and into the city streets.

The detective pulled down a one-way side street only a few blocks from the police barracks. The road narrowed, and Lisa felt claustrophobic. No sidewalks—just the old brick walls of industrial buildings built near the end of World War II.

Trash dumpsters lined the street, and the detective slowed down, swerving left and then right to avoid them. The speed of the car dropped to a crawl.

Lisa turned and looked through the back window. Another car had pulled into the street behind them—a black van a hundred yards back. She turned around and stared through the front window, looking around the passenger headrest. A cross street with a four-way stop was ahead.

Ron stopped at the sign and looked left and then right. A large trash truck on their right slowed and stopped at the sign. The detective made sure the trash truck driver saw him and pulled slowly into the narrow intersection.

The trash truck lurched forward.

Lisa screamed as the truck smashed into the right side of the car and kept going. The passenger's-side windows shattered instantly, showering shards of glass over the dashboard and leather seats. Ron yelled. Lisa was knocked toward the center of the car. Her seat-belt tensioner ratcheted down, and her neck and spine were caught in the whiplash.

The smell of diesel was strong, and clouds of gray exhaust billowed through the shattered windows as the tempo of the truck's engine increased.

Lisa shook her head, dazed, and looked blurrily through her door frame where a glass window had been just moments before. She saw nothing but the grill of the truck.

The car began to slide across the narrow alley until it was pinned between the left wall and the relentless trash truck. The frame of the car groaned under the stress.

Ron slammed the car into reverse, but the truck kept coming, pushing the car into the wall and continuing to crush its frame. The car's wheels squealed and smoked, but the truck's position and mass kept the vehicle from escaping its grip.

Lisa turned and looked through the rear window of the car. The black van had stopped directly behind them. Two men exited the sliding side door and ran toward the car—wearing black ski masks.

"Detective! Behind us!"

This was no accident. Lisa knew it in an instant. They were going to take her, or kill her—probably both.

Lisa reached into her bag and found Sheridan Preston's business card. She felt the sharp corners of the thin card and pulled it free, holding it in her sweating hand.

Ron shifted in the driver's seat, his right arm passing between him and the steering wheel, and pulled a pistol from a leather holster. He twisted back in his seat and pointed the gun over the driver's seat toward the rear window.

"Get down."

Lisa obeyed, putting her hands over her head and bowing her body so that her forehead almost touched her knees.

Ron's gun went off. A cannon-like roar filled the cabin of the car. Lisa's ears rang with the reverberation of the gunshot.

The rear window exploded outward, but for Lisa there was no sound, just a high-pitched ring.

Another shot—this one from behind.

Ron slumped over the wheel, and the horn of the car sounded. His foot came off the accelerator, and the motor returned to an idle.

The trash truck pulled away as rapidly as it had appeared.

One of the masked gunmen stood outside Lisa's door with a black pistol aimed straight at her face. The laser beam from the gun blinded her and refracted from the tears in her eyelashes.

"Get out!" he screamed in a thick Eastern European accent. The ringing in her ears was still at full volume. Lisa could see the man's eyes flare with hatred, emotion, and intent, but she couldn't hear his words.

Lisa trembled and struggled with the seat belt. The man cursed and kicked the door.

"I said get out!" He fired into the air. Finally her struggling fingers pressed down on the button, and the seat belt released its grip. She tried to open the door, but the crushing blow from the trash truck had jammed it closed.

The man pointing the gun at Lisa swore and reached through the empty window, grabbing Lisa roughly under the left arm as he lifted her through the window frame.

Lisa screamed in pain and fear, not sure which emotion had the upper hand. She prayed. She had no idea what these men were going to do.

The man stuffed a rag onto her face. A strong odor filled her nostrils, and her eyes watered and stung at the same time. She felt her arms and legs grow heavy.

Her last few conscious moments were a tangle of emotion and senses that were quickly shutting down.

The acidic smell of diesel fuel overwhelmed her.

Phil! Will I see him? Are they taking me to him?

She saw black military boots moving over the glass-covered asphalt.

She felt her legs dragging on the pavement and felt her hair falling over her face.

She heard footsteps and the sliding sound of the van door.

God, please protect me.

And then everything went dark.

Chapter Thirty-Five

Intersection

Detective Mark Rizzo scribbled in his casebook as the last few employees at the office park were interviewed. They knew nothing—mostly. He suspected that Lisa Baton would be the gold mine of information, but so far, the link between David Rohm and the assault at Axcess was elusive.

He was playing a hunch—something he had learned to trust after twenty years on the force. A good detective saw connections where others didn't. The trick was keeping your mouth shut about it until it was obvious to the others. If you called it too soon, you came across like an overanxious rookie who had seen too many murder mysteries on cable.

Rizzo pulled his cell phone out of his pocket and dialed Ron's number. He wanted to know what Lisa knew, and he knew she would need his help. Martin's connections with the commissioner would make this investigation difficult. He needed Lisa to become an ally.

Ron's phone rang but dropped to voice mail after seven rings. Rizzo growled in frustration. More than likely, Ron's cell phone battery was toast after the calls he'd taken on this busy day—a day that had started unusually early in the parking lot of Axcess Energy. Rizzo's message was short and precise. "Ron, call me."

He yelled at another officer, "Find out when Ron and Miss Baton arrived at the precinct."

The young officer grunted and walked toward the window, pulling the transmitter from its clipped position on his arm. "Dispatch, what's the 10-81 on Lisa Baton and Detective Ron Cantor?"

A brief silence.

"We have no record of arrival," came the voice over the radio.

"Hey, Detective Rizzo. They haven't arrived yet," said the young officer.

Rizzo looked up from his scribbling and rolled his eyes. "Yeah, I know—I overheard dispatch—everyone in the building did."

"Maybe they stopped for doughnuts," joked another officer.

Rizzo ignored the lame joke. *No arrival—that's not good.*

He tried Ron's cell again. Nothing—his voice mail picked up again.

"We're going," said Rizzo, making for the exit.

In the pit of his stomach, he knew something was terribly wrong.

This is bigger than we think.

Rizzo exited the corporate floor and flew down the stairs three at a time, heading for the lobby. He pushed through the revolving door and into the bright sunlight, throwing himself into his car and calling the precinct. "Dispatch, give me the position of Detective Cantor's car." All the Austin police cars had been LoJacked two years ago. They could be located by GPS anywhere 24/7.

There's more than one way to skin a cat.

"One moment," came the response. "Car number 432 is located at the intersection of Cole Avenue and Swisher Streets."

Rizzo visualized the intersection and began to think like bad guys do. *An alleyway—a perfect place for an ambush.*

"Is it moving?"

"One moment . . . no, it's stationary."

Rizzo cursed and squealed the tires as he headed for the precinct. He called dispatch one more time. "Contact Interpol and DHS. Put a watch/stop on the passports of Lisa Baton and Philip Channing. Get some black-and-whites over to that location—possible officer down."

Rizzo pushed the accelerator to the floor. It wouldn't matter anyway. These guys weren't taking a commercial flight to wherever they were heading. He only hoped he could save the lives of those two young people.

As Rizzo pulled off the expressway and headed for the last-known position of his colleague, he saw a traffic jam ahead. He pulled a portable police light from the glove compartment, rolled the window down, and slapped the magnetic base on the roof of the car. The drivers ahead of him did what they always did when a flashing red light appeared in their rearview mirrors.

They ignored it.

Rizzo laid on the horn at a particularly oblivious woman who was updating her Facebook status or texting her daughter or something else of incredible importance that took priority over getting to the side of the street to let a member of municipal authority through. She moved, and he turned down a street.

The mashed hulk of the Crown Vic appeared ahead—the car that Ron and Lisa had taken just an hour before.

With the attack so close to the police station, the coroner had just arrived, and a dozen crime-scene techs and other officers were already scouring the area. Rizzo parked his car as close to the side of the alleyway as he could and stepped out into the smelly, trash-filled alley. Glass from the car's windows covered the pavement. Gunshot impact points pockmarked the pavement and the frame of the car. Empty brass shell casings littered the asphalt.

Rizzo squatted near a particularly large pile of shell casings and carefully picked one up by inserting his pencil into the empty end of the expended shell.

His expertise told him much more about the empty shells than the average person would know: *9x19mm Parabellum cartridge—the world's most popular and widely used military handgun cartridge—full metal jacket of copper nickel.*

He counted the empty casings: thirty-three shells.

The local tech sniffed at Rizzo's quaint and old-fashioned style. Rizzo ignored the smirk.

"Uzis, huh?" asked Rizzo.

The tech nodded.

Rizzo swallowed. Sorrow was pushing at him, but he couldn't let it overpower him now. *Ron ran into trouble he simply couldn't win against.*

Rizzo approached the passenger's side of the car. The crushed chassis had green paint and scratches all over it.

Dull green paint, not expensive—cheap—utilitarian paint.

The right rear passenger door was jammed shut and he moved to the front door on the same side. The door had been forced open. He squatted down and looked into the interior. A white sheet of polystyrene was hung over Ron's inanimate form—hunched over the driver's wheel. Spatters of blood were on the front window, but there was no blood on the rear seats. Just glass and fluff from upholstery that had been hit during the shootout.

The similarity of the attack on Phil Channing's car was not lost on the detective.

Rizzo fought with his emotions as he saw his friend slumped over the wheel. Images of Ron Cantor's wife and children, whom he had seen at the office holiday party, rushed into his mind. He put his hand on his fallen friend's shoulder, and the plastic barrier crinkled in response.

"Ron, I'm sorry, buddy." His lip quivered a moment, and he put his hand over his face to regain his composure.

He turned around and looked at the back seat, covered with shards of glass and dried droplets of blood. As he looked down, he saw a white business card lying facedown on the floor mat.

"Hey," he yelled at a tech a few feet away. "Did you see this yet?"

The tech shook his head and came over. The detective traded places with the tech, who snapped on a pair of gloves and carefully lifted the crisp, white card from the floor mat with a long pair of silver tweezers.

"This seems a bit out of place, doesn't it?" asked the examiner.

Rizzo simply nodded. He cocked his head and followed the card as the tech pivoted it and flipped its printed side face up.

"Sheridan Preston, *Austin Chronicle*," said the tech. "Hey, that's the gal who does the local business scene, right?"

"Yeah," said Rizzo, deep in thought. ". . . the local business scene."

Lisa's a smart kid—just like Phil. Did Lisa leave this like a breadcrumb for me to follow?

He pulled out his well-used notepad and wrote down Preston's number.

Another tech approached the detective. "The tire marks over there look like they belong to a heavy-duty van."

A corporate jet roared overhead. Rizzo looked skyward, wondering if he was too late and Lisa or Phil was aboard that plane.

He clicked his radio. "I need an address lookup. Name? Sheridan Preston. It's probably unlisted."

Chapter Thirty-Six

Lisa

Lisa moaned and opened her eyes drowsily. Her memory flared to life. The trash truck lurching forward—the back window exploding in slow motion.

The detective being shot in front of her.

The smell of ether filling her nostrils.

Her eyes widened as the horror of her situation gained context.

Her mouth was covered by a hastily tied cloth. She was sitting in a leather seat in a corporate jet. She looked out the oval windows, flinging her head a bit to move the curls of her brown hair out of her eyes, and saw the cloud base far below.

Where are they taking me?

She heard voices behind her. Voices she didn't understand. Voices thick with Russian accents. Were there two or three or five men? The accents swirled together. She couldn't tell—the voices were too similar.

Her hands were bound by a plastic zip tie, but her legs were free. Panic filled her frame.

I have to get out of here!

She stood up and rushed down the aisle, trying to keep her balance, but still dizzy from the ether.

The voices raised in volume and urgency. Lisa lost her balance and pitched forward onto the gray carpet of the jet. She struggled to stand up again, and a strong man with blond hair grabbed her roughly, flipped her onto her back, and straddled her midsection. His arms came down like anvils on her shoulders, pinning her to the floor.

One of the men in the back of the plane said something to her attacker in Russian. The tone was unmistakable—urging him on—baiting him. Even without knowing Russian, the man's meaning was clear. Lisa could only hope and pray that the man above her wouldn't follow his compatriot's advice. She struggled beneath his weight, twisting her body left and right.

The man yelled at the men behind him. His tone was urgent, demanding something from his colleagues. Lisa, taking advantage of the distraction, brought her knees up with a jerk. The man on top of her doubled over, groaning in pain. Lisa rolled to her side before another man rushed forward with something shiny and metallic. She twisted her slender body under the man, squirming under his weight. He slapped her hard across the face. Lisa stopped struggling as the sting of the slap faded in a blush of heat.

The second man brought a metallic object to his eye level. It glinted in the sunlight that was streaming through the oval windows of the jet.

A hypodermic needle.

He tapped the side of the syringe expertly with his index finger while applying pressure. Serum squirted in a needle-thin arc through the air. The air was pierced with the smell of it.

Then she felt a sting—a prick in her arm. The serum rushed from the syringe into her bloodstream. She felt it traveling through her and her heart rate accelerating. The luxurious cabin of the jet began to revolve around her.

A wave of nausea rushed through her, and then everything went dark—again.

"You're such an idiot," growled the man who had been kneed in the groin. "Why didn't you just kill her? Bringing her with us is a mistake."

Gorin threw the syringe on the closest leather seat. "Her fiancé has information we must stop, and after your blunder at the corporate park, we have to leave America. It's too dangerous to stay long enough to find the boy."

Gorin pointed at Lisa's unconscious form. "But now we have something he loves, and we will have his undivided attention. He's going to come to us."

Chapter Thirty-Seven
Rogue

The white corporate jet carrying Gorin and his prisoner roared across the Mediterranean at six hundred miles an hour. They were headed for Izmir, a port town on the western coast of Turkey. They would meet the weapons shipment and ensure it was properly disguised and protected for shipment to Syria.

Gorin walked from the cockpit toward his comrades, who were playing cards in the back of the plane, using a thick piece of cardboard resting on an ottoman as a table. He stopped and looked down at Lisa's unconscious body lying across three leather seats. The anesthetic had done its job well. She would sleep for the remainder of the flight.

The plane rattled for a moment as it flew through the turbulent air rising from the warm waters below. Gorin steadied himself by placing his hand against the ceiling of the fuselage.

He unzipped his jacket and walked back toward the guffawing men who were half-drunk and laughing at the misfortune of a particularly bad hand of cards.

214

The men looked up at Gorin standing behind them and encouraged him to sit down and join them. Gorin smiled and held out his hand—he was too stressed to think of playing cards right now. He turned and headed back up the aisle toward Lisa.

His right hand snaked across his chest and pulled a pistol from a leather holster mounted under his left arm. He carefully lifted the gun and spun around, facing his friends.

Bleep, blip, bleep.

Two of the men slumped forward onto the makeshift card table, and the third was knocked backward into the curved wall of the fuselage, eyes wide with surprise and a red hole centered in his forehead.

Gorin glanced toward the cockpit. He could see the pilot's right arm working a dial on the console, apparently unaware that the passenger manifest was now lighter by three.

He took a quick swig of the alcohol the men had been drinking and collected each man's credentials: wallets, passports, even rings and watches that could be used to identify them.

On the way back up to the cockpit, Gorin straightened Lisa's limp body across the seats and wrapped a seat belt around her midsection, making sure it was snug on his precious cargo. He reached under her seat, pulled out an oxygen mask, and carefully snapped it over her mouth and nose. He cracked the valve on the oxygen bottle until the gauge on the regulator matched his desired amount.

Gorin stepped into the cockpit and slipped into the copilot's seat.

"How's the view from up here?" asked Gorin, buckling his seat belt.

"What are you doing?" asked the pilot. "You shouldn't be up here."

Gorin glanced at the altimeter. *Ten thousand three hundred feet—close enough.*

"I've made a small change in plans," he said, pulling out the pistol and pointing it at the man's head.

His finger squeezed the trigger. The window on the pilot's left side burst into shards even as the pilot slumped over the yoke, and the plane began to depressurize. Loose papers, charts, and flight plans swirled through the air and were sucked out the smashed window. Gorin reached under his seat for an oxygen mask, fitted it tightly over his mouth, and pushed the yoke forward. The plane dove toward the earth. Gorin watched the altimeter spin counterclock-wise. He was heading under radar range.

The mountains of Turkey appeared in the windscreen ahead as the jet broke through the clouds. Gorin continued the dive but began to put the plane into a turn as well. He watched the bearing of the plane change slowly until it was heading southeast.

■ ■ ■ ■

Lisa rolled over and opened her eyes. She had a five-alarm headache, and her shoulders hurt from being in the same position for hours. Her vision was blurry; she saw halos around everything. She shook her head and blinked her eyes.

A voice boomed over the top of her. "Good morning."

Lisa looked up groggily and saw a man smoking a cigarette. "Who are you?"

"My name is Gorin, and I'll be your host for the next thirty hours or so." He had a thick Russian accent.

"What are you going to do with me?" She knew she probably didn't want to know the answer.

"My dear, I'm using you as bait. Now, come with me." Lisa began to struggle, but as Gorin scooped her up and laid her over his shoulder, she saw the men who had been in the back of the plane. Each one had a bullet hole in his head. She stopped fighting.

Gorin set Lisa down on the floor of a black van and rolled the door closed. She sat up and looked out the back window. Another man was helping Gorin. He wore a blue jacket with yellow letters that read "Parezim Petroleum."

She looked left and right. The jet was parked between aircraft hangars, seemingly abandoned. The metal on the structures was rusting and in disrepair. A dust devil spun on the deserted pavement between the buildings. She looked back at the men and watched Gorin hand the other man an envelope stuffed with money.

The man in the petroleum-company jacket flipped through the bills, nodded in satisfaction, and stuffed the envelope into his pants pocket. The two men pulled a gray object out of a box that was sitting by the open hatch of the jet. They fiddled with it for a few moments and then headed back toward the van.

Lisa ducked down, hoping they hadn't seen her. She lay down on the dirty carpet of the van and prayed.

God, please protect me.

The doors of the van opened, and Gorin slipped behind the steering wheel and started the vehicle as the other man slammed the passenger's-side door. The van's tires squealed as it pulled out, knocking Lisa backward onto the floor of the vehicle.

The van slalomed its way through a maze of hangars and support buildings for the airport before exiting the site and heading down a two-lane highway.

Lisa sat up on her knees and looked out the rear window again. She watched an orange mushroom cloud explode behind the fence that outlined the airport. An oily smoke column began to rise into the air over the hangars that were getting smaller and smaller in Lisa's sight. A few minutes later, she watched as firetrucks rushed past the van toward the blaze that was consuming the jet that had brought her here against her will.

Chapter Thirty-Eight
Going to Press

"A re you sure you want to do this?" asked Sheridan's editor. He was leaning forward on his heavily used wooden desk, which was scratched and scarred, as he always did when she produced a column like this. His eyebrows were like bushy white clouds that floated over piercing blue eyes. Barry Golden looked like he had spent a lifetime in the news business, which he had. He knew why he was asking this pointed question.

Sheridan Preston wasn't sure she wanted her story to go to print, but she wasn't about to show insecurity or weakness in front of her boss. He was the last person on earth she would allow to see her second-guessing herself. She crossed her arms and leaned against the wall adorned with Golden's newspaper awards.

"Absolutely," she answered.

The editor's wrinkled hands hovered over the crisp white paper that was still warm from Sheridan's laser printer. "You've had hard-hitting pieces before,

Preston, but this—" He tapped the papers with his hands. "You've never done anything like this. This could really make life miserable for you and me during the next twenty-four hours."

Sheridan's tone was insistent. "I've been working on this story for over a year. You of all people know how big, how important this is."

The editor sat back in his worn leather chair and smiled at his star reporter. "I just wanted to make sure you really believed in this story."

Sheridan stopped herself from smiling with relief. *I guess I passed the test.*

"We go with it tomorrow—front page. It's easily your best work yet." He pressed a button on his phone, and the speakerphone sounded with a ringing tone.

"Press." The sounds of the offset printing press churning through reams of paper could be heard in the background.

"Peter, we've got the front-page story for the morning edition. Sheridan's going to e-mail it to you right now. Let's get it ready, and call me at home if we have any issues."

"No problem." The call terminated.

"Okay," said Golden, standing and looking at the old clock on his desk. "Eleven-thirty—it's late. You'd better get some sleep, because I think tomorrow's going to be a big day—for both of us."

Her boss extended his hand, and she shook it—professional—nothing personal—just the way she liked it.

Sheridan left the editor's office and nearly ran to her cubicle. Her step was light with excitement. The energy of sending this story to press pulsed through her like a secret only she knew—but the world would know it in a few short hours. She quickly e-mailed the story to the press supervisor and waited for the delivery receipt. Almost immediately, the receipt popped into her inbox. She closed the lid on her laptop and grabbed her purse, heading for the parking garage.

The ride home was fast, and her mind was on to other things—like her acceptance speech for the Pulitzer Prize. She thought through the day and the treasure trove of material Lisa Baton had given to her that morning. The missing links . . . the parts she had searched for that had eluded her in the maze of state government and federal bureaucracy.

She had despaired when she heard about David Rohm's strange death late last night. Sheridan had thought the story was over, a path with a literal dead end. And then Lisa had dropped this into her lap. She placed her hand into the computer bag and touched the manila folder the young woman had given to her as if it was part of a dream and might evaporate from her grip.

What a roller-coaster ride this day has been.

She pulled into her long driveway and slowed as she approached the satellite garage in the large yard. The garage door opened, and she parked the car and walked toward the front door along a winding paved pathway. She fished her house keys out of her purse and had just inserted them in the lock when she heard footsteps behind her.

"Miss Preston?"

She turned to find a tall man with a black mustache coming up the walk. Her heart rate increased, and she began to back away.

He raised his hands and stopped walking. "I'm not here to hurt you." He pulled something from his breast pocket and held it out to the side. "This is my badge. I'm a detective with the Austin Police Department. My name's Mark Rizzo."

"What's this about?" Sheridan demanded. Her eyes glanced at the badge.

"We have reason to believe you might be in danger," he said calmly.

"What makes you think that?" asked Sheridan.

"Because you met with Lisa Baton today, and she's been kidnapped. My partner was killed trying to defend her from the people who took her."

Sheridan's countenance changed from belligerence to concern—the emotional response Rizzo had been hoping for.

"Lisa? Where is she?" Sheridan whispered, her eyes flicking up and down the road.

"We don't know. That was something I was hoping you could help us with. Can we step inside and talk for a while?"

"Just as soon as I call my editor," said Sheridan.

"Whatever you want." Rizzo's lip curled beneath his bushy mustache, and he jammed a fresh toothpick between his teeth.

Sheridan began to work the lock while Rizzo walked the remaining distance. He looked up and saw a strange green wire running from the top of the door through the thin tolerance between the door and the jam.

"No! Wait!" screamed the detective.

The lock clicked, and Sheridan pushed open the door. Rizzo rushed up onto the porch, placing his body between her and the door, sweeping her away from the house in the same motion, and diving headlong into a mulch bed with his body over Sheridan's. His long field coat sailed out behind him.

Inside the house, the circuit from the copper contact on the door closed, and a black satchel sitting ten feet back against a load-bearing wall exploded, shattering the wall and sending a shock wave throughout the entire residence.

Windows shattered, and bricks blasted from their firm nest in the white mortar of the walls. An explosion and shock wave blasted outward from the living room and rolled out of the windows before turning into a roiling black cloud that dissipated into the night sky.

Rizzo waited an extra second before lifting his head and looking back at the destruction. The house was demolished. Wood splinters that had been the door were spread all over the front lawn, along with bricks and the glass from the blown-out windows.

Car alarms sounded all through the housing development, and windows began to illuminate as the neighbors were jarred from slumber and late-night TV talk shows.

Rizzo rolled off Sheridan. She pushed up from the mulch bed and brushed her blonde hair out of her eyes, staring in horror at the place she had stood just a minute before.

Her voice trembled. "I would've been killed."

Rizzo looked at the shattered doorway. It looked like a grenade had gone off. "For sure," he said.

Rizzo stood up to full height and looked down on the reporter. "How 'bout this . . . you tell me what you know, and I'll tell you what I know. Maybe we can still save Lisa and Phil." He cocked his head toward the remains of the house. "These guys play for keeps."

The normally unflappable reporter nodded. In the distance, sirens headed toward the remains of her house could be heard in the night air.

Chapter Thirty-Nine
Gideon's Spies

P hil was bumped out of sleep by the warm air gliding over the land of
Israel and colliding with the cooler air off the Mediterranean Sea. He
grabbed the armrests on his seat before he realized it was just turbulence.

Caleb laughed as his friend gripped the chair with white knuckles.

Phil wiped his hand across his face and rubbed his bloodshot eyes. He
looked out the window of the jet and saw the city of Tel Aviv scrolling by beneath him. Skyscrapers and modern buildings were in good supply, and Phil
was surprised at how much Tel Aviv resembled any other city—certainly not
like its ancient sister, holy Jerusalem, to the east.

The pilot's Hebrew words broke the droning sound of the two turbine
engines to announce the landing. Just a moment later, Phil heard the whirring
sound of the landing gear being lowered and locked. The runways of the Ben
Gurion International Airport came into view, and the tires squealed as the
Gulfstream touched down and rolled to a stop.

"Now what?" asked Phil.

"A quick trip to Mossad headquarters," said one of the scientists who had drilled him with questions about the reserve during their flight over the Atlantic.

The Gulfstream taxied to a stop, and Phil, Caleb, Amir, and the scientists disembarked. Three black SUVs arrived and parked close to the plane. Phil jumped into the back seat of one, sliding to the middle, and Amir and Caleb flanked him. The windows were tinted black, and the drivers had earpieces and no sense of humor. As soon as Caleb pulled his door closed, the locks on the doors popped down, and the convoy sped off.

■ ■ ■ ■

Twenty minutes later, the line of SUVs pulled up to a modern-looking building that would have been at home in any city—with one small exception.

"Why are the windows that color?" asked Phil. Every window on the building was tinted with amber. They stood out in odd contrast to the other buildings on the block that had normal windows.

"That's a special copper sheathing that keeps conversations in and snooping laser microphones out," said Caleb.

A number of guards armed with Tavor Tar 21 assault rifles were in the lobby, and Phil stayed close to Caleb as they made it through the security gauntlet. For the first time, it started to sink in that he was in the company of spies.

The group of scientists along with Caleb and Phil walked down a long, pristine hallway lined with doors that had mysterious labels and security badge scanners.

Code names, no doubt, thought Phil.

The scientists finally grouped around a doorway with a label in Hebrew.

"What's it say?" whispered Phil. He felt like his voice echoed in the white hallway even as he tried to speak softly.

"The Promise," Caleb replied under his breath.

The door clicked, and the men walked into a command center. Flat plasma screens lined the walls, and computer workstations were in abundance. Then Phil saw something he didn't expect. In the center of the room was a mess of Playboxes, cords, and zip ties. An exact replica of his handiwork in Austin.

Phil walked up to it. "You built a grid just like mine."

"It's nearly a perfect replica, Phil. It's only missing one thing: the data you were going to mail to the archives last night."

A scientist took the digital tape out of a package of Bubble Wrap and loaded the data.

A few minutes later, the Maximal Reserve was floating before everyone on four screens, instead of the three that Phil had rigged up back at Axcess.

"Sorry, Phil, I had to add another one. I wanted to do it right."

"No apologies needed, Caleb. I was on a fixed budget—my personal budget," said Phil. "How long has the Mossad known about the reserve?"

"That's a long story, but for about a year we've been tracking the Russian pipeline's construction and political progress. Russia was placing industrial spies in key positions with all of the contractors that were involved with the pipeline. When I joined the team last year and saw some of the radar returns and the track of the anomalies, we began our own crash project to understand where it led. Unfortunately, one of the projects we secretly funded was also penetrated, and Jack was killed."

"*You* placed Jack on the lava tunnel project that he e-mailed to me?"

Caleb looked down at the floor. "Yes. He was so excited, and I knew it was important for him and would do wonders for his career. Aliya doesn't know. It's a decision that will haunt me for the rest of my life."

An officer dressed in a pale green uniform walked over and handed a printout to Caleb. "We've been scanning Philip's e-mail, and he just received this." The patches on the man's uniform identified him as belonging to Israeli intelligence. Caleb glanced at the printout and handed the still-warm paper to Phil.

It was simple and frightening to read.

I HAVE SOMETHING YOU WANT.
31° 19′ 31.92″ N
35° 21′ 09.85″ E
Come by way of the Dead Sea and the Ziggurat. You have three hours.
P.S. The second attachment is for my friend, Caleb. Enjoy.

The e-mail signature was from Gorin Vladofsky.

"He sent this to my corporate e-mail account at Axcess?" Phil asked. "Is he nuts? He has to know that the Austin authorities will be monitoring my e-mail and my phone."

Caleb nodded silently—this was a new wrinkle.

"Come with me to watch the video and see the other attachment." The officer who had brought the disturbing note walked back to his workstation.

The intelligence officer double-clicked the video, and it sprang to life on his screen. The quality was terribly poor. Phil thought it was probably taken from a cell phone—frames dropped in and out of the feed, and the motion was jerky with snow and interlace problems. The images were dark—very low lighting—but with a strange amber quality to them. Orange shades and high-contrast shadows lay on the floor and the walls of the environment the cell phone's camera was capturing.

Finally, an image came across the screen that made Phil's emotions move in two directions at once: joy and horror.

"Lisa!"

Her face was down, chin on her chest, and she was curled into a near-fetal position with her arms behind her. Her eyes were covered in a blindfold, and her dark, beautiful hair spilled down over her face.

Gorin's voice came over the background, taunting her. "What's your name?" His voice cracked. It sounded different from Phil's memory: more maniacal.

Lisa said nothing.

A blur smeared across the video as Gorin slapped her face. "Speak—you insolent minx!"

Phil's heart filled with rage as he heard his fiancée gasp from the blow and watched as her face slowly returned to center from the whiplash of the assault.

Lisa's lip trembled as she spoke her name. Phil could hear the despair in her voice as if she were reading the tombstone of her own grave. "Lisa Baton."

The camera tilted and faced upward toward Gorin. His eyes were wide, and his face was smudged with dirt and grime. "Don't wait too long, Phil." He began to laugh, and then the video ended.

"The e-mail was sent by Vladofsky's cell phone," said the intelligence officer. "I hate to state the obvious here, but the fact that this man is using unencrypted e-mails and sending messages like this from registered cell phones can only mean that he wants to be found and caught—not the best sign of a man thinking straight."

"Can you triangulate the signal of the phone now?" asked Caleb.

"That's the strange part. No. The coordinates he gave are just near the Dead Sea, here." The officer pulled up a map on the computer and pointed at the location with his mouse. "It's nothing but a plateau—just part of the plain near the Dead Sea. Anything coming off there would readily be picked up by our signal intelligence network, but we can't even pick up the phone polling for e-mail or text messages."

"That's because he's underground," said Phil.

Caleb reread the short message from Gorin. "Show me the second attachment."

As the image appeared on the officer's display, Caleb's stomach fell. A picture of a young man's body lying on dark grassy field with a bullet hole in his forehead filled his vision.

Phil's voice was just barely audible as he looked at the haunting image of his friend and imagined his last moments. "Jack . . . "

Caleb looked at the time of the transmission and glanced at the clock on the wall. "We're wasting time. Let's go."

"I'm coming with you," said Phil.

Caleb shook his head. "No, Phil. This is too dangerous, and you're too close to it. The Mossad trains for this sort of thing."

"You're too close to it as well, Caleb," said another voice.

Phil and Caleb turned to find Amir adjusting a strap on his backpack. "I want Phil to come. He knows Gorin, and he's seen the tunnel structures and understands the underground environment. You should stay. You can help us more from here."

Caleb remained silent. Phil put a hand on his friend's shoulder. "If it were Aliya, I wouldn't be able to hold you back."

Amir smiled. "Let's go, Phil."

The three men walked to an elevator and took it to the top floor of the headquarters where a heavy-duty helipad waited. As a military helicopter approached from the distance, Caleb gave Phil a pat on the back. "I'll be monitoring your progress. At the first sign of trouble, the entire Israeli army will be on that mountain range."

Phil embraced Caleb, and then Caleb stepped back and watched with his arms folded.

Two more Israeli commandos joined them on the ramp, and Amir introduced them to Phil. "This is Nuri Gantz and Tal Yadlin. They're going to help us get Lisa out."

A helicopter landed on the helipad just as Phil returned handshakes with the other members of the team. Nuri and Tal led Phil to the helicopter. Amir jogged behind them and was stopped by a tug on his backpack. It was Caleb.

Caleb leaned in and yelled over the helicopter's turbine. "You know this is a trap, don't you?"

"Of course it is," said Amir with a smile. "Don't worry, Caleb. I'll take care of him."

Caleb nodded and patted Amir on the back. The Israeli commando turned and ran after Phil, who was climbing into the cabin of the helicopter waiting to take them to a base near the Dead Sea.

Chapter Forty
Salt Sea

P hil stared out into the blue expanse of the Dead Sea that filled his vision on the left side of the road. Trails of minerals bloomed into the open water from their salty, mineral-encased harbors along the side of the sea, branching and creating a series of mineral reefs in the cyan and turquoise water. Nuri and Tal were sitting in the back of the jeep, going over a map of the area and conversing with Mossad headquarters about the latest satellite and sur- veillance footage of the mountains over the coordinates Gorin had provided.

"We have a drone flying over the area. There is no evidence of any other force on radar or on the ground. Gorin is definitely working alone," said Tal.

Amir frowned. "I'd rather have the entire Syrian army on radar. Who knows what this madman has in mind?" The two commandos in the back shared the same sentiment.

"The lowest spot on earth," said Amir, gripping the steering wheel of the jeep and glancing at the sparkling water. "The Dead Sea is over thirteen hun- dred feet below sea level." The commando followed the curves of the coastal highway that delineated the body of water from the desolation on the passenger's side—rugged, mountainous terrain leaped from the sand and rubble.

A white tourist bus rushed past, carrying visitors to the tourist sites around the Dead Sea. The healing properties of the highly buoyant waters were well known, and they attracted everyone from cancer patients seeking healing to movie stars looking for that extra edge for flawless skin.

As Amir drove around a bend in the road, Phil's breathing halted for a moment. The colors of the rock, which had been rich in shades of terra-cotta, red, and purple, were interrupted by a lighter range of color, nearly white. The color change seemed to burst from the landscape and continue up and down the coast for miles.

"Why is the color of the terrain so different here? It's not from the minerals in the Dead Sea, is it?"

"That's Gomorrah, a city so wicked that God destroyed it with fire from the sky. Another four cities to the north were also destroyed," said Amir, noting Phil's fascination with the ashen formations.

Phil's mind reviewed the references he had learned in Sunday school about Lot and his departure from the doomed cities. "There were five cities? I thought there were only two."

Amir nodded. "The five cities were called the Pentapolis: Sodom, Gomorrah, Admah, Zeboim, and Bela, which some people call Zoar. They were also known as the Cities of the Plain."

Phil was astonished. He had heard this story his whole life, but here in front of him were the ruins. "This is where Lot and his family escaped from?"

"They're the only ones who made it out—the only righteous people in the city," said Tal, one of the commandos in the back of the jeep.

Nuri, seated next to him, snorted and laughed. "Which is tragic, because within a few days, Lot's daughters are so sure they're the only ones left in the world that they get him drunk and have children with him."

Nuri's cynicism made Phil wonder whether they believed the story or if the ancient escape was just a myth to them.

Amir slowed down and pulled off the paved road onto an unpaved frontage road that headed toward the ghostly structures. He drove for a few minutes before the ground became deep in ash and sand. He stopped the car and looked out across the stark landscape. "We walk from here."

Phil jumped out of the jeep, ready to get into the mine. The sooner they got started, the better. Time was running out for Lisa.

Amir began pulling equipment from the back of the jeep and stacking it into a pile. He handed Phil a climbing harness made of thick black nylon and covered in carabiners, quick draws, and rotors, the basic tools for making secured connections to rock walls. A bright blue descender hung from the front of the harness.

"It's smart to be prepared," said Amir. The multicolored climbing rope Amir was stacking on the tailgate looked like a nightmare of rattlesnakes and coral snakes. Phil lifted two of the rolled ropes over his shoulder.

"How much climbing have you done?" asked Amir.

"Quite a bit, actually," said Phil. "I did a bunch in undergraduate during trips to the field—it kind of goes with the territory."

"Good enough. Two more things, Phil," said Amir, reaching into the back of the jeep. He pulled out a helmet with a headlamp strapped to the front and tossed it to Phil. While Phil juggled his increasingly gangly collection of climbing gear, Amir reached into a small box and brought out an instrument wrapped in protective Bubble Wrap. "This one's important."

It was a gas monitor, a device for measuring toxic gases in the air.

Amir handed it to Phil. "This was a sulfur mine, and we must be careful of hydrogen sulfide. There are blooms of H_2S all over the Dead Sea area."

Phil turned the instrument over and found a clip on the back as well as a small cord with a clasp to prevent him from dropping the precious device. He placed the monitor on his harness and secured the cord to his belt buckle.

"If you smell rotten eggs, you'll find a mask in your backpack. You'll only smell it for a few moments before you lose consciousness, so you'll need to move fast."

Amir reached over and pressed the "test" button on Phil's gas monitor. The display lit up with a graphic bar and a number and chirped.

"The display will beep if it detects anything, and the display will show you how much gas is in the area."

"When should I be worried?" asked Phil as he put on his climbing helmet and adjusted the chin strap.

"Hydrogen sulfide will initially be detected by its odor, but that quickly stops as your olfactory nerves become paralyzed. It doesn't take a lot to mess you up—around five parts per one hundred. Then your nervous system will start to come apart: tremors, shaking, that sort of thing. Eye irritation shows up right after that, and then pulmonary edema. Your lungs will fill up, and you'll drown in your own fluids. With any luck, you'll pass out before you drown."

Phil gulped and reexamined the device. "Did you put fresh batteries in before we left?"

Amir let out a hearty laugh and slapped the top of Phil's helmet. "Of course! You ready?"

"As ready as I'll ever be."

"Then let's do it!"

As the team trudged across the rough terrain, the soil became craggy, filled with rocks bursting through the dirt and laced with white alkali, and rock salt, which glinted in the sunlight. Amir stepped across a particularly large dome-shaped feature and turned to find Phil examining the rocky mount as he walked across its crunchy surface.

In the center of the salt dome, a set of rusty pipes with valve coverings protruded. A corroding chain with a padlock was wrapped around the device to keep the unauthorized from opening the valve. A dozen wooden frames were stacked like palettes, warping in the arid environment.

Phil recognized the arrangement immediately. "They were mining sulfur here. Why'd they stop?"

Amir kept walking, and his response was ominous. "You'll see."

The Israeli commando pointed toward the south at a large mountain barren of any vegetation. It was a plateau—a table-like structure that soared above the plain that ran to the Dead Sea. "That's Masada up there."

Phil looked up at the distant fortification sitting atop of the imposing mountain. He thought of the Jewish Sicarii, who had held off the greatest army on earth, the Roman Empire, before committing mass suicide rather than being taken captive. Masada was a source of pride and resolve to the nation of Israel—an example that sometimes there were things worth dying for.

Some things—like Lisa. Phil set his jaw and continued on, hoping with all his heart that he had what it took to get through the next few hours.

Chapter Forty-One
Brimstone

P hil, Amir, Nuri, and Tal hiked through the gray material that enveloped the landscape. The ground was deep with ash, chalk-like flakes that became deeper and deeper as they neared the larger structures of the doomed city. Within minutes, the black and blond leather segments of Phil's climbing boots were indistinguishable from the whiteness around them, and walking became difficult, like walking in deep sand.

The two men passed by a strange column, standing alone and very out of place on the barren landscape. Its sides were alternating layers of gray and white, which was eroded by centuries of wind and sand and water brushing up against it.

"This is man-made," said Amir. "Look at the base."

Phil looked at the bottom of the odd, sphinx-like shape. The base was distinct, jutting out before narrowing into a column that protruded about five feet up and became conical on the top.

"What was it?"

Amir rubbed his hand along the vitrified edge of the column. "Who knows . . . it could've been a pagan symbol or a statue of a god. It was probably something erected to bring the city fortune and luck or to keep evil spirits away."

Phil looked from the sphinx of layered ash back to the larger remains of the city behind him. "Whatever it was, it didn't work. Let's keep going."

The sand and ash became deeper and deeper, and the sun's heat increased with every step. Phil examined the landscape for anything that would tell him he was still on Earth and not on some other planet in another galaxy. Nothing was growing here, not even a blade of grass. It was as if God had cursed this ground from bearing any fruit, vegetation, or life of any kind.

As they walked, the haunted atmosphere of the place worked on Phil. He wondered why God had put him in this situation, why He had allowed Lisa to be abducted by Gorin, why Jack had to die. This city felt like his faith right now as he struggled through the deep ash.

Shoulder-high mounds of white began to appear as they hiked toward the mountain range. The edges were straight, approaching ninety degrees and betraying that they weren't natural structures, but walls made by the hands of men. Sheets of stone and ash covered the ground between the mounds.

Small spheres of white covered the powdered ash of the floor like hailstones, some even embedded in the walls. Phil pulled out a small rock hammer and knocked one of the spheres loose. It popped away from the ash layers without effort and left behind a dark, scorched cavity.

"What've you found?" asked Amir, looking at the strange ball in Phil's hand.

"Brimstone," said Phil, and with a short, jerking motion he brought the hammer down on the equator of the small crusty sphere.

"The ancient term for—"

Crack! The sphere broke apart.

"—sulfur,"Amir finished.

Phil dabbed his finger on the inside material and touched his tongue. He coughed and spit out the bitter, acidic taste. He handed the broken hemisphere to Amir, who held it to his nose and sniffed. The unmistakable odor of sulfur spiked into his nasal passages.

The four men looked at the walls of the ancient city and the streets ahead of them. Hundreds—no—thousands of the spheres ranging from marble-sized to softball-sized littered the landscape. Along the walls of the city like bullet

holes, black, discolored rings outlined the white balls of brimstone, which had
rained from heaven and consumed the city in a conflagration.

Amir pointed at a structure ahead of them that broke free of the low-slung
walls and towered over the rest of the rubble. "There's the landmark Gorin
named: the ziggurat."

Phil picked up the pace at the mention of Lisa's kidnapper and was the
first to reach the massive structure after jogging through a recess that encircled
the ancient building. The crumbling edifice was massive, square, and the size
of a city block. Each of its walls was about six stories tall. A conical pyramid of
flaky white debris capped the structure.

"Look at that," said Phil, pointing to the walls of the ziggurat. The pattern
of ash on the wall of the ziggurat was different from the sphinx on the outskirts
of the doomed city: instead of layers of ash sandwiched together, the ash here
was captured in a frozen swirl like the vortex of a whirlpool captured in a pho-
tograph. The swirls were tiled across the surface of the crumbling wall, each
swirl traveling in the opposite direction from the ones adjacent to it.

Phil touched the delicate ashen wall, interpreting what he saw out loud.
"These swirling patterns are from ionization. The temperatures here had to be
so hot that the magnetic fields of the electrons in the air were attracting and
repelling one another." The surface beneath his fingers immediately gave way
and fell into a pile of dust at the base of the wall.

"How hot does it have to be for that to happen?" asked Amir.

"About six thousand degrees," replied Phil solemnly. "This whole place
was vitrified—rock walls, wooden fences, people, animals—nothing had a
chance." Nuri let out a low whistle. The wall almost seemed to come alive
before them. The men could imagine what it must have been like in that moment when a swirling cauldron of death in the form of super-hot gas swept
through the streets, incinerating the city's inhabitants as molten balls of sulfur fell from the sky.

"Where to next?" asked Phil.

Amir glanced at his GPS, which was holding the coordinates from Gorin's
e-mail as its destination. "Northwest—there!" he said, pointing at a nearly vertical city wall that towered over the doomed landscape three hundred yards away.
Phil ran toward the ruins with renewed vigor, knowing that Lisa was close.

The walls of the ancient metropolis rose far above the desolate remains of
the once-proud city. A hill of rubble and dust sloped from the ninety-degree

walls covering the base of the defensive structure. As Phil and the Mossad agents got closer to the wall, they saw faint rectangular outlines on its stratified face. A rectangle here, the faint outline of a doorway there—once Phil spotted them, he saw doors and windows everywhere.

The sandy, ash formations were haunting, as if he could see children, women, and men staring back at him, warning him—begging, pleading with him to leave the city.

An arched doorway rose from the debris and dust of millennia, encrusted in salt and melted, glassy rock. A flat, cracked rock lay near the arch. A scrawl of writing was barely visible on its smooth face. Phil kneeled and brushed the ash and alkali from the inscription. He recognized the alphabet and the language as Hebrew.

סיהולא עבצא

"What's it say?" he asked.

"*Etsba Elohim*," whispered Amir. "The Finger of God." The commando's voice had a touch of reverence.

Amir made his way around the fallen stone that blocked their path and stepped into the darkness of the arched doorway. "That's what the workers here called this cave. When we get inside, you'll understand why."

A large, rusting panel of metal covered the passage. Amir pulled a pair of leather gloves from his pack and bent the thin, corroding metal away from the cave wall.

"In you go," he grunted, straining to hold the metal. Phil quickly scampered inside and then helped Amir with the rusting sheet metal as he made it into the passage. Nuri and Tal followed close behind.

As the metal snapped back, the four men were engulfed in the pitch darkness. Amir struck a flare on the wall and it flamed to life, burning incandescently and lighting up the tunnel's walls. They walked for a little way before the flare burned to its end, and the team clicked on their headlamps. The dust they had brought in with them was settling, snowing down onto the chipped aggregate beneath their shoes.

"Come on," said Amir.

The men walked through the throat of the cave and into the darkness beyond.

Chapter Forty-Two
The Passage

Phil and Amir's headlamps danced on the smoothly cut stone walls like Hollywood spotlights. Nuri and Tal were hanging behind a little, keeping watch in case trouble followed them in. Thick timber and iron beams that helped support the ceiling made appearances periodically, but the mine was essentially empty.

Ahead of the men, the mine shaft turned to the right and ended abruptly. The smooth walls and angular man-made cuts against the stone ended, and craggy boulders with fissures began to appear.

A wall of rock closed off the shaft. Only a small, three-foot hole had escaped an avalanche of boulders that had to weigh five tons or more.

"This is where the mine ended," said Amir.

"Why did they stop? Did they go out of business?" asked Phil.

"No. When the miners found this entrance and what lay beyond, they said this was cursed ground and left."

"You mean they walked off the job?"

"Yes, to a man," said Amir, getting on his knees and sliding into the open-ing. "Come on."

Phil tried to think of the times in his life when he had done dumb things, but all of them paled in perspective to crawling through a hole in a wall under-ground where dozens of stoic miners had been so scared they had quit their jobs. Phil closed his eyes for a moment, summoned some courage, and found his love for Lisa enough to propel him to follow Amir into the hole.

It was a tight space. Phil squirmed and squeezed between rocks and through miniature canyons until he reached the end, where the claustrophobic passage opened into a large cavern.

Phil struggled through the portal and stood up covered in dust. The cav-ern was enormous. Beautiful mineral veins meandered through the limestone and granite of the cavern walls. The ceiling of the cavern formed up into a huge dome, but the ceiling was not smooth.

Phil grabbed Amir's flashlight and twisted the rim, narrowing the beam. Miniature ripples of rock, like ripples in a pond frozen in time, covered the vaulted ceiling.

"They're lavacicles," said Amir. "This isn't just a cave system. It's a lava tube. The heat from the lava got so hot that the ceiling began to melt."

Amir pointed across the space of the cavern to the walls toward the begin-ning of the dome. "Look over there; you can see the marks on the cave wall where the lava reached."

Phil scanned the rock face and saw what looked like watermarks every few feet. The lava level in the passage had created etch marks that changed the color of the rock.

"Let's get Lisa. She's gonna hate being in here," said Phil. Normally the cavern would have fascinated him—but the danger to Lisa was all-consuming. He felt hollow without her—like the cavern that stretched high above them and plunged to the depths below. He started to tie the rope into a strong an-chor. "Come on; let's get to the bottom of this thing."

Beneath the ledge that Phil and Amir stood on, a huge pillar formation stretched down into the depths of the cavern. The pillar was one massive sta-lagmite covered in grooves and pits from lava flows a thousand years before.

Phil tested the rappel anchor and fastened up a backup. The words of his climbing instructors in college echoed in his mind: *Tie the anchor like your life depends on it.*

Next, Phil tied a double figure-eight knot into the end of the anchor, creating an equalized point and sharing the load between the two tie-down points. After he double-checked that the rope wasn't lying on sharp edges, Phil looked over the edge and yelled into the darkness, "Rope!" He tossed the coil of rope into the blackness and heard it hit the ground of the next level.

Phil tied himself into the rope and arranged his descender. He saw the almost-amused look on Amir's face. "The sooner we get down this cliff, the sooner we get to Lisa."

He unclipped himself from the anchor, leaned back into his harness, and walked off the cliff backwards, letting slack move through his descender slowly at first by moving his right hand, the brake hand, to the front, and braking the rope by simply moving his right arm away from the center. His own audacity surprised him—but it helped to know that Amir and later the other two Mossad commandos would follow.

He rappelled down the wall's face. The gray and brown rock material scrolled beneath his feet, glittering every so often with small minerals peeking through the basalt.

Halfway down the pillar, Phil noticed a strange change in the rock face. The random, irregular edges of the boulders and rock began to become more angular, more regular, more predictable.

It was a man-made wall.

Phil moved closer to the wall face and traced the edges of the bricks with his finger. The wall was a menagerie of lava flow, mineral tendrils, and ornate bricks swirled together. As if a city had literally sunk into a lava pool.

"Amir!" Phil yelled up the rock face. A moment later a headlamp peered over the edge. "Get down here!"

In the upper blackness a call echoed through the cavern, "Rope!"

A coiled rope flew past Phil, fifteen feet to his right, and slapped against the wall, wiggling as Amir tied into it and began his descent to Phil's position.

Phil released a bit of the rope and moved down the face. The stones were expertly carved and polished. The stark difference between the natural rock and the smooth, man-made stone was otherworldly.

He turned his head to the left, and his headlamp illuminated a man's face, screaming into the void. An outstretched right arm jutted out of the rock face.

Phil let out a startled but muffled scream before he realized the man wasn't alive.

The arm was broken off at mid-forearm, but it was not solid like a statue in an art gallery or museum—it was hollow inside. A wafer-thin second skin of rock lay over what must have been the doomed man's actual skin. Phil looked into the face of the macabre statue. Its eyes stared straight ahead, wide in horror, and its mouth was frozen in mid-scream. Phil looked downward and to the left of the statue, aiming his headlamp at the wall. There were bodies everywhere he looked, all writhing in agonizing pain, frozen at the point of death— death that must have been instantaneous.

Amir's voice pierced the darkness. "This was what scared the miners who discovered this place. This was one of the Cities of the Plain. It was destroyed by fire and brimstone."

"It reminds me of what archeologists found in Pompeii," said Phil, staring at the tangle of dead bodies. He twisted on his rope to face Amir. "Why hasn't anyone excavated this site? How come the world has never seen this?"

"The nation of Israel has many secrets, Philip. The world doesn't need to know about all of them."

"Let's hope this city doesn't claim any more victims. Let's find Lisa and get out of here," said Phil, continuing down the cliff face.

Chapter Forty-Three
Double-Cross

T he senator's cell phone rattled on the inclined wooden desk. He lowered his bifocals to the bridge of his nose and glanced at the name on the glowing display: Janelle Capland. His intern was paging him.

It must be important. Janelle knows where I am.

Senator Camran, the senior senator from Texas, looked up from his phone. He was surrounded by a dozen senators listening to a four-star general drone on about why a long-awaited, newfangled weapons system the army wanted wasn't ready yet.

Senator Camran did this twice a week. It was an occupational hazard of being on the Armed Services Committee: a prestigious position, but sometimes terribly boring.

The general finished up with a particularly agonizing answer about the costs of the project that was already three years late and two hundred million dollars over budget.

Upon conclusion of the rambling answer, Senator Camran smacked the gavel on his desk and called for a recess of fifteen minutes. The general's face filled with relief, and he took a much-needed sip of water from a nearby tumbler.

The senator folded his glasses, placed them in his suit pocket, schmoozed his way across the platform, and pushed the thick wooden door of the chamber open, heading into the hall of the Capitol. His expensive black shoes, polished to a mirror shine, clacked on the marble floor as he walked toward a young woman who was talking on her cell phone.

The senator's eyes crawled over her—his intern, his object. He no longer saw her as a young girl or even as another person with her own dreams and plans. His selfishness had transformed her into an object of pleasure for only himself.

Janelle heard the sound of the senator's expensive shoes and recognized his gait. "I'll call you back," she said, terminating the call.

"Senator," she said, turning to face Camran and rising up on her toes a bit, leaning into him. "This message came for you via fax." Janelle handed him a crisp piece of white paper with a short message.

"Fax?" said the senator, pulling his glasses from his breast pocket. "How quaint."

As he reached for the paper, he purposefully touched the intern's slender fingers, letting his hand linger. He glanced at Janelle's face. Her reaction was obvious and predictable. Her eyes flared and her neck became red.

Power is the ultimate aphrodisiac, thought the senator, smiling at the response from the young woman. How far he would travel down this road was still uncertain.

Camran read the fax.

Our asset at AEC has gone rogue.
Pipeline is in jeopardy. Package is en route to Syria via Crete.
Advise on situation.

He looked at the top of the fax transmission. The country code was international, and he recognized it as originating in Russia.

The senator folded the message in thirds and placed it into his inside suit pocket. "Did you take this off of the fax machine, or did someone else hand it to you?"

"I pulled it off myself," said the intern.

Camran smiled and touched her shoulder—with more than a simple touch. "Good. Let's keep this one between you and me."

"Yes, senator." The intern walked away with a near skip in her step, and the senator's mind returned to business.

Camran looked up at the columns that towered over him and ran through the powerful address list on his phone. People of power—people with means—people who could get him out of his precarious situation.

They've already gotten to Rohm. It's all unraveling.

He thought for a moment and then dialed Governor Wyngate.

Roger Wyngate answered immediately, his voice pleasant. "Yes, Senator, what can I do for you?"

The governor's lackadaisical attitude took the senator's annoyance meter from zero to enraged in one second. "Can't you do anything right?"

Wyngate's casual demeanor fled. "What are you talking about?"

"I'm staring at a message that was sent over an unencrypted machine, over international phone lines, that says the Russian agent we had at Axcess has gone off the reservation. He's doing his own thing. Do you know what that means?"

Silence boomed on the other end of the phone.

"It means that most likely the NSA and DEA have already read my fax, and this whole operation is a bust."

"Don't do anything for five hours; I can fix it," stammered the governor.

"You have four hours—not five—four. Make this go away—right now!"

Senator Camran terminated the call.

Camran looked out across the city of Washington and watched the flights on final approach preparing to land at Reagan National. The red lights blinking in the windows at the top of the Washington Monument seemed to be sending Camran a coded message. He thought about how long he had worked to get to where he was and how much he had to lose.

This isn't worth an oil pipeline. Not to me it isn't.

He flipped open his cell phone and dialed a different number. "I need the number of Charlie Jacox at the CIA." A moment passed, and the connection was made.

"Jacox."

"Charlie, this is Senator Camran. You and I have done business before, right?"

"Yes, sir."

The senator smiled at Jacox's response—his acknowledgment of the Washington code for "I'm cashing in all my chips." It looked like Jacox was willing to accept the political transaction. He was glad he was talking to a player and not some Boy Scout who still believed in ancient ideals and black-and-white patriotism.

"I have come across some information, some deeply disturbing information, about an illegal arms shipment that's heading toward Syria as we speak. How would you like to see your star rise a little in the next few hours?"

"I would, indeed," said the CIA operative.

"Listen carefully . . . "

Flexibility is the key to politics, thought Camran. *That and the ability to stab anyone in the back who endangers your career.*

Chapter Forty-Four

Brimstone

A mir led the way through the narrowing rock formations. The once-jagged edges of the rocks were noticeably smooth from water, which had dribbled and trickled through the passageways for hundreds of years. Finally, after thirty feet, the passage ended in a dead end.

"Now what?" asked Phil.

Amir aimed his lamp on the floor of the cavern and illuminated a small crawlway no bigger than a dog door.

Phil was already claustrophobic, but this was another level altogether. He stared at the obstacle with determination and gritted his teeth. This was only one of many barriers between him and Lisa. He'd do anything to get to her.

"I'll go first. Give me a ten-foot head start and then follow," said Amir, taking off his backpack and attaching a nylon strap to tow the pack behind him in the small space. Amir knelt down in front of the opening, and after a moment of studying the first few feet, he dove in and disappeared into the crevice.

Six feet above the men, a small black sensor measured a disturbance and sent its signal through a thin wire strung across the ceiling of the passageway.

■ ■ ■ ■

"They're here. The tumbler on the outside passage just picked them up," said Yoshi. He pointed to a small orange flashing light on a portable instrument panel.

Gorin smiled at the instrument. "They came through exactly as you said they would."

"Of course. There are only two ways in here, and almost no one knows of the way I brought you."

Gorin pulled out a pistol that was tucked into the front of his pants and worked its action. "It's time. Go ahead and blow the charge."

■ ■ ■ ■

Phil wiped the sweat from his face. It was getting hotter the deeper they went. He followed Amir's lead and dragged his pack behind him through the crawl space. Dust and rock particles hung in the air and floated persistently, illuminated by the lamp mounted on his helmet. Phil could taste the sand in the air and smell the dirt particles in his nostrils. The grit was landing in his mouth, where he could feel the sandy particles when he ran his tongue along his teeth.

An enormous cracking sound rumbled overhead, and the walls of the passage trembled. Phil scrambled forward through the narrow shaft. Dust and debris rained down in front of him, and then a roar filled his ears. He heard a muffled scream from behind him and then nothing.

A moment later Phil was in complete blackness. His headlamp was smashed and his lower legs were immovable, covered in stone and sand.

Phil's headset squealed and screeched with Amir's voice. "Nuri—Tal! Come in?" Phil rubbed the dust from his face and called out to Amir. Static was the only response.

"Amir?"

Amir's voice came over the headset. "Phil? Thank God you're alive! What's your condition?"

Phil felt stabbing pains in his legs. He felt like he was cocooned. "My legs are buried. I think the passageway behind me caved in. I—I don't think Nuri and Tal made it." Phil pulled himself forward in the passage and began to shake and jiggle his legs. Little by little they gained more room to move as the rocks fell to either side of his body.

As he pulled his legs free, he felt the remaining loose remnants of the passage behind him cave in.

His headset echoed the plea from Amir again and again. "Nuri, come in. Tal, what is your condition?"

Static filled the headset.

Amir's voice was filled with sadness and resolve. "We have to keep going. Focus on the mission." Phil could tell by the tone of Amir's voice that the commando was speaking to himself as well as to Phil.

Amir moved through the lemon-squeezer passage on his back and pulled himself out of the opening. He flashed his lamp circumspectly into the new passage.

"I've made it to the end. There's a larger cavern." Amir looked down and saw a bottomless pit yawning below him. A series of footholds and volcanic pocks in the wall allowed for transit around the edge of the deadly orifice.

"Watch your step when you come out, Phil. First one's a little steep."

The Israeli commando began hammering pitons into the wall and making his way across as Phil reached the end of the passage, pulled himself free, and looked down into the abyss. "Whoa!" Phil kicked a small rock off the lip of the pit and watched it disappear into the blackness. He didn't hear it hit the bottom.

"Yeah, be careful there," said Amir, working his way hand-over-hand across the gaping hole. He was halfway across the pit and had rigged up a guideline, which passed through a number of pitons secured to the wall.

"We're headed for that over there," said Amir, pointing across the void to a rocky ledge that opened into a larger passage.

Phil leaned against the wall with his back and carefully clipped his safety rope onto Amir's bridge line. He began to pick footholds along the smooth-curving cavern wall. His hands were slippery with sweat as he made his way across, moving his feet carefully, searching for small toeholds and methodically testing them before moving his weight over the minute edges.

As Phil moved his left foot to another crevice, a shot echoed against the tight walls of the cavern. Phil flinched at the roar and nearly lost his balance, retreating back to his last good position. He looked back toward Amir.

He wasn't there.

The space where Amir had been standing just a moment before was empty. The commando's guide rope strained, moving left and right like a pendulum. Phil looked into the darkness, watching the multicolored rope stretch into the deep. It was taut and trembling as it sustained Amir's full weight.

Phil tried to move closer to the safety rope that his friend was dangling from. "Hang on, Amir!"

"I don't think your Jewish friend will be answering you, Phil." A man stepped from the shadows of the cave ahead.

"Gorin!" The name escaped Phil's lips and seemed to linger in the stale air of the cavern.

Gorin held a pistol in his grip. A light with a laser sight ran under the barrel, and a cruel smile crept across the Russian's face as he watched Phil's surprise become a look of disgust.

Phil turned from Gorin and yelled to Amir, dangling helplessly from the end of his line. He couldn't see him, but the strain on the climbing rope and the slight tremble of the line told him that Amir was still connected.

Gorin aimed the pistol at the knot that was attached to a carabiner, which was sliding perilously between the two pitons that secured the guide rope. A red dot from the laser site danced nervously on the multicolored line.

Phil put his hand out. "*No! Wait!*"

A muzzle flash lit the craggy walls of the cavern, and the rope unraveled instantly, releasing its heavy payload into the bowels of the lava tube.

"Amir!" screamed Phil.

No response.

"It's a deep hole. Maybe you should scream louder, Phil."

Phil gritted his teeth, overwhelmed with grief. "You—you murderer!"

Gorin pointed the gun at Phil. "I'm not done yet, Phil. Get over here."

Gorin fired another shot into the stone face just above Phil. "Now," said Gorin, narrowing his eyes.

Phil flinched and began to make his way across the guideline, lingering for a second where the frazzled end of Amir's climbing rope hung uselessly from its carabiner connection.

Phil reached the end of the perilous shelf and jumped onto the landing with Gorin. "Where's Lisa?" he demanded.

Gorin laughed at Phil and pointed the gun at his midsection. "You are not in any position to make demands. Turn around and put your hands behind your back."

Phil faced the craggy wall of the cave. The rock wall was smooth and glassy, a typical lava tube.

Gorin pulled out a zip tie and put it around both of Phil's wrists, zipping it tightly. Phil grimaced as the thick plastic cut into his skin and constrained his circulation.

"Now move, straight ahead." Gorin pushed the muzzle into Phil's back, nudging him deeper into the cave.

Phil moved hesitantly in the direction Gorin indicated and glanced one last time into the dark, yawning hole that had consumed Amir.

The volcanic rocks crunched underfoot, and the orange and red dust from the pulverized rock tinted the top of Phil's leather boots. His steps were echoed by Gorin's, following right behind him, gun pointed at Phil's back—finger twitching—at the ready.

The passage was short—just fifty yards. Phil tried to calm his fears, to focus his energy and thoughts. The passage walls changed from a single rock type to multiple kinds of rock. Zebra-like stripes painted the walls in a marbling of color.

As they stepped out of the passage, the cavern opened up into a huge expanse. Phil was astonished by the size of the opening—at least a hundred yards across. The sides were smooth, glassy, and volcanically formed.

This is it, thought Phil. *Etsba Elohim—the Finger of God—the lava tube that goes all the way down to the seal, just above the Maximal Reserve.* Even in his own danger and his worry for Lisa, Phil couldn't help feeling awed.

Minerals wound through the smooth walls and sometimes spilled out of the walls into a waterfall of stalagmites and stalactites, forming crowns and caps on top of each other. The rock looked frozen in flight.

The ceiling was high and vaulted in a massive dome overhead, like St. Peter's Cathedral, but comprised of glittering minerals instead of beautiful paint by a famous artist. Stone formations, built over centuries by single drops of water, hung down from the ceiling.

Phil looked down into the lava tube; there was no discernible bottom, just sheer walls and darkness. No narrowing, just a vertical cliff face that trailed into the blackness.

From the left side of the chasm, a rock formation jutted out and built up like a pinnacle, filling the center of the massive void. It reminded Phil of one of the pedestals in Monument Valley that he and Lisa had visited together a few years before.

There was a gap, a void between the ledge that he and Gorin stood on and the pedestal's cap. A set of aluminum ladders were bound together with climbing ropes and laid across the gap. Gorin pushed the muzzle of the pistol into Phil's back and forced him forward to the edge. Phil winced and moved toward the brink of the chasm.

Phil looked back at Gorin. "You're kidding, right?" Phil nodded toward the ladder. "How about you go first and show me how this is done?"

The humor was lost on the Russian. "Go," Gorin said, cocking the gun and pointing it directly at the base of Phil's skull.

Phil had seen this before. Climbers often took ladders to the Himalayan ice falls and bridged gulfs with them. It was a common approach to getting over the treacherous ice falls of Nepal for a chance to summit Everest or K2. A wrong step or a weak ladder—whether at the Etsba Elohim or the Himalayan mountain range—would amount to the same result. Death.

Phil carefully edged up to the ladder and looked into the yawning void. The darkness was all he could see. He closed his eyes and summoned his remaining courage, opened his eyes, and stepped onto the first rung.

The ladder creaked as it took on Phil's weight.

Phil moved carefully. With his arms tied behind his back, he had no way to balance as he stepped across the ladder. He blocked out everything—Gorin's taunts and threats, the orange rock, the formations that seemed to morph into animals and men's faces, even his concern for Lisa. It all got pushed to the back of his mind as he made his way across.

Phil stopped and counted the rungs left to cross. *Halfway across.*

Sweat poured down his neck and back, pooling and tracing its way around the points where his backpack came into contact with his shoulders and upper back.

Phil began to feel dizzy, as if the darkness below was swallowing him and the ladder was spinning like a propeller. The ladder shifted and groaned under each step as he crossed the last remaining rungs and stepped onto the orange dirt of the pinnacle's cap.

His legs were jellylike, and his muscles burned, but Gorin wouldn't let him rest—yet.

"Move over to that side," said Gorin, motioning at Phil with his gun. Phil stepped over to a large boulder that was adorned with a crown of quartz that had dripped drop by drop from the ceiling for hundreds of years. Phil fell to his knees. He didn't have the strength right now to contemplate escaping.

Gorin put his arms out from his side, imitating an acrobat, and made his way across the ladder like a pro, almost dancing across, as if every motion was a taunt to his exhausted prisoner.

As Gorin's boots hit the pinnacle, Phil stood back up, stumbling to catch his balance. "Where's Lisa?"

"You'll see," Gorin grinned.

Gorin turned and picked up the aluminum ladder, heaving it into the abyss. Phil watched as the silver bridge clanged against the smooth wall of the lava tube and disappeared into the depths of the earth.

"I guess there's more than one way in here," said Phil.

Gorin cackled and motioned Phil beyond the rock formation. Phil stumbled forward and followed Gorin. Just around the bend from the boulder, Phil saw construction boots, jeans, and a nylon jacket with a large emblem on the back: "Parezim Petroleum." The man was face down, and his hardhat was lying on the ground a few feet away from his head, which was spattered with blood and gray matter blown out by a point-blank encounter with Gorin's gun.

"Yoshi here showed me an easier way to get in," said Gorin with a smile.

Phil looked at the grim sight and back at the murderous Russian. "And it looks like you rewarded him for it."

Across the darkness of the pinnacle came a voice—hoarse and soft—barely discernible, but Phil recognized it immediately.

"Phil? Is that you?"

Lisa!

"Lisa! It's me. I'm here!"

Phil ran toward the voice, and Gorin followed, still pointing the gun. Beyond a forest of stalagmites, Phil found his fiancée sitting on the sandy ground of the pinnacle near an old gas generator with large lights that were pointed in opposite directions, their wide beams making the veins of quartz gleam and sparkle on the walls of the lava tube.

Lisa's arms were tied behind her, bound by the same kind of zip ties that restrained Phil. She was blindfolded, and her dark, beautiful hair cascaded over her face. Her black blouse was smudged with orange dust and soaked through with perspiration.

Phil knelt in front of her and kissed her forehead. "I'm here, Lisa. I'm here."

Her shoulders began to shake, and she buried her face against his chest.

Gorin laughed in the background.

Chapter Forty-Five
Executive Decision

G lenn Martin walked into his executive office as the morning sun
began to blaze through the windows of his wood-paneled office. A
stack of local and national newspapers was arranged in a neat cas-
cade on his desk. Martin flipped from paper to paper and stopped at *The Austin
Chronicle*. The front-page headline made his blood chill.

CONSPIRACY
Axcess Energy and Governor's Office Implicated in
Syrian Arms Deal for Oil
BY SHERIDAN PRESTON

The entire front page was dedicated to the story. Black-and-white photos
of David Rohm and Governor Wyngate were flanked by line after line of text.
A graphic depicting the planned natural-gas pipeline layout over Turkey and
Syria was also included. And there in the middle of the page, a picture of Glenn
Martin himself, grinning and looking confident.

252

His fingers shook as he flipped through page after page of the story.

A knock at the door of the executive's office interrupted his realization that life as he knew it had just come to an end. "Come," his voice cracked.

One of Martin's many assistants came in with tears in her eyes. "I probably shouldn't do this, but you should see CNN right now," she said as she walked over and clicked on the flat-screen TV that was mounted on the wall. She exited without another word.

The TV came to life with a reporter standing in front of a harbor. Two ships—a large supply ship and a navy cruiser—were anchored behind the man.

The audio kicked in. "Just an hour ago, the United Arab Emirates seized a ship carrying weapons that were allegedly purchased at a Russian arms bazaar in Kharkiv, Ukraine. The ship was apparently bound for Al Ladhiqiyah, a port in Syria. This shipment is a clear violation of United Nations sanctions, according to UAE diplomats. The weapon, a high-precision, advanced cruise missile with classified capabilities, is manufactured by Wyngate Corporation, the Texas-based defense contractor. Sources close to the situation say that the governor of Texas, Roger Wyngate, who is also the founder of Wyngate Corporation, used his political power to trade these weapons in exchange for the construction work on the natural-gas pipeline that will feed much-needed natural gas into the Middle East. The main contractor for the natural-gas pipeline is Axcess Energy Corporation, which has been in the news recently with its bombastic chief executive, Glenn Martin, who only a few days ago generated enormous wealth for shareholders based on a theatrical news conference announcing the pipeline."

The interview continued, but Martin's attention was pulled to the window of his office. A cacophony of sirens preceded a line of police cars that spilled into the parking lot of Axcess Energy. He watched the policemen and men wearing blue FBI jackets pile out of the first car. He recognized one man: Detective Mark Rizzo.

Rizzo adjusted his wrinkled shirt and tie and glanced up at the executive wing. Seeing Martin at the window, he gave an abbreviated wave and pulled a toothpick out of his front shirt pocket, burying it behind his bushy mustache.

As Martin tried to figure a way out of the situation, the TV news report continued in the background, like some kind of horrible soundtrack to a dream he couldn't wake up from.

He stepped behind his desk, opened the bottommost drawer, and pulled out a wooden box. He opened it; a nickel-plated pistol gleamed in the morning sunshine. Martin picked up the gun and chambered a round. Reflections from the shiny metal body of the weapon danced across the paneled walls of the executive suite.

Martin pressed the muzzle of the gun to the roof of his mouth.

A moment later a gunshot echoed through the executive wing, and Martin's assistant put her hands to her mouth as she ran to the door of the CEO's office.

Chapter Forty-Six
Back from the Dead

A hundred feet down the sheer rock wall of the lava tube, Amir clung to a razor-sharp outcrop just barely thick enough to jut from the side. Blood coursed from his palms as the volcanic glass dug into his skin. A red line slowly traced his wrist and began to move down his trembling forearm.

His headlamp had smashed against the wall as he had fallen into the abyss. He hung in the darkness between the certain death beneath him and uncertainty as to where to go from here. Amir shifted his weight to his left hand for a moment while he fished through his climbing bag.

His muscles ached, but his military training took over, pushing the goal of survival to the forefront of his mind. His pain and fear went to the bottom of the list.

He had to survive. Nothing else mattered.

His right hand ran over numerous items: carabiners, pitons, and a small flashlight. The light's metal body was knurled and easy to grip.

He twisted the brim, and the lamp came on. He stuck the flashlight in his mouth, biting down on it and relieving his left arm of his weight by returning his right arm to the sharp outcrop. Amir glanced upward, moving his head slowly and deliberately across the black, glossy face of the cliff.

Nothing on the left side looked promising; there were just the reflection of light from his flashlight and a smooth surface that climbed upward. He scanned to the right, and the light beam followed his gaze. Suddenly the disc of light shining on the rock formed an eclipse as it passed over a gaping void in the volcanic wall.

Amir squinted and studied the hole. It was large, another cavern or perhaps a lava tube. Whatever it was, it was his only option.

Again he removed his right hand from the outcrop, balancing his weight on his left hand, and reached into his climbing bag for a piton. He mashed it into the wall, twisting it left and right, trying to get a good hold.

The black rock flaked away and began to coddle the high-tensile steel into its face. The silver piton tentatively gripped the rock. Amir grabbed his climbing hammer and carefully tapped the piton's head, driving it deeper into the rock with every swing.

Amir's left arm began to cramp, and he shifted his weight to his right hand and tested the piton for strength as best as he could.

If this thing lets go, it won't matter anyway. I can't hang on here much longer, he thought.

He reached down, grabbed the severed climbing rope that had given way to Gorin's gunshot, and threaded it through the piton's eye. He pulled it through and tied it into a loop about five feet long. Amir put his left foot into the loop, pulled it taut with his weight, and finally released his left hand from the rocky outcrop. His muscles and back felt instant relief.

After a moment of rest, he began pounding pitons into the glassy wall and made his way up to the cavern opening.

He would survive. A new goal took hold. *I have to help Phil.*

Amir's muscles bulged as he pulled his aching body up the rock face.

I hope he's still alive.

Amir gripped the lip of the cavern opening and pulled his muscular body into the opening. He turned and looked deep into the passage, which narrowed ahead and seemed to meander around and through boulders and mineral formations. He picked up his pack and began to move slowly up the cavern passage.

. . . .

Phil sat next to Lisa, exhausted, watching Gorin type on a laptop. A small device with an antenna was plugged into the USB port of the computer. Phil recognized it as some sort of transmitter.

"Making reservations for a hotel in a country with no extradition policy?" asked Phil.

Gorin kept his back to them. "You're a slow thinker, Phil. I don't have to go anywhere. In a few minutes the evidence of this whole abomination will disappear, and LukZag and the pipeline will be the only choice for Israel's energy needs."

"You can't cover up everything, Gorin. People know about the reserve now," said Phil.

"You mean like David Rohm and Jack Sanders?"

The words took a minute to sink in. "Rohm's dead?" asked Phil. Lisa nodded.

Gorin shook his head, looking back at the laptop. "I don't know what Chambers ever saw in you. You're really playing catch-up here, Phil."

"You're going to destroy the biggest oil reserve in history because of your stupid pipeline?"

Gorin stopped typing. "This isn't just about energy, you idiot," said Gorin. "It's about control. Once we have control of Israel's energy, we can march in here and take this oil. No one can stop us. America is weak, tied down with what the rest of the world thinks. We don't care what the rest of the world thinks. We never have."

Gorin walked over and knelt in front of Phil. "Here's some more catch-up, Phil." Gorin leaned close to him, savoring the news he was about to deliver. Phil could smell cigarettes strong on the Russian's breath.

"I killed Ward and Chambers, too."

Phil clenched his eyes shut and rested his chin on his chest, Gorin's words pounding on him. He wanted all of this to go away.

As Gorin moved away, Phil reopened his eyes, looking down at his toxic gas meter. The protective covering on the front of the meter was cracked and splintered. A long piece of sharp, clear plastic was still held by the edges of the gauge, but it jutted out across the device—knifelike.

Phil looked back up at Gorin, who had walked back over to the laptop and was typing on the keyboard, fully absorbed in whatever he was doing.

Phil rocked and watched the sharp piece of plastic fall forward. He shifted his weight to the right, and the shard slid out of its tentative position on the instrument's frame and onto the sandy rock where he was sitting.

He looked back at Gorin. The Russian was glued to the computer screen.

Phil pivoted his body, picked up the shard with his right hand, and sat back down next to Lisa. She looked resolved to whatever fate awaited them.

He began to saw up and down against the zip tie that bound his hands. He moved the blade of plastic a dozen times before he felt the serrated edge of the shard begin to get a bite on the ridged plastic spine of the zip tie.

He leaned close to Lisa's ear and whispered, "I think I may have a way to get us free."

Lisa nodded and prayed.

■ ■ ■ ■

Amir continued working his way through the twisting, undulating passageway. He saw light ahead and heard a reciprocating engine, like a generator, coming from the space ahead of him. He moved in and out of the narrows of the tunnel and finally reached the end. He heard muffled voices.

Amir peeked over the edge and found he was face to face with an enormous lava tube that seemed to have no bottom. A hundred feet below him, a small rocky pinnacle jutted out from the side of the tube. He saw two people huddled near one another—obviously prisoners of the one huddled over the laptop. The light from the generator was blinding, but he could tell that Phil was one of the prisoners. He assumed the other was Lisa.

Amir cocked his head and looked left and right. He was in a curved, dome-shaped rock formation that covered the top of the lava tube. Stalactites hung from the ceiling like dripping ice-cream cones. Some of the formations were enormous—the size of five- or six-story buildings.

Amir formulated a plan to help his friends as he pulled rope from his pack and watched Gorin.

I wonder what he's doing with that laptop.

Chapter Forty-Seven

Struggle

P hil continued to saw through the tough nylon zip tie that bound his hands as he watched Gorin rummaging through a stack of equipment twenty feet away. Gorin was unhinged—full of murder and hate.

I have to find out more about Gorin's plan. I have to slow him down, he thought. He cleared his throat.

"Gorin, let Lisa go. You have me now. I have knowledge of the reserve. You can use me to bargain for whatever you want."

Gorin turned from his laptop. "Bargain? How arrogant of you to assume you know what my plans are or what I want."

Gorin picked up a device that looked like a walkie-talkie, with a small antenna protruding from the top of a black handheld case, and walked over to the two bound captives.

"This is not a hostage exchange, Philip. This is a cover-up." Gorin began to laugh at his own words: a sick and unintended pun. "That's right—it's a giant cover-up." He raised his arms as if imploring an assembly of believers. "This whole mountain won't exist in thirty minutes."

Phil tried not to grimace. The pit of his stomach began to hurt. *He's mad—completely insane.*

"What are you talking about?" asked Phil.

Gorin held out the strange transmitter. "This is the shovel that will bury both of you and the knowledge of this infernal place."

He danced up to the two prisoners, taunting in his steps. Phil thought back to the Gorin he had met on the ship—annoying in his own way, but not like this. This was beyond any reason.

"Look up there." Gorin pointed to the dome-shaped roof of the cavern. Phil squinted in the bright lights, powered by the generator. Directly above them on the stalactite-covered ceiling was a net of steel cables. It bulged down from the rocky ceiling like it contained some sort of strange spider's egg sack. Its edges were pinned into the rock.

"What is that?" asked Phil. Even as he spoke the words, he thought, *I don't think I want to know.*

"C-4—enough to bring this entire cavern down and fill it up."

Phil swallowed hard as he looked at the nest of explosives high on the ceiling.

"Aw," said Gorin mocking. "Don't look so glum. You'll be dead soon!" He laughed uproariously.

"And how are you going to get out?" asked Lisa, still blindfolded but defiant.

Phil smiled at her rebelliousness. Not a quality he normally admired, but here, in this circumstance, it was welcome and wildly attractive.

"Why, my dear, I'm going to waltz right out the passage I came through." Gorin motioned over toward a rock bridge that jutted out to the pinnacle surface. A large passageway on the lava-tube wall was just beyond it. Phil could see the drag marks that Gorin and the late Yoshi had made dragging equipment onto the rocky plateau.

An alarm sounded from Gorin's watch, and he glanced at the face. "Oops. It's been nice talking to you two, but I'm afraid it's time for me to go."

Gorin glanced at Phil. "Oh—and Phil, when I arm this detonator, it can't be stopped. See that laptop over there?"

Phil looked over at the small computer Gorin had been typing on earlier.

Gorin pressed a button on the transmitter, and a digital clock with large red digits appeared on the black screen.

20:00
19:59
19:58

"I wanted you to have something to watch before the big show," said Gorin. "You Americans all love entertainment, so think of it as the pregame show."

"That's a nice touch," said Phil, his eyes glued to the countdown.

"I thought so too. You two enjoy yourselves for the next eighteen minutes." Gorin laughed as he clipped the transmitter to his belt and began walking toward the stone bridge and the passageway to freedom and safety from the blast.

At that moment, the ground shook. The generator hiccuped and sputtered, and the lights flickered on and off and then lowered in intensity before snapping back to full power.

Another rumble shook the cavern—this time louder and more intense. The walls trembled with seismic intensity, and the razor-sharp rocks that had grown minutely over hundreds of years on the ceiling of the lava tube sheared off and headed downward, creating a gallery of killer knives. One of the craggy shards slammed into the plateau just twenty feet from Phil and Lisa. Phil did his best to shield his fiancée from the flying shrapnel as the rock shattered into a thousand pieces.

Dust and sand began to snow down into the cavern, and cracks appeared in the wall of the glossy lava tube. Gorin struggled to stay on his feet as he made for the stone bridge, dodging the sharp lances of rock that shattered on the pinnacle's surface.

"Phil, what's going on?" gasped Lisa.

"It's an earthquake!" Phil tried to position his body over Lisa's to provide some safety, all the while continuing to saw through the zip tie. He was almost free; he could feel the rough edge of the portion he had cut through. The entire pinnacle shuddered underneath them.

Then a roaring like a freight train passing through an echo chamber filled the air of the lava tube, and the pinnacle vibrated. A stalactite the size of a four-story building snapped free from the ceiling and fell toward the pinnacle like a giant dart. It smashed through Gorin's escape bridge, shearing it off into the depths of the lava tube.

The swirling dust cloud concealed the damage for a moment before the roiling particles drifted aside to reveal that the entire structure had been erased. Gorin ran to the edge of the plateau and spun around, his hands on his head, and pulled on his hair. Terror was present in Gorin's eyes for the first time. The gap was too far to jump across. The passageway across from him—his only way out—was now filled floor to ceiling with rocks and boulders the size of cars.

"No. *No!*" screamed Gorin. He raised his fist into the air and cursed.

Phil looked back over at the laptop. It had fallen off its perch and was lying sideways on the rocky floor, still counting down.

16:45
16:44
16:43

Gorin ran over to Phil and Lisa and pulled his pistol out of its holster, pointing it at Lisa's head.

"You're going first!" Gorin screamed.

"No, Gorin. Do me first. Kill me!" Phil yelled. Gorin shifted his attention to the young man, confused by his request. At the same instant, Phil flexed his forearms for all they were worth and snapped through the shorn zip tie.

Phil brought his hand around quickly and grabbed the muzzle of the gun, pushing it to the side. Gorin, surprised, squeezed the trigger. A gunshot fired into the darkness of the cavern, the sound echoing wildly across the glassy walls.

Lisa, unable to see what was going on, pulled herself into a fetal position and tried to become a small target. "Phil!" she cried.

Phil punched Gorin in the face, knocking him backwards, and then dove headlong into the Russian's midsection, knocking him on his back. Gorin rolled to his side and kicked Phil in the stomach, knocking the air from his lungs.

Phil went to his knees gasping, rasping for air.

Gorin stood up and wrapped his arms around Phil's throat, preparing to wrench it and snap his neck. His eyes gleamed with hate.

■ ■ ■ ■

Amir was watching the whole scene unfold from his perch high on the ceiling. He had thought the entire salt dome would pancake on top of him at the last quake, but now he knew he had to help Phil, who was on his knees a hundred feet below him.

He was missing his gun, lost in the fall down into the abyss, but he pulled his commando knife from its leather binding on his calf and flipped it over, holding it by the tip. This would have to be a perfect throw. Lying on his side, he pulled the top of his body free of the rock. He felt like he was skydiving directly into the pinnacle. He wedged his legs into the passageway behind him, supporting his upper body.

The Israeli commando raised his right arm and let the knife fly with all the strength and skill he could muster.

■ ■ ■ ■

Phil could feel the tendons in his neck stretching and his vertebrae straining under the pressure of Gorin's twisting hands. He gasped for breath.

It was all going to be over. His vision began to narrow, and a gray tunnel materialized in front of him.

Suddenly Gorin let out an anguished scream and released Phil, who fell face forward onto the pinnacle. Gorin reached for the back of his left thigh. The silver blade of Amir's commando knife was embedded in the muscle, its serrated tip deep in his thigh bone.

Another tremor rocked the cavern—larger than the last. The cable net drooped from the roof of the cave and strained on its steel grommets, which connected the netting to the pitons in the rock face. The grommets slowly began to deform under the stress, and one by one they popped free.

The quake had knocked the screaming Gorin to the ground. He grasped blindly for the knife that was now cutting through the muscle wall of the back of his leg. After a painful pull, he finally pulled the knife free and flung it to the ground. He swung around and emptied his magazine clip at the passageway where Amir was positioned. The bullets sparked off the rock and ricocheted around the cavern.

Gorin turned back to Phil and Lisa with murder welling in his eyes and hatred contorting his countenance into that of a goblin. He limped toward them with his lacerated leg while snapping another magazine of ammunition into his gun.

"I've had it with you. Now you'll watch your fiancée die, and then you're next!"

Gorin cocked the gun and pointed it at Lisa.

Thunk!

The massive netting fell on top of the pinnacle, flattening Gorin to the floor and burying him in steel netting and dust.

Phil ran to Lisa's side, removed the blindfold, and cut her bonds with the commando knife stained with Gorin's blood.

A groaning sound came from under the heavy metal net, and a bloody arm snaked out from beneath its metal cords, brandishing a gun. Gorin strained under the weight of the net and the thick rectangular blocks of C-4 that were tied to it with zip ties like those that had bound Phil and Lisa's hands.

The whites of Gorin's eyes, peeking through the rusted cabling of the net, were filling with blood, and his nasal passages and mouth were streaming red. His arm trembled as he pointed the barrel of the gun at Phil, who turned his body to cover Lisa.

Suddenly the net of cables began to move, sliding over the slippery, mineral-covered pinnacle cap with Gorin trapped underneath. It went slowly at first, until half the netting and explosive blocks lay off the edge of the pinnacle and hung into the void of the lava tube. The smooth mineral secretions on the top of the pinnacle only hastened the retreat of the net, and Gorin released the gun and clawed at the smooth surface, grasping for anything to stop his slide. He scratched at the glass-like surface but was denied at every inch.

Gorin and Phil's eyes met for one last time before the Russian slipped over the edge, entangled in the net.

Then he was gone.

Chapter Forty-Eight
Down to Get Up

Silence seemed to scream in the moments after Gorin was pulled off the pinnacle. Sentenced to his doom by his own devices—his own madness.

Lisa rubbed her raw wrists, which had been cut by the zip ties, and glanced at Gorin's laptop. It was still counting down.

10:03
10:02
10:01

Lisa turned to Phil. "The timer's still going, Phil. What does that mean?"

"It means we have ten minutes to get out of here before this whole cavern implodes."

Phil looked back up at Amir, hanging out of the recess in the ceiling of the cave. "Amir, can we get out that way?" Phil's voice echoed against the ancient stone.

Amir shook his head as he tied an anchor against a stalagmite in preparation to join Phil and Lisa on the plateau below. "There's no way. This passage caved in during the last aftershock."

Phil nodded and paced the pinnacle, thinking. He looked over the edge into the dark canyon that Gorin had been pulled into. It was quiet in the cavern, but it wasn't completely silent.

Drip. Drip. Drip.

So much had been happening that Phil hadn't had a chance to listen to his surroundings. A trickling cacophony now filled his senses. The impact of thousands of water droplets hitting rock was everywhere. Phil looked at the lava-tube walls: they were slick with water. There were even some miniature waterfalls cascading down the volcanic walls.

"Amir, do you have any flares?"

The Israeli rummaged through his climbing pack. "Yeah, three of them."

"Throw them down here. I have an idea."

"What are you going to do?" asked Lisa, moving to his side.

Phil pointed at the slick walls of the lava tube that reflected the generator's lights. "Water. It always seeks the lowest level. It's been trickling downward like this for centuries, perhaps for a millennia. We might have to go down to go up."

"You mean there's a lake down there?" asked Lisa, peering over the edge of the pinnacle into the darkness.

"Maybe."

Amir dropped a pack of flares that were wrapped tightly in red wax paper onto the pinnacle's cap, and Phil ran and picked them up.

"That's not exactly the confident answer I was looking for," said Lisa.

Phil popped a flare on his knee and was blinded for a moment by its ignition. A red cloud roiled from him as he walked back to the edge of the tube and lobbed the burning flare into the darkness.

Phil counted to himself as he watched the intense light of the flare diminish in the vast darkness of the lava tube. A muffled splash followed a few second later. The flare floated for a moment on a pool of blackness before it was snuffed out.

"Water," said Phil. "About three hundred feet down."

"How can you be sure it's water?" asked Lisa.

"Because if it had been just oil, there'd be a wall of flame around us right now, and we'd all be fried extra crispy."

"Again, not so happy with that answer," said Lisa.

Phil popped another flare, walked to another edge, and dropped the burning light. Again the flare fell, and Phil counted slowly to himself until he saw it impact. This time, before it was extinguished, he saw white foam. "Just what I thought! There's a current!"

Phil ran to the opposite side of the pinnacle and threw the last burning flare in the direction of the current. The flare flew through the darkness and then smacked into a barrier and ricocheted downward into a foamy whiteness. It burned for a moment longer, and Phil could see a curtain of white surging against the rock face of the lava tube.

"There's a river down there that runs under the rock wall. That's our ticket out of here."

The swishing sound of rope traveling through a metal carabiner filled the air as Amir rappelled from the closed passage at the top of the domed ceiling to the pinnacle's slick cap. Amir quickly pulled the rope through the descender and then yanked the loop clear of the piton he had driven into the roof of the cave. A moment later, two bundles of braided Kevlar rope, each measuring two hundred feet, fell in a pile at his feet like oversized pythons.

Amir picked up his commando knife, still stained with Gorin's blood. He wiped the blood on the thigh of his pants and refitted the weapon in its leather sheath.

"You take Lisa down first, and I'll follow," said Amir as he began to fasten the ropes in a double anchor to a thick stalagmite formation that glistened under the lights of the electric generator still chugging away in the background.

Phil glanced at the overturned laptop.

8:45
8:44
8:43

"Don't spend too much time sightseeing up here, or you'll end up a permanent resident," said Phil, placing his hand on the commando's back.

Amir nodded. "You don't have to worry about me. The moment you two reach the lake below, I'll be on my way."

Phil quickly outfitted Lisa with a thick nylon climbing harness that he pulled out of Amir's pack. Amir walked to the edge of the pinnacle and tossed a rolled-up rope into the darkness. The rope unfurled and smacked the water far below. Phil followed suit and lobbed his rope into the abyss. A distant splash followed.

Lisa looked downward into the yawning darkness. "I don't think I can do this." Her hands were trembling, and sweat covered her palms.

Phil pulled her close and ran the inside of his palm along her smooth cheek. "Hey, we'll do it together. No problem." He backed to the edge. Lisa followed him with an unsure look on her face.

"Okay, Lisa, this is the hard part," he said, carrying out his own instructions as he talked. "You're going to have to trust the harness and the rope. Just sit back into the harness and walk off the edge. As long as you have the rope pulled to the right of the descender, you won't go anywhere."

Lisa gulped and tried to sit back into the thick nylon webbing, but her body and mind were at odds on this task, and she began to swing downward too far. Her feet were higher on the cliff face, and her back was sinking too far down. "Help!"

Phil swung on his rope across the rock face and positioned himself behind her. "Okay, bring your feet down slowly." Lisa steeled her jaw and walked down the cliff face until her feet were directly below her. "Now let out some slack by moving your arm toward twelve o'clock," came his voice from below. Lisa obeyed, slowly moving her right arm from a three o'clock position to midnight. The rope began to slide through the descender.

Phil tugged on a strap and double-checked the alignment of the rope through the descender ring. Phil patted Lisa on the arm. "You're doing great!"

Lisa closed her eyes, steeling herself for a step into nothingness, and began to walk down the cliff face and work the descender simultaneously.

"Now, push out from the wall and let the rope out as well." Phil showed her how, and he bounded down the cliff face twenty feet before his feet landed on the face of the volcanic wall. He looked up with a grin.

Lisa gulped and tried it. Fifteen feet later, her shoes impacted the black glass wall of the pinnacle.

"See, you have the hang of it!" yelled Phil.

"Hey!"

Lisa and Phil stopped what they were doing and looked up. Amir was looking over the edge at them. "We have about seven minutes, so if you're done with Rappelling 101, I'd like to get off this rock before I get blasted to Mars."

Lisa nodded and led the way—twenty feet the first time, thirty the next. Ten more times of bouncing along the wall, and Lisa's feet splashed into the black water that had been collecting in the lava tube since the time of the Roman Empire. Phil was right behind her, and he landed in the water.

Phil's body twisted and jerked as the current swirled around him. "Be careful, this current is wicked. This river must be huge," he said, helping Lisa unlatch from the rope. She held on to a handhold in the rock wall, a smooth ripple of rock.

"Ready?"

Lisa nodded.

"Let's go!"

They both released the handhold and splashed into the water. The current gripped them and pulled them away from the pinnacle's foundation.

The white foam gleamed in the dim light and acted like a primordial beacon.

The rocky floor beneath Phil's feet began to shallow. He flailed his feet, looking for the bottom, and felt it after a moment.

"I can reach the bottom," said Phil, his head barely above the water.

Lisa, who was treading water, looked over and tried to reach the lake bed. "I can't reach it yet." Phil reached out for her, grabbing her by the hand and pulling her along as he walked up the shallowing rock shelf.

■ ■ ■ ■

Three hundred feet up the cliff face, Amir was working on an Australian rappelling sling—a dangerous but rapid way to rappel by running down the cliff face-first instead of back-first. He had no choice; time was running out. Only six minutes remained on the laptop's display.

Amir walked to the edge of the pinnacle and gave a quick tug on the strap that ran through a large carabiner extending from his mid-back on a thick nylon sheath. He took a deep breath and leaned forward, walking over the edge and carefully feeding the rope ahead of him through the looping arrangement around his body. He was face-to-face with the abyss.

He took a step and let the rope thread through his gloved hands. Twenty feet slipped away in an instant as he ran like a marathoner along the vertical face.

A vibration chased upward from the underground lake along the pinnacle foundation and continued into the ceiling of the lava tube. Stalactites began to break off of their fragile bases on the ceiling of the cave and fall into the underground lake. Like spires of a medieval church, the five-story spikes smashed into the river, shattering into piles of glistening rock and sending water high into the stale air of the cavern.

Amir did his best to keep his balance and his pace as he continued his vertical run down the pinnacle's face. The pinnacle trembled beneath him and suddenly split—a crack ripped through the formation from bottom to top and began to widen.

Amir's foot slipped on the rocky, oscillating surface, and his body slammed into the rock face. The rope wrapped around his midsection and twisted over his muscular forearm, then slowly began to slip through the carabiners. The rope became like a surgeon's knife, digging into the Israeli's skin.

Suspended thirty feet above the lake, Amir screamed out in pain, hanging in the harness and tangled in the high-tension rope. Another stalactite sheared from the ceiling of the cave and came down just inches from Amir, grazing his free arm and knocking him into the pinnacle wall yet again. Amir struggled with the rope and moved his body in an attempt to gain some relief from the painful binder. He twisted and turned his body, grasping, reaching for the commando knife in its leather sheath around his right calf.

"Stay here, Lisa. I have to help Amir," said Phil, plunging into the black current and swimming toward the pinnacle wall.

Lisa headed toward the rocky wall, moving her feet blindly on the river floor between boulders that ranged from the size of pumpkins to softballs. The floor seemed to roll beneath her feet; nothing felt solid.

Stroke after stroke, Phil continued swimming. The current was strong, carrying him off course and causing him to realign numerous times across the expanse.

Amir was struggling for breath in the burning pain of the climbing rope sliding against the inside of his forearm and his back, bruised from multiple collisions with the pinnacle face. He took a deep breath and focused. Stoically ignoring the pleading of his nerves, he reached down and pulled the knife free. He brought the blade across the climbing rope and watched as the Kevlar housing began to shear away, revealing the inner cords of the expensive rope. The tension of the rope split away as Amir pulled the blade over the tense lines. Finally, the rope broke, and Amir fell headlong into the black lake coursing thirty feet below.

Phil heard the splash of Amir's crash landing. "Amir!" he screamed into the blackness, half gargling the water that was raging around him. Amir's head finally broke the surface, and Phil pulled him on to his back and free of the tangled rope.

The two men began to make their way across the current toward Lisa.

■ ■ ■ ■

The current seemed to accelerate around Lisa, and she watched as the foam curled around her body and then slipped beneath the rocky face. She squinted through the darkness, trying to catch a glimpse of Phil and Amir. She looked upward. Three hundred feet above her, the halo effect of the generator's lights on the top of the pinnacle flickered like a candle.

Lisa called into the blackness. "Phil!" Her voice echoed three times, the volume reducing each time.

She shifted her weight on the boulder, and the rock slipped from beneath her. Lisa's head plunged beneath the dark water, and her legs flailed as she tried to stand up. The smooth rocks were like ball bearings, sliding and rolling beneath her, denying her traction. Her face breached the surface, and she gasped for air and pushed against the roiling floor of the riverbed. The cold water rushed by her ears and the bubbling foam spurted in her nose and eyes.

And then the full danger of the situation hit her. As she pushed up through the surface of the raging water, she saw she had drifted. She was close to the rock wall the foam and water were being slurped beneath.

Lisa craned her neck backward in the direction of the pinnacle and screamed, "Phil! Help!" Her voice was raspy and her volume muted. She tried to swim against the current, but she was slapped back up against the rock wall. The water made a terrible slurping noise as it slipped past the wall.

She pushed off again, swimming with all of her strength. Her muscles burned.

The strength of the current quickened, and she felt the suction of the vacuum that was pulling the water as it reached out and wrapped around her thin body. Her feet began to drag through the softball-sized boulders on the riverbed.

The rock face was close; she could see the volcanic pockmarks on its black surface and the drizzle of quartz and tendrils of minerals that danced through it.

Lisa put her hand up and grasped the face. The sharp features of volcanic rock felt like a dozen knives. Her body was moving out from beneath her, moving under the wall.

She pulled up on the rocky grip with her remaining strength and screamed into the cavern, "Phil!" A moment later she was gone.

Chapter Forty-Nine
Fire and Water

"**D**id you hear that?" asked Phil. Amir groaned, the sound barely audible over the current lapping around them. "Lisa!" called Phil. Nothing.

Phil peered through the darkness, looking for Lisa's profile against the rock wall where he had left her just minutes before.

There was no sign of her.

Phil saw the lapping water and gurgling foam of the current raging beneath the wall, and as he got closer to the spot, he felt it pull more and more urgently on his waterlogged body.

"Oh, no!" Phil let go of Amir and swam as fast as he could toward the wall, glancing frantically left and right. There was no other place she could have gone.

"Go after her," came a garbled command from Amir. "I'll be right behind you."

Phil didn't even respond. He breathed in and out rapidly four times, inhaled as much air as he could, and dove headlong into the foaming madness.

Chapter Fifty
Breath

*B*urning. Longing. Desperation.

Lisa's higher functioning brain was quickly shutting down. Her need was primal now.

Oxygen.

Air.

Now.

Lisa tumbled head over heels in the blackness, struggling to orient her body and swim with the current. The passage was smooth, totally devoid of sharp edges. For centuries the water had sanded the lava tube into a perfect, glassy conduit.

Her lungs burned, and she squeezed her eyes shut, focusing all her energy on keeping her mouth closed and preventing the water around her from forcing its way down her throat and filling her lungs.

She couldn't hold out much longer.

Her eyes flickered open and looked into the black sea that was carrying her. There was no end, at least no end that could make a difference to her.

Then she felt heat. Her hand being held. She recognized the fit of the hand—the touch—the sheer intent communicated to her as clearly as words. It was Phil. She could see him now. His lips were pursed tight, and his dark hair swirled in the water. His eyes were confident, but filled with concern—for her.

He had come for her. He pressed his lips to her mouth, completely covering her lips, and breathed out air.

Lisa's lungs accepted the precious air, but it wasn't enough; she needed more oxygen right now.

Her lungs were in agony and beginning to operate erratically. They gratefully took in the new air but continued to pressure its host for more.

Lisa knew this was it. She felt it—desperately felt it.

Suddenly, serenity seemed to overtake her—as if here, at the end in a horrible death, she still had hope.

Lisa felt her strength leaving her. Somehow she had the clarity to pray.

God, I thank you for my life. Please let Phil make it. I love you.

Lisa's body trembled—struggled—shook. Her last defenses against the blackness around her fell down.

Her hands grasped for Phil, pulling him close. She had no choice, no will in the matter. She had to breathe. She opened her mouth and breathed in the cool water coursing over her. Her body shuddered in Phil's arms, and her muscles convulsed.

Lisa's body bucked as the water continued to pour down her throat, and then she stopped moving. Her arms and legs went limp, and the struggle against the current ceased.

■ ■ ■ ■

No!

Phil kicked his feet and hugged Lisa close, feeling the life leave her as her body convulsed and struggled against the menace that was flooding into her and stealing her life away. If he didn't find a way out, he would soon follow. But he couldn't leave her.

His heart was pounding in his ears. His head felt like it would split open. He kicked harder, and then he saw it: an eerie blue glow a dozen yards away.

Phil thought he was hallucinating, seeing things that weren't there from lack of oxygen, but the closer he got, the brighter the shade of blue became. The tunnel became shallow, and Phil could reach the smooth rock floor of the lava tube. Finally, the underground tunnel of water broke the surface, and Phil gasped for air. His lungs stung as he inhaled. Small stars floated before his eyes, and the cavern spun around him.

Phil picked up Lisa's thin, limp body and rushed out of the water, carrying her to a flat area just out of the water.

"Lisa," he gasped. "No! Don't do this."

Her face was pale white, and her lips were tinted blue, beautiful in a strange way, like a porcelain doll. Phil felt for a pulse.

Nothing.

"Come on honey, give me a sign." Phil straightened her body and tilted her head back, trying to clear her airway. He leaned over her silent form and listened for breath. Her chest was still. He put his mouth over hers, held her nostrils closed, and quickly breathed three breaths into her body. He watched her chest raise and lower with each breath he put into her. He felt for a pulse again. Still no heartbeat. Phil found Lisa's sternum and carefully measured two fingers up from the bottom of her rib cage, so as not to break off a sharp bone and lacerate her liver.

Phil gave five compressions and then three quick breaths. His arms trembled as he performed the sequence over and over again.

Lisa—please, honey! You can do it!

Gasping for air, he pleaded with God and Lisa. "Come back to me!"

He breathed into her again. Lisa's chest trembled, and she half sat up with a cough. A quart of dirty water bubbled from her mouth.

Phil laughed and hugged her and cried. Lisa sputtered and wiped her mouth, and then she opened her eyes and saw Phil smiling at her.

"What happened?" she rasped.

"Welcome back," Phil whispered, and then he just laughed and held her with tears in his eyes.

Phil heard a splash and glanced behind them to see Amir emerging from the water, gasping for precious air the same way Phil had just moments before.

Lisa sat up all the way, coughed roughly, and pointed ahead of her. "Look."

Amir and Phil followed the direction of her finger. She was pointing at a sunburst of light, two hundred feet away.

"It must be an opening to the outside," said Phil, squinting at the light source.

Amir looked at his watch. "We don't have much time. Let's get going."

Phil, Lisa, and Amir made for the opening as the underwater river behind them continued to churn and splash as it had for hundreds of years.

Chapter Fifty-One

Tremors

"What are you talking about?" asked Caleb, making his way to the front of the command center. The high-tech room was a beehive of activity. Plasma screens lined the room at eye level, and rows of workstations were manned by members of Israeli intelligence. The light level of the room was dark, and the screens illuminated each soldier's face.

"Our seismographs are picking up deep-earth tremors," said the tech.

Caleb skirted around the man and looked at the video display. A series of lines with sawtooth edges, increasing in amplitude, were scrolling on the screen.

"How big are they?"

"They started at around 1.2 on the Richter scale, but they are increasing in magnitude. The last one was around 4.3."

"Where's the epicenter?" asked Caleb.

The tech typed for a moment, and a map flew up on the screen. "It's just southwest of the Dead Sea. Hey, that's right where Amir and . . . "

The tech turned around to find Caleb gone. He had run down the aisle and was on the phone.

"General, we are about to have a really big deal occur near the Dead Sea," said Caleb.

The response on the other end of the call was predictable. Caleb rolled his eyes and sighed with exasperation. "There's no time to talk about this. Pick me up on the helicopter ramp, and I'll brief you en route." Caleb slammed the phone down.

On his way up the steps and out of the darkened command center, he caught the intelligence officer by the arm and ducked into a small alcove. "Listen to me." The intelligence officer bristled at the command from someone he didn't report to directly, but he listened. "If that oil reserve breaches the surface, the entire planet will know we are the new Saudi Arabia. Do you get that?"

The man nodded hesitantly and looked out of the corner of his eye at the rest of the room. They were watching the conversation but trying to pretend they weren't.

"If the tremors continue increasing, don't waste time analyzing it. You put the military on alert and scramble air cover and patrol the country's borders. This will be the biggest opportunity for our enemies to attack since our founding in 1948. Do you get me?"

"Yes, sir."

Caleb released the man's collar and exited the room, taking the metal stairs two at a time until he reached the roof of the building. He pushed the door open, stepped to the edge of the helipad, and looked out across the city of Tel Aviv, which curved against the blue waters of the Mediterranean.

A moment later, helicopter blades chopped through the air overhead, and a spiderlike shadow appeared over the ramp. A gray Sikorsky MH-53 hovered for a moment and touched down, the joints on its landing gear bent like mechanical kneecaps. The massive transport had a long refueling probe, which extended from the front of the vehicle like a jousting lance from a mounted medieval knight.

An Israeli soldier slid the door to the passenger cabin open and helped Caleb into the cramped fuselage. It was packed with soldiers—all with deadly expressions and weapons that were locked and loaded.

The twin turbines of the helicopter howled with power, and the craft lifted from the ramp, rattling windows in the buildings that surrounded the intelligence building. It wheeled on its axis, snapping to face the southeast, and raced toward the Dead Sea. With a top speed of one hundred and sixty miles an hour, it would be a short trip.

Chapter Fifty-Two
Revelation

Gorin's body floated down through the inky blackness of the petro-leum-laden water. The heavy net of metal cables wrapped around his breathless body pulled him downward and trailed its pitons behind him like some unclassified species of squid. His eyes were wide in death, staring ahead at the rugged lava cap he was sinking toward.

The tangled mass of primer cord, C-4 explosive blocks, and industrial cabling cocooned his body, and finally the tangled mass settled onto the cap of the plugged lava tube—fifteen hundred feet from where it was originally set to go off. The lights on the flashing detonator blinked on and off like a deep-sea angler fish. The cool water bubbled with flammable petroleum that was leaking through the porous lava cap and trailing upward through the dark water.

Red, orange, and yellow cracks of molten rock periodically peeked through the gray of the rough rock before being cooled to a black crust by the icy water. The cap had been building like this for centuries, undisturbed, unknown, undiscovered.

It was waiting for this moment. The only barrier between the highly pressurized Maximal Reserve and the surface was this thin rocky seal.

High up on the pinnacle, the laptop's display continued its inexorable march to zero:

5

4

3

2

1

0

A green light on a small black box connected to the metal netting that had captured Gorin and dragged him to the depths blinked twice, then the igniter in the detonator fired, sending an electrical charge through all the primer cords instantaneously. The temperature around the explosives instantly flared to fifteen thousand degrees, vaporizing Gorin and the metal net and sending expanding shock waves from the explosion that ruptured the lava dome.

The lava cap was forced apart by the explosion, and the petroleum that had slowly been finding its way through the meandering crust of rock suddenly came into contact with its age-old enemy: fire.

The petroleum ignited, flashing the millions of gallons of water that had cascaded down the smooth sides of the lava tube and collected over the plug into steam. A massive pillar of water vapor fired upward toward the surface, continually flashing the liquid water into vapor that rushed downward to fill the empty space around the super-hot petroleum flare.

Again and again the water gave in to the embrace of the heat and graduated to its next physical state: steam.

The water around the steam pillar crushed down upon it, causing a tornado at the base of the pillar, the gargantuan tunnel of water twisting and rotating around the base of the flashing event like the drain in a giant sink. The intense counteraction of energy began to vacuum the water in the giant structure to the now-ruptured salt-dome cap. The waterline, resting on the crust-covered walls in the Etsba Elohim structure, began to lower as the water became steam and drained the ancient tube of its liquid inhabitant.

. . . .

Phil heard the rumble and felt the tremor pulse through his body.

"We're out of time," he said, helping Lisa make her way over the rock-strewn floor of the cave. The opening was only seventy feet away.

"That blast must have been the charge going off!" said Amir, running ahead of the couple.

Within moments the humidity of the cave changed. The arid, dry air was now full of moisture, and a wind began to blow through the cave. It came from the opening to the daylight ahead of them and blew through the cavern back toward the underground river.

Phil grabbed Lisa's hand and pulled her across the rough stones. "If we don't get out of here right now, we're all dead. Run!"

As the three ran for the exit illuminated before them, the temperature in the cave began to rise, and a hissing sound came from behind them.

They didn't look back; they just ran.

. . . .

Fifteen hundred feet below the trio, the physics of the explosion had flash-evaporated all the water in the cave. The forces that fed upon one another began to ebb, and the tornadic energy slowed and then stopped.

The lava tube was empty, eerie, like a subway tunnel waiting for a train to speed through and give it meaning and purpose.

The rocky cap bulged and expanded, pushed by the pressures from beneath it beating upon the undergirding of the plug, removing every barrier between its prison below and freedom above. The downward pressure of the water in the tube was gone. There was nothing to counteract the titan that dwelt below in the oily darkness.

. . . .

The roaring behind Phil, Lisa, and Amir was becoming deafening, and the temperature was reaching broiling.

The ground trembled. The three stumbled on their feet, swaying from side to side as they made for the exit. Sunshine burst through the opening like a shaft of sunlight through a cloud bank as they made their way through the opening, shielding their eyes from the intense light.

They were finally free of the caverns of Etsba Elohim.

As they blinked in the sunlight, the roaring behind them became deafening—like a locomotive. Phil looked over his shoulder and saw a curtain of white blow from the underground cavern. He pushed Amir to the right and grabbed Lisa's hand, pulling her away from the front of the cave entrance just as a shaft of blistering steam exploded through the opening. The trio covered their faces as the steam rushed by for five seconds and then died down.

■ ■ ■ ■

The lava cap strained and trembled, and then a rock the size of a man's hand speared high into the air as if had been shot out of a howitzer. It flew to the top of the lava tube and disintegrated against the vaulted ceiling above the pinnacle. A stream of black oil blasted right behind it. The hole began to erode, giving up more and more of the surface of the cap to the stream of oil. The walls of the lava tube were slick with black and spattered and stippled with the new wealth of Israel.

The hole became larger, now the size of a geyser.

Moments later the hole was the size of a car, then a house, then a building, eating up and eroding the lava cap with every increase in its breadth. The pressure did not abate, and it began drilling its way out of the top cavern that Phil, Lisa, and Amir had escaped from just minutes before.

■ ■ ■ ■

Just outside Etsba Elohim, Phil, Lisa, and Amir stood in the ashes of the cities that had once lined the Dead Sea. The mountain began to tremble, more violently than before. High up on the slope above them, fragile formations of rock snapped from their bases and began an avalanche of sand, rock, and sharp fragments, raining into the ash-covered valley below.

"It's not safe here. Let's go!" yelled Amir, leading them down the ash-covered slope toward the Dead Sea, a mile away.

And then they heard the loudest noise any of them had ever experienced.

Phil looked over his shoulder to see the top of the mountain containing the Etsba Elohim split in half as the vaulted ceiling inside its crown disintegrated under the grating pressure of the oil that was escaping from the Maximal Reserve. The oil shot through the top of the mountain and continued vertically for another four hundred feet before succumbing to gravity and falling back to earth.

Black rain began to dot the landscape; the white ash of the Cities of the Plain painted with the brush of an ancient prophecy being revealed to the world.

A river of oil blasted through the empty underground river that had attempted to claim Lisa's life. It shot through the opening the trio had escaped from and poured through the ashen streets of the ancient city.

Phil pushed Lisa forward onto an ancient ledge just as the slimy river reached out and overtook him. Phil lost his balance as the thick oil rushed around him, and he splashed into the muck that was taking over the street.

Lisa stopped and reached out to him. "Phil!"

"Go! Don't stop!" screamed Phil, his head barely above the dark brown crude. More oil rushed into the street, and Amir grabbed Lisa's hands and yanked her forward just as the ground of the ledge fell away. Phil disappeared into a swirling stream of ebony.

Lisa ran with Amir to an ancient brick wall and climbed to the top of the edifice. Suddenly the chopping sound of helicopter blades overwhelmed their hearing as a gray military helicopter flew in from the south around the oil geyser. The helicopter hovered just over the wall, and its rear ramp lowered to the oil-spackled ground. Amir helped Lisa board the chopper, and he looked at the landscape behind him that was being swallowed in oil.

There was no sign of Phil.

The mountain that loomed over them continued to vaporize under the pressurized oil, which was surging out of the earth. The pilot of the transport did his best to dodge the clods of dirt and small rocks that were clanging through the rotating helicopter blades, threatening to destroy the helicopter.

The pilot's shaken voice came over the intercom, barely audible over the clods vaporizing in the rotor wash. "We have to leave now!" The chopper pulled up and began to head toward the Dead Sea.

Lisa sat in a seat along the fuselage, her head in her hands and her shoulders shaking uncontrollably. Caleb sat down next to her and put his arm around her. She laid her head against his shoulder and cried out, "I love you, Phil!" Then she buried her face in Caleb's chest and sobbed.

■ ■ ■ ■

Phil felt the river rushing around him—eroding the sand and ash beneath his feet—making it impossible to keep his head above the turbulent surface. His head bobbed under the surface, and his body swirled in the undertow of blackness. His body spun, and he kicked his legs, but it was impossible to gain control—like swimming in a raincoat. Finally, as his lungs were about to explode, he broached the surface. He gargled and gasped a deep breath of air, wiping the oil from his eyes.

He saw the helicopter hovering seventy feet away and screamed, but his voice was raw and hoarse. They couldn't hear him anyway over the screaming of the geyser and the twin turbines of the military transport.

Phil's eyes stung with the grit and oil that was caked in his eyelids, but ahead he saw a city wall—stout, made of thick stones. He swam to the wall and pulled himself out of the pool of oil that was rising beneath him. He reached the top of the wall and stood and waved at the helicopter that was heading toward the blue sea across the valley.

■ ■ ■ ■

Amir squinted through the oil vapor and saw a figure standing on a wall. Rivulets of oil coursed all around him as the escaping petroleum snaked through the ancient, doomed city, looking for its end in the Dead Sea.

"Wait! Go back! I see Phil!"

The pilot tried to debate, but Caleb and Lisa both turned toward the cockpit and in unison screamed, "Just do it!"

The helicopter banked to the left and headed back toward the ash city, which was quickly submerging beneath the oil of the Maximal Reserve.

The wall beneath Phil began to rumble and quake as its foundation, laid four millennia ago by human hands, dissolved under the onslaught of oil and debris that was grinding the brick into sand and grit. Phil struggled to keep his balance as bricks and fragile mortar disintegrated beneath him.

The helicopter pushed forward through the rain of oil and the hailstorm of stones ejecting from the crown of the mountain. It wheeled on its axis just as it reached Phil, narrowly missing chopping him into fish bait with its massive tail rotor. The wall trembled and gave way. Phil jumped for the rear ramp, just catching the tailgate of the chopper as the wall collapsed beneath his feet. Phil's hands desperately grasped the metal, but he began to slide off the back of the tailgate. Amir leaped forward and grabbed Phil's oil-slick forearms. He hauled him into the helicopter, which was already flying away from the geyser.

Lisa kneeled next to Phil and threw her arms around him, wiping the oil from his eyes. She was laughing and crying at the same time.

The helicopter gained altitude and flew away from the sign of Israel's new significance and strategic value to the world.

Overhead, three Israeli fighter jets screamed by, circling the oil geyser.

White dots began to bloom against the azure sky as the parachutes of the Israeli army filled the sky. God's promise to his people was fulfilled.

Inside the cabin of the transport, Phil and Lisa wiped the oil from their faces, and Caleb walked over and sat down next to the couple. "I've been on the phone with both our governments, and we have something to offer the two of you until this all blows over."

■ ■ ■ ■

Three hundred and fifty miles above the Dead Sea, a KH-17 U.S. spy satellite floated in low Earth orbit, making a pass over the Middle East. The craft was the size of a school bus, with two large solar panels that stood out from its cylindrical frame. Sunlight glinted off its solar wings as it trained its powerful camera lens on the body of water far below it. The aperture spun clockwise first and then reversed, bringing the turquoise water of the inland sea into greater focus.

The water began to change color. Slowly, almost imperceptibly, the cyan and azure water began to darken as if ink had been dropped into a glass of water. The scalloped edge of the darkness curled and pushed forward through the water.

Another fifty miles above the classified U.S. Satellite, a Slovak-11 Soviet–era spy satellite snapped photo after photo as it observed the change in the body of water on the Jordan plain.

The invisible secret of the Maximal Reserve, concealed for millennia in the bowels of the earth, was now in the open. Israel was now the most oil-rich nation on earth.

Chapter Fifty-Three
The Beach

L isa Channing sat in the pure white sand and brushed some of the granules from her wedding dress. The shadow of the palm trees growing nearby provided cool shade from the sharp rays of sunlight. The sound of the ocean waves rolling in and crashing against the beach and a few seagulls were the only sounds that could be heard.

She looked down the beach where a series of footprints were still discernible. The footprints in the sand were from the wedding that had occurred just a few hours before. She looked at the circle of shoe prints that encircled three main sets: hers, Phil's, and those of an unfortunate federal judge they had found at a nearby resort, who was on vacation.

One of the encircling prints was deep in the sand with sharp indentations. Lisa smiled as she thought about her mother wearing ridiculous spiked heels and constantly sinking in the sand during the brief ceremony. Her mom had cried, as all mothers do at weddings, but Lisa wondered if it was because of the hastily thrown-together ceremony and venue instead of the life change of her little girl.

Her memories moved to her father's warm embrace and Phil reciting his promise to her—his vow to honor, cherish, and love her for the rest of her life. *Her life . . .*

She thought about the irony of those words. Her life and Phil's life were no longer what they had thought they would be. The relocation package offered to them had essentially erased them from the registers of society. Soon they would have completely new credentials. The Israeli and American governments felt this was the wisest move. The conspiracy that had consumed Gorin, Governor Wyngate, Senator Camran, and Glenn Martin could still be there, looking for vengeance.

"Thank, you, Caleb—for everything," said Phil, hugging his friend.

"It's Israel who should be thanking you, Phil. Now my job is more difficult. Everyone on earth will want a piece of us," said Caleb, walking to the doorway of the seaplane and stepping inside.

"If anyone's up to the challenge, it's you," yelled Phil as the doorway closed.

■ ■ ■ ■

The sound of a prop-driven seaplane starting its engine pulled Lisa's attention down the beach. Detective Rizzo, Sheridan Preston, and Aliya had been flown out for the quick wedding on the beach, and they were now departing. She watched Phil, her husband, jog up the beach toward her as the seaplane turned and flew into the perfect sky, dipping its wing, flying around the island, and disappearing from view.

The waves continued to rush ashore, beginning to erase the circle of footprints and the remainder of her previous life.

The warm Caribbean breeze blew her wedding veil in slow motion as Phil approached her, still dressed in his tuxedo, but without the coat.

"Well, they're off," said Phil, sitting down next to Lisa. "Sheridan and Detective Rizzo are working together to expose Senator Camran's part in the weapons exchange."

"Do you think they'll get him to confess?" asked Lisa.

Phil smiled. Lisa's tone was more cynical than he remembered, as if this entire adventure had dulled her naivety about the safety of living in the United

States. "Sheridan said that one of his interns came forward and said she was involved in some, um—" Phil searched for the appropriate word "—improprieties with the senator."

"Well, maybe that will help," said Lisa, watching the tide roll in.

With a strange smile, Phil pulled out a newspaper article.

"What's that?" asked Lisa.

Phil grinned. "Our obituaries—want to read them?"

"Maybe later," said Lisa. Her expression said it all. She was already sick of this cloak-and-dagger stuff. It was all too new—too fast—too different and too unexpected.

"It's really not all that bad, is it?" asked Phil. Lisa smiled at him and leaned her head against his arm, and he placed his hand over hers.

"I know it's not what we talked about and dreamed about, but only one thing really matters," said Phil.

"What's that?" she asked, her eyes giving away the fact that she already knew the answer.

"We're together. That's all we really wanted anyway."

Lisa leaned in against him, tracing his jaw line with her finger, and then guided his lips to hers.

Phil swept his bride off the sand and pulled her close, kissing her deeply, and then turned and trotted up the sand, carrying her toward the honeymoon bungalow, leaving footprints of the new life they were starting together.

That was all Phil wanted now.

References

The Abiogenic Oil Theory, prominently discussed in this book, is not fiction. It is strongly held and fiercely debated by numerous scientists, especially those in the Russian science community. An American scientist, the late Thomas Gold, was considered the champion of the theory here in the West and has been admired by his peers for possibly cracking the code of how oil is produced deep in the earth. Some of his fans and supporters include brilliant scientists such as Freeman Dyson, the theoretical physicist and mathematician, and Hans Bethe, the Nobel-winning laureate and world-famous physicist. Both have proclaimed their belief in the Abiogenic Theory.

When I wrote my first novel, *Wayback*, I ran into numerous issues that raised my curiosity. A few of these were related to the internal structure of the earth.

- Why did God create the earth with the look of age?
- Were there sedimentary rock layers before the flood?
- God commanded Noah to apply pitch for waterproofing the ark. Was pitch petroleum-based, as many waterproofing chemicals are today? If so, where did this petroleum come from?
- Did all of the petroleum reserves we leverage as a global society today come from the biological debris buried by the flood?
- What is God's view of our use of hydrocarbons for powering our civilizations?

Wayback was not focused on these questions, and I answered them as best I could. As I researched this book, I found that the answers may be much more interesting than fuels simply being linked to the Great Flood. Please understand that this has not impacted my faith in the actual occurrence of the flood and its association with global petroleum reserves. It has, in fact, made me more appreciative of God and His architecture of our planet. My unwavering belief in the flood and its effects on our world is clearly portrayed in my first book. (I have the hate mail to prove it.)

If the Abiogenic Theory is true, and I do believe it answers more questions than the theory of buried biological debris being reworked by geologic processes does, then the processes of the deep earth are just as much a display of God's handiwork as the oceans, mountains, and sunrises that inspire such awe. From the core of the earth, which generates the electromagnetic field that protects our planet uniquely from the ill effects of our sun, to a possible "engine" that provides abundant and inexhaustible petroleum, mineral, and metal deposits that underlie our economies, the deep earth is a marvel. And everything about our planet is designed to be under our dominion—including the resources hidden in the interior of the planet.

It is interesting to speculate that God provided this engine and expects us to use it, just as agriculture and animal husbandry were put under our dominion. I do believe that God expects us to use common sense and wisdom in how we use these resources. Clearly, we have the ability to destroy the world's fisheries, but we still have dominion over them. Defaulting to either side of the argument in an extreme fashion seems to break the laws God has given us. Worshiping the creation instead of the Creator does not allow us dominion over the ecosystem He has given us, and on the other side of the spectrum, reckless use of resources destroys our ability to exploit them for the advances of our civilization. The Abiogenic Theory raises questions with the power to affect us all. If petroleum is abundant and a function of deep-earth processes, then what is the impact of this upon what we now consider to be the major oil-producing nations of the earth? What happens when the basic unit that powers our society turns out not to be scarce and is found to be literally available beneath the feet of all nations? As I contemplated these questions, it occurred to me that there was a great story just begging to be told.

What follows is a list of references that were useful in the writing of *Maximal Reserve*. Any errors in the descriptions of technology, theory, oil exploration techniques, or recovery methods are solely mine. The reader should not assume that the authors of these papers and references hold to anything described in this work of fiction. Any mistakes are mine alone.

Adelman, M.A. *The Genie out of the Bottle: World Oil Since 1970.* Cambridge, Massachusetts: The MIT Press, 1995.
—"The Real Oil Problem." *Regulation*, Spring, 2004: 16–21.

Barnes, Joe, Amy Jaffe, and Edward L. Morse. "The New Geopolitics of Oil." *The National Interest*, Winter 2003/2004: 7–15.

Birney, Leroy. *Journal of the Evangelical Theological Society*, Winter, 1970.

Campbell, Philip. *Rebuttal of Article in Nature Reports (12 August 2002)*. http://www.gasresources.net/Nature(Editor01).htm (date accessed: February 1, 2010)

Craig H., W.B. Clarke, and M.A. Beg. "Excess 3He in Deep Water on the East Pacific Rise." *Earth Planet*, 1975: 125–32.

Flanigan, James. "Russia Is World's Key to Having Oil to Burn." *Los Angeles Times*, May 30, 2004: C4.

Gold, Thomas. *Power from the Earth: Deep Earth Gas—Energy for the Future.* London: J.M. Dent & Sons, 1987.
—"Rethinking the Origins of Oil and Gas." *Wall Street Journal*, June 8, 1977.
— *The Deep Hot Biosphere*. New York, NY: Copernicus Books, 2001.

Goolsbee, Austan. "Dependency Paradox: How Conservation Could Actually Make Us Gulp—Even More Reliant on Foreign Oil." *Fortune*, August 22, 2005.

Jenkins, W.J., J.M. Edmond, and J.B. Corliss. "Excess 3He and 4He in Galapagos Submarine Hydrothermal Waters." *Nature*, 1978: 272:156–58.

Judd, A.G., M. Hoveland. *Seabed Pockmarks and Seepages: Impact on Geology, Biology, and the Marine Environment.* London: Graham and Trotman, 1988.

Kenney, J. F. *An Example of the Little-Moron Logic & Mendacity of BOOP: The Carbon Isotope Ratio Nonsense.* http://www.gasresources.net/THECAR-BONISOTOPERATIONONSENSEcorrectedbyElyzabethforWashConference.htm (Date accessed: February 1, 2010)

—"Comment on 'Mantle hydrocarbons: Abiotic or biotic?' by R. Sugisaki and K. Mimura." *Geochim. et Cosmochim. Acta, 59/18,* 1995: 3857–3858.

—"Gas Resources." http://www.gasresources.net/ (Date accessed: February 1, 2010)

—"Principle Results of the Major Scientific Investigations for Hydrocarbons in the Swedish Deep Gas Exploration Project." *Proceedings of the VIIth International Symposium on the Observation of the Continental Crust Through Drilling,* 1994.

Lupton, J.E., G.P. Klinkhammer, W.R. Normark, R. Haymon, K.C. MacDonald, R.F. Weiss, and H. Craig. "Helium-3 and Manganese at the 21N East Pacific Rise Hydrothermal Site." *Earth Planet,* 1980: 50: 115–27.

Mills, Peter Huber and Mark. "Oil, Oil, Everywhere . . . " *Wall Street Journal,* January 27, 2005.

Nakaya, Andrea C. *Oil—Opposing Viewpoints.* Farmington Holls, MI: Greenhaven Press, 2006.

Ourisson, Guy, Pierre Albrecht, and Michel Rohmer. "The Microbial Origin of Fossil Fuels." *Scientific American,* August, 1984: 251(2):44–51.

Szevtzyk, U., et al. "Thermophilic, Anaerobic Bacteria Isolated from a Deep Borehole in Granite in Sweden." *Proceedings of the National Academy of Sciences, USA,* 1994: 1810–1813.

Sozansky, V.I., J.F. Kenney, and P.M. Chepil. *On Spontaneous Renewal of Oil and Gas Fields.* http://www.gasresources.net/OnSpontaneiousRenewalVasyl.htm. (Date accessed: February 1, 2010)

"The Fraudulence of Claims of Spontaneous, Low-Pressure Generation of Petroleum." http://www.gasresources.net/EssayforWebPageFaudulantClaim-sreSponEvolutionPetroleumCompounds.htm (Date accessed: February 1, 2010)

Acknowledgments

As always, I have people to thank. First, thank You to God for Your faithfulness and Your unconditional love to me.

To my loving family: Susan, my wonderful wife, to whom this book is dedicated; Samantha, my beautiful daughter; and Parker, my curious and inventive son. I couldn't do this without your support—thank you.

Thank you to my supportive family. Mom and Dad and Marnie, thank you for always cheering me on and supporting me in my writing. To my mother-in-law, Donna, and my sisters-in-law, Bonnie and Laurie: your encouragement means so much.

Thank you to Melissa Adamski who helped me with the Hebrew-to-English translations early on.

A special thank-you to my early readers, who helped me find clarity from the confusion of a first draft: Chris Caldwell, Randy & Monda Holleger, Dawn Pleasants, Nadine Isabell, Dina Hoskinson, Drew Morris, Nathan Gifford, Phil and Lydia Martin, JR McGee, Tim and Carla Meell, Carol Cobb, Henry Miller, Barry Moyer, Rebecca Misuira, Pat Webster, Bud Bender, Kevin Nickerle, Phil Spence, Connor McCauley, Jeff & Joshua Rapp, Giosi Derleth, Patty Koechig, Amy Paskel, Bonnie Leithmann, Laurie Nunez, and Kelly Bullard Unruh.

Thank you to my final proof readers: Dylan Trievel, Danielle Schlichtmann, Emily Davis and Nadine Isabell.

There's an axiom for writers, and it states that you should write what you know. While I mostly agree with this principle, the parts of this book that deal with Phil's troublesome mother- and father-in-law are not familiar to me. I am blessed that my late father-in-law, Joe Leithmann, was a great friend to me—literally a second dad. He never pressured me and never made me feel that I wasn't good enough for his daughter. The same is true for my mother-in-law, Donna. Unlike many others, my marriage is richer and more fulfilling because of my extended family. I miss you, Joe. Thank you, Donna.

I must also call out my great conversations with Barry Moyer, a Pennsylvania police officer and a good friend, regarding the crime scenes and police/detective work that was way outside of my comfort zone. In addition to

Barry, my friends Jeff Rapp, an aerospace engineer, and JR McGee, engineer extraordinaire and all-around wicked-smart guy, looked over the manuscript to keep me honest with the technical concepts. Thank you, Jeff and JR!

A huge thank-you goes out to John Haynes, a master of the English language, who did the initial editing on this manuscript. Despite my abuses of the English language, he still saw through my mistakes and helped polish the story in ways I could never do alone.

Again, I have to express thanks to my production editor, Rachel Starr Thomson, who edited Wayback and has pushed me to produce the best manuscript possible. You're amazing, Rachel! Thanks to Bill and Nancie Carmichael and Lacey Hanes Ogle at Deep River Books for making the road to publication easy and pain free.

Reader, thank you for taking this journey with me. I hope we can take another one soon.